Book One of the Trilogy:
The Last Scroll

THE EDUCATION OF TEMPLE FOX

Patricia S. Christy

ISBN 978-1-935689-71-3
Library of Congress Control Number 2014936585

REVIEWS

"...probably the most ingeniously skillful and creative writer I have ever read... An amazing wordsmith...Very captivating, alluring, suspense filled and funny!"

~ **Marisol Cervantes**

★   ★   ★

"…As allies and enemies alike conspire with him and against him, Temple learns much about love, sacrifice, the intricacies of life, and the destinies of the souls that surround him…This story is more contemplative, more moody, and cleverly subversive…. His spiritual journey is engrossing…and many other characters are written with delightful complexity…It's nice to keep this in mind—that these characters feel alive and true…Simultaneously exciting and contemplative, Temple Fox is a thought-provoking story that honors its characters. Christy's imaginative scope is daunting, thrilling, and just plain fun."

~ **Kelsey Vetter, Blogger/Pagegirl**

★   ★   ★

"Christy is a genius. This powerful story is delicious…rich, hopeful, insightful and spiritually expansive."

~ **Mimi Kates**

"Spellbinding…No housework got done while reading this book. So many life lessons imbedded within. So many interesting characters. What a wonderful imagination and talent this author has and I look forward to more of her books."

~ Carol A. Taylor

★　　★　　★

"I gobbled up the pages and fell in love with the characters. It was like taking a thrill ride through an expanded version of reality that included the presence of past-lives, ghosts, primitive creator gods, a power lusty shaman, and even aliens! As Temple Fox expands his own consciousness through the story, you find that his awakening process is not so unlike our own. Wonderful!"

~ Stacie Coller, Author of Awake in Angelscape

★　　★　　★

"Although this reader generally shies away from publications of a spiritual nature, I was pleasantly surprised by Patricia S. Christy's first tome in the Last Scroll Trilogy… Christy expertly weaves a sublime and fascinating plot, …comparing favorably with works by Douglas Preston, Lincoln Child and Clive Cussler…The pleasures of "Temple Fox" are not ephemeral, but like any good work of art, remain with the reader, encouraging thought and instilling wonder…"

~ J. Michael Modlin

★　　★　　★

"Welcome to the magic. Christy takes her readers by the hand and sweeps us into a strange land. The rules of life are as different as the characters who live here. The joys, the love, the tragedies and the hate, however, sound a familiar chord. This book brings both fantasy at its best and reality at its most poignant. A spellbinding read and a great first book of Christy's long-awaited trilogy."

~ Bob O'Connor, Author of Unholy Ground
– A Max Steele Thriller

"This is a very fast paced spiritual fantasy that I didn't want to put down. I've read it 3 times already, and each time I find something new I missed before. I highly recommend this book to those who are eager to push themselves to grow, or who just want a great story! The author is skilled at drawing you in, and causing you to challenge yourself to honestly examine your own life… A great read!"

~ **Suzanne H. Kahn**

FOR

My Mother,
Mary Theresa Hannon, known as Elaine Christy
(1920 – 2002)

Kit Moorehead,
whose love, devotion, commitment and generosity
sustains me every day.

Phil Sherlock
who encouraged me to write,
taught me discernment
and enriched my life for many years.

And finally,
for the Spirit Which Moves In All Things

ACKNOWLEDGEMENTS

It's been 16 years since I resurrected this book from a forgotten box in my dusty storage room. Consequently, I find it hard recalling who may have helped me form the thoughts that fill this book. Ideas are formed over a lifetime of living and contemplating what's been lived.

Experiencing a single word spoken, the sight of some unexpected beauty, surviving a betrayal or injury, even catching a fleeting thought that seemingly came out of nowhere – anything can spark ideas. And, before you know it, whole dramas unfold before you like a movie. Life is like a walk in the woods where you get lost many times and retrace old paths until you find your way home again. When you're finally out of the woods, you find the path looks like a Celtic knot. So, I apologize if I missed acknowledging any one person, spirit guide, thing or event that may have helped this novel to unfold.

For certain, I'd like to acknowledge my parents, Chris and Elaine, and my brother, Jim, who provided enough tragedy and vaudevillian comedy in my early years to supply a lifetime of writing ideas and a sense of drama.

The wisdom of Ramtha, channeled by J.Z. Knight, and the works of Machaelle Small Wright *(from Perelandra)* also very much influenced me, as did the works of Budd Hopkins, Whitley Strieber, John E. Mack M.D., and Raymond Fowler, who all wrote important books that added to the knowledge of the extraterrestial and UFO phenomena. I also thank Bob and Betty Luca for their conversations on the same subject and for sharing with me numerous unpublished drawings of Betty's otherworldly experiences. I'd also like to acknowledge James Redfield and his book *The Celestine Prophecy*, plus some of Gregg Braden's thoughts from his books.

When I look back, I see just how much I grew under the tutelage of Lenora Foerstel, professor of Ethnological Art History at the Maryland Institute, College of Art. She was the first to introduce me to the richness of world culture, e.g., Hopi prophecy and African Dogon, Australian Aboriginal, and Ancient Mexican culture and history.

Although I didn't know about shamanism when I wrote Book One, except through anthropological studies, I'd like to also thank Shaman Jaes Seis, whose healings on me were invaluable and whose influence and teachings will be more noticeable in Book Two.

I'd like to thank Mary (Muff) Imboden and her daughter, photographer and dear friend, Connie Imboden, who generously paid for my trip to Kenya and the Seychelle Islands in 1979. That amazing trip provided much of the background scenery for the book.

This book was also greatly influenced by knowing and loving my beloved friend, Olga Perewersew, a wise, old, Russian miracle healer who lived in Boronia, Australia. Her wisdom provided a model for the character Tani, although Olga was a class act and never crude like Tani often was. Tani's bawdiness came from me.

The Education of Temple Fox would not have been written without the influence of author Dacre Hill, who encouraged me to keep writing. I also thank my former husband, Phil Sherlock, for his brutal assessment of my skills as a new writer. I learned more and learned faster after enduring his criticisms. I thank him for deepening my knowledge of "Near" Death Experiences, and I am in gratitude for his patience when I would wake him in the wee hours of the morning to ask, "How do you get bats out of a cave?" and numerous other weird questions.

I would also like to mention Shelley Mateson, who found many "Patisms" throughout my manuscript and other grammatical errors. Thank you.

Thanks go to my first editor, who I will refer to as "Jane". "Jane" kindly accepted a payment of numerous rides to her doctor and her probation officer plus one used vacuum cleaner to critique my first draft. Her comments and encouragement were priceless.

I'd like to thank my first writing teacher, Jean Rubin, and, most importantly, my two editors: professional photo journalist, editor and friend, Roberta Binder, and also friend, Suzanne Hinton Kahn, for their expertise in editing and their suggestions on how to improve the manuscript. Roberta, thanks for your friendship, your wisdom, and for the "family discount", although a used vacuum cleaner was clearly not part of the deal. My old friend, Suzanne, I thank you for your keen eye and your never-ending humor and encouragement during the final polish. I'm so glad you fell in love with Temple. I owe you a vat of mint chocolate ice cream and a keg of margaritas.

Acknowledgement goes to Webmaster, Joni Stone of Stone by Stone Marketing, NC, for her technical assistance and also Brian Schwartz, Pres. Colorado Independent Publishers Association, and his assistant, Veronica Yager for their expertise. Many kudos also goes to the multi-talented, visionary artist, Barbara Lakshmi Kahn, for her brilliant cover design.

Many thanks also goes to a benevolent benefactor and old friend, Barbara Flick Jones-Smith.

The biggest thanks goes to my present life partner, Kit Moorehead, who supports me in countless ways. Her financial support, her honesty, her willingness to allow me the room to create, shows her true and generous heart. I also thank her for coining the word, "Patisms".

Finally, I give utmost gratitude to the Spirits of the Four Directions, Mother Earth and all Her creatures, Father Sky, Grandmother Moon and People of the Star Nations. I thank the creative spirit that moves through me, and all Life in all its varied forms, who, like my supportive friends, continue to enrich my life.

Pat Christy 2011

THE LAST SCROLL

BOOK I: THE EDUCATION OF TEMPLE FOX

TABLE OF CONTENTS

PART – III THE ASPIRING MASTER

PART – I
THE RECRUIT

CHAPTER ONE

A Shedding of Shadows

"A voice, like thunder skipping over ice spoke with piercing clarity. 'You will remember. You will know all,' It said."

Temple Fox
Makolese Scroll on Death & Dying #1
The Makolese Scroll on The Education of Temple Fox #1

"Now read it back to me," Temple insisted.

The Scribe brushed aside a strand of hair that had fallen into his eyes. He tilted the barkcloth scroll toward the light of the oil jar. "One of my first boyhood memories from England," he began, "was wetting my knickers when I was ten. My friends never forgot this. When they were in the company of girls the memory would suddenly resurface. My friends would look down at their crotches in imitation of me and they'd scream like a girl and hobble around bowlegged."

"Make this one my first memory," the old man said.

The Scribe, Maśon, paused and looked up from where he sat, scrolls of barkcloth paper surrounding him on the blanketed ground. The last of the day's light had long since faded to a dusty rose in the hut constructed just as Temple Fox had remembered it seventy-five years before. Only this wasn't the island of Makol. And it wasn't 1927. The compound where Temple dictated his memoir sat deep in the old forests of western North Carolina and felt as out of time to him and out of sequence as his memories.

The Scribe looked into the face of the robust centurion, wincing slightly from the cramps in his hands and thin legs. He was tired. The centurion was not, however, and ready for more work.

"Are you ready?" Temple asked.

"You are tireless like the ocean tide," Maśon said.

Temple paused, his gaze soft. He let out a short, sharp blast of air from his nostrils. A ball of light shot out of the old man's midsection and illuminated the hut in a soft pink glow. A warm pulse of energy raced through Maśon's limbs eliminating his pain and rejuvenating him.

"Thank you," Maśon said.

The mountain village was established in a *living zone* off the electric grid where no cell phone signal could penetrate, shielded from the thick inculcated cluster thoughts from the outside world. Most importantly, the compound was settled in pockets of the higher mountain's *no brainwash zone* to magnify the Gravitational Responsive Anomalous Vacuum Energy they had created, which was known affectionately as Gravy. This is where the new masters sought solace together or alone and where many lived together collectively.

Naturally, no one needed to be there. Not if someone was able to tap into the Gravy Field. They communicated telepathically from anywhere in the world. It was their choice to come for the sheer joy of affecting the land, the weather and the collective thoughts of others near and far, and be in groups with friends. Mostly, it was about getting together with old and new friends, to teach and learn more about consciousness, to share experiences and to drink a lot and tell jokes. And, yes, there were the usual sexual adventures to be experienced. It was the perfect place for Temple to have his memories recorded for those who hadn't yet learned to enter the Gravy Field.

For Makol's best Scribe, however, it was work. There would be no computer for this traditionalist who used a simple bamboo brush and ink pot. Maśon knew he would have to reorder this vast work later by hand, copying and recopying the text and creating cross references. He grunted softly under his breath at the task ahead of him. When this was completed only then would Temple Fox dictate the last and final scroll.

Maśon drew in a deep breath and nodded for his Master to continue.

"Even after my parents relocated to East Africa in 1913 the reputation of being a coward, an outcast, clung to me like a pair of wet knickers. No English boy, even a half English boy like myself, ever hated cricket. But I did. That's a sport, by the way, not the insect," Temple noted, being careful not to confuse the Scribe, who smiled back knowingly. "And I absolutely loathed hunting, which, for the son of a big game hunter spelled death."

Temple acknowledged the Scribe's need to refill his ink jars while the old man refilled two cups of warm wine from a simmering pot in the center of the hut. He handed the Scribe a steamy cup and sat back down on a cushion of blankets.

"Regardless," Temple began again, "when you're a young man of fifteen and you're beginning to look less like a plucked chicken, it's time to enter the world of men." The old centurion's eyes suddenly took on a faraway look. He paused and an awkward span of silence enveloped the room. In that instant Temple became a wounded boy again and, although the distant event had long since been healed, the memory burnt itself into his tender soul once again like a hot brand. Temple sat in the quiet of the room transfixed on his distant past. "We didn't speak. That is to say, my father and I never spoke again after the incident. In his eyes I was no longer his son."

The Scribe raised his head and looked into Temple's rheumy eyes as a witness and friend.

Temple looked up, his voice tight. "Maybe I'll skip this part until later."

Mason nodded and waited for Temple to continue.

"By my mid-twenties I had earned money doing odd jobs, mostly as an airplane mechanic. Blake was my business partner and co-pilot. We put our savings together and bought a new 1927 de Havilland Moth aircraft. We did fairly well doing supply runs."

"The Moth, right?" the Scribe said with a quiet chuckle.

"Yes, the famous Moth," Temple responded smiling. "I tell you when I climbed inside that plane I felt like a man. I loved the smell of machine oil, the creak of my leather suit, the sound the engine made when it popped over. And when the wind pushed hard against my goggled face as I soared above the earth like a bird, I felt I was in heaven. And no one would dare question the guts it took to fly a rickety airplane made of canvas and wood and then try to land it on some dusty, dirt strip dotted with zebra, gazelle and elephants. I felt I was king of the air!"

★　★　★　★　★　★

The tree frogs sang in their hypnotic rhythm as the last of the moonlight hid behind a shifting cloud. Temple had long since been put to bed. The Scribe, alone now, paused before the litter of scrolls scattered on the ground. Maśon did more than take dictation. He was Makol's Supreme Poet, interpreter of a full century of events, and born with the gift of clairsentience, which helped him capture every nuance of his Master's emotions, sometimes to his own anguish.

Having learned the art of entering individuated fields of consciousness, only by invitation of course, Maśon received the next round of the memoirs by entering Temple's lucid dreams. He moved the fire pot closer, this time for warmth, and his brush moved rapidly across the barkcloth. And as he finished the first part of the scroll, he read it aloud as much to himself as to the ancestral spirits in the room.

"Fate crouched in ambush, tensed to deliver the final purposeful blow that would throw Temple Fox into a destiny as fixed as the monolithic stones set into the ancient chalk plains of England; immutable like the Sphinx, face scoured and broken by water, wind and man, but the stare unchanged. Above all else, Fate was patient, aware and watchful as the Spirits of the Wind, Rain, Lightning and Thunder, all Its conspirators, moved into action."

"Agaluga, Spirit of the Tornado, moved as the breath of god across the face of the deep."

★   ★   ★   ★   ★   ★

Sheets of water hit the propeller and shattered into bullets of heavy spray, causing the plane to quiver like a wounded beast. The pilot and co-pilot's goggles filled with rain, blinding them, but both pulled back hard on their joysticks and bumped through the storm like bronco busters.

The warning came in seconds when Temple's scalp prickled beneath his leather helmet and his nostrils filled with ozone. He let out one long scream, but it was lost within the din of wind and rain against wood and canvas; lost within the wild pounding of his heart against his soaked leather flight suit. Lost when a blinding spear of lightning seared through the fuselage, forcing the plane to lurch downward and pitch sharply. The de Havilland Moth rolled into an irreversible spin.

Strips of canvas flew past Temple's face and he yelled for his co-pilot to jump. He unhitched his own restraints and started to leap out of the plane when his eyes lighted on the vaccine crate and he, without thinking why he did so, grabbed it as he fell. As he flailed in midair a sudden memory played in his mind.

Damn that African! If it hadn't been for Izaan, who gave them the crate, they wouldn't be floundering over trackless ocean. It had happened at the last possible moment. The Moth had been rocking and trundling along the dirt strip, ready to take to the air, when out of a dust devil the African had emerged on horseback. The small, black Moslem in the white burnoose and red fez had waved them down. His co-pilot, Blake, had throttled back and cursed.

"Dere bad yella fever in Seychelles, boss man," the man had shouted over the idling engine. "Doctor Bower say fly dis medicine immediately and give to Doctor LaFlamme." He handed Temple a thick envelope and a wooden crate.

The pilot quickly read the note enclosed and counted the bundle of cash. The rear compartments and rear cockpit were crammed to capacity and he took the box reluctantly, placing it between his feet.

"God is grreat! God is vedi grreat!" the man said, bowing and bouncing as he spoke.

"Your God has nothing to do with this," Temple breathed annoyingly between his teeth and shouted for his companion to kill the engine. "We'll have to plot a new course," he announced and glared down at the little man beaming up at him. "Tell Doctor Bower we've accepted his offer. Now get that damn horse out of the way! Now!"

During the whole trip the crate had slid back and forth cramping Temple's feet, and he had cursed Izaan from the time they had left the white beaches of Mombasa until now.

★　★　★　★　★　★

Temple somersaulted through the mist and never saw Blake and his de Havilland Moth vanish into the rain cloud. There was no direction, only the shriek of gray noise and the rush of air. *"Pull the cord! Pull the damn cord!"* He fumbled in panic, found the ripcord and yanked.

The chute opened with a sudden updraft of wind. Temple's body jolted and the crate wrenched upward hitting him in the head. It seemed to happen in slow motion. His body tensed, but his hand went limp and he let go of the crate. He watched it passively as the box slipped away, becoming smaller,... forever falling,... falling.

The pilot descended at a sharp diagonal when the heavy rains subsided. A cool spray billowed against his face, mingling with something wet. His head stung and his senses blurred. He raised his hand slowly to his brow and winced. Blood. He lifted his head and saw red droplets rising into the air.

"I'm raining blood!"

The white silk chute mushrooming above him was reassuring to

Temple. It gently caught his blood for him. And with that last muddled thought he lost consciousness.

Temple Fox was dragged through the heavens like a lifeless puppet, dangling by his destiny and guided by the will of the lawless wind.

★ ★ ★ ★ ★ ★

On the island, patches of blue broke through the white fog as people gathered on the shore. Mothers took account of their children who had been kept by other families when the storm broke. Men assessed the damage of several thatched roofs, which had given way in the squall. Palm leaves were strewn everywhere.

It was the children who first noticed the strange white cloud in the sky. It was a small cloud, very round on top with a flat bottom and a dark spot beneath it. It didn't move like the other clouds. It was moving toward them, but was descending rapidly. Mothers argued with their children, ordering them to clean up the beaches. With palm leaves in their hands the children clustered at the water's edge and pointed skyward. The women shouted for the men and the men gathered too.

There was a great commotion on the shore when High Shaman Mefakani ordered the men into their boats. A dozen dugouts nosed into the breakers of the rough sea with the Shaman yelling in the shallows for his own boat.

The Priest positioned himself in the prow of his dugout with the spray slapping him. He held his crooked staff up high and mumbled a prayer of thanks to his Lord and the Spirits of the Mountain.

"Could it be," he prayed, *"that our Lord Tagheetu and his legion of Spirits have at last answered my prayers?"*

Mefakani held on tight, his long, gray hair lashing in the wind as the boat rocked unsteadily in the choppy sea. Beyond a break in a wall of heavy fog, he watched the falling figure plunge into the sea with its strange cloud trailing behind it.

★ ★ ★ ★ ★ ★

There was no struggle, no panic when Temple Fox shed his body like an old set of clothes. He simply lifted out of the top of his head and watched his physical body, hardly recognizable in its leather suit, float upwards with the bubbles to the surface of the water.

Temple floated upward and hovered over the churning sea, calmly eyeing the lifeless shell he once inhabited.

"So this is death? What a gentle exit it is, not the drama one would imagine with thrashing arms or gnashing teeth."

With his newly discovered freedom he looked around him in a surprising three hundred and sixty degrees. Temple felt strange that his vision was so unrestricted and that he still had a body of some kind, though his instinct told him it was non-physical. Without a warning, his lifeless body in the sea below vanished, and he found himself surrounded by a deep black void and the feeling of wanting to move deeper within it, as if he knew what lay ahead.

And then it happened. It was like a great womb opening and a tunnel appeared before him, its surface swirling with a nacreous glow. Temple was sucked into it, drawn to a magnificent Light beyond.

He stood alone, awestruck before the Light, sensing its unearthly familiarity. It was all Love – a divine, uncomplicated Love and a Peace of the greatest intensity. All the Love he had encountered in his mere twenty-five years seemed but a pitiful imitation. This Light was a Love that had never been soiled by the dogmas, the false religions created by superstitious men. This was limitless God in Its purest state and to Temple's eyes It was brighter than a million suns.

Temple looked into It with a joy he never imagined he could feel. The intensity of It didn't hurt his eyes, but soothed him and seemed to beckon him to open up to more.

"Could there be more?" he wondered.

At the thought that he could exceed this state of incomprehensible bliss, the Light drew closer and completely encompassed him. Every cell, if he still had cells, suddenly filled to capacity. He became a conduit, a sun, a spark from the creative essence, and the essence Itself, and he glowed like an alabaster chalice overflowing with liquid light. To Temple it was less a filling up and more a sense of release that he felt. It was as if some tough, stubborn, shadowy substance had suddenly dissolved its boundaries and was at last reabsorbed into the essence from which it had been birthed millennia ago. It was a letting go, a dropping away, a shedding of shadows. Temple Fox's spirit overflowed with a deeply felt calm and knowing and, as he became one with the Light, his new body flashed and sparkled in response to the Divine Light, like one star talking in an unknown language to the master of all suns.

It was simple, but profound. It was everything he had known before, but had forgotten. It was Heaven. It was Peace. It was the ultimate reunion.

At last he had returned home!

In the next instant his memory quivered out of focus and he found himself watching the Light pulsate. A voice, like thunder skipping over ice; a voice neither male nor female, spoke with piercing clarity. *"You will remember. You will know all,"* It said, as It receded back into the void.

"Don't go! Take me with you!" he pleaded.

"You must return to complete yourself," the Light said as It vanished into the distance.

The pilot was suspended in the blackness, his heart aching from bewilderment and rejection. A voice moving like lapping water broke the silence.

"Please tell my family I am well."

Temple wheeled around to face a well-built, middle-aged man with a large spiral tattooed on his chin. His skin was the color of burnt almond and so completely covered with indigo spirals from his nipples to his knees that Temple thought he was looking at blue lace until the patterns seemed to wink at him with an unearthly shimmer.

"Who are you?" Temple asked.

The name Noko echoed in the void, and the figure broke into scattered wisps of chalky light and dissipated.

★ ★ ★ ★ ★ ★

The young mute, Tiv, was alone in his dug-out, searching for the creature, when he spotted it bobbing face down in the water with a white membrane wrapped around it. Although the teen was slow thinking, he beat his paddle against the boat to signal the others, then grabbed the thing and hauled it in, placing it face up in the bottom of the boat. Wasting no time he pulled the blood splattered caul from its face. Tiv stared down in horror, his mouth gaped wide with no sound issuing out. He raised his paddle to defend himself, but the creature with the thick, brown hide and enormous eyes filled with blood didn't move.

Temple's spirit watched high above the water as the fleet of dugouts rocked in the waves. In the bottom of one boat lay a masked man who was covered in dark, brown leather. Temple felt drawn to the helpless figure and, without knowing why, drew himself down inside him. But the instant he popped inside he realized he was stuck. The body was too dense, too cramped, and he let out a silent scream, feeling much like he once did when as a child he had slipped through the outhouse hole into the warm, dark, stinking slop below.

It was in the next moment that he ceased remembering and fell into a silent blackness. But awareness, a different awareness, began to stir in him again with the feeling of the salty sea rising in his throat.

Mefakani's hazel eyes filled with wonder as he watched Tiv resuscitate the creature and the creature gasp for air.

"Never has the Spirit Father of the Heavens and the Spirit Mother of the Sea ever produced such a thunderous labor. What am I to make of this man-like creature who fell from the sky?"

The Shaman knew exactly who Temple was.

Mefakani watched the sun come out of hiding and melt the last of the fog. He held his twisted staff up high and led his tribesmen back to shore. The steely-gray water, flicked with blue now, slapped against the belly of his boat with a lulling rhythm. And he smiled to himself knowingly with the wet and unconscious creature cradled in his arms like a newborn babe.

CHAPTER TWO

The Prophecy

"A human God, who comes from the Heavens, will be Teacher and Prophet to the Makolese. The Holy One will come at a time of peril and help to conquer the enemies of the Makolese. This magical Being will be the High Priest's greatest ally in conquering his enemies...(damaged text/short section missing)*...One without the other is empty. Power multiplies tenfold and then again tenfold, again and again until the time of Purification and Redemption. To be recognized, the Divine One must bear the sign of Wisdom, which is the mark upon the holy brow. Beware of impostors, who can fool the elect."*

Prophet Unknown
Makolese Prophecy Scroll #12
The Makolese Scroll on The Education of Temple Fox #2

Queen Palomei's anger was as imposing as her size, all eight feet and four hundred pounds of her. The High Shaman always kept her waiting and, when he did, she always found herself doing exactly as she did the last time he held her captive by his indifference to her dictates. She paced and seethed. She shook the timber floor of her tall pavilion with each step, until, feeling somewhat defeated, she walked back to the obsidian dais. The giantess sat back down on her huge rattan chair, cushioning her feet on the two skulls she used as footstools. She had heard the rumors about the Creature, several different versions of them. Now she needed someone who could give her facts and see beyond the fog of hopeful expectation.

The private partition slid open causing a swarm of bees to scatter from Palomei's crown of blossoms. A warm sea breeze filled the room. The Shaman entered and lowered his head to the timber floor. "May the Lord Tagheetu bless you with many children, Most Respected," he said as he leaned his staff out so the Queen could kiss it.

Queen Palomei glared at him from beneath lowered brows for a few interminable seconds, then leaned forward and kissed the staff. "As usual, you have kept me waiting," she growled in a tight voice.

The Shaman looked up at the Queen with irritation. *"Where would Palomei be without my spiritual advice? How many battles have I won for her? This is not a time for impetuosity. What I am about to tell her now will change the very course of her life, all our lives,"* he thought.

"Haste muddies the pond," he responded lightly. "In truth, I could not leave."

"I do not care," she growled even louder. "You should have come to me immediately."

Mefakani fell silent for a brief moment, too concerned about recent events than to waste time bickering. The Queen, noticing her sudden tiredness, did the same. And so, there was a reining in of tempers and a yearning for a truce.

The Queen gave in first. "So what is this Thing that fell from the sky?" she finally asked.

Mefakani's energies renewed and his hazel eyes came alive. "The Creature is a miracle and a marvel to see, Most Respected. Its hide is thick and dark brown, and it sheds it like a butterfly sloughs its cocoon. I have brought Its scalp and eyes for you.'

Mefakani clapped his hands together and his Apprentice, a boy of eighteen, rushed from behind the tall sliding panel. The thin boy with a shaven head bowed reverently to the matriarch. He unwrapped an ornately painted parcel made from barkcloth and raised it to the level of the Queen's face. She eyed it narrowly and gestured for the Apprentice to pick up the items. Jabal lifted the leather helmet and goggles in the air as if holding dead body parts.

"Inside the dark cocoon," the Shaman intoned with a sense of awe, "was a man, a man whose skin is like the midday sun."

"A white man!" Palomei shouted as if sounding an alarm then dismissed Jabal with a hurried hand.

The Apprentice shuffled backward bowing. He opened the sliding screen, stepped through and closed it quietly.

"Not quite so," the Shaman said calmly, waiting for the partition to close completely. "This pale Creature," he let the words draw out slowly, "is a man-god."

Palomei's cheeks puffed out and she gave a look of shock in return.

"He is a gift conceived by the Spirit Father of the Heavens and birthed from the Spirit Mother of the Sea."

"But a white man can never be a good thing," she stated flatly, reproaching him with a scowl. "Shaman, I am shocked you have drawn such a hasty and dangerous conclusion."

"Most Respected, I, above all, would not hold this opinion unless I was absolutely certain. When we first peeled off his outer hide and saw his unfortunate hue, we were as alarmed as you were. But then we saw it." He spoke as if remembering the happiest day of his life. "He received a wound when he fell from the sky. It has left him with a scar—here ." He drew a finger to his own forehead and rubbed it gently above a point between his brows.

Palomei pursed her lips together. Her voice was sober, clear. "You, of all people, know what this means."

"Yes," he intoned with equal seriousness. "This fulfills the oldest prophecy: A magical Being, a Teacher, would someday come from the Heavens. But he must bear the sign of wisdom, which is the mark on the brow."

The Queen, in a state of wonderment, rocked on the fulcrum of doubt between acceptance and total disbelief. She leaned back deep in thought, her massive flesh filling the contours of her chair. As she did this, she pondered the Shaman's words in her mind, *The prophecy foretold of a Great One who would appear during a time of profound adversity. These were treacherous times, indeed. But what can I make of the prophecy that also forewarned against impostors, false prophets who could fool even the elite? It is my right and duty to play the skeptic.*

She leaned forward and the chair creaked as it strained beneath her weight. "Does he say why he has come here?"

"No, Most Respected. He lies asleep due to the injury to his head. He does speak while unconscious, however, yet the language is strange. Tani says it sounds like the language of the Whites."

Mefakani was sorry he let the last words slip out, but it was the truth.

The Queen raised an eyebrow, got up, and paced the chamber, raising a fury among the bees who chased her across the room.

"Why is Mefakani so certain that the creature is not a wizard, but a god? But a white god! Perhaps the stress had finally cracked his mind wide open."

The chair issued its squeaky complaint when she sat back down and she looked at her Spiritual Advisor with scrutiny. "Go on," she said.

"There is, as you know, Most Respected, only one who knows the language best and she has become widowed by the storm."

"I have heard this and my heart is greatly saddened. I am very fond of Losha, as you know. This house has already made provisions for her and the last of her kin. Her husband's niece, I believe."

"Then you also know that we are uncertain if Losha is truly widowed. Amron's body has yet to be found."

"I want to learn what the Spirits say about this matter later, but for now...." She thumped a heavy foot against her footrest.

Mefakani continued. "Losha agreed to hear the words mumbled by the man-god. He repeats a phrase over and over again which she interpreted as, "I lost the medicine. I am sorry.""

The Queen leaned forward again with her forearms pressed heavily against her fleshy thighs. "What do you think it means?"

The jagged tattoos across his cheeks pulled taut and his brow tensed. "The Gods sent him to bring us their magic, but, while becoming human in the process of birth, he has forgotten the magic."

"An impostor's trick?" she asked.

"Wise question, Most Respected. Was it not for the sacred sign upon his head I would think otherwise." His eyes locked deeply into hers and his tone softened. "Palomei, you must trust me."

When the Shaman addressed his sovereign in the familiar, the tension, which had congealed into a stubborn knot in her stomach, loosened and her suspicions slackened. "I do trust you, Mefakani. I trust you and Owane above anyone else. Still, you must realize how serious this is. We must be certain beyond any doubt. The prophecy warns about impostors."

"Yes, My Beloved Queen. I have taken that into consideration."

Palomei rubbed the three interlocking spirals tattooed on her fat chin. "And Elder Tani, what does she say about this?"

"The same," he replied. "She feels absolutely certain he has fulfilled the old prophecy."

"I should be happy," she said in a distant tone. "Perhaps suspicion is simply part of my nature."

"As it should be for any Queen," the Priest declared. "Wisdom is discerning."

Palomei straightened up and the chair creaked beneath her in protest. "As you might have guessed, I am not deciding on this matter until the Elder Council and I meet with the Stranger." Agitated, she got up and paced the room once more, sending the bees into another frenzy. She stopped and towered over the Priest. "What advice can you offer me for now, High Shaman?"

Mefakani had worked out a plan in advance and he prayed to Lord Tagheetu that nothing would shake it. He gazed up at the Sovereign. "Patience, My Queen. We must all exercise that first when we set about the task of healing him. Only then will he remember what he brings us from the Gods."

The High Shaman moved his plan into place. "As for the sacred placenta that nourished him on his journey here, it is very strange. It is made of an incredibly fine, white skin and is as light as air itself."

"Well, where is it? Let me see it!" The Queen clapped her hands together in anticipation. There was a glint in Mefakani's eyes as Palomei swallowed the bait. "Well?" she asked, staring down at him.

Mefakani exhaled loudly. "I do not have it and there is nothing I can do about it. Elder Tani is the finest of Healers, who I bow before in humble admiration, but she has become too... well, cautious in her old age. She will not let me inspect the sacred skin."

"What?" Palomei raised an imperial eyebrow.

"I, too, was surprised, Most Respected. Not only will she not let me touch it...me, who pulled it out of the womb of our Mother Sea, but she has placed her own unjustifiable taboo on it for all males. And yet," he pointed out, "it is a male man-god the Lord Tagheetu has arranged for the Sky Spirit to send to us. Is it right to keep taboo this sacred tissue, which nourished the Lord's messenger? I understand she guards the man-god day and night. I assure you, Most Respected, she does this out of duty to protect him."

Palomei sat back down and the bees circled round her head. "I have not decided yet in whose care he will be placed," she spoke with rising indignation.

"In all truthfulness, Tani's was the nearest hut. In light of the Being's injuries it made sense to take him there at the time." He leaned forward with his staff. "Like Elder Tani, I, too, am duty bound to protect this vulnerable creature from demons. I pray that his well-being will not be jeopardized."

"I will make certain of that," the Queen assured. "When the man-god is able to be moved safely, he will reside at your compound."

"Thank you, Most Respected." Mefakani knew the Lord and his Spirits had at last seen things his way. "But what of the holy afterbirth?"

Palomei tapped her chin in deep thought. "I see your point, Mefakani, yet I also see Tani's. It is certainly beyond the power granted to me to give spiritual advice to our own High Priest, however, it seems that this Spirit creature comes not for males exclusively, but for all." She handed the leather helmet and goggles back to the Shaman. "Would it please the Lord Tagheetu and his High Priest if the men keep the creature's shed skin and eyes, as they would a piece of priestly foreskin; and allow the women to keep the placenta as their sacred relic?" she asked.

Mefakani nodded in agreement and bowed. "You are truly wise, Most Respected. Yes, it would greatly please the Lord Tagheetu."

"You will keep me informed as to the creature's progress?"

"I will, Most Respected."

Palomei rose from her chair signifying that the meeting was over. Mefakani bowed again, then left.

When he was alone outside, Mefakani faced the direction of the swamps and bowed once. Then, he turned towards the twin peaks of the sacred hollow mountain, where the spirits of the mountain hid, and said a prayer of thanks. He allowed himself a smile.

"Soon, I will be the mediator between the man-god and the Queen, and without compromising my bittersweet relationship with Tani. But, more importantly, this Stranger, who has dropped from the sky, will now become my most powerful ally. Yes," Mefakani thought, *"the Lord, indeed, has finally seen things my way."*

CHAPTER THREE

The Allies

"I was a milksop from the time I was born until I died in the waters near Makol Island twenty-five years later. To return to life was my first act of courage. This was a sacrifice, which I first regretted."

Temple Fox
Makolese Death & Dying Scroll #1
The Makolese Scroll on The Education of Temple Fox #3

Temple woke with his head throbbing and a feeling of nausea. He found himself lying on the wooden floor on a soft bed of ferns, his body draped in a red and black barkcloth. In front of him, a curtain of the same cloth moved gently in the breeze. It was quiet. Temple rolled his head uneasily to the right and focused his eyes the best he could on the far corner of the room. There, he spied a small metal pot simmering above a quiet fire in a shallow pit of sand and stone, the scent of sandalwood permeating the air. High above him in the rafters hung rows of dried fish and plants. He turned stiffly to his left and eyed a small enclosure sectioned off by a curtain parted just enough so Temple could see bamboo shelves filled with a vast menagerie of smoky glass jars, dried roots, and a mortar and pestle made of volcanic rock. A row of dusty human skulls sat on the floor below this.

Temple could feel a new wave of nausea rise in him and his head pound harder. He touched his aching head where the blood had dried just as an enormous spider climbed out from one of the skull's eye sockets, dragging a dust mote on one of its spindly legs. Temple watched as it scuttled by his side, then disappeared under a piece of cloth beside him. He tried to beat the cloth with his fist to kill the intruder, but the slightest movement caused his pain to come alive and he moaned with the effort.

Without warning, a pair of tiny brown feet caked in sand came into view under the barkcloth curtain. A thin bony hand appeared and pulled the curtain aside. Out popped a white fluffy head of disheveled hair attached to a tiny leathery woman with a flat nose and a honey-brown complexion. Her earlobes hung loosely to her shoulders and her dried-up breasts hung to her waist. A strange tattoo, a large spiral, marked her chin and stretched when she gave a toothless smile that seemed to reach from ear to ear. She bowed, then raised her head and asked, "Ah, good?"

"Head hurts," Temple said, startled and confused. "Who are you?"

Tani squatted beside him, her black liquid eyes dancing with life. "I, Tani. I no talk good white words."

"Do you speak Creole? Parlez vous Francais?"

Understanding was absent from Tani's eyes.

"There was a plane. A plane?" he explained in slow English, but Tani just stared back. "And there was another man." She shook her head. She did not understand. The old woman held a coconut shell to his lips for him to drink. Temple swallowed hard and frowned at the bitter taste.

"Good pujo. Eat!" she demanded, and placed a large leaf with some kind of sour mashed plant under his nose. But the white man's eyes rolled back inside his head and he fell back into unconsciousness.

★　　★　　★　　★　　★　　★

The pilot drifted in and out of consciousness till the next evening, remembering little of Tani and nothing of the Priest. When he finally woke to full consciousness, he lay still with his eyes closed, listening to soft chanting in the room.

Temple knew that something had changed deep within him. It wasn't simply that he had survived death, or even that he had lost his best friend. He knew Blake was dead. Yet, how did he know for certain? He searched his memory for the last time he had seen Blake before they set off on the trip together.

The Englishman had been in his tattered overalls leaning against an acacia tree. He had rolled a cigarette neatly between his oily fingers, lit it and took one deep drag. The last vivid memory Temple had of Blake had been of his impish grin through the great shock of gray beard that stuck out beneath his leather helmet. He remembered how Blake had squinted up at the cutting African sun as a vulture circled unsteadily overhead. "Soon, after we're up there, we'll have some peace, mate," he remembered him saying.

Peace indeed. Blake was dead. And yet it wasn't grief for his old friend that troubled Temple now. Rising within him were fragmented memories of the storm, the Moth spinning helplessly and his cart wheeling through space. Still, there was something else. It was a memory of something huge; an event so penetrating that lost planes and torn flesh meant little in comparison. But compared to what? What could be so large and encompassing that even the death of a friend seemed small?

Temple felt a sense of profound loss. If it wasn't for his adventurous friend, then what? He'd lost the medicine crate, which he realized could jeopardize many lives in the Seychelles, and yet it wasn't that either. The feeling of losing something lay elsewhere deep within his heart.

The pilot let the tension ease from his battered body and allowed his mind to roam. Slowly, ever so slowly, he remembered the Light; a Light so powerful and filled with bliss that it was eternity itself. He remembered it in fragments: the void, the tunnel and the Light. How could a man in his mid-twenties, who was relatively stable, sane, accept what had just happened to him? Death. Rebirth. And what of that profound Love he had experienced right down to the invisible cells of his invisible body? Love was something he had never given much thought to before. Yet he had felt Love, real Love, and he knew it was the most real feeling he would ever know. So, there he was, lying in a thatched hut somewhere on a tropical island, swimming in the heat of his own sweat, a one-time arrogant atheist now thoroughly altered by his own death.

Temple's jaw tensed and his eyelids fluttered. But what of his former self? Where had the old Temple Fox gone? Where was the young man who tried liquor swilling, plug spitting and imitating the swaggering talk of men, but never fooled anyone into thinking he was anything but milksop? Where was the Temple Fox who attempted the perpetual smirk only to let his quivering lip triumph? No broad shoulders or muscled thighs, or even his practiced manly stride, ever fooled those who knew, because they had heard the stories, that

Temple Fox was a coward, a Momma's boy, a girlie-boy. So who was he now?

Temple would have burst into tears had it not been for the fact that, milksop or no milksop, he was half English, and the English never cry. He felt the presence of others around him and bit his lip to hold back the tears. If he let go he knew the tears would never end because, for some unknown reason, he had mustered the courage to return to life, which, to Temple, meant the loss of that deeply felt peace. Life felt like death!

★   ★   ★   ★   ★   ★

The shadows shifted slightly as Tani lit another oil jar in the twilight of the room. Mefakani stared down at the sleeping God, whose forehead was wrapped with a thin strip of cloth, his sandy brown hair still streaked with dried blood. The Shaman waved his crooked staff over him, causing a shadow to slide across Temple's swollen face.

Temple opened his eyes far enough to see the carved head of a crocodile on top of a wooden staff. Wrapped round it was a live snake. A shiver ran up his spine and he closed his eyes tightly thinking he was dreaming. When he opened his eyes again, cautiously this time, the snake appeared a part of the stick and nothing more. He squinted in the half-light and a strange man, barely past his prime, came sharply into focus. The man's liver-brown face was tattooed with dark blue zigzags; his face and head were clean shaven, and the only thing he wore, besides a cloth wrap-around, was a long, slate-gray ponytail at the base of his skull. The man stared back at Temple with hard hazel eyes. Realizing that this strange man was not your typical inhabitant from the Seychelles, the pilot stared back at the two people staring down at him, wondering who they were.

"Must have had a bloody good bang on my head," he groaned softly, blinking his eyes painfully.

The Healer and the Priest looked at each other with raised eyebrows, then prostrated themselves before the young God. Then Mefakani got up and waved a bundle of feathers across the length of Temple's body while Tani removed the cloth from the pilot's head and gently dabbed something greasy on his wound.

Temple moaned louder when Tani fed him a gruel using her own fingers to push the food into his mouth. When the man-god protested by pushing her hand away, they knew he was getting better.

"God, that's awful stuff," he complained, with his mouth full. He reached for the bowl of liquid Tani held to his lips, but his hand trembled and fell weakly to his chest. He drank greedily from her hands then asked, "By the way, where the hell am I?"

The Shaman rose to his feet, bowed to Temple again then walked to the window to issue a boisterous command to someone outside. Temple could hear the pounding of running feet fading into the distance.

Within minutes, the floor vibrated and the door opened to the stilted hut. In walked a young woman who stood in the lamplight by the foot of Temple's bed mat. She had a fine nose, thick lips and almond shaped eyes. She was much darker than Tani or the Priest, a chocolate brown with a dash of cinnamon. Her long bushy hair fell past her bare breasts, and around her skirted waist she wore a sash of yellow feathers. When she saw Temple, she lowered herself to the floor.

"Why does everyone do that?" Temple grumbled, trying not to stare at her breasts.

"It is a sign of high respect," she answered in a peculiar English accent with her head still touching the floor.

"You speak English!" The rush of excitement set his head throbbing again, but he managed to sit up in bed stiffly.

Losha rose and flung back her unruly hair, giving her a wild appearance. She peered into Temple's eyes. They were a startling blue like the sky from which he had fallen, she thought, and yet, now that this divine creature was awake, he looked more like a man than a god. "Am I permitted to speak?"

"You can sing if you like," he said, more alert now. "What's your name?"

"Losha. Losha Ninti," she answered and watched the Shaman stir out of the corner of her eye.

Temple stared back for a quiet moment trying to reckon with the peculiar feeling of familiarity he held towards her. He rubbed his head. "Any idea how I got here?"

"You fell from the sky and were pulled out of the sea by our High Shaman," she answered, giving Mefakani a sideways glance.

Temple eyed the proud tattooed face. "Please thank him for me. I'm in his debt." Losha translated and the Shaman gave a stern nod in acknowledgement. The pilot looked to the woman again. "You're English is very good," he said.

"My mother was an interpreter and translator of many languages. I learned much from her and from an Englishman from India."

"Well, thank God you're here because I need to know where Doctor LaFlamme is and how I can get back home?"

Losha gave a puzzled look to the others then turned again to the Stranger. "I have been asked to act as an Interpreter until you learn our language."

"Oh, I won't be here long enough for that," he said, still staring at the woman. "So tell me, which island am I on?"

"You are on Makol Island."

"Makol Island?" Temple held his head searching his feeble memory. Makol was not in the archipelago of the Seychelles Islands. He knew that for certain. A heat ran through him and he broke out in a new sweat as his memory began to clear. A shroud of mystery surrounded Makol Island, if indeed it actually existed. Young merchants in Mombasa often quarreled with people who thought the island didn't exist, and argued about it with the older seamen who knew it did. The younger merchants told tales of headhunting savages who liked the taste of Arab flesh. But the old men spoke reverently of the archipelago of Seven Isles, the wealth of its obsidian, greenstone and onyx, the beauty of the main island, and its generous people who, it was rumored, were endowed with magical abilities. Many of the old men claimed they had sailed back to find the magical kingdom, only to be driven home by blinding fog and treacherous storms that had taken too many of their companions' lives. Temple laughed to himself quietly, nervously.

He had heard some of the stories from the persistent seamen, the ones the people used to call "the mad men of the sea," who went so far as to employ astrologers and holy men to chart their courses for them, having failed many times in their attempts to find the misty isle. It was only rarely, very rarely, they'd say, that Allah would allow them to find their way back to Makol. But this was, of course, all legend.

"That's impossible," Temple finally said. "This place isn't supposed to exist. I mean, The Island of Mists is only a legend." He eyed the human skulls sitting neatly in a row on the dusty floor behind Tani. Then, he looked at Tani's deep black eyes and the hardened lines on Mefakani's face. All eyes were fixed on him. He looked back to Losha with defeat. "Makol isn't the name of one of the islands in the Seychelles, is it?"

"No," she said.

Temple's swollen face reddened. "Who exactly are these people?"

"This is our respected High Shaman, Mefakani," she said with a slight bow to the proud Priest, "and this is Elder Tani, a Healer. They want to know how we may address you."

"My...my name is Temple Fox." He tried to shake off any outward sign of worry, but his voice cracked slightly. "How often do ships come to this island?"

"Why, I believe the last ship came six moons ago. I can show you the remains of it when you are well," she answered plainly.

Tani's medicine rose in Temple's throat and he swallowed hard to rid himself of the putrid taste.

Mefakani, growing impatient, asked for a translation. And, while Temple lay there listening to the strange language, his heart sank and the light in his eyes slowly died.

"Six months! Would it be another six months before another ship arrived – if it survived?" he thought. *"Would anyone even bother to send a search plane this far to search for Blake and myself, and if they did, could they even find the island? How can I hold out for several months with head hunting cannibals as hosts? Is there another way to get off this island?"*

"This white man you mentioned, the Englishman, where's he now?" he interrupted.

Hearing the English words for *white man,* Mefakani broke in abruptly and demanded an interpretation.

"Let the girl speak with him," Tani said, with a light touch on the Shaman's wrist.

Mefakani pulled away from the old woman. "Ask him how he got that scar on his forehead?" he insisted of Losha.

The Healer and the Priest listened intently to Temple as if they were able to understand every word, but it was Losha who heard and understood the tale of how the Stranger had been hit by the medicine box and how he had lost it while floating through the sky.

When Temple was finished with his story, Losha turned to the others and relayed what she had been told. Mefakani grinned and the black slits of Tani's ancient eyes widened until the whites showed. The Shaman's smile slowly faded and his eyes squinted with faraway thoughts.

"One more question," Mefakani inquired. "Tell us about the other scar, the old one that wraps around his waist?"

Again all three leaned forward with keen interest and Losha interpreted.

Mefakani leaned back in a more calm repose and gave a thoughtful glance to Tani. "The others will not understand," he said.

"By the power of the Divine, they must!" the old woman replied with defiant optimism.

Mefakani looked down at the Stranger. "How old is he?" he asked without looking at Losha.

"He says he is twenty five seasons."

The Shaman's brow furrowed in surprise, "A boy? They sent us a mere boy!" he scoffed.

A moment passed and the Shaman came to understand why the Gods had planned this so. *"The younger the man part of him, the more like clay he would be,"* he thought. He gave Tani a callous sideways glance. *"And far more malleable than Elders who are stubborn beyond reason!"* Mefakani smiled at the God's wisdom.

Losha looked from the happy Priest to Tani and back to Temple. She had been instructed as to what must be done. "Shaman Mefakani says before you meet with any of our people you must first meet with both the Queen and the Elder Council to explain why you have come. I will act as Interpreter."

"A Queen!"

"Until you are accustomed to your new home, Shaman Mefakani suggests I tutor you in our language in his lodge."

Before Temple could protest, Mefakani clapped his hands twice and two muscular men, wearing chest bands made of crocodile hide, appeared in the doorway. The marooned pilot paled to dead white. The men entered and bowed, then rushed over and took hold of Temple's arms and legs.

"Wait a minute!" he protested. "This is uncivilized!"

The two men lifted Temple who flayed about weakly and laid him on a litter carrier. Mefakani and Tani murmured quiet prayers and blew smoke from a burning bundle of herbs into his face until he coughed. The Shaman then shrouded the Stranger in a long robe of black iridescent feathers to render him invisible to the demons of the night.

CHAPTER FOUR

The Interrogation

"You must know beyond belief; trust without doubt, and be courageous beyond thought of consequence. And above all else, forgive and love..."

Temple Fox
The Makolese Scroll on The Education of Temple Fox #4

Temple lay dreaming in the twilight of Mefakani's private lodge. In his dream he was alone searching an island beach for something he had lost. He looked everywhere, yet couldn't fathom what it was he was looking for. It had just stormed and an apricot light broke through heavy black clouds. Scattered on the beaches were hundreds of palm leaves. He was worried and frantically looked under every frond. Where had he lost it?

Suddenly, a white bird appeared in front of him and perched in his open palm. It spoke softly to him. "I am not lost," the bird said, "I have been here all along." Before Temple could respond he caught a movement out of the corner of his eye. His skin prickled and his blood ran cold when a lion appeared out of a yellow sea. It shook the sea loose from its mane then trotted towards him, causing the ground to vibrate beneath him. The beat quickened as the beast finally charged across the beach at him. The dreamer, seized by a sudden panic, froze in place. Then, without knowing why, he quite suddenly grabbed the dream bird and swallowed it whole, feeling it slide down his gullet like a slippery oyster. All at once a profound peace came over him, filling him up like warm oil. The dream ended with the brawny lion sitting by Temple's side licking his hand.

The pilot woke on his sleeping mat in a state of euphoria, his palms wet, his heart racing. As his attention focused onto the room, the contentment dissolved like vapor, replaced by an uneasy feeling of deep dread. He opened his eyes to find the Priest looming above him and rambling in rapid Makolese.

Losha stepped from a dark corner, crossed her hands over her breasts and bowed to Temple. "The High Shaman asks how you are feeling today."

A slice of dawn light slipped into the room and a glint of metal hit Temple's eyes. An Arab dagger, a helmet of Spanish design, and an array of chest armor hung on the wall behind the Shaman's head. On the floor sat a dusty sextant and a neat row of skulls similar to what he had seen at Tani's. For a split second he thought he was still dreaming then remembered the events from the day before. He looked up at the dark woman. "I've got a bit of a headache, but I do feel stronger," he finally replied.

"The Shaman would like me to teach you some Makolese to prepare you for a meeting with the Queen's and the Elders' Councils today."

He blinked at her in a daze. "Well, okay," he said.

Mefakani leaned over, clasped Temple's elbow and pulled him to his feet. The pilot groaned with the effort. The Shaman pointed to the window and the pilot walked over to it stiffly and gazed out. Spread before him was a village compound comprised of round thatched structures with conical pitched roofs and timber pilings as their base. The complex was oval in shape and built around a huge, moss-covered cedar that grew several yards from a central fire pit. To the southeast, a muddy river flowed by. The Shaman made an elliptical gesture in the air with his staff then pointed to himself.

"This is all yours. Is that what you're saying?" Temple asked, using the same gestures and pointing to his host.

"Yes," the Interpreter said, answering for the Priest. "And that small hut he is having built will be where you will live," she added.

Temple's shock and confusion started to stew into a complaint. He stood for a moment, mustering just the right measure of diplomacy and strength to express his gratitude and decline the generous offer when a group of men ran to the middle of the complex and shouted for the Priest. Mefakani called back in response and strode out of his lodge and down the stairs towards the panicked voices.

Alarm flashed across the Interpreter's face and she rushed to the window where Temple stood. Mefakani marched across the compound over to a growing mob, shouting above the explosion of voices as he went. When they parted to make way for him, he found four men sitting on top of a fifth man who twitched uncontrollably. The Shaman shook his staff, shouting at the crowd to disperse, but a rise of murmuring voices followed and some of the villagers pointed to Temple at the window.

The blood behind Temple's eyes pounded against his brain and he clutched the windowsill. "What in bloody blazes is going on?"

The Shaman shouted across the compound at Losha and she let out a quiet, but sharp cry. She spoke in a faraway tone without taking her eyes off the convulsing man in the distance. "A lost spirit has taken over this man, Tolowan. Shaman Mefakani says the men think it is the spirit of my dead husband, but he says it is not." She struggled to catch her breath.

Temple's jaw tensed and he stared back at the sullen woman.

Tolowan screamed like a wounded animal and his eyes rolled back and flashed white. When the men carried him past the window, Mefakani barked a few words up at Losha as they passed, then led the men up the stairs into a nearby hut.

The Interpreter took a deep breath to gather herself then turned to the marooned pilot. "The Shaman says he is sending for his Apprentice to help cast out the spirit."

Temple's eyes were fixed into a stare as he watched the sudden chaos before him. People rushed to the banks of the muddy river and placed baskets of fruit, fish, and bundles of reed into a dugout.

"What are they doing?" he asked nervously.

"When Jabal, the Shaman's Apprentice, draws out the lost spirit, he will put it safely inside the funeral boat. Then he will take it to the swamps," she said, calmer now that she had caught her breath. "Upon death, all must enter the jaws of Tagheetu. Tagheetu is the Eater of Men's Fears. He is the intermediary between the people and the gods." Losha pushed a tuft of hair off her face and tucked it behind her ear. "We must return to Him when we die. Still, some do not conquer their fears before the Lord and escape Him. They become demons who roam the island, waiting for someone to prey upon – like poor Tolowan."

Temple felt vulnerable in this alien place, vulnerable and

thoroughly alone.

Losha saw his discomfort. "It is not uncommon for this to happen," she added with such nonchalance that it sent a shiver up Temple's spine. "Mefakani wishes to show you the exorcism himself, but there is no time. Today, we must go to the Great Round House where the Queen's Council and the Elders' Council meet. I have never been there myself," she said with a little apprehension. "The Great Round House is a holy place: The Place Tagheetu Last Rested." She gestured for Temple to sit, signifying she had much to explain to him.

She leaned against the window frame and caught the sun in her unruly hair, remembering her history from childhood. "It has been told long, long ago the Mountain Gods had a great battle and blew the top off the mountain. Hot ash and smoke choked off all life on the many islands, except one.

"After the gods had their war, it is told that they flew back into the sky and left this ruined world forever. There was one, tiny island not far from here, however, where one, very old man survived. His name was Gadji."

Temple felt a gentle tingle creep across his brow. He touched his wound lightly with his middle finger, then again gave the Interpreter his full attention.

"There was no one alive but Gadji," she continued, "save for one big crocodile named, Tagheetu."

"Tagheetu. A crocodile?" he murmured under his breath.

Losha became animated as she told her people's history. "Tagheetu was very angry with the gods. And He did not trust humans, who were the most destructive of all the god's children. He would not talk to Gadji, but the old man slowly coaxed Tagheetu into a friendship. And so, the Crocodile became his brother.

"Still, life was very lonely for the both of them. One day, Tagheetu returned from hunting. He told Gadji he had seen the old mountain island. He said there was a beautiful palm tree bearing many coconuts there, perhaps the only one that had survived. Gadji was excited and Tagheetu agreed to carry him there to see it for himself.

"When Gadji beheld the tree, a great light shone from it and turned the land, sea, and sky a milky white. The old man was blinded and dizzied by it. When he recovered his senses, the sea and sky had turned blue and the land charred black. The magnificent tree had gone. In its place stood an old woman who greeted the two with a dance and an offering of coconuts. Her name was Hianna. Hianna said she had flown to Makol from a great people to the northwest in the Land of Sin-Ni. When she saw Makol and how barren it was, she set about the task of making it fertile again, for she had the power of the Su to bring about life. She needed a companion to help her, she told them, and so she had lured the two brothers to her shores by magic."

Losha changed her voice to fit the characters as she told the ancient tale. "'How is it that we can make life again on this barren earth?' Gadji asked, knowing that Hianna was a magical being and he was not.

"'Make love to me, Gadji, and from my womb all life will flow,'" Losha continued in a firm, yet delicate voice.

"'But I am an old man,' Gadji protested, 'and you an old woman. The years have taken the life out of my seed long ago.'

"Before the old man's doubt could deepen, Hianna turned herself into a beautiful young woman and Gadji into a young man. It is from their seeds that all life has sprung." Losha ended her tale by clasping her hands together and giving a respectful nod. She sat down on the floor in front of the man-god. "Tagheetu," she added, "was granted Lordship and given the power to govern humans so they would not wander from the true path."

Beneath Temple's silence there was a hidden, nervous smile. *"A primitive tale,"* he mused. *"But a crocodile god?"* In truth the story made no sense to him.

Losha handed the Stranger a slice of breadfruit. "Please eat," she said. "We have been delayed enough and I must make you ready to meet with the Queen and the Counselors soon."

★　　★　　★　　★　　★　　★

Losha secured a yellow blossom behind her ear and tried to tame her hair again with a tortoise shell comb. By the time the Queen's personal guards arrived, she had smoothed her yellow, feathered sash so many times the ends began to shed.

"We must go now," she said to Temple nervously and dashed quickly down the lodge stairs with her charge behind her.

The pale Stranger was met by a troop of twelve guardsmen wearing chest bands, skirts, and buskins made from crocodile hide. Each carried a spear, and, by their side hung a two-pointed sword with a broad curved blade. Temple was puzzled by the curious shields they carried, if indeed they were shields, for they had been forged into a thin, circular, metal frame with only a small, round, polished quartz crystal at its center.

Losha saw Temple tense. "They will protect you," she said.

The castaway gave a shallow nod to the tattooed guards then took a startled step back when Mefakani stepped from behind the wall of warriors.

The High Shaman, dressed in the full skin of a crocodile, dragged his long tail behind him creating one long winding track in the sand. In his hands he carried the most important tool of his profession – his crooked staff with its crocodile head and snake carved round it. By his left side hung a scimitar; on his right hung a war club carved in the same curved design. Mefakani's eyes remained caged behind the crooked teeth of the crocodile's upper jaw when he lowered his head in a respectful bow to the Stranger. Without a word, he held his staff high and motioned for the procession to follow.

The troop marched silently through the Shaman's compound in a northern direction and entered a shady forest trail with a high latticework of hanging lianas, thick as a man's thigh, arched above their heads. Colorful birds flickered from vine to vine screaming in protest at the sudden invasion. They marched on for half a mile past giant ferns and cypress choked in vine, until they came to a bright, open area of beach. There, they passed a large village of round huts grouped in circular clusters. Women, balancing baskets on their heads, abandoned their labors and joined the curious onlookers who had gathered. Some villagers hissed, some bowed with respect, but all were kept at bay by the flash of metal swords.

Before they took a turn towards the interior to the east, Losha pointed along the coast to the Common House, a long rectangular building in the distance built on top of massive pillars by the sea.

"That is where people gather to cook and eat the days catch. Next to it is the Children's Lodge," which, she explained, was the new school and living quarters for children seven years and older, an idea that their Shaman had recently implemented. "My husband's niece lives there. She is the only kin I have left now," she said.

The pilot only gave a strained smile in reply.

Losha walked in silence, chewing on a strand of her hair. She caught occasional glimpses of the Stranger. *Am I or am I not in the presence of the Great Teacher?"* she pondered. *"He appears so harmless, so frightened. If the dark spirits were able to conjure a wizard to fool the Makolese, would they send one such as this? Perhaps. After all, he is White. And yet, he seems to be only just a man. But a man who had fallen from the sky?"*

The pilot's feet blistered from the burning sand. With every step his nerves began to fray and he trembled inwardly with anticipation. *"What exactly is going to happen to me? Would anyone back in Mombasa dare to send a search plane this far? But where? I don't even know exactly where Makol is."*

Temple side stepped into some shade and glimpsed at Losha to see if she'd noticed. It was at that moment that he rose out of his miasma long enough to see the burden he had put on the young widow. For her, there was to be no mourning, just the anxious feeling of being as lost as the roaming spirit of her dead husband. Lost spirits. The notion turned his stomach. The only lost spirits he knew were himself and now Losha. Temple slowed his pace a bit so she was walking by his side. He didn't know what he was going to say to her. He gave her a sideways glance and cleared his throat to speak when Mefakani stopped at the bottom of a steep, sandy hill littered with large boulders and shattered Temple's effort to say something, anything.

Losha looked over at Temple, sensing his discomfort, when the Priest signaled for the procession to continue up the ragged pathway. Before Temple caught her eye, the widow looked away again.

Temple fell back into his own silence with his attention focused on his own discomfort. His feet went from blistered to stone bruised, yet he dared not complain or slow the pace Mefakani had set. When he reached the summit, he eased himself down onto the hot ground to catch his breath and positioned himself in Losha's shadow to shield him from the glare. He watched the rest of the procession climb the hill and viewed the island from a distance. Spread below him was a view of four distinct villages, all much larger than the Shaman's own compound. All the huts were circular in design, all thatched, and set on rock and timber pilings. He spied villagers, ant-like in their movements, as they meandered to and fro. There were men in boats and children chasing seagulls while others cleaned the morning catch. Temple's thoughts were interrupted when the guardsmen circled round him and motioned him to move on.

The Widow and the Stranger were escorted through a thicket of gnarled trees where the light grew green and dimmer and the air thicker with humidity. They brushed past the creepers and fronds with Losha catching the last of the morning dew in her untamable hair. Temple found some relief as his feet sank into the cool spongy moss that carpeted the ground and noticed the dark whispers behind him when he paused to untangle Losha's hair from a vine. Here, there was a sense of both sacredness and fear. Here, all was alive, pulsing with life, yet trembling with dread.

The murmurs came to an abrupt halt when the trail ended at a wide, flat rim of sand, marking the edge of a hidden caldera, and the sight of Hollow Mountain far in the distance.

Temple and Losha wandered over to the edge to peer over the

precipice. Far below, a resplendent dome rose out of the center of a deep crater of verdant green. Burnished stone captured the sun and cast out luminous rainbows in the humid air. Losha snatched her breath in delight. She turned her head and smiled at Temple like a child who had shared in some secret discovery, but they were motioned on and the smile faded. Though the sense of wonder remained for both, their nervousness grew as they wound their way down wide stone steps and drew closer above the strange dome. Colossal pillars supporting a massive, black base of ponderous stone came into view. Like a giant table fit for Titans, the structure sat better than three stories high. On top of this monumental plinth sat the shimmering dome. Through the haze of rainbows, the Stranger and the Interpreter caught the glint of moving water under the structure and a small flock of white swans swimming lazily about. But what made both of them even more edgy now, other than this awesome sight, was the crowd spread round the Great Round House below, all eyes focused on them.

Temple was grateful for the moist grass beneath his blistered feet when he reached the bottom of the stairs. However, the deeper he was escorted into the crater the more uncertain he became. *"What will they do to me? Sacrifice me?"*

Nothing prepared him for what was before him now. The Shaman took hold of Temple's arm, led him past the wide semi-circle of old people and positioned him twenty feet in front of a crocodile – a large one. Behind the beast stood a line of guardsmen with scimitars in hand.

Temple felt the blood drain from his head. He caught himself in a near faint and quickly put his head to his knees to steady himself, making it look like a respectful bow. No greeting was returned. Instead, the guards moved in unison, like a curtain parting, to reveal an enormously fat woman sitting behind them on a huge rattan chair.

When Queen Palomei rose from her throne-like chair, the people chanted in unison and an instantaneous buzz that sounded like bees filled the crater. Towering over her guards at eight feet tall, it was obvious this was no ordinary woman. In one hand, the Titan held an intricately carved wooden scepter that was taller than her and inlaid with pearls the size of Temple's fists. In the other hand, she balanced an unusually large human skull. When she raised these into the air, the bright yellow, feathered cape she wore over her red barkcloth skirt shimmered in the light, and a few frantic bees flew from blossom to blossom on the wreath that crowned her head. She lowered both scepter and skull and the buzzing chorus came to an abrupt halt.

Temple eased himself off the ground and met Queen Palomei's waiting eyes. She had been well informed as to the Shaman's findings in regards to the Stranger. Behind the cluster of interlocking spirals tattooed on the folds of her heavy chin, there was a hint of a half-smile.

Temple gazed down at the crocodile, which was uncomfortably close, then looked up at the Queen again, trying to hide his fears. In her eyes, he saw a trace of kindness, and a curious air of both dignity and deep, deep, despair, the kind of despair, he pondered worriedly, that could turn a person cruel. Temple wiped the sweat from his brow and found his heart calm a beat when the Interpreter was brought to his side.

"Queen Palomei is from the Si Te Cah blood line and is the last of her line," Losha explained in a half whisper. "Four of the men who are seated are her husbands."

On either side of the towering sovereign sat five men of normal stature on smaller rattan stools. One man, in particular, was so ancient and frail his skin hung from him like brittle parchment.

"Who's the little guy?" Temple whispered back. *"Probably lunch,"* he mused nervously.

"The old one is Okon, Great Grandfather to the Father of Palomei. He is nearly one hundred and sixty seasons old, the eldest on the island. All the others are the Elder Council."

Surrounding the Queen's Council were almost one hundred Elders. The men wore necklaces of bone and shell. Some had dangling feathers in their gray ponytails. The women wore their hair long and loose, and their earlobes long and floppy, mimicking their sagging breasts. Temple looked for the healer Tani, but only met the cold, hard stares of brown faces tattooed like blue lace.

A conch shell wailed and Mefakani leapt in front of the Queen and cantered around the crocodile, teasing it with his staff and forcing it to open its jaw to show a row of its needle-sharp teeth. He prayed aloud and hissed at the creature, then lowered himself to the ground and crawled close enough to shake his staff over it. The creature didn't move. Then without knowing how or why, Temple saw the Crocodile Priest raise himself off the ground holding the bloody head of the beast high in the air. The crowd cheered.

The Queen glanced down at Temple and smiled.

Temple drew an unconscious hand up to his unshaven throat. He moved his mouth to speak. "How'd he...?" Losha gave him the hush sign.

The Priest lowered the head down to his mouth and flicked his tongue against a flap of ragged skin. Temple watched in horror as he chewed a bit of raw flesh.

"To eat the crocodile, is to become one with Lord Tagheetu," Losha explained. "We are nourished by it." Then in a lower, cautious voice that marked her disapproval she said, "It is an archaic rite."

Temple's stomach flinched in revolt. *"Their god is a crocodile, their Queen is a giant and the souls of the dead invade the living! And where do I fit into this? Am I going to end up as some sort of meal?"*

The Priest placed the crocodile head at the Queen's feet, then smeared a bit of blood onto his staff and held it up towards her. Palomei kissed the Priest's staff and bowed her head reverently. With his blood stained hand and his beastly headdress tilted skyward, Mefakani raised his war club in the air and pointed it towards the Queen. The crowd hushed. Mefakani hit his club and his staff together three times; the knocking sounds ricocheting a moment later off the shiny dome.

Everyone in the circle dropped to their knees before the giant.

All eyes watched as Losha nudged Temple forward. When the Stranger knelt, the crowd hushed into a deeper silence that seemed to press all thoughts into one emotion – anticipation. Without showing the slightest twitch of uneasiness, although he felt quite the contrary, the pilot recited the phrase he had rehearsed with Losha earlier then slipped back into total nervous exhaustion.

The crowd gasped. Queen Palomei stood motionless with her head held high. When she nodded, the High Shaman beat out a rhythm to set her people upright again.

The Crocodile Priest's eyes sparkled behind the crooked teeth and again he danced into the center, this time waving his war club and staff around the Stranger. Then, the High Shaman did something not even Tani or the Queen expected. He aimed his staff in Temple's direction and beat out the familiar rhythm. Everyone stood, staring in confusion except Losha, who fell to her knees.

Cranik, an old man with long yellow teeth and a jaw too big for his face, leaned over to another Elder. "Does he expect us to bow to this white creature? I have heard that it is not even human. Has the Priest finally lost his mind?"

There were whispered protests from the Elder Council who could not find any good reason to kneel before the man-thing. They were gathered today to question the creature, then, to kill it. What more was there?

A short fat Elder shouldered his way through the crowd, making his way over to Cranik. "This display of respect is outrageous," said

Elder Gabu, with his hands placed defiantly on the round of his hips.

Senior Elder Sahdon, a handsome man with thick, gray, hair, leaned heavily on his cane and cast an eye beside him at Gabu. "Our Priest seems to have already made his mind up about this Thing. But why?" he whispered in a strangled aside.

Thinking he had been too impatient in hastening the Stranger's acceptance, the Shaman growled a quiet complaint and bowed to Temple himself.

There was a profound stillness in the air and a scattering of Elders, one by one, lowered themselves to the sand, hesitantly…reluctantly.

Temple was left eye-to-eye with Palomei, and her drilling stare and half-smile. Slowly, amid the gasps of confusion, she gave a shallow bow and a distinct nod in his direction.

Cranik ground his teeth together then spat.

When the few who had prostrated themselves were ordered to rise by the sound of Mefakani's signal, Temple stood there feeling naked.

"I understand we are to address you as, Temple. Is that so?" the Queen finally spoke and Losha interpreted.

"Yes, Most Respected," he answered directly in Makolese. Then in a clumsy, anxious moment, he added in English, "Where I come from, there have been many great Queens. Our last great ruler was named Queen Victoria."

Losha paused in sudden shock. *"Queen Victoria was an English Queen! A white Queen! The Stranger is no god as prophesied, but a barbaric Englishman! Yet he bears the sacred mark!"*

Losha didn't know what to do. She wanted to warn the Queen right then, but after the open display of respect, she was afraid it would make the Shaman, even the Queen, look foolish.

Losha reckoned this was not the time to disclose her discovery. She looked up at the imposing figure that waited anxiously for the interpretation. "The Stranger says, in the Heavens there is a great ruler called the Queen of Victory," she finally said with no more time to think and feeling foolish for the embellishment.

"Ah, a good name for any Queen," Palomei said, and cast her gaze down at Temple again. "The Elders and myself are anxious to ask you many questions about your origins. I have been made to understand you are well enough to answer our inquiries, are you not?"

Losha interpreted.

"Yes, Most Respected," Temple answered.

"Well then, we will go inside and share some sha together." Queen Palomei raised her scepter, turned, and walked up the mammoth staircase of worn stone into the Great Round House. Behind her the apprehensive Elders followed along with a cloud of strained murmurs and dark whispers.

Temple turned to Losha. "What happens next?" he asked worriedly.

Losha gave him a harsh look and then looked away quickly. "Now you must answer why you have come here," she answered curtly. *"Then they will discover you are an impostor,"* she thought.

"And, if they don't like my answers?" he pondered aloud, glancing at the headless crocodile on the blood soaked grass.

"They will know you are an impostor," she said, with a trace of acid in her tone.

"An impostor for whom?" he pondered, yet dared not ask.

Before Losha could say another word, the Priest moved between them and escorted Temple up the huge staircase to the platform of stone, which led to a low archway. There, they entered, one by one, on their hands and knees into the great hall.

It was vastly cooler inside, and Temple shivered slightly when he stood up. He was unprepared for what he saw. This place was old, infinitely old. He could feel it through the soles of his feet. It was as if the chamber held the history of the world in its belly. The frame of the dome was constructed from what looked like ribs of a great beast, notably their Lord Tagheetu, only Temple could see that the tapered beams were carved from granite. The walls themselves were composed completely of abalone shell cut into complex geometric shaped tiles. Like a rainbow colored oil slick, the walls shone with an ever-changing iridescence, forming large murals of strange symbols that seemed to appear, then disappear in the flickering light.

Temple noticed the play of light and searched around for its source. Seeing no windows or oil jars, he looked down at the curious floor. The slab was not a dense black at all, but a translucent smoky gray that confused his senses into thinking he was walking on something as substantial as marble and yet as intangible as a puff of smoke. The floor was as luminous as the nacreous walls in response to the dictates of the sun and the wind that combed the shallow reflective pool below them.

Inside the vast chamber, there was a buzz of voices as the Elders settled onto fat, round cushions. Okon, the Great Grandfather, steadied himself on his servant's arm as he stopped before Tani. He gave her a little nod. "You are like a cool breeze on a blistering day," he smiled. "It is always so good to see you, Tani."

"You are so old, you old shark, it is good for you to see at all," she chortled.

Okon laughed back and winked. "I know you are busy like a hungry titwee, but come to the compound sometime before the final dusk and we will share a cup of sha, you and I."

"For you, Okon, I will always make time, even if ten women wait in labor."

"Ahh. If only our women could be so," he sighed sadly.

The old Healer nodded in sympathy and Okon motioned for his servant to move him to his seat beside his Great, Great Granddaughter.

Mefakani positioned Temple and the Interpreter on soft cushions opposite the center of a semi-circle where the Queen's Council sat. The Queen herself sat on a huge throne carved smooth from a single block of rainbow obsidian, her feet resting on another set of skulls. On the perimeter, a circle of weathered and tattooed faces from the Elder Council moved in unison to their ghostly reflections on the polished floor. They murmured among themselves uneasily as the Crocodile Priest took a seat on a cushion to the right of the Queen's Council.

Losha pointed to the man and woman on either side of them seated on their knees before low tables. Each had several bamboo brushes, bowls of ink, and scrolls of bark paper laid out in front of them. "They are scribes," she explained. "One records everything that is said. The other describes the feeling and mood of the speakers and listeners. Nothing goes past them unnoticed," she added in a prickly tone and looked into Temple's frightened eyes. However, it wasn't an impostor's fear of disclosure that struck her eye. What she saw was simply a frightened man, which confused and bewildered her even more. *"Perhaps that is all he is,"* she thought. *"Maybe he is just a frightened mortal, like the shipwrecked survivors."*

Palomei clapped her hands and a servant appeared with a bowl of steaming brew. "Will you join me in some sha?" the Queen asked.

Temple nodded in consent. The servant ladled a spoonful into a bowl made of coconut shell and placed a banana leaf, with something unidentifiable on it, before him. He waited until the Matriarch drank first then sipped from his cup slowly.

"It's very good," he said to Losha. "What's this?" he said, pointing to the banana leaf.

"Those are the tongues of titwee birds. They are considered a delicacy," she said in a voice that had gained some normalcy.

Temple's throat constricted, but he forced a few into his mouth. He swallowed them whole, chasing them with the warm wine. Owane watched Temple from across the hall and let out a humorous snort. "That is Owane, the Queen's first husband and highest Advisor," Losha said, with a tilt of her head in Owane's direction.

Owane, who was considerably older than the Queen, was a tall, robust man with a natural ease in his movements. He bowed from where he sat. "I bid greetings to you, Stranger Temple, and hope our curiosity does not wear thin your patience."

"I pray you have a healthy life, Councilman," Temple spoke in the little Makolese he had memorized. "I thank the brave Makol people for saving my life."

Owane nodded with respect, then began. "We would like to know why you have come here, Temple Fox?"

In spite of the coolness of the chamber, Temple wiped the sweat from around his neck. "I came to bring a vaccine – a powerful medicine to the people of the Seychelle Islands. While I was flying, I got lost in a storm." All eyes looked to Losha for coherence and she interpreted slowly.

"How did you... fly here?" he asked.

"In a biplane; a de Havilland Moth," he stated.

"He says he flew here on some kind of moth," Losha interpreted and gave a brief shrug.

"*A moth?*" the Queen asked with a perplexed frown.

"A plain one," she answered.

A confident voice issued from behind the crocodile jaw. "It is true," Mefakani explained to the Counselors. "Tani has kept the moth's silk as a relic for the women. I possess the thicker cocoon, which he emerged from like a wondrous butterfly. I hold this relic for all male initiates."

"May we examine the sacred relics?" an Elder asked excitedly from the far reaches of the chamber.

Cranik's attempt to rein his temper back by clenching his teeth and grinding them together were futile. His anger spilled out into the great hall in one loud impulsive burst. "You fools! Why are you calling these things *sacred*?" he blurted out. "We do not even know who or what this creature is, but, for certain, he looks to be a white man! He is an impostor! Be done with him now!"

The Matriarch raised her hand to silence the rising clamor in the room. "We will continue with the questions without interruption and exam these skins later. So," the Queen looked down at the helpless pilot and asked, "you were not sent here? You were sent elsewhere?"

"Yes." Temple felt lost in the confusion of voices.

"Yet the gods of Heaven blew you to us. Why is that?"

"Our prayers are stronger," Mefakani said with confidence etched with a touch of arrogance.

Cranik rose to his feet and pointed. "Then our Priest will be held responsible for this treachery."

Cranik's disrespect was cutting, but Mefakani did not rise to anger. His training was one of control and restraint for his every action, even his thoughts and desires. He spoke in a stern and steady voice. "I do not expect you, Cranik, to understand all the ways of the Lord and his Spirits. I will, however, pray that you might reach at least a reasonable level of understanding."

Cranik noticeably bristled. At great risk to himself, he pointed again at the Shaman. "The Lord Tagheetu and His Spirits will punish us if you are wrong, High Shaman! And, you are wrong!"

"Silence!" Palomei ordered. "We will have no more outbursts," she looked to Elder Cranik with a glaring contempt, "or displays of disrespect to our High Priest. We are here to question and to debate later. Now, I would like an answer to the question." The Queen gave Temple an equally stern look.

The pilot blotted a trickle of sweat that streamed down his face with the back of his hand. "I told you, we got lost in the storm."

"We?"

"Yes, Blake and myself. There was another flying with me." The pilot swallowed hard.

Queen Palomei leaned over to her Great Grandfather. "There is nothing in the prophecies saying two would come."

Okon leaned closer. "Great Granddaughter, the scroll this particular prophecy was written on is damaged. It is also written in archaic Makolese. The subject, therefore, is indistinguishable as either singular or plural." The old man shrugged. "Who knows, maybe the gods sent two in case one did not make it."

The scholar in Mefakani interrupted. "Traditionally, this prophecy has been interpreted to mean only one would come and, as you see, only one is before you now."

Palomei seemed satisfied with the explanation and looked back at the frightened pilot. "Well then, Temple Fox, please tell us about your journey here?"

Temple saw a flash before his memory. He remembered seeing the Light – the powerful, peaceful Light. It was something he hadn't altogether reckoned with yet. Did he dare mention it? He spoke hesitantly. "I remember floating through the sky... and I remember dropping the medicine."

"You dropped it?" she asked.

Mefakani leaned sideways towards the giant Matriarch. "It is a poor translation. He means it dropped from his memory. He *lost* it."

The Queen nodded in gratitude, then looked back down at the pale

Stranger. "And, do you remember being born again?" she asked.

Temple was baffled by the question, and yet, it triggered the memory of the day he died and was revived from the waters. Again, he remembered the incredible Light. Could this possibly be what she meant? If so, how could she have known of his experience? He chose his words carefully. "No one remembers being born in the flesh, but I do remember being born in Spirit."

There was a rising murmur in the room.

The Queen raised her hand to the Counselors. "So, you admit you have been born twice, once in Spirit and once in flesh?"

"That's correct," he answered, swallowing to keep the bird tongues from rising into his throat.

"And, do you recall how you were injured?"

Temple gently touched the scarred knot on his forehead and spoke with a puzzled look on his face.

Losha, more bewildered now than ever, spoke, "He says he does not remember. He thinks the medicine hit him there. He says it is the last thing he remembered before he lost it."

Again there was a buzz of voices.

Senior Elder Sahdon rose painfully from his cushion with his cane supporting his grotesquely scarred leg. He bowed to the Sovereign with effort. "Most Respected, may I also ask a question?"

The Queen nodded and the Elder moved with prideful dignity, despite his infirmity, to the center of the floor. "All Elders know about the sacred mark in relation to the prophecies," he began. "There is little to dispute in regards to this magical sign. Still, I must be allowed to question this stranger so there remains not a wisp of smoky doubt in our minds in respect to his divinity." All the Elders nodded in agreement. "May I ask the Stranger to stand?" Temple rose as requested, feeling like a lab specimen under glass. "I have noticed that the Stranger has another mark upon his body – a great scar around his waist." All the Elders, particularly the very old ones, leaned closer and squinted.

"Make a light," snapped the old Great Grandfather.

Mefakani stood up and motioned to Sumuro, the Head Guard, to leave his post in front of the chamber door. Sumuro, a large, muscular man, walked over to the Priest and handed him his spear, then backed away. Mefakani mumbled an incantation and touched the tip of the spearhead to his staff. The head of the crooked staff sparked into flames and the Councilors gasped in delight.

"My god!" Temple exclaimed. He looked down at Losha. "How'd he...?"

"Hush," she insisted.

One of the servants grabbed a large oil jar and placed it by Temple's side for the Priest to light.

"Losha!" he called out wide-eyed with fear.

"The impostor, if he is an impostor, is about to be found out," she thought gleefully, believing he certainly was an imposter. "Shhh! Be still!"' she said in sharp rebuke, firmly convinced that this would be the end of this sham.

Temple was ordered to lift his arms up and to turn his side towards the flames. The deep, horizontal ridges of the massive scar were thrown into sharp relief.

Sahdon cleared his throat. "Temple Fox," he said in a smooth voice, "tell us how you got that scar?"

"He says he got the wound from fighting a large hairy beast called a *li-yon.*"

Temple gestured with his arms outstretched, showing the size of the animal.

"He says it weighs three times as much as a man. He said he killed it."

Sahdon settled into a strategic calm, patiently waiting on Cranik's impulsiveness. He was not disappointed. "You old fools!" Cranik exploded. "He has The Mark of the Beast! He is not only an impostor! He is a wizard!" he shouted.

The old voices rolled like the turbulent sea on the distant shore. Before Palomei could raise a hand, Sahdon beat his cane on the glassy floor to quiet them. "The prophecies do say to be wary of false gods, do they not?" he said, and the Elders nodded, muttering to each other. "Surely, one that bears both the marks cannot be the Great Teacher."

Losha looked up at Temple, the confusion distorting her face. He gazed back at her, his frightened eyes pleading for understanding.

"What should I do? What should I say? Should I tell the Counselors now that he is an Englishman? And yet...." She mulled over her thoughts and searched for clarity. Losha looked back at the Stranger whose intense blue eyes were filled with more than fear. They spoke of his innocence and profound isolation.

Palomei listened mindfully as the Elders' voices reached a roaring pitch and her Counselors unshakable trust in their Priest began to waver. Bit by bit, Palomei's own trust started to dissolve into uncertainty. She looked over at Mefakani with a disparaging, but shielded eye, as the sudden fear overtook her.

Mefakani rose and waited for the Counselors to quiet again. He spoke calmly. "I see there are few here who have the eyes to see this wondrous blessing. Sahdon, I admire your eloquence and sound skepticism. You would have made a good Apprentice."

Not addressing the Elder as *Elder* was insult enough, but Sahdon controlled his anger with silence. He lifted his chin higher with pride and glared back with distain.

"It so happens," Mefakani continued, "that there are details to the old prophecies that you are not aware of. Only Elder Tani, Great Grandfather Okon and I, know the secrets of the signs – signs which have been passed down from our ancestors for many generations."

The Elder tightened the grip on his cane, the indignation rising hot within him. "Will our High Shaman enlighten us as to the detailed meaning behind The Mark of the Beast?" he asked in mock politeness.

"No," Mefakani answered flatly.

"No?" Sahdon struck his cane violently against the floor and the sound echoed round the chamber. "And you expect us to blindly believe you without any explanation?"

"It would be extremely dangerous for the people if too many of us knew the exact meaning behind each and every sign. I am your High Priest. You must trust me."

Cranik shouted from the back of the chamber with impulsive candor. "Then prove his divinity!"

"He is right, High Shaman," Sahdon said, again holding the attention of the Councilors. "If you are certain that we, the Elders, cannot be trusted with your knowledge, then we beg you to prove this creature's divinity. If this white man is truly a new god, tell him he must perform a miracle before us now."

Mefakani took a step forward. "You still do not understand these matters, Senior Elder. It may be months before he remembers his medicine. Every Shaman knows the trauma of rebirth. He is only a boy of twenty-five seasons – still a wet chick who must relearn his magical ways. I am here to rekindle his memory."

Again, Cranik's anger burst through the chamber. "Oh! So, for months we must sit and wait like pregnant sea turtles on a crowded beach, and chance to see if his white Outsider friends come and make war on us?"

All of the Shaman's discipline suddenly unraveled and his eyes flamed with fury. He pointed his staff towards Cranik and jabbed the air between them. "All Outsiders will perish! And, Makolese troublemakers, who defy the plans of the Lord, will also perish!"

Cranik and Mefakani burst into a fiery quarrel. The power of their voices bounced off the pearly walls and rolled around the chamber until the sharp sound of Palomei's scepter, banging against the floor, could be heard above the echoing din.

"Enough!" she shouted, pulling herself up to her full size and fury. Her voice echoed in the sudden silence. "I will have no more of this!"

Temple looked down at Losha sheepishly. "I'm not doing too well, am I?"

Losha didn't answer. She attempted to, but she nervously gulped the air around her instead.

Temple hid his own fear by squeezing his hands together to stop their trembling. Then, as if a blow was given to make his quivering cease, he was brought to a sudden understanding of the events around him when Queen Palomei asked the next question.

The Matriarch's gaze bore down on him. "If you are truly a god, we would like to know why the Lord has sent a white god to be our Great Teacher?"

"God? Me?" Although he was stunned that she should think he was anything but a man, a cowardly man, nothing on his face betrayed his knowing otherwise. He stared back at the Queen, trying to imagine himself through her savage eyes. They had never seen an airplane before. He was a creature that had sailed through the heavens like a god. He gazed at the skulls propping up the Queen's feet, their vacant sockets silently warning him to save his head at all costs.

Pure fear breeds invention. The idea came to him quickly. "The Divine Light, where God resides," he started slowly, "sends the darker skinned Teachers to the white people in the far west. The Light also sends white Teachers to the darker skinned people, like the Makolese, in the east. It's a test." Temple caught his breath.

There was truth in what he said. Most of the prophets had said that they had come from other lands and many of them were from different cultures, although up to this point, none of them had been white.

The Queen grimaced. "What kind of test?" she asked.

Temple did not falter. He simply remembered the Divine Light. "A test in your acceptance and love for one who is different from yourselves."

A scattering of the older faces and their shiny reflections nodded in agreement.

"It is how it was seasons ago, when we still had the Su," Okon nodded in approval.

Owane leaned forward with greater interest. "Tell us about this Light you speak of?" he asked.

While Temple paused to collect his thoughts, Tani shuffled over to the Stranger and gestured for him to sit again. She handed him a cup of warm sha, bowed, then sat back down and folded her leathery hands in her lap to wait with the others.

There was one thing Temple was certain of. He could not conceive of seeing his head displayed like one of his father's game trophies. If Makol was to be his new home, until he chanced upon a ship, then he would have to be convincing as a god. He sipped the last of his sha and felt a cool tingle glance his scarred brow. He prayed, yes, he prayed; something he had never done before, so the Divine Light would guide him.

He spoke slowly so Losha could catch his every word. He described the tunnel, and the void, and explained what it felt like to become a part of the One; the indivisible, invisible wholeness; the space where all that exists is present and yet indistinguishable from anything else.

Temple got lost in his own story as he relived the depths of unearthly love he had experienced when he first encountered the Divine Light. He became animated and moved his hands about, trying to describe the Holy Essence and how it had imbued his body with a sacred Light; how It contained all knowledge and wisdom. He explained that there were no adequate words to describe the experience, but that the experience would change forever ones feeling for all things created.

Then, much to his surprise, he felt his Spirit rise slowly out of his body. It was the same weird sensation of buoyancy he felt when he first left his body bobbing lifelessly in the sea. He thought he wouldn't be able to control his movements, until he stopped, one foot from the domed ceiling because he thought he'd crash into the stone rafters. A slim, green lizard,, that clung upside down on one of the rafters, rolled one dispassionate eye towards Temple's spirit and blinked. The pilot looked far below him, startled to see his physical body still sitting cross-legged on the floor, gesturing with his hands. As if being in two places at once was the most natural occurrence in the world, his Spirit passed through the rainbow shell ceiling and up into the azure sky. Higher and higher he soared like a bird until the Council Round House was nothing more than a blazing ball in the distance. The village rooftops, too, became small brown dots and he watched the treetops move like a sea of grass.

In the distance ahead of him he saw one large cloud mass drifting in the upper atmosphere, sweeping the sky like a magic carpet. Beyond it were the stars. Their brilliance caught his wonder, but no sooner had he leaned his interest towards the magic of the stars, when his spirit began to descend rapidly.

Further and further, he floated effortlessly, until he spotted the glimmer of tiny campfires and the faint hint of white caps moving towards the dark shore. The round roofs in the villages filled his field of vision once again, only this time they were barely discernable in the rosy twilight of dusk.

Like a mysterious magnet, his spirit drew itself down to the center of the vast crater. He passed through the domed hall, shining like pewter now in the half-light. Temple watched the tops of all the peoples' heads until he found his own. He descended through the crown of his head and lodged with a sudden jerk inside his physical body. A static whining grated against his ears sharply until he raised his hands to his ears to ease the pain. He shook his head like a wet dog and readjusted his eyes to the twilight of the room.

Temple was keenly aware of a pronounced difference in the chamber. The peoples' shiny reflections on the polished floor shone brighter and there was the flickering light of several oil jars, which had been placed in huge pots on short tripods around the chamber. The Elders' shadows, too, splashed behind them like huge black fingers against the opalescent walls. The obsidian floor was now a solid, impenetrable black. The light from the open doorway shone red and there was a dead stillness in the room. The only sound was the labored breathing from several Elders and the sputter of dying flames.

Temple looked at Losha whose lips were parted as if she had stopped in mid-sentence. "Did I doze off?" he asked. "I kind of got lost there for a second. What was I saying?"

"You were speaking to Great Grandfather Okon about his eyesight. He was thanking you for healing him."

"Healing him?" Temple paused and looked at the silent row of wrinkled, tattooed faces. "I didn't..." his thoughts stumbled. He strained to see Losha's eyes in the lamplight. "How long have I been talking and...?"

"You have sat here the time it takes to burn one large oil pot and have spoken to both Councils about how it feels to be a spirit. You have also given us an insightful explanation behind both the sacred mark upon the brow and 'The Mark of the Beast'." She gave a sideways glance to the Counselors and continued. "You have also given us a prophecy." She lowered her voice. "I have been told to tell you what you have done when you returned. The god that speaks through you told me this. I was told to tell you that, without your bravery, this could not have happened. It also told me to tell you these words, 'You must know beyond belief, trust without doubt, and be courageous beyond thought of consequence. And above all else, forgive and love; love the one who threatens you most and throws you into disbelief, doubt and fear'."

The pilot stared back in silence, watching the play of light on the dark woman's face, when she returned the look with equal intensity.

Palomei pressed the girl for an interpretation, but Losha turned to Temple instead and added quickly, "The others are not to know that the god only speaks through you, and is not you. I am the only one who knows."

Temple sat dumbfounded as he listened to Losha rattle off a quick interpretation.

"Temple Fox has told me that our people and their ways are still strange to him. He asked me how I thought the Counselors responded to him."

"I hope you have interpreted well our deepest thanks," Palomei said in all seriousness.

"Yes, Most Respected,'" she said. "He also says his memory has been badly impaired as a result of his traumatic birth into flesh and has asked that we be patient with him."

"Is there any other medicine Temple Fox wishes to give to the Counselors before I close this meeting to begin our debates?" the Queen asked.

Temple rubbed his beard stubble absentmindedly, as if waking from a long sleep. "There's one thing that's bothered me. Before I was rescued, I saw a Makolese man in spirit." He gestured with his hand. "He was covered with strange, spiraling tattoos from his chest to his knees and I think he said his name was Noko."

One old woman screeched when she heard the name and the Elders chattered anxiously.

Losha leaned forward and studied Temple's face. "Is this the god who speaks again or is it ....?"

The people yelled to Losha for her interpretation.

"Temple Fox says Noko is safe and at peace. Noko wants his family to not worry."

Cranik spat out his words from under his breath. "I could have said the same thing. It is only words! Pure trickery!" he whispered harshly. "I believe nothing."

"I agree," Sahdon said in a conspiratorial hush. "There were no real miracles performed here. Mefakani can do healing just as well, if not better. And, Losha must have told the Stranger that Noko was killed in the accident along with her husband."

Losha held her hands together out in front of her as if pleading. "Please, please tell me Temple Fox, did you see my husband, too? He has an unusual tattoo, a series of chevrons that mark his left cheek and run down his arm. Was he with Noko?"

Temple turned to Losha and saw the tears brimming in her eyes. "I'm sorry, Losha. I only saw the one man."

Tani rose and scuttled over to Losha and rested her ancient arm on her shoulder. "You have done well, Little One," she said patting her.

Losha forced back the tears before they had a chance to fall. "We must go now. The Queen says she will call us again if the Counselors need to question you further."

Half the Counselors prostrated themselves before Temple as the two rose to leave. A band of armed guards were summoned and they escorted Losha and the Stranger through the low archway, out into the humid evening air.

CHAPTER FIVE

The Makolese and the Breaking of the Su

"The Universal Laws were immutable, but prophecy was not... The Beast, however, would spread lies to the contrary... Temple knew the Beast's plans were alterable by two simple things: vision and initiative. Fire that within even one individual and the world changes!"

Temple Fox
Makolese Prophecy Scroll #901
The Makolese Scroll on The Education of Temple Fox #5

The villagers became swiftly moving shadows when the band of armed guardsmen cleared the way for the Interpreter and the white Stranger. Losha waited till she was well beyond any villages, walking beside Temple in the warm evening air, before she spoke again.

"I will not lie to you, Temple Fox. There was much arguing going on among the Counselors. They are trying to decide if you are the man-god foretold in our ancient prophecies or if you are a wizard."

Temple rubbed his sore head. *"A few short days ago I learned that I had a soul, or rather was a soul, an indestructible, eternal soul. Now someone wants me to play god. I'm understandably confused and more than a little frightened."*

"Aren't they rushing things a wee bit? I mean, I just landed?" he said peevishly, hoping Losha didn't suspect he was a complete fake.

"Perhaps. After all, you are English although your accent is a bit strange." She stared at him in such a way as to let him know she knew about his secret. She waited for a reaction.

Temple let his head drop. *"I've been found out and this could cost me my life."*

"Actually, I'm... an Anglo-American. The Anglo part is English," he rambled nervously in confession. "My mother was a Brit. That's English too. My father was an American, a big game hunter in Kenya. Can you follow all of this?"

"Anglo-American or not, once the Counselors finally turn to reason, they will accept you without question," she said, trying to convince herself.

"But Losha, you told me yourself that a voice spoke through me...and that I'm really not ..."

"There are many things I do not yet understand. You are a servant to a greater God, yet you are still a man, are you not? And, a white man at that?"

He stopped dead in his tracks, ignoring the small band of armed guards who surrounded them with torches. "But Losha, that's exactly what I am,...just a man. And I'm afraid the others will forget that. Why in God's name do you want to help me? You know I'm an impostor."

Losha wanted desperately to believe as Tani did and to believe her own words now. "You are the Great Teacher," she said slowly and reassuringly. "Only you have had your memory broken." She looked him squarely in the eye until he could see the liquid reflections of golden torches behind him. "Do you not want to be the Chosen One?"

"No!" he shouted in desperation. "All I want is to go home!"

Her questioning eyes flamed brighter. "Then you would rather be beheaded?"

"What!" Temple's mouth flew open. *"Savages! Greasy savages! All of them!"* "Is that what they do to impostors?" he asked.

The guards started to mumble to one another as the two argued on the beach.

Losha glared back at the reluctant god, her brown oriental eyes flickering with the flame of sudden doubt. *"If a god speaks through him then why does it not know where my husband is?"* she thought. "It can be arranged," she said aloud, turned and walked briskly away.

"Blackmail!" "What is it that you want, girl?" he called out. He ran to catch up with her creating confusion among the guards. "It seems to me that you're the one who's in control here. Answer me!" he yelled and grabbed her shoulder sharply.

Losha spun around, the fire in her eyes like molten copper. "I am Widow!" she snapped. "Do not touch me without permission!"

Temple was taken back by her sudden contempt and stood there speechless.

Losha left the Stranger standing alone with his guards as she stormed down the dark beach. One of the guards lumbered over to her carrying a torch, but she motioned him away. When she was engulfed by the twilight again her shoulders slumped. The weight from days of tension had finally caught up with her.

"Who am I to press this man? Maybe he isn't the Prophet." Losha rebuked herself for forcing Temple into a situation he obviously didn't want any part in. *"Perhaps I should have told the Queen he was an Englishman before this all began and be done with it. Yet,...he seems so innocent. And there was that voice that spoke through him. It is not his fault he is trapped here... trapped like me... trapped like Amron's lost spirit. God or no god, perhaps I have been too harsh on someone who does not know our customs, someone who dared to touch a...."*

Tears started to fill her eyes. One tear found its way down her cheek, but she grit her teeth and held the rest back. *"After this is over I will deny grief no longer."*

"It is true," she whispered to herself, allowing the hurt to well up inside her again. "I am indeed a...Widow." This time she cried out loud without restraint.

Temple stood quietly with the guards for a minute watching the dark figure by the sea. The waves teased Losha by stretching themselves on the shore like skulking fingers, chancing to catch her ankles and pull her in, but they would hesitate and withdraw. *"Touch her?"* he thought. *"I'm scared to death of her. Since she has my life in her hands the real question is, can I trust her?"*

He watched as she slipped into the darkness, the only sound the sea breathing. He walked over to her slowly, cautiously, until he was standing by her side again. The guards followed with their torches. "Look," he started, "I'm sorry I grabbed you back there. Would you please accept my apologies?"

She turned towards him briefly and nodded. "It is accepted."

"I ...I don't know what's happening to me. You say a voice spoke through me. I don't remember a thing, but I believe you. All I remember is leaving my body and floating out towards the stars. The next thing I know – I'm back!" He scratched his head and then his raspy whiskers. "Curious. You said I bear The Marks. You also said the Voice gave an explanation of them?" he raised one eyebrow.

Losha told the guards that the Stranger needed to rest awhile, so they stopped beneath a coconut tree on the edge of a dark jungle. They formed a circle around him with their spears and strange shields. It was in this tense, but quiet setting that she relayed much of what had transpired in the Great Chamber.

'The Voice said that all people bear an invisible, holy mark upon their brow and the invisible Mark of the Beast. It said that your marks were visible to remind us that we are half god, half beast. The Voice said it is up to the Makolese to conquer the beast within themselves and allow divine wisdom to flow until one can see with a singularity of vision."

One of the guards hacked the end off a coconut with his broad sword and handed the nut to Temple.

"Then It gave a prophecy." She knelt, and with her finger drew five, evenly spaced, vertical lines in the sand. "The Voice spoke about a time when this sign will appear all over the world. It said the beast that produces the mark of the claw trusts only itself and never depends on the Divine from which it came. Because it does not know how to connect with the Source, it must obtain power by robbing the energies and resources of others. By this sign it will conquer and enslave because it is the only way the Beast knows how to survive. It is a very ignorant creature, a sad Being who, as The Voice explained, is still a divine child of God.

"The Voice said the high merchants, who serve the Beast, have already put a system of exchange firmly into place that would seem foreign to the Makolese. To obtain goods you must first work to get a round piece of flat metal or a piece of painted bark cloth. These you trade for goods, but the high merchants will scheme to make this metal and cloth worthless. When that happens they will do away with the metal and cloth completely and use The Mark of the Beast as their trade sign. The Voice was very specific and our best scribe has committed Its words to paper."

Temple wiped the milk from his chin and offered the nut to the Translator, who declined with a wave of her hand.

"The Voice," she continued, "said the people who work for the Beast have set up this system so no one can create their own cloth or goods. They will not be able to even grow their own food or gather their own medicine. In order to buy and sell goods, everyone must carry or wear the beastly mark. People will do this because their knowledge of the Divine will have been stolen from them. Instead of trusting in the Spirit that dwells within, they will trust in the values put forth by the Beast and his servants. There will be some, of course, who will succeed in bartering for their necessities."

Temple didn't know if he even believed in prophecy, and yet the depths of him knew there was something to what she had said. He could feel its truth, although somewhat distorted through translation, prickle up his spine into the base of his brain, triggering something he knew the Light had hidden deep within his subconscious. The Universal Laws were immutable, but prophecy was not. It was alterable if there was enough power to change it. The Beast, however, would spread lies to the contrary, filling with futility those who held the sacred vision. Temple knew the Beast's plans were alterable by two simple things: vision and initiative. Fire that within even one individual and the world changes!

"The Voice," she explained, "said the Makolese are the Chosen People. It said we must never lose the knowledge to make cloth, and to hunt for fish and healing plants, and never lose the knowledge to commune with the animals and plants. If some of us do lose the knowledge in the End Times, however, It said to be like the dolphin and the bird, which do not worry about where their next meal comes from. Trust in the Divine."

Losha noticed the guards were becoming restless. "Finally, The Voice said the beastly mark will be placed upon the back of the wrist. That is why Shaman Mefakani knew you were not the Beast or one of his wizards. The scar from your li-yon was clawed into your side, the side your heart rests." She nodded to the guards, acknowledging that she would not keep them much longer in this vulnerable place. "Then The Voice gave a riddle. It said, 'As for the future signs upon the flesh, the Mark of the Beast may be as visible as a Makolese tattoo or as invisible as a sliver of clear crystal.'"

"That's very strange," Temple said. "Did It say when this is supposed to happen?"

"After the Great Iron Wall has fallen, and about fifty seasons after the second Great War."

Temple's mouth fell open. "Second? We've only had one Great War and its unlikely there'd be another of its kind."

"It spoke of many signs saying this will all occur slowly at first, but become more noticeable when the Eagle and the Bear mirror one another, and become temporary allies again. Or later when the world is divided into three, but controlled by twelve families. This small clan of white men is the high merchants. I do not understand what is meant by this," she said.

"Nor do I."

"The Voice said It was telling us this now so that we would not live in ignorance and sleepwalk through life. At the same time, It said It didn't want us to live in either blind expectation or fear of this prophecy. That is because great light and understanding takes place when all of this happens – so much so that the prophecy itself can be changed." Losha paused for a second and searched Temple's face. "Do you understand what duality is?" she asked.

"I think so."

"The Voice spent an enormous amount of time explaining what that meant in regards to the End Times ahead." She stopped to collect her thoughts.

"Well, what did It say?"

"We are not to fear the high merchants who will cast a net of energy over the Earth that sends out inaudible drum beats of polarity and fear. They are children of God who have simply lost their path to the Divine. If we should fall into fear, we will fall into a deeper duality than we are already trapped in. Do you understand?"

"Well... kinda."

"Many of us will falter at first. But many will be able to hold this light It spoke of. Our people are to preserve the spiritual truths and keep the vision of a better world intact while the world struggles with the changes The Light brings…for there will be much conflict as people climb out of what The Voice called, 'the illusion of separation' or 'duality' into the light of oneness."

Losha motioned for the guards to gather their torches. "The last thing The Voice said was to remember that the most dangerous beast is the one inside you. That is the beast who keeps you prisoner. And that beast is fear."

Temple gave a thoughtful grunt then spoke quietly as if the guards might understand him. "And the people think it was me saying all of this?"

"Yes. And The Voice stated that there would be many others who would prophesize in the same way, which would later lead to something greater."

Temple felt a sudden surge of energy shuttle through his nerve pathways. There was a twinge of momentary understanding as if someone had opened a great door, a cosmic portal, then shut it again quickly, allowing him only the briefest glimpse inside. He shivered visibly.

"A message for The Chosen," he half whispered to himself.

"What message?" she asked, noticing his unease.

"Teachers... Volunteers... The Awakened Ones," he said, remembering something from long, long ago. "They hold the light for others while the others allow the light to grow within themselves."

With this last utterance, Losha felt what seemed like an enormous hand, made of a finer substance than moonlight, pass right through her body. The sensation left her slowly like a fading mist and she looked to the Stranger with half understanding eyes.

He caught the look. "Are you okay?"

"Tai," she said in Makolese, feeling somewhat embarrassed, then looked all around her noticing the guardsmen were ready to leave. "We must be moving on. It is getting late."

The band continued on a short distance until the path ended at the edge of a thick forest of tall bamboo. Losha stepped forward and stood before the bamboo, asking in prayer for permission to enter the forest. The Stranger drew back in surprise as a swath of stalks leaned to and fro on their own, rattling and clacking together noisily. A narrow, but neat pathway was formed.

The little band passed through the bamboo forest and the stalks rearranged themselves upright again behind them, closing the pathway and rendering it impassable. The small troop marched on in silence until they came to the edge of a secluded grove of enormous banyans. The circle of trees wore shawls of heavy moss and their outstretched arms extended as if greeting the small band like long lost grandchildren. The warriors stepped mindfully over masses of tangled roots carpeted in velvet green until the forest loomed above them, blotting out the moon and the stars. Beyond them lay Tani's round hut resting on timber and stone pilings that were covered in lush moss, its soft edges facing west, fringed in the last purple light of dusk. Temple remembered it well.

"This is a sacred grove. You must show respect before we continue."

Knowing he must act like a god, the Stranger walked slowly with a kind of reverence to the center of the grove until the black canopy was broken enough to allow glimpses of the moon and stars. Feeling too scared to feel foolish, he spoke to, and then bowed to, each and every tree. The guards thought this was hilarious and laughed out loud.

"No, no, no," Losha smiled, easing the tensions from before. "Until I teach you our prayers, simply acknowledge the spirit of the grove in a silent way."

Temple couldn't have kept up the act for long, even without the mocking laughter. He almost laughed himself. He couldn't believe what was happening to him. *"A Voice has spoken through me spouting spiritual platitudes and riddles, little of which I understand. I almost get slugged because I touched a woman. And now I'm talking to trees."*

"What if the trees don't want me here? Are they going to fall on me or beat me with dead limbs?" he quipped.

"Even if you are divine, and especially so, it is not wise to show disrespect to things older than yourself...which also includes myself," she said, walking away and leaving Temple standing in bewilderment.

All but two guardsmen positioned themselves around the edge of the grove, settling in for the evening watch. The remaining two waited patiently as Temple entered a brief silence to honor the old banyans, then caught up with Losha on the stairs of Tani's hut.

"Wait a minute, girl!" His boyish tongue rushed ahead of his brain. "You've got to be much younger than me. I do apologize for grabbing you before, but don't expect me to bow to you like I had to do with those toothless crones back there. If anything, you should be bowing to me because I'm a god now. Remember?"

Losha rolled her eyes. "This is the man who speaks now, is it not? Even so," she said, "I am thirty-three seasons of age and expect to be treated with respect." She rearranged her skirt and smoothed it out as if it had just been mussed up, then opened the door with a creak. One of the guardsmen entered first to light some oil jars.

When they stepped inside Temple's eyes darted over her firm, ripe breasts. "You don't have to play games with me, Losha. If you want more respect out of me, you've got it. After all, you have my life in your hands. But for God's sake, you don't have to lie about your age to get it. Why, where I come from the girls lie and say how *young* they are."

A tiny lizard scurried behind one of the skulls as Losha placed an oil jar close to Tani's cluttered shrine. "Your ways are strange to me, but one thing you should know. I never lie."

Temple plopped himself down on the soft mat that had once been his sick bed, too exhausted and confused to argue. One way or another, he had to find a way out of the deep mess he found himself in.

"Losha, I'm too tired to think straight anymore. Tell me, whatever happened to the white man who taught you English?"

Losha cast a look over her shoulder at the one guard who remained standing at the door inside the hut. She lowered her voice. "It is taboo to speak of him."

"Why is it taboo?" He looked over at the guard, then back at Losha. "He doesn't understand English, does he?"

"No."

"Well then?"

"Do not speak his name or the guard will know who we speak of."

"Why are you so afraid? Are all white men considered taboo... or just that one white man?"

Losha pulled her tangled hair off her face. "All white men and all Outsiders are considered taboo. Is that not why the gods have sent you: to teach us magic to fight the Outsiders?"

Temple's head began to throb again. *If I'm expected to fight the very people I wish would storm the beaches with an arsenal of cannons at this very moment, how am I ever going to be rescued? And, what else am I expected to do besides fight my own rescuers?*

"But you say I'm a god who's forgotten my magic. Remember? Unless, of course, that voice comes back and speaks through me, telling me what to do."

Losha lit another oil jar and the lizard slithered behind a bundle of herbs. "I am sure Shaman Mefakani and Elder Tani have planned to help you remember. The gods do not make such grand efforts in sending a man-god without there being a purpose in it."

"You spoke about the marks on my body as signs," he said. Temple was curious, but cautious. "How else can you and the Counselors be so certain I'm what you say I am?"

The Interpreter sat down in front of the young man-god. "The manner in which you arrived and how your marks were received were foretold to us two thousand seasons ago. It was foreseen that you would come in the time of greatest sorrow."

Temple looked into her brown almond eyes. "I know you've seen sorrow, Losha."

The woman dropped her eyes and stared into her lap, allowing her private side to hide in the shadows.

"Is this a time of sorrow for your people as well?" he asked.

"Here there is much trouble," she said, lifting her head to meet Temple's strange blue eyes. "The Outsiders have been coming to Makol more often. The man I spoke of was one of them, but Tani and Mefakani foresee there will be many more."

"And what's suppose to happen when they come?"

"There is only trouble when the Outsiders come now. But before..." she stopped to gather her thoughts and began again. "Many seasons ago, friendly Arab Traders came from the north. Mefakani, who was only a small boy, was befriended by one sailor who taught him astronomy and mathematics. Mefakani was a very intelligent and curious boy. Even then he possessed special spiritual gifts and was able to foresee when the seamen would arrive. Unlike now, our people looked forward to these times, not only for trading, but in preparation for the making of the Su with Outsiders."

"Su?"

"The making of the good seed. The mating ritual. It used to be the Makol way to make strangers a part of our family. The Arabs were always made welcome," she said. "Our people traded cinnamon, jute and obsidian. The Traders brought us metal knives, axes and nails. It was a good and prosperous time for us. But then...

"The History Tellers have said that at one time, when Mefakani was still young, he foresaw the ships coming and the people made ready with their trade goods. But, instead of his friend, ten strange Arab dhows arrived." Losha matched Temple's penetrating stare. "The strangers killed Mefakani's father and kidnapped his mother. They took his aunts and uncles as well. The same happened all over the island. Palomei's mother, who was then Queen, was killed with all her seven husbands. Palomei's sisters and brothers were also taken, although we know not where, but we know they were taken as slaves." Losha took a wisp of her hair and secured it behind her ear. "It was a horrible time. Many of the surviving women were made unclean and the Su was broken."

"What'd you mean *unclean*?" he asked hesitantly. "You mean...they were raped?"

She nodded. "Afterwards, the offspring became marked as Su Shapa."

"Su Shapa?"

"The bad seed," she explained. "Tagon was the High Shaman at the time. He had the children of rape purified – fed alive to the crocodiles. Tagon would have had the women cleansed as well had Tani not put a stop to it."

Temple was horrified. "I don't understand."

"Rape," she explained, "had never been known before. Because of it, barrenness plagues the Makol woman and the land to this day. Since the Su has been corrupted there have been fewer births and the old die younger. Even our weather has changed and entire species of animal have died off." She paused to catch her breath. "I was not yet born when this started, but I have seen the consequences."

Temple started to see the connections with the timing of his arrival. It started his head pounding again.

Losha continued under the light of a flickering oil jar. "After the massacre, mostly the very old and the very young remained. Mefakani had already been thinking about entering the Priesthood, but after this he swore he would use his magic to protect the people. He has kept his promise, but it has been hard for him, for he has had to form an army and the Makolese have never had need for an army before." Losha paused, deep in thought. The sound of tree frogs filled the night.

"Many seasons ago, Queen Palomei's only daughter was killed in battle. Having no heir to the throne has left our people with a feeling of hopelessness. We all know that the army and Mefakani's magic cannot keep the invaders from our shores. Although his magic is great, he is only one person and there will be too many of the Outsiders to defeat."

"So he considers me a powerful ally who has been sent to help him protect the people?"

"You are beginning to understand, yes?"

"Yes," he thought, *"but I won't fight anyone's war. I have no plans to fight my rescuers. I must buy time until they arrive."*

"Can't the Priesthood you speak of help Mefakani fight his war?"

"Mefakani *is* the Priesthood," she emphasized. "All but two old Shaman Priests were killed in the massacre. Mefakani became an Apprentice to both, but Tagon was his Master. These Priests are dead now."

"And Tani? Does she have magic to fight Mefakani's war, too?"

"Tani only uses her power to heal, but you speak a great truth. It is both Mefakani's and Palomei's personal war, which the people support."

"I'm at a dead end and yet I've got to find a way of getting off this bloody island."

"You never finished telling me about... the man you are forbidden to speak of," Temple asked with renewed curiosity.

Losha looked up at the guard and spoke in Makolese, gesturing towards Temple. The guard nodded and left the hut.

"I told him our guest is hungry. He will bring us food, but he will not be long."

"Thanks. You're right. I'm starving," he complained and reached for a dried piece of fish that hung from a bamboo pole nearby.

"Nooo!" Losha lurched forward and hit his arm so hard he lost his balance and tottered to the floor. The dried meat went flying across the room past the tiny lizard. "That is puffer fish! It will kill you!"

Temple sat back up and wiped his hands off on his wrap-around until he was sure they were dry. "Well, what in the bloody hell's it doing here!"

Losha picked the fish up and hung it back on the rack with care. "Some of the fishermen use it to stun larger fish. Tani uses it for medicine. In tiny doses it numbs pain. Right now it could kill a thousand people!"

Temple took a deep breath to quiet his racing heart. "You saved my life. Seems you're always looking after me," he said. When he noticed that Losha diverted his gaze, he felt awkward and stupid, and the sweat ran off him in spite of the coolness of the night.

"As I said before, the guard will not be long." She sat back down on the floor, regaining her composure. "You asked about the white man?" She spoke uncensored now. "His name was Captain Kneller. He was a British officer from India. Thirteen years ago he and his companions set sail for a pleasure cruise, but got lost in a terrible storm. The currents and the winds blew the remains of his shipwrecked boat to Makol. He was the only survivor and not expected to live. Tani and Mefakani say there are no accidents. If the spirits meant for the Captain to die he would not have been blown all the way to Makol. So both set about the task of healing him. In spite of Mefakani's hatred of Outsiders he felt the spirits had sent this single Englishman to inform him about the power of the white enemy.

"My mother acted as an Interpreter and often served as a mediator between him and the Queen. Captain Kneller was grateful to his rescuers, but he refused to help defend the island when Portuguese slavers appeared. After this, he was treated less a guest and more a hostage."

Losha rose and checked out the window as she spoke. "The Captain was quick to anger and had many blows with the High Shaman Priest. Mefakani accused the Captain of using white man's magic on him to try and kill him. The High Shaman wanted him beheaded. The Queen did not see things his way, however, and there was much quarreling between Palomei and the Priest."

She paced the floor as she spoke. "The Queen decided to be merciful. The Captain, and the wife he had chosen, were both banished to a tiny, remote island northwest of here. He was exiled for more than ten seasons and she still remains there."

"Is he dead?" he asked, concerned now that he too might end up a captive or worse.

Losha stopped and looked down at Temple who appeared as meek as ever. "Yes. Mefakani said that the Captain hated our people so much that he even bewitched his own Makolese wife. It is rumored that she was made crazy by him and murdered him. It has always been strictly taboo to go to that island where she still lives."

"How did he die?" he asked nervously, thinking he might follow a similar fate.

"I told you. Winyon, his wife, went crazy and killed him."

He rubbed his sweaty palms together. "But how...how did she kill him?"

"By witchcraft...of course."

Temple squirmed where he sat. "Is there a lot of sorcery practiced here?"

Losha took a thick shock of hair and tried to coax it behind her ear unsuccessfully. "Not anymore," she responded. "Mefakani put a stop to it by collecting a piece of everyone's Ka. That way, no one can commit witchcraft against another, and law and order is maintained."

"Ka? What is Ka?"

Losha pondered. "I do not think there is a word equal to it in English. Captain Kneller called it *prana*, a Sanskrit word for breath or vital life force. The Shaman, you see, collects a piece of everyone's vital energy and has it in safekeeping. See?" she pointed to a tiny pockmark between her breasts which was barely discernable in the twilight of the room. "This is where he takes the Ka."

Temple gazed at the spot then snatched a quick glance at her nipples.

"At first," she explained, "Tani fought against this ruling, and for a long while she and the Shaman became bitter enemies. But the Shaman argued that the people had corrupted the magical laws and that was why the Invaders had come. It was the Great Lord's punishment."

"And the Queen," he asked, "did she have a piece of her Ka taken too?"

"She elected to be the first to have it done to show the people how safe it was."

"And when did this happen?" he asked, sneaking a peek at her breasts again when she had turned her head to glance out the window.

She spoke hurriedly, anxiously, when she turned back again. "About thirty-three seasons ago when I was born. It took many seasons before Tani and the Priest ever spoke again. But you see Tani is a great Healer, and Mefakani is the only Priest and desperately needed her help."

"And do the people think this... this taking of a bit of Ka works?"

"Very much so. The island has not been plagued by sorcery ever since. Some people are still allowed to use their powers, of course, but only under the Shaman's guidance, like in the case of his Apprentice."

Temple pretended to swat an invisible mosquito when his face twitched nervously.

"*A voice speaks through me. There has been talk of spirit*

possession, beheadings and now witchcraft!" A random thought flew through his head. *"Perhaps I'm still dead! Maybe the Light never sent me back to the Earth plane and I'm trapped somewhere else!"*

Losha searched Temple's face. "Are you not well?" she asked.

The pilot's mind reeled in circles. He felt dizzy. *"Hell is here! Right here! The Light has sent me straight to bloody Hell!"*

"My head hurts a mite, but I'll be all right," he finally said in a thin voice. "I'm fine, truly. I was just thinking about your Shaman. He's a decent sort of bloke to want to try to keep the peace. I'm just sorry your people are plagued by so many other problems." He wiped a trickle of sweat from his cheek with the back of his hand.

Losha hesitated for a moment with unexpected doubt. She thought to herself, *"Who exactly am I dealing with? I believed Temple is the Prophet and yet an ounce of disbelief lays buried deep within me. I am astounded at how The Voice spoke through him. Yet, judging from his behavior, he did not hear or remember what The Voice said. It had said:* **He must 'know beyond belief.'** *Can I do the same?"*

Temple looked into Losha's intelligent eyes for some semblance of warmth and ached for the familiarity of the old Temple Fox. He smiled at her the best he could.

She reciprocated with an awkward smile, which quickly faded when the floor vibrated beneath them. The door opened and the guardsman entered and bowed. He placed a steaming basket before them and Losha thanked him with a nod. Her eyes shone with gratitude as she unfolded a huge banana leaf, letting the steam rise into her face then waited for Temple to do the same.

"This is rock cod with wild plums," she explained. "When you cook it in banana leaves, it disintegrates the bone."

"Magic," he breathed, and bit into the fish.

During supper Losha gave Temple a lesson in Makolese, and explained the personal symbols tattooed on their bodies and the clan symbols that marked the people's chins.

"I noticed you don't have any tattoos," he interrupted.

"I am darker than most, but mine are still there." She leaned forward and pointed to a barely discernible spiral on her greasy chin.

He smiled a genuine smile this time and looked into her warm brown eyes. "Losha, I never had a chance to say this before, but... I'm sorry about your husband. You said the man I saw in the spirit world wasn't him?"

Losha put the remains of her meal aside and smoothed out her skirt. "Noko was fishing with my husband when they were caught in the same storm that brought you here. Noko's body was found, you see, but my husband's body was not. We know now from what you told us that Noko rests in the spirit world. My husband's body is lost, however. We think his soul remains lost."

"Losha, believe me when I tell you this," He spoke softly as he continued. "Just because his body was never found, and just because I didn't see him in the spirit world, doesn't mean his soul is roaming around somewhere." He paused to gaze at her for a moment. Temple sensed there was something odd about her husband's death, but intuitive hunches were new to him and he couldn't say why or what exactly he was feeling. "Unless, of course, you think he's still alive somewhere?"

She furrowed her brow. "I fear he is truly dead, but cannot find his way to Lord Tagheetu. If that is true, then Amron may soon become a demon of the night like so many others," she paused. "Or, perhaps his soul cannot find the way to the Light you speak of." When she cast her head down to conceal her pain, her hair loosened about her face and with it the yellow flower from behind her ear fell softly by her side.

"I'm sorry, Losha. It must be hard not knowing one way or the other." Temple picked up the flower and gently placed it into the woman's hands. "If I could only remember my magic, I'd gladly help you."

Losha wiped away an unexpected tear. Her voice was controlled. "Thank you, Temple Fox."

CHAPTER SIX

The Widow

*"One can be too open minded…Some are so open
minded that I fear their brains will fall out. And
what a terrible mess that makes!"*

Elder Tani
The Makolese Scroll on The Education of Temple Fox #6

After more guards were called in for a night watch, Losha left Temple for her own private lodge so both of them could get some much needed sleep. Her mind, too agitated from the turmoil of several days, ached for the very thing she could not find – sleep. She lay on her sleeping mat, which felt strangely empty without Amron, eyes wide open in the darkness, watching a confusion of images play before her eyes.

In her waking dreams she played the same scenario over and over again until she thought they would fray the fabric of her mind. She imagined waves as they rocked and battered the prow of Amron's fishing boat. Her husband and Noko braced themselves against the salty spray that angry gusts snatched from the waves and drove into their faces. Suddenly, the boat dropped so steeply it seemed the squall would sweep away the water and leave them on the bottom of the sea. Amron looked up in horror at the walls of water that surrounded them like the walls of the great caldera. The heavy sky vanished. One mountainous wave split off from the rest and curled, suspending itself above like a hungry cobra. It struck swiftly, shattering the boat, and swallowing its tattered prey.

Losha turned over on her sleeping mat and closed her eyes. Her thoughts rolled over inside her head like the endless turning of a great wheel. She imagined Amron gasping for air and, just when she thought she saw him rise and break the surface of the sea, a veil of mists swirled round him and in his place she saw Temple. Over and over again she envisioned the Stranger's pallid face and piercing eyes until her will pushed to see the face of Amron and hold his image steady in her mind. The curious line of Amron's strong jaw and the depth in his hazel eyes, came into sudden focus and she held her breath as though the very act could sustain the memory. No sooner did her breath escape than Amron reached out and grasped her arm. She woke with a start with the door rattling and her heart pounding.

In walked Tani who shuffled over to Losha's bedside. "Child. Get up! You cannot sleep the day away! There are matters to discuss!"

Losha's heart was still racing. "I have not slept for days," she complained.

Tani folded herself into a squat, all bones and leather on the floor by Losha's bed mat. "None of the Councilors have slept either. We were up all night debating." There was a sparkle in her eyes. "After the meeting the Queen met with Mefakani and myself in private. She and her entire Council voiced full support of Temple as the Master Teacher." Her smile turned sour. "Sahdon and that whale dick, Cranik, led many of the Elders in their opposition to the Stranger last night. Many believe he is a false prophet and want blood. You," she pointed with a crooked finger, "are being called to explain your actions yesterday. Those who are yet undecided will listen well to what you say."

"Explain what actions?" Losha sat up with sudden alertness.

"'Child, know you not that there are ears and eyes everywhere? I have just been given word that you were seen arguing with the Teacher on the beach last night. The Queen will find this out soon enough."

The young woman caught herself with her mouth open.

"You would be wise to keep your temper, Losha," the old woman said with a keen glare. "Can you not see the Unbelievers take over?" Her face pulled into a maze of wrinkles. "Oh, what I would give to rip out every hair from Cranik's bushy brows with my teeth, if I had any. But, Bi Kana, it is Sahdon who worries me most. He mimics reason and turns everyone's brain into a twist. We must be cautious. Careful what you say, Little One, when you explain your actions."

"But Tani, I do not know if...." Losha let the sentence dangle in front of them. *"Maybe I am too analytical, or perhaps it is the fatigue, which causes me to doubt now. Still, there is every reason to doubt the Stranger. Is it possible for the gods to send a complete mortal, and a white one at that, to teach the people? And could it be he dropped from the Heavens, but is still from a far off land as well? And why does Temple seem not the least bit interested in proclaiming himself the Teacher? If anything he only acts the part, and poorly, in order to save himself from an impostor's impossible fate."*

"You do not know what?" The old woman leaned forward sensing the confusion in Losha's energy field.

"I do not know yet about this man," she said, surprised at her own admission. *"Why did the Voice insist I tell no one that It spoke through Temple? The Voice obviously wants the Councils to believe otherwise. Perhaps this white man is no more divine than I am and is being used by some malevolent force. Maybe it is using me!"*

Tani took the young woman's hands in her leathery palms. "Child, it is good to question."

"Yes, but if I doubt too much, am I not being like the Elders Cranik and Sahdon?"

Tani gave the dark woman's hand a firm squeeze. "Child, they are crazy skeptics. There is no reasoning in their reason. They are like pieces of stone. Only in time, when the wind and sea have worn away their doubts, will they know. And then it will be too late."

"Do I dare tell Tani that the Voice and Temple are not the same?" Losha breathed a heavy sigh. "But he is so human. Perhaps he is not a god. But maybe he is not a wizard either. Could he not be just a man?"

Tani patted Losha's hand. "It is healthy to question. There is such a thing as being too open minded. Believe me, child, there are some who are so open minded that I fear their brains will fall out. And, oh, what a terrible mess that makes," she cackled.

Losha managed a weak smile. "Yes, but you said so much depends on what I say today to the Councils and I have not yet made up my mind. What will I do?"

"You have till late morning to ask your heart. Have no doubt that you will receive your answer. I must go now. The Counselors wish to meet together before you come."

Losha looked up at the old woman as she rose stiffly from the floor. "But Tani, if I make the wrong decision, will they kill the Stranger?"

The Healer looked down at the girl. "Are you answering your own question?"

Losha looked up at the old woman in deep silence.

"We expect you later. I believe you will have your answer by then," Tani said, and shuffled out the door.

CHAPTER SEVEN

The Intimidator

*"All the doubts, and even anger, churned into a
dark cloud of suspicion, which engulfed the
frightened Interpreter."*

Council Scribe
The Makolese Scroll on The Education of Temple Fox #7

There were several small groups of Counselors clustered inside the Great Round House waiting for the meeting to begin. Sahdon's group sat a distance from the others, sipping sha and arguing.

Gabu leaned back and swallowed a mouthful of wine, then rested his cup on his fat belly. "I do not trust this mysterious informer you speak of," he warned.

Sahdon sat with one leg folded and his withered leg sticking out uncomfortably in front of him. He shook his head in mild irritation. "Do you not see? The Queen has her spies. We are only doing as she does by knowing where the white man goes and what he does."

Cranik's permanent frown deepened on his heavy brow. "I agree with Gabu. How do we know this informer does not spy on you and report to the Shaman or the Queen?"

Sahdon tried to move his bad leg to a less painful position, but was unsuccessful. "Because, I give him no information. I only listen,"

Sahdon said, controlling both his impatience and his pain.

"Still," Cranik grumbled, "I am suspicious of his intentions. Might he not give us misinformation to his liking instead?"

"We will know more when we hear what the girl has to say," Sahdon said.

"If you are wrong, Senior Elder, we could end up looking like fools," Gabu cautioned, his voice cracking slightly.

"We will end up being worse than fools if we do not persuade both the Councils," Sahdon said. "This barbarian must be destroyed, and yet I can not think how to do so without first convincing the Queen."

"There are other ways," Cranik said with a dangerous smile, and the others fell silent.

Elder Kulo, a large man with wooly white hair, cleared his throat. "Truly Elders, I must speak." The Elder's knotted, arthritic hands placed his cup of sha before him, signifying a need for sober thinking. "I appreciate your diplomatic approach, Sahdon, but I agree with Cranik. It would be best to simply get rid of the Stranger ourselves."

The old man beside Kulo shook his gray head and spoke, his deep gravelly voice in direct contrast to his small rodent-like face. "But that would drive an even larger wedge between Believers and Unbelievers. It could create civil war!" Elder Ikus said.

Sahdon nodded. "You are quite right, Ikus. This must be done here and it must be done with the Queen's consent."

A call to order echoed through the chamber and all the Elders took their cushioned seats on the floor. Gabu downed the rest of his sha before he rose. He looked down at Cranik who was stewing in silence alone. "May the Lord and his Legions help us," Gabu prayed.

Cranik's black bushy eyebrows hid the sinister, far-away look in his eye as he stared into his cup of brew. *"What the others do not know will not hurt them. It only takes a tiny spark to create a huge bonfire and that spark has long since leapt from flint to kindling. For the few of us who know without a doubt what the Creature represents, I offer that one small flame of assurance."*

Cranik smiled knowingly to himself and cast his gaze upon the Senior Elder who had resumed his position on the floor. *"All that is needed directly from our faction of the Elder Council is the cover of diplomacy, and for that the others and I will depend on Sahdon."*

★   ★   ★   ★   ★   ★

One of the old women stepped in front of the Queen's Counsel and bowed deeply. "Before we begin, Most Respected, I would like to give you the short report you asked for." The Sovereign nodded and Sahdon stepped back to give the woman her say. The Elder spoke with a distinct quiver in her voice. "It has been reported that the wild lettuce pond has dried up without apparent cause. Along with its destruction lies the death of the entire species of bald egret and snake kite."

One lone bee probed the blossoms Palomei wore in her hair, making an audible buzzing in the chamber. "It is grim, deeply grim," she said. "Thank you, Elder. Perhaps the matter for which we gathered today may mend the Su soon enough."

"You hear that, Sahdon? The Queen favors the Stranger," Gabu whispered, and the Elder statesman nodded his head in deep thought.

When Losha crawled into the Chamber the same awe overtook her as it had the day before. This was the place her mother often spoke of, but could never describe. Within the sacred hall it was easy to feel small as if she were deep inside the hidden chamber of a nautilus. The smoky floor illuminated the weathered faces from below, casting an eerie, luminous light. She straightened her black widow's sash. It was the first time she had worn it, a clear sign that she was accepting her recent loss. Feeling uncertain she strained to find Tani among the pearly ghosts of faces.

"Here," the guard gestured to the same cushion the Interpreter had sat on the day before.

Palomei sat high on her black polished throne with her yellow, feathered cape draped loosely over her shoulders and her huge breasts hanging over the enormous round of her belly. She tapped her scepter against the obsidian floor, and the sound echoed in a muffled facsimile.

"We bid you a bright morning and wish you good health," the Queen began.

Losha lowered her head to the cool polished floor then sat up keeping her head bowed in respect. "Thank you, Most Respected."

Palomei eyed the woman's widow sash from a distance. "Losha," she said in a gentle tone, "the Counselors would like to extend our deepest sorrow for your loss. We wish to acknowledge the hardship we impose on you at this time."

"I wish only to be a humble servant to you, my Queen, and to my people."

"Very well." Palomei's tone changed and there was a restless stirring among the Elders. "The Counselors wish to ask you a few questions. The Counselors have chosen our High Shaman, Mefakani and Senior Elder, Sahdon, as spokesmen. There is no need to remind you, I am sure, of the consequences of dishonesty."

Losha felt a sudden chill rush to the surface of her skin as she gazed upon one of Palomei's footstools.

Palomei nodded to the handsome statesman. "Elder Sahdon, please begin."

The Senior Elder stepped forward, brushing a polished hand through his thick gray hair. He leaned heavily on his cane with his head held down, mind deep in thought. Although he limped, he moved with a stately elegance to the center of the hall. He paused briefly and looked at Losha. "Young woman," he began, his smooth, deep voice filling the hall. "All of the Counselors feel that you know the Stranger better than anyone else. You know his language and have certainly spent more time conversing with him than any one of us." The old man wasted no time. He pointed his cane at Losha. "You, young woman, do not even believe that this white savage is a god, do you? You were seen last night arguing on the beach with him. If this man is to be considered a man-god, do you not think that he would deserve more respect? Yet, it has been reported that you stormed away from him in a fit of anger. It is because you know he is an impostor. Is this not true?"

Losha bit her lip and glanced at Tani who was praying. She bowed her head in humble submission. "I regret my actions Elder Sahdon and wish to make amends."

"But why? Why such anger to *a god*?" he spat sarcastically.

She licked her lips nervously, knowing she had been snared in a political trap. Yet, secretly she felt the act of being publicly humiliated was perhaps due her for she found her own behavior appalling. Only now there was more at stake. Her honor and loyalty to the Queen had been called into question and that was a most serious offense.

"I regret that I have allowed my own personal problems to get in the way of my duties, Respected Elder. I did not believe that my husband was truly dead. I had hoped..." she paused to calm the tremor in her voice. "I had hoped that at least his body would yet be found. The Stranger was trying to convince me to accept his death. He was trying to comfort me." It was the perfect lie.

Sahdon's voice echoed through the chamber. "Comfort? It has been reported that this white man struck you! Is that not true?"

"Certainly not!" She met Sahdon's glare with forcefulness and clarity. "He never struck me! It is a lie!" she pleaded as she turned towards the Queen.

Palomei called the meeting to a halt to confer with her Head Guard, then turned towards the assembly.

"I do not know how Elder Sahdon received his information," she said, with a black look aimed at the Elder. "From the report I just received, it is a great exaggeration. It has been told to me, however, that you did argue with the Stranger."

Losha held her eyes against Sahdon's in a steadfast stare. "The Stranger did not strike me. He grabbed my shoulder to turn me around. He did not know it was forbidden to touch widows. It was then that I realized that I was, indeed, a widow. In truth, I yelled it at him. If it were not for his breaking the taboo I never would have seen the truth of my situation. I am a... a widow," she declared, with her eyes cast down in a sorrowful look of finality, and with the secret knowledge that, at least, part of her tale was true.

Sahdon hobbled forward exerting pressure on the girl by his mere proximity. "He acts like no god I have ever heard of. He was yelling at you like a barbarian!"

"I would like to answer, Respected Elder," Losha responded firmly, then turned towards the Queen, "even if it means the Queen rules that I am unfit to serve her Counsel any longer. I confess that I was so unsettled about the news of my husband that I would not listen to reason. The Stranger argued with me to see reason. I am indebted to him."

The Counselors mumbled to themselves until the chamber was filled with loud echoes.

"Silence!" the Queen demanded.

"May I?" Mefakani gestured, and the Queen nodded. "Losha, having spent as much time with the Stranger as you have, would you say he is a man-god?"

This was the very question Losha feared. She envisioned Temple's head impaled on a bloody stake, another future footstool for the Queen.

"May the gods forgive me if I am wrong," she whispered silently inside her heart. "I would." She stole a glance at Tani who rocked back and forth with her eyes closed tight.

"Why?"

She remembered the mysterious Voice. "He speaks with wisdom and compassion. His words are gentle when gentle words are called for and confronting when confrontation is needed to see the truth of a matter." Losha's words rolled over the round chamber walls and returned in a muted echo. "Forgive me for speaking so forthright, but the Stranger *is* half human."

Sahdon interrupted. "Is that so? Will this be the excuse used to explain his inconsistency of behavior? One minute he acts like a clever wizard, the next he acts like a white savage?"

"He complains of headaches," she intervened, holding her argument firm.

Palomei looked to Mefakani. "You have stated that the Stranger's memory has been affected by the blow to his head, have you not?"

"Yes, Most Respected. This would account for his erratic behavior. Losha is correct. It must not be forgotten that the Stranger is still half human."

"Excuses!" Sahdon grumbled loudly. "The Makolese cannot afford to have an ounce of doubt about this creature. May I remind you all that if we are wrong, our people will suffer, even die? Our very culture is at stake."

"We are all here for the same reason, Sahdon," Mefakani shot back. "If you are wrong we could very well be putting The True Teacher to death. And then, Senior Elder, our very culture *will* be at stake."

There was a low murmur of voices in the great hall.

An Elder who was undecided coaxed Sahdon over to him. "Sahdon," he whispered. "The Queen will rule in favor of this Temple Fox anyway. Why make tensions any worse?"

"You heard the Queen," Sahdon replied in hushed tones. "If this wizard is declared The True Teacher he will be expected to mend the Su. And when he does, our women will be coerced into birthing babies – fresh supplies of Makolese for the slave markets. We are looking at the possibility of having a white man on our throne!"

A look of horror darkened the Elder's face. "I had not seen it in this light before. My apology, Senior Elder."

Sahdon cleared his throat and the echoes faded. "May I continue, Most Respected?" The Queen nodded.

His words hit like a cold slap of wind. "Young woman, it is not my intention to expose why you are lying. I am only here to prove that you are. You know this Temple Fox is an impostor! It has been reported that while in Tani's hut you attacked him!"

Voices rumbled within Mefakani's circle of allies and within the Queen's own Council. Palomei fumed in anger and turned towards her first husband. "Why had I not been told of this? I will put this foolish woman to death if she is lying!"

All the doubts, and now anger, churned into a dark cloud of suspicion, which surrounded the frightened woman. Losha moved her mouth to speak, but not a word escaped.

"Answer the Elder!" the Queen ordered with a gruffness that shook the air.

Losha's eyes brimmed with tears of humiliation. Her words lodged behind a growing knot in her throat, but pulled free when she allowed her anger to rise. "It is a lie!" she finally blurted out, and a hush came across the hall. She tried to pull back her tears, but try as she might her words came out in fits and starts. "The Stranger said… he was hungry. There were fillets… of fish… hanging on a rack to dry. He reached for one. It was puffer fish!"

Tani raised her hand to her mouth in shock and turned to face the Shaman.

"He was about to eat it! I knocked it out of his hand!" she said pleading.

Cranik got up and pulled Sahdon off the floor while there was a clamor in the chamber. "You old fool! She is telling the truth. You see we can not trust your precious spy."

Fury rose beneath Sahdon's embarrassment. "Shut up, Cranik!" Sahdon snapped. "Our informer reported on exactly what he was able to see."

Mefakani stood up. "This is the very thing I feared would happen, My Queen. I insisted that Temple be moved to Tani's hut last night so he would not meddle with my own potions in my absence. I take full responsibility for this error in judgment."

"No, no, no!" Tani cried as she flattened herself on the floor. "It was my idea and so it is my fault. I hung the puffers to dry. I did not stop to think of the dangers."

Palomei held her hand up and the chamber fell silent. "It seems there have been many errors of judgments made these past few days." The Matriarch gave a long penetrating stare to Mefakani then Tani who was still folded on the floor with her white tangle of hair splayed out before her. The last stare was saved for Sahdon who raised his head proudly in the air to rebuff Palomei's silent reproach.

"Until this matter of the Stranger is settled, he will reside under my protection within the royal compound," she declared. "Furthermore, I believe the girl's story," she continued, then looked down at Losha. "I had second thoughts about imposing the task of Interpreter on you in light of your recent tragedy. But we are all pressed into service for the good of our people. In the future, I suggest you take better control of your emotions." Losha gave a sheepish nod and kept her head lowered. "I might add that the Council is in debt to you for saving the Stranger's life."

Losha's voice was shaking and barely audible. "Thank you, Most Respected."

The Queen turned to look at Mefakani again. "As for you, High Shaman, I want you to make time for this matter of Losha's husband. It is better to be finished with this business now since there are more important things to attend to.

"And you, Elder Tani," Palomei shook her head in dismay. "If you do not tidy that cluttered, dirty little hut of yours, I will have it razed to the ground! Understood?"

"Thank you, Most Respected. Thank you," the old woman breathed in a raspy whisper.

Queen Palomei raised her head above the crowd. "Is there anyone else who wishes to speak at this time before I rule on this matter?" she challenged.

Sahdon whispered to Cranik. "Our only weapon is to demand more evidence. If we are not granted that, then the only thing we can do is to stall her decision."

Sahdon limped forward as if nothing had occurred before. "My Queen, I speak for many Elders. Our hearts so want to believe this great thing and yet our heads tell us otherwise. We believe with all our souls that this white man is a master of deception. Would the Most Respected at least grant us one small wish to help us all bring this matter to the light of truth?"

"And what is this request?"

"Bring the Outsider to us once more so that he may perform a miracle."

"I have no objections to this," the Queen said. "If this Temple Fox is the True Teacher then this is why he has come – for miracles." The Sovereign rapped her scepter on the floor and called for a break for some sha and breadfruit before continuing.

Owane looked jovial as he whispered into his wife's ear. "Perhaps a miracle or two will convince Sahdon and his boneheads."

"My thoughts exactly, husband," Palomei smiled.

Mefakani didn't rise to leave, but looked to Tani who was shaking her wispy white head in deep worry.

CHAPTER EIGHT

The Unbelievers

"Before the Slavers came, the Makolese were known as great traders. There was one trade item the women loved best – metal cooking pots. As I recall, these pots had numerous uses."

Temple Fox
The Makolese Scroll on The Education of Temple Fox #8

It was a calm day on Dolphin Bay. The children played tag in the receding tide while the women harvested oysters that had become ensnared in the stilted roots of mangroves. Work was finished early so the women could gather to bathe and discuss the recent rumors. Although baring their breasts in the tropical heat was their custom, they were modest when it came to complete nakedness, except around other women. With baskets full, one by one they abandoned their labors and their barkcloth skirts, revealing the intricate spirals that adorned their flesh, and plunged into the warm crystal waters.

The women laughed and splashed one another, when, suddenly, one woman dropped her basket and let out a startled scream. The white Stranger, with a band of seven palace guards, marched purposely in their direction onto the collar of beach. The women made a frenzied dash from the water and flung their skirts around their waists, then quickly gathered their children. There they watched with either fear or awe as the pale Stranger washed, then fell back in line with the guards.

Leading the band towards the island's interior was Sumuro, Palomei's Head Guard, a large man with a powerful build and a massive jaw tattooed so intricately that it took on the appearance of a beard. Crowds flocked around the Stranger and Sumuro's narrow eyes moved quickly to and fro beneath his pugilist's brow. He barked an order and the people stepped backwards, all but the little children, who drew closest to Temple until their mothers snatched them back.

By the time Sumuro had pushed the band around Makol's largest village, the humidity sidled up against the Stranger, nuzzling him like a pesky dog.

"Sure could use a cold Yankee beer right about now," Temple said, but Sumuro gave no response. The pilot smiled wearily at the villagers who bore down on him, swallowing him with their curiosity, but couldn't find Losha, the Shaman, or the old Healer. A crippled man staggered up to him and one of the guards held up one of their odd shields to push the man away.

"You won't do much good with that thing, mate," Temple said to the guard, pointing to the hollow, wheel-like shield. No sooner had he said this when, out of nowhere, a large metal pot dropped from the sky. The soldier held up his shield and the pot bounced four feet off in front of the strange shield and into the air without the pot having touched the shield.

Temple wiped the sweat from his eyes and squinted into the glare, uncertain of what he'd just seen.

One guard drove the crowd back and picked up the battered pot. He moved swiftly through the crowd to find the culprit, a small middle-aged woman, who wound her way out of his reach and emerged from the other side of the crowd. She shoved her way to the edge of the procession where the Stranger stood staring in bewilderment, then pulled her skirt up and thrust her bare buttocks out towards him. A small crowd cheered to goad her on.

"White beast! White beast!" she shouted, as the guards forced her back into the crowd. "When they cut off your white head, I will boil it in my pot!" she spat, hitting Temple in the face, then retreated grumbling and cursing.

Temple wiped the spittle from his sun burnt cheek. He looked up into Sumuro's oriental eyes, but could draw nothing from the Head Guard's dispassionate gaze. "What's happening? Where are you taking me?" he asked nervously above the angry voices. The shaft of a spear pressed against the small of his back, urging him to move on. "Where's

Losha? Where's the Priest? I'm your god! Do you hear me?" But his words fell on deaf ears.

Sumuro's men quickened their pace. They marched around the villagers, past a thick grove of palms, and came to an abrupt halt. A mob, armed with clubs and rocks, blocked their passage.

"I am moving the Stranger, by the Queen's command!" Sumuro shouted. "Move out of the way!" The warriors formed a spoke of spears around Temple.

A voice in the crowd yelled out, "You hold the white Wizard. Release him to us. Now!"

Sumuro shouted back. "This man's fate is to be decided only by the Queen. Leave immediately, or you will be holding your own entrails in your hands!"

The rebel leader yelled orders at his people to attack. There was hesitancy at first then a restless stirring, until someone from behind the wall of villagers threw a rock, which missed the small procession by a few yards.

Sumuro restrained his men as they drew their spears back into throwing position, their muscles tensed and ready. Dozens of rocks were thrown and one rolled past a guard's shield, hitting him in the foot. With only raw instincts to guide him, the angry guard pitched his spear with a vengeful force. The spear arced in the air and the mob scattered. When it hit the ground there was a flash of white light and blue sparks, and a deep thunderous rumble. The sand quivered slightly, causing a rippled effect across the beach, and the screaming villagers dove for cover.

Temple stood silent and wide-eyed in the sudden quiet that followed. A burnt, electrical smell permeated the air.

The rebel leader glared bitterly at Sumuro. He retrieved a burning portion of the spear shaft from the vitrified spot on the beach, holding it up as a flaming beacon for his followers. The rebels slowly rose and regrouped themselves into a wider semi-circle of frightened and angry people.

"Throw your spears on my orders only," Sumuro commanded. "And make ready for a run."

Temple stiffened.

The Head Guard moved his men quietly, without provocation, past the excited mob, holding their leader in his sights. The urgency seemed to ease at first as the band wound their way into the foothills, but the trail was leading into dense forest and Sumuro sensed the mob might follow at a safe distance behind them.

The soldiers moved at a fast clip, eyes darting this way and that through the heavy foliage, ears alert to the snapping of twigs they heard far behind them now. Temple was poked a couple of times and forced to keep the pace. The sweat poured off him, the rustling of leaves behind him providing the main impetus to keep up. Minutes moved in sluggish time.

The pilot sighed with relief when they stepped out from the trail's end into a wide clearing, knowing the stairs that would lead up and over the crater was just ahead around a cluster of trees. His optimism proved premature, however. Through the trees they spied a group of men crouched over the bodies of two guards. The men were armed with clubs and fishing gaffs, and blocked the boulder path. Sumuro issued a few whispered commands then pushed Temple, forcing him to break from the cover of trees and run up the sides of the crater. But Sumuro's strategy came too late. The first mob broke from the forest trail behind them and the second mob advanced.

The eight scurried up the steep incline on all fours until they found a level foothold. Temple's throat constricted when he saw a heavy stone arcing through the air.

"Now!" Sumuro yelled, and all the warriors threw their spears with split second precision. "Run!" he ordered.

The stone hurtled down and ricocheted three feet off of Sumuro's shield, but the sky was still dotted with more. There was an explosion of light where the spears fell below, and the sound of screams and stones hitting sand could be heard beneath the rumbling earth. The tiny band scrambled up the steep slope, creating an avalanche of earth behind them as they hurried.

Temple was sheltered from dozens of successive blows, all repelled by the strange shields and the guard's precise movements. But luck and skill were not lasting, for one rock fell from an odd angle and slipped through the guardsmen's defenses. Sumuro caught the blur from the corner of his eye, pivoted and glanced the stone with the edge of his shield without time to use its repulsion field. A metallic ring pierced the air and the rock ricocheted an inch past the pilot's head, leaving sharp fragments in his hair.

Temple was folded into a crouch, his muscles cramped and his breath shortened. He raised a hand to his face to wipe the powdered stone from his cheek, but his hand was stopped by a forceful grip on his arm and wretched upward. He struggled against the seizure to gain his balance. His feet clamored for a firm foothold on the yielding terrain, one hand clutching fistfuls of earth and the other being dragged by Sumuro. But the Head Guard pulled too hard. Temple fell face down on the slope, gathering a mouthful of dirt and a loss of several yards and several seconds.

When Temple slid backwards below his protector, and deeper into the mob's newly gained territory, there were shouts of panic and a sharp grunt. He dug his fingers and toes deep into the hot soil, slowing his decline, until he collided with something. He turned his head for a split second, enough to see the body of a guard beneath him.

Seeing the Stranger was defenseless, there was a new wave of rock throwing. Temple grabbed the dead man's shield and buffered himself behind it, shoulder pressed against the crystal sphere. But he didn't know how to use its power and several rocks fell through, one hitting him in the back, knocking the air out of him and forcing him to the ground. He lay helpless now, too occupied with his struggle to breathe to fight off his attackers, when he felt someone below grab his ankle. And he was pulled down the rock-strewn hill at a rapid speed, his chest grating against sharp stone. He struggled for a full breath through the new wave of pain, and the cloud of dust that choked him, when someone above him snatched a crop of his hair. He thought his scalp would rip from his skull as a tug-of-war ensued, with both thugs and guardsman as enemies now. Sumuro yelled a command and two guardsmen grabbed hold of each of Temple's arms, grunting as they pitted their strength against gravity and the rebels below.

Temple's sinews stretched beyond the limits of his endurance. Thinking his limbs would be torn from their sockets, he cried aloud for mercy. The last thing he heard, before he fainted, was wailing and the rattling of swords around him.

CHAPTER NINE

The Teaching

"All successes are yours. Failures, too, are your own. But, in the larger truth, there are neither successes nor failures, only learning."

Temple Fox
Makolese Prophecy Scroll #902
The Makolese Scroll on The Education of Temple Fox #9

All eyes fell on Sumuro when he rushed over to the Queen and threw himself on the floor in supplication. All gasped in horror when they saw his back smeared with blood and dirt.

Sumuro tried to catch his breath. "We were ambushed, Most Respected. A mob of fifty or more... near the crater. We provoked no one," he said, panting with his head held down.

"And the Stranger?"

"We lost three guardsmen and..."

"The Stranger!" she snapped loudly. "What has become of him?"

"He is outside, My Queen. He passed out, but we revived him. He received some cuts and bruises. That is all."

"Bring him to me now!"

"He refuses to enter and calls for the Interpreter. He is washing in the pool below." Palomei looked through the chamber floor. Below, a pale, hazy figure moved, its form barely discernible through the thick volcanic glass.

"Losha, attend to the Stranger. Now!" she ordered.

The Interpreter rushed to the chamber door with the sound of the Queen's voice echoing with rage.

★   ★   ★   ★   ★   ★

The swans scurried away from Temple when he stepped into the reflecting pool. He tried to wash the grit from his open cuts, but started shaking. He scrutinized the heavy tablet of smoky stone above him. Nestled inside the round chamber, in the quarry of death, were all the little minds who would discuss his fate. What would their decision be? He looked out across the crater's rim, almost expecting the mob to reappear, but all he saw was a line of guards at full alert. Towering above them were the royal palms, their green tops swaying in the wind like the heads of Roman spectators who had just cast their vote at the games. The marooned pilot began to weep silently.

"Temple!" a voice called out.

He splashed his face quickly and looked up at the panicked Interpreter.

"Are you all right?" she said, eyeing the cuts on his cheek and chest.

"No! They tried to kill me!"

"Temple, the Queen is waiting. You must go inside."

"No! I can't! They know I'm a fake!"

"You are no impostor. You must find that Voice again," she insisted.

Temple passed a wet hand through his gritty hair. "Losha, I can't. This is all a lie. Do you understand? Everything is a lie! I even lied to you about this." He pointed to the old scar around his waist. "I never killed that lion. I couldn't kill it! I'm not some god! I'm a coward! You hear me?" he started to yell.

"Please, Temple, you must listen. The Queen favors you. If she issues a decree, no one will harm you."

"Tell that to the mob that just tried to stone me to death!" The short grunts of swans filled the air as Temple sloshed through the water. He plopped himself down on the banks of the pond. "Did you see those spears and those shields the guards carry? No Voice speaking through me is ever going to protect me from that kind of power. I'm finished!"

Tani suddenly appeared and shuffled over to the Stranger. She scowled at him in disgust. "Bi Kana! You are a mess! Do you not have enough scars already?" the old woman groaned as she pulled a satchel from beneath her waist band. She pried it open, dug her fingers into it pulling out a glob of some greasy ointment and dabbed it onto Temple's chest.

"What's she saying?" he asked.

"She says if you get one more scar you may fulfill yet another prophecy, so please stay out of trouble." She gave a feeble smile.

Tani pulled an obsidian vial from under her sash and made the Stranger drink it. "What is this stuff?" he asked, frowning at the bitter taste.

Losha gave the vial a quick sniff and looked at the old Healer. "Tani, what are you doing?" she whispered with alarm.

"Hush girl! It will help him to get out of his body again."

Losha's mouth flew open. "Then you know?"

"Of course I know, girl. I slipped a few drops of this potion in his sha yesterday. And I know it worked 'cause I watched his spirit leave and a greater one take him over. He will be expected to do it again today, so I thought he might need a little help," she winked.

"Bi Kana!" whispered Losha. "Does the Shaman know of this?"

"No, I distracted him so he did not see it. He knows nothing of my conjuring."

Losha bit her lip. *"Tani knew all along that Temple's spirit had left and was taken over by another! Furthermore, she helped him to do so, and yet, she still believes he is the Prophet!"*

"Tani," she whispered, "this is the last of the potion."

"I know, but can you think of a better time to use it, child?" she whispered back. "Do not worry. In six months time the juk will blossom again and I will brew more."

"But Tani, if...?"

"There is much left to learn, Little One." The old woman's eyes twinkled and she grabbed the Stranger's hand and coaxed him to his feet.

"Bi Kana lo!" Losha repeated under her breath.

★   ★   ★   ★   ★   ★

There was a sudden hush when the Stranger was brought into the great chamber. He brushed his dripping hair aside, revealing a thin trickle of blood on his stubbled cheek. His eyes swept across the hall at all the ghostly old faces. The only movement came from one of the scribes whose brush was moving rapidly. Tani motioned for him to sit.

The rapping sound of Palomei's scepter ricocheted around the chamber and all were brought to order.

Losha interpreted. "The Queen says the Councils greet you once again and to please accept our apologies for the inconvenience."

"Inconvenience!" he said gritting his teeth.

"Temple, Hush! Please," Losha pleaded.

"We will trouble you no further with protocol, but ask you only for one request," the Queen said.

"Yes, Most Respected," Temple said, bowing low with great reluctance.

"We ask for yet another miracle."

No one could hear Temple's stomach churn violently. A sudden flush came over his body, but it was concealed by the iridescence cast by the chamber walls. He placed his hands squarely on each thigh to balance himself. "I think I'm going to get sick," he said.

"It is only the pujo – the medicine. You were given a heavy dose. The queasiness will soon pass," Losha explained.

"Will you abide by my wishes, Temple Fox?" the Queen asked.

"Yes, of course," he spoke out, then turned to Losha. "I'm a dead man, Losha."

"No. No. Wait," she whispered. "The potion will take effect very soon."

"What do I do?" he asked feeling slightly lightheaded.

"Breathe deeply and steadily," she instructed. "Picture yourself viewing your body from the ceiling. Imagine yourself lifting."

Tani sensed her potion working on Temple. Distracting Mefakani was paramount now, so she handed a scroll to the closest servant and told her to give it to the Priest.

Mefakani unloosened the strips of bark cloth that bound the scroll, unrolled it and read. And while he did this, Temple's spirit slipped out of his body and glided across the room to where Tani sat. He pulled on one of her long ear lobes, and swore he saw the old woman wink and wave him away from her like a pesky fly.

Temple hovered just below the ceiling and looked down at his body, watching it breathe without him. The hall was alive with anticipation. Suddenly, a shower of unworldly colors filled the air and a ghostly blue form appeared floating before him. The wispy figure came into sharp focus. A man wearing leather overalls and a gray tangled beard hovered on the lip of the familiar silver tunnel.

"Blake!" Temple called out in his mind. "Get me outta here!"

Blake grabbed hold of his friend's hand and the two vanished inside the safety of the tunnel.

The Voice suddenly let out a raucous laugh, which thundered through the chamber. "And so you need another miracle, do you?"

Mefakani looked up from the scroll amid the flurry of voices from the Councils.

When the bustle died down, the Voice began and Losha interpreted. "When will you ever see that *you* are the miracle? Ah well, I will give you another miracle if only to gain your attention for greater things. Listen well islanders, I will give you a prediction. In three moons time, forty ships will come."

There was an immediate rumble of panic in the room. The Queen looked sharply at Mefakani. "Have you foreseen this?"

A rush of heat turned Mefakani's face the color of dried blood. "I sensed something of enormity coming, yes, Most Respected...but I had thought it was the Stranger's arrival. But now..." he stopped and cast a drilling eye at the Stranger.

"Forty ships! That is an entire armada!" exclaimed the Queen. "What kind of ships?"

"All large. All with lateen sails."

"Arabs!" the Queen exclaimed. "Forty booms?"

"Yes, Most Respected," answered the Voice.

A rise of turbulent voices rolled around the chamber until the Queen rose from her throne, her towering height dwarfing the Elders. She took a step towards the Stranger. "Will you help us defeat the enemy?"

"Name your enemy," the Voice replied.

"Help us to defeat the Arab slavers," the Queen requested.

There was a brief silence, then the Voice responded, "No," flatly.

The Matriarch almost lost her grip on her scepter. It was as if someone had lodged a fist in her solar plexus. "NO?" Her voice echoed throughout the hall in shock and disbelief.

"Your *fear* of the Arab slavers is your enemy, island Queen. I will only help you to conquer your **fear**."

The Titan stepped nearer the Stranger. "The Makolese people are not afraid," she stated. "We worship the Lord Tagheetu and confront all our fears through Him."

"Then what do you need me for?" the Voice asked. There was a short shock of silence. "Island Queen, you must realize it is *everyone's* fear that draws the slave traders to your shores. Do you not know that there is an escalating campaign of fear which rules this island?"

"*I* rule this island," the Queen corrected. "And **I am not afraid**," she declared, still standing tall. **"I am the sovereign power here!"**

"Island Queen," the Voice asked in an even tone, "how is it that you can serve as Master over your subjects when you have not yet mastered your own Self?"

In truth, the Queen had no answer for a question she did not understand.

"Do you wish to possess more power? True power?"

"I am the secular power on this island," she answered with indignation. "I wish only to defeat the Outsiders," the Queen declared, with head held high and pulling her self to her full height.

"Ah, but with *true power* you could defeat all your enemies."

"Then, that is what I wish for. I wish for *true power*."

"Then, in time, it will be so."

The Elders sat staring at their giant Queen and the Stranger who held her with his words. "Then, it is granted to me?" she asked. "This true power you speak of?"

"Beloved Queen, if it is true power that you want to defeat your enemies, I will arrange for you to learn this power. Do we have an agreement?"

"Yes," she said, somewhat in awe. "If you can grant me that, then you are surely the Master Teacher."

"And so, I am," the Voice laughed.

"And so, my rump!" Cranik muttered for the ears of his allies close by.

The Queen stared into Temple's strange blue eyes looking for something more. "Temple, I am Mother to my people. Our Su has been broken. Both the land and our women are becoming barren. I have lost my only daughter and have no heir. Can you also mend the Su?"

"I can only help you to heal the Su yourselves. I give you the tools; you and your people will need to do the work. Do you understand?"

The Queen slowly nodded her head.

The Voice spoke. "All successes are yours. Failures, too, are your own. But, in the larger truth, there are neither successes nor failures, only learning. Do you see?"

"He contradicts himself," Sahdon thought to himself.

Temple's head was sharply turned towards the Senior Elder, and the spirit that peered through the pilot's eyes looked directly at Sahdon. "There lies the paradox for having to live in this plane of duality," the Voice explained. "You see, there are no rewards or punishments either, my old friend, only consequences for actions taken... and always, always learning."

The Senior Elder met the Stranger's gaze and squirmed

uncomfortably in his seat.

The Spirit behind the Voice turned to meet the Queen's eyes again. There was softness in Its tone and manner. "Woman, you speak from a great heart. It is no small thing that grieves you. Know you that the Su begins to heal once you conquer your fears? The gods who created you have great plans for your people. Do you think it is a senseless tradition that the Makol people have made Su with strangers for thousands of seasons? It has been a celebration of life and has been to enlarge your sense of family. It has, also, been by the god's designs, for your people hold the sacred Su, the perfect seed, for all humanity.

"You see, respected woman, your people are near their biological completion. Know you that you are biologically tied with the entire outside world in spite of the law that keeps you inside the Barik Limits. Those limits were set up thousands of seasons ago so we, who you understand as gods, could select the seeds of your new kin carefully. Your isolation also became law so certain traditions could remain intact. Yet, in spite of all our efforts, you still bring about your own destruction and the destruction of life on this precious island."

"But it was the Arabs who first broke the Su," the Queen stated.

"It was broken long before that," the Voice explained. "Know you, island Queen, that even Arab blood runs through your veins? They are your brothers and your sisters, too. When they enslave you, they enslave a portion of themselves. And, when you fear and hate them, you fear and hate a portion of your own beautiful being."

There was a sudden change in the Teacher's voice taking on an almost lighter tone, which grew more somber as It spoke. "Now, Island Queen, do not think I mean for you to rush up to your oppressors and kiss them when they come. Before they arrive, I want you to do something....I want you to *be* them. I want you to ride their ships in your mind. Think their thoughts. Feel their feelings as if you were really them. You will see just how desperate they are...the same as you. How they are pained creatures who are often joyless...the same as you – who only know confrontation – the same as you and who are enslaved by their own want for control, the same as you. To understand them is to understand *yourself*."

The Queen's jaw tightened. She remained silent.

"You see, you are very much like your Arab kin who have yet to master their emotional selves. It is why your people attracted the slavers to your shore to begin with. They will act like mirrors for you."

The Queen found her voice again. "And the gods allowed this?'

"We forever hold in our mind your true essence, which dwells in the original state of grace in eternity. It is your divine spirit we always see and know, and hold in love prior to your choice to separate yourself from the Greater God, and even after that choice. We inspire. We do not interfere."

"Are you not interfering now?"

"You did pray for me to come, did you not? Although in truth, I have been with you always and forever. But, just as you attracted the slavers, you have attracted me. Like attracts like. You asked for someone to come and speak the truth you needed to hear. It has been in your heart to hear what you already know. Yet, you could not open to the truth. You needed someone to come and help to facilitate the knowing. It is for you to choose what you do with this knowing."

The Queen stood staring again in silence.

"You and your ancestors have kept the prophecies pure. That has been a great accomplishment in our eyes. But not all has been kept pure. We foresaw a time when you would need hope and guidance after you lost your way. And now, in truth, is the time to mend the Su, for the gods have larger plans for you."

"Then, I will have an heir?" she asked.

"Yes."

The giantess relaxed her stance a bit. "The people will be much relieved. I thank you."

"Be patient, great woman, for the time is not yet ripe."

Palomei glanced at all the old faces as she returned to her throne. She was lost in her own thoughts.

"I must rest now," the Voice said, and Temple's shoulders slumped forward.

Before anyone could react to what had transpired, Temple's spirit slammed back into his body with a jolt. He bent over with his elbows on his knees and held his head in anguish. "My head," he groaned.

"Are you back?" Losha asked.

"Yes, yes." He made an attempt to suppress his moaning and rocked on his haunches to ease the pain. "There's too much pressure in my head."

Losha looked at the Sovereign with alarm. "He is in pain, My Queen!"

Palomei looked to Mefakani. "Can nothing be done?"

"Most Respected, Elder Tani and myself have arranged to bring about a more complete healing for the Stranger. Only then will his pain ease and his memory become fully restored, but it will take some time."

"Very well," she said. The Queen looked to the pale Stranger first, then to the rows of startled faces. "I wish to rule on this matter before I grant you all leave," she announced. Palomei quietly walked to the center of the great round hall again and turned to address the semi-circle of Elders. She thought for a moment as she watched the refracted ripples of light make strange patterns on their wrinkled, tattooed faces. Her voice softened. "In spite of the unfortunate hue of his skin; in spite of his recent injuries which impairs his memory, and in spite of the fact that he is merely a boy, I hereby declare this Temple Fox as the True Teacher." There was a sigh of relief from the majority of Elders. "He is to be held by all with the highest respect. Those holding opposing views are to be silent!" she ordered. "And those who dare to challenge this decree will be exiled or put to death!"

"What's happening?" Temple whispered quietly aside.

"She has declared you as the True Teacher," the Interpreter whispered back. "Acceptance of you is now law."

"Must have been a whale of a magic show," he said.

"Not exactly," Losha murmured under her breath. "Look at Sahdon and his faction."

The pilot looked around the chamber. Most of the Elders showed a twinkling of reverence in their eyes, a sense of wonder for the divinity in him. But more than he cared to count sat in quiet stillness and appeared to be grieving as if the very end of their lives were drawing near. This was more than mere doubt or disbelief, which clouded one area of the hall. Behind their shielded eyes and wooden stares was total terror.

Sahdon sat quietly amid the murmurs of his band, his expression changing from one of bewilderment and shock – to a suppressed anger slowly hardening on his face.

Ikus spoke, his beady eyes taking on the look of defeat. "What can we do now, but make certain every effort is made to enlarge our army to fight the Outsiders? All of us can pressure the Councils into doing this."

The others nodded in agreement, except Sahdon.

"And of course," Ikus said, "we must make certain that our own Priest, misguided as he is, keeps his promise to deliver the new weapon he has been working on before all of this happened."

Again heads nodded, except Sahdon, who turned to them quietly and whispered coldly, "Kill the Beast."

PART – II
THE INITIATE

CHAPTER TEN

The Test

*"All lies within the divine breath, like the day in
the beautiful dawn. It is this you need to learn."*

Elder Tani
The Makolese Scroll on Healing #129
The Makolese Scroll on The Education of Temple Fox #10

The stone walls of the underground chamber held the cold, permeating
Mefakani's bones. He placed another oil jar next to an ancient scroll
on his writing table, causing the shadows to shift slightly. He rubbed
his hands over the flame to shake off the damp chill that had invaded
him, then got up to search the vast wall of shelves for yet another
scroll chest. He let out a churlish snort. "Jabal!" he yelled. In moments
the library door flung open and a brown-skinned boy of eighteen
entered and bowed.

"Some of the prophecy scrolls are out of order!" Mefakani
snapped accusingly.

"I reorganized them six moons ago, Master, just as you told me to.
All the real prophets are here," the boy gestured to the shelves before
him, "and all the lesser prophets, the women, are there." Jabal pointed
to the darkest, dustiest corner of the room.

The Shaman growled annoyingly. "Then why am I sensing that

one is missing?"

Jabal scratched his shaved head in thought and scanned his Master's table. "Since the Stranger arrived, there has been a renewed interest in the particular prophecy scroll you have before you now." He shrugged. "But, any other scrolls, I have no idea. Perhaps one of the Elders has borrowed..."

"Borrowed?" He almost screamed.

"I do not know, my Master. When I finish with the six exorcisms this week I will search the scroll chests, all nine hundred of them, if you wish." He lowered his eyes, and in a cautious voice he said, "Perhaps my Master has simply misplaced the scroll."

The Priest cast a weary eye over to his Apprentice and grunted. "I want the Prophecy Library kept locked from now on, just as we do with the History Library. If anyone wants to see any of the scrolls, they will have to come to me first. Do you understand?"

Jabal gave a lethargic nod, bowed and left the room.

Leaning over the moldy scroll the Shaman's fingers traced over the archaic glyphs lightly, being careful not to tear the fragile fibers. *"Ever since the Stranger fell from the sky, I have felt that I am not seeing the entire picture yet. And, yet, this particular prophecy seems clear. So why do I feel so uneasy?"*

He muttered to himself. "It clearly states there will be a time when 'One without the other is empty. Power multiplies ten fold and then again ten fold, again and again.' The man-god will help to," and he quoted, "'conquer the enemies of the Makolese.' And, it states here, in bold glyphs that this new god will also 'be the High Priest's greatest ally in conquering his enemies.' It states I am destined to share in this god's power. So, what is there to be concerned about?" he asked aloud.

This the Shaman pondered into the early hours of the morning until his Apprentice interrupted.

Jabal, weary and irritated from overwork, entered the stone chamber cautiously. He bowed low to his Master. Seeing his Master had been studying through the night, he gathered his resolve, too frightened to complain of his own fatigue. "Master, it is time we headed for the swamps."

"Very well," Mefakani said, as he carefully rolled up the ancient scroll and slid it into its long, narrow casing of shark's skin. He placed it with reverence back into its proper stone chest and set it on his shelf with great care. And there he left it behind the locked library door in his compound, along with any of his previous doubts.

★　★　★　★　★　★

The jungle was drenched in a soft cool rain forcing Losha and Temple to wrap themselves tightly in their capes, he in white feathers and she in a simple brown barkcloth. The pale Stranger blended into the morning mists and disappeared with his dark companion into a little used jungle trail draped in liana vine. There were occasional hoots, whistles and howls from unseen creatures, and he swore he saw an owl swoop by him.

Losha stepped carefully over a tangle of roots, which had grown over the windy path, her movements nimble and swift. The pilot stumbled behind, nursing his bruises from the day before and now his cold wet feet. When he caught up with her, he paused for a moment and tried to peer through the foliage and fog. "Are you sure I don't need protection anymore?" he asked, worriedly.

"Shhh! Do you wish for them to hear you?" she said, in a reprimanding hush.

Temple shivered from more than just the dampness. "I thought you said I was safe now!" he replied in a harsh whisper.

Losha stopped on the path to face Temple, her unruly hair bejeweled with rain. Her whisper was barely audible. "The Queen's decree is absolute law. No harm will come to you from our people, but today the spirits in the mountain are watching through the mists. This is a time to be silent and show respect. They may be elusive creatures, but they can be dangerous."

The pilot turned as pale as his cape. "What creatures? What do you mean, *dangerous*?"

She whispered behind her as she walked. "Do not worry, Temple Fox. They only come in contact with those who seek them during the mountain rite." She paused and brushed a wet fern out of her way. "Except, of course, those they kidnap."

Quivering, he looked over his shoulder, trying to see beyond the barrier of milky whiteness that enveloped them.

"When our youths come of age, they pay homage to the spirits by taking gifts to the entrance of the sacred mountain. Although it never insures their complete safety, it always seems to insure fertility, until the Su was broken, of course," she added. "But today is most special, for, whenever the mists appear on the first day of the new moon, the Mountain Spirits come out to watch."

The Initiate's foot came down on a thorny sapling. "Ouch!" he yelled out loud. "Sorry," he whispered back. "Watch what?"

Losha stopped again and held a look of reproach. "It is the time they come to witness an important event; usually some great victory or defeat."

"Terrific. You don't suppose you know the outcome today, do you?"

She shook her head and motioned for Temple to keep the pace on the ever-narrowing path.

Temple pulled his white, feathered cape over his head, leaving only a small opening from which to peer through. The drizzle rolled off the oily feathers, but the moisture still penetrated his bones.

"Careful where you tread," she whispered behind her. "There are root snakes in this region."

"Root snakes?"

"They lay across trails and take on the color and texture of nearby roots," she explained.

"Oh great!" He took a wide step over a suspicious looking root expecting it to almost lunge at him. "God, I hate snakes... almost as much as I hate lions," he muttered aloud to himself. "Lions and lost spirits, and now...."

"Shhh!"

The two rounded a bend in the path, which widened into a field of pangola grass. There was no wind, no birds, only the sound of rustling grasses. They sloshed through a marsh spiked with reed and clotted with algae, until they passed a forest of sorrel and blood wood. In the distance ahead lay the mudflats dotted with cypress draped with moss.

Losha shook the brackish water off her cape. "This part of the Snake River is drying up," she lamented.

Temple remembered what Losha had said about Makol's changing weather, which, he reasoned, would account for the numbness he felt in his feet now. He walked cautiously around the cypress, their fluted bases groping in the mud like desperate hands clinging to life. He cast a suspicious eye at the strangler fig trees that twisted around the cypress, making certain their snake-like roots didn't move.

Losha pulled a curtain of hanging moss aside and they entered a narrow tunnel of brambles. When they reached the other side, they found themselves on a shallow bench of soggy earth just above the swamps. Before them stood the Priest, dressed in his crocodile garb, with his back to them. A misty curtain hung in the air turning the Priest's features into that of a beastly ghost. He stared in the direction of Hollow Mountain and spoke without turning.

"Today the Spirits will be watching a grand victory." The head of the crocodile turned with a deliberate slowness towards the white Stranger. Mefakani bowed, then pointed to his right. "That is Jabal, my Apprentice. He is preparing the potion for you."

A short distance away, a ghostly figure crouched next to a smoky campfire. Flames licked the mist, casting an eerie orange glow in the thick air. A burst of steam suddenly enshrouded the figure and the Apprentice disappeared from view.

"Now we begin the work of helping you remember your greater magic. The greatest power comes from the Spirit of Lord Tagheetu. He will be your teacher. But first, you must cleanse yourself of impurities."

The Initiate and his Interpreter followed the Crocodile Priest to where Jabal was feeding the fire with coconut husks and dried patties of crocodile dung.

Temple peered down into the bubbling concoction. "What am I to do?"

"You must drink this potion first. It will cleanse you," she said. "Then you will drink the sacred yage. That will help you to see beyond the fog."

The Shaman brushed his Apprentice aside and motioned for his new Initiate to come and sit beside him by the fire. Temple loosened his cape and drew the warmth of the flames into his body, letting his tension subside a moment.

Losha, feeling like an intruder into the affairs of men, stood a considerable distance from the fire. She pulled her cape over her head to stem the growing cold inside her, wishing only to be alone with her feelings.

Mefakani spoke to Losha without looking at her. "Tell him to hold onto this and never let it out of his possession during the ritual." A mammoth crocodile tooth of considerable length and weight was pressed firmly into Temple's hand. The Shaman blew smoke from a bundle of herbs into the white man's face while Temple stared numbly at the mammoth tooth. Losha continued conveying the instruction she had been given.

"Now you must drink the potion," she urged, when Mefakani handed him a small bowl of steaming brew.

"Smells putrid." He coughed as much from the smoke as from the acrid smell, which singed his nostrils.

"He insists that you drink it quickly."

Temple gave Losha a wink and downed the potion in one gulp. "God, that was awful."

"It is only a matter of seconds before it takes affect. You must take care to...."

Before Losha could finish, Temple felt his intestines twist spasmodically until a sharp pain seized him, forcing stomach bile to rise in his throat. The Shaman smiled with satisfaction when the

Initiate retched uncontrollably, the bile from Temple's empty stomach smothering a portion of the cherry bed of coals.

The Anglo-American hunched down on all fours over the hissing fire and vomited for what seemed like forever until his guts were raw. When his dry heaves had subsided the Shaman pushed a bowl of water towards him.

"Now wash," he ordered.

Temple splashed his face and rinsed his mouth making no effort to still his trembling hands.

"Now, drink another," the Priest insisted, holding another steaming bowl before him.

"Is this some sort of sick joke?" he drooled.

"You must drink it, Temple," Losha pleaded softly.

"And what happens after I retch my guts out again?"

"Then you will drink the yage. Then you will do battle with Lord Tagheetu," she answered.

"What?" He rose on his haunches, a string of drool still hanging from his lower lip. He stared up at the woman. "I suppose he wants me to slay the beast with my bare hands as well."

The woman paused, staring down at the frightened god, watching him sway feebly by the fire. "It is true you will have no weapons. You must battle the Lord with only your mind."

Temple rose unsteadily, glaring now at his Interpreter. His stomach balled into a tight knot. "Does he demand a sacrifice? Is that what I am?" he asked in a sudden panic. "You're god damned savages! You hear! I'm not going down there with live crocodiles! You think I'm a fool!" He turned sharply away from her and threw the heavy tooth into the fire, causing the Apprentice scrambling frantically to retrieve it.

"Bi Kana! Is he crazy!" Mefakani called out, as his pupil staggered back into the tunneled path of brambles. The Shaman yelled to his Apprentice who was still combing the ashes. "Go and bring him back!"

Jabal grinned as he handed the giant sooty tooth to his Master. "The Stranger is a coward."

There was a sharp, dry split in the moist air between Mefakani's quick hand and Jabal when the boy's legs flew from under him and he plummeted to the ground. "Arrogant boy! Go and bring Temple back!"

Losha was sympathetic, but also frightened when Jabal returned minutes later with Temple marching reluctantly in front of him.

"Tell your boy to untie me!" he demanded.

The Shaman nodded and Jabal walked in front of Temple. The boy spit into his palm and murmured an incantation, then waved his hand in the air in a circular motion near his captive's navel. Temple's hands pulled free from behind him. He looked down at his wrists. There were no ropes, no marks or bruises, no sign of anything having bound him.

He looked to Losha. "How'd he do that?"

"The Shaman says there is a lot to learn. Years of learning in so little time. Only you are too impatient and impulsive."

"Isn't there any other way to learn without getting my legs bitten off? No!" he stopped. "Don't tell him that. Tell him gods are not accustomed to this ritual."

"He says, what could be more powerful than the power of the Lord Tagheetu? He thinks you should have already known this."

"The Light. Tell him the Light is more powerful."

"Mefakani says to get to the Light you must first go through Lord Tagheetu. And to go through Lord Tagheetu, you must do battle with Him. There is no other way."

Temple fell silent. *"The only thing I can do now is stall until the armada comes, even if they are slave ships and they take me with them. Anything is better than the horror before me now. But stall? How can I stall this Priest for three months!"*

The pilot's thoughts tangled in the curtain of moisture that hung before him, preventing him from seeing beyond his own fear. He thought about the raging mob, and the power of the strange spears and shields, the elusive spirits in the mountains, snakes disguised as roots. And now, there was Jabal's awesome power that could bind him. The image of crocodiles thrashing around him shook him to his core. His inner voices struggled within the web of confusion, pushing his mind this way and that, but none of the voices could agree on any course of action. He shook his head in defeat, recognizing that all the voices were his; and his advisor, the Unknown Voice, lay smothered and silent somewhere within the jumble inside his head.

"Why can't I just disappear?" Temple's body ached for escape and longed for familiarity to his old life. *"After I died and returned, what is left of my old life? A quiet chat with Blake by a warm fireside on one of those starry African nights is like another lifetime. No more flying in the clouds. Not even a good cup of tea."*

Temple eyed the potion Mefakani had prepared for him. His mouth went suddenly dry and his body began to cast off wisps of steam in the cool morning air. In spite of the sudden heat that filled his body, he shivered uncontrollably.

The Shaman stood waiting with his Apprentice quietly gloating by his side.

"Losha," Temple finally spoke in a soft whimper like a beaten animal, "It's no use. I'm a dead man. Tell your Priest I'll go through his barbaric ritual. I'm not a religious man, but, all the same, I want a decent burial with a proper wooden cross on my grave. Understand? I don't care about my life anymore. All I want is to go to the Spirit World to be with the Great Light again."

"No, Temple. Listen. I know you will pass this rite. Do as the Voice who speaks through you says. 'Believe beyond doubt. Trust beyond fear. And have courage beyond thought of consequence.'"

"I can't. I can't. I'm too scared," he said meekly.

"I will suggest that you need more time to prepare for this."

Mefakani's face hardened when she explained Temple's feelings. He began to pace.

"All right," he conceded after much thought. "We will crawl before we walk." The Crocodile Priest stopped and turned to Temple. "By this evening, I will have a lesson prepared for you to ease you into this rite. Until then, go out into the jungle with my Apprentice, here, and collect some plants I will need. Understand?"

Losha spoke for Temple, saying he understood then said a silent prayer.

★　　★　　★　　★　　★　　★

"Oh Jesus! Where the bloody hell is that kid?" Temple wandered aimlessly in the jungle. "Jabal!" he yelled, but heard no reply only the startled cry of a khala bird.

The pale Stranger made his way to a clearing and dropped his sack of roots beside a tall Banyan tree. He scraped the mud from his hands against the crusty orange fungi covering the skin of the Mother Banyan then lifted himself onto her lowest branch, flinching a bit from the new soreness of his stomach muscles. When he raised himself onto the sturdy branch he eyed his surroundings. Before him lay a dense thicket of giant groundsels; to either side, the swamps steamed in the fine rain. He climbed several branches higher to search for the missing Apprentice.

"Hey Jabal!" he yelled several times, and waited for a reply.

Temple never saw the spear arc through the air towards him. There was only a whistling rush in the air and a crack like thunder when the spear split the air and bore itself into the limb above him, sending sparks in all directions. A bolt of blue fire struck the top of Temple's head. His hands loosened and he fell onto the branch below, only to slip off until he was caught by another arm of the Mother Banyan. He clung there helplessly, his muscles recoiling involuntarily from the shock, but his hands were slippery and they lost their grip. The small of his back hit hard against the lowest branch before he landed knee deep in mud. He was shaking, oblivious to his pain, when he noticed the burning. Temple beat the top of his head with his muddy hands, the stench of singed hair and burnt wood permeating the moist air. He watched in shock as the top of the Banyan blazed above him and sizzled in the cool rain. Closing his eyes against a shower of hot ashes, just as the pain in his back came alive, he tried to calm his broken nerves, knowing he couldn't stand there as an easy target. He lifted his leg to move forward and sank a little deeper into the thick mud.

"Does the assassin know I am still alive? Or is he waiting for my body to sink into the earth?"

Temple tried to raise his leg again to climb out of the muck, but sank up to his hips. Realizing his vulnerability, his eyes darted to and fro looking for sudden movements among the heavy foliage, anything to tell him where the assassin might be hiding. Temple's heart nearly bounded out of his chest when a bird made a quick movement in a nearby bush and caused him to flinch and slip deeper into the ooze.

"Help me," he whispered. "I implore the Light to please help me!" The only sound that answered back was the sucking sound the Earth made.

Death was welcomed, but he didn't want to die like this. Not like a trapped animal. Not like the coward he knew he was. He had to try something, and the only thing he could think of was to push the pain and panic aside and refocus his mind wholly onto the Light again. He breathed evenly, deeply, calming himself enough to think clearer. He pleaded again to the Light, but this time emptied all his frantic thoughts so he could listen quietly for an answer. It was then that he felt a cool tingle spread across his forehead. Beneath the normal level of hearing, he thought he heard the deep, drawn out groan of a long sustained heartbeat. Then he heard the sucking sound again, which drew him deeper into the bowels of the Earth. Yet there was something in the sound that spoke to him and he knew what he had to do. Temple pushed his knee back and forth in the heavy mud to create a hollow space around him. He forced his arm down through the black ooze until his hand touched his knee. When he pulled his arm out, the air pocket below connected with a sudden rush of surface air and the suction was broken! With mud dripping into his eyes, causing him to become momentarily blind, he leaned forward, hands trembling as he groped for a nearby Banyan root to pull himself free. To his surprise, a helping hand, which had appeared out of nowhere, slid into his hand.

"Jabal," he thought.

He blinked back the mud that had encrusted his eyes. On the banks stood a dark figure wearing a white wooden mask that stared blindly down at him. When Temple stretched further to get a firmer grip, the hand pulled away teasingly and a muffled laugh came from behind the mask. Without warning, the figure picked up a large rock above his head and aimed it at Temple.

Temple held his hand up in defense. "No! Please don't!"

The masked man laughed again, then, without Temple knowing why, his assassin let out a startled howl. One of the Banyan roots lunged and twisted itself around the assassin's ankle. The man let his rock fall to one side and the Initiate watched in both horror and relief as the figure became entangled in a nest of roots snakes. There was a shuffling sound and a muted cry, then the sound of a heavy body hitting the soft Earth. All Temple could see from his vantage point was a churning mound of snakes and the flailing of limbs.

The moaning stopped and the pilot was alone again, lost and dizzied. He grabbed tufts of saw grass, seizing his hold on reality, something solid, something known, and pulled out of the primordial mud onto the opposite bank. He lay there quite unable to move and listened to the distant sounds of the sputtering fire overhead, horny scales jarring against one another, against human flesh, and the rustling grasses by the opposite bank. He struggled to stay conscious.

There was a snapping of branches deep within the swamp and a voice rang out. Jabal ran towards the smoking Banyan, yelling as he went.

Temple felt a warm, callused hand grab his arm and pull him from the burning debris onto more solid ground.

"I'm okay," he managed to say in Makolese, but he was visibly shaking. "Just... just stunned is all," he stammered in English, then pointed to the prone figure on the ground on the other side of the swamp as it rolled off the bank into the swamp and slowly sank beneath the mud.

"There is nothing I can do for him now," the Apprentice said. "I will take you back to the Priest." The boy lifted Temple and steadied him onto his feet.

★　　★　　★　　★　　★　　★

The Healer and the Widow sat in the center of Mefakani's compound beneath the great cedar. The Priest moved into the shadow of the tree and squinted down into a bowl of oily liquid. "I am sorry Losha. It is all I can conjure for you now," he said, as he skimmed more film off the surface of the brew. "I see nothing more about your husband."

"Then his soul is lost," Losha said with her eyes cast down.

Tani put her wiry arms around her young friend and rocked her gently. There was an uneasy feeling in the air, a peculiar energy that puzzled the old woman in regards to Amron's accident. *What is it I am sensing? And why can I conjure no clearer picture than the Priest?"*

Brisk footsteps broke the muffled quiet of the compound as Temple and Jabal appeared through a curtain of drizzle and smoke. Temple's reddened face was covered in small blisters and mud, and the front of his hair was missing in patches.

"Here, Mefakani," he asserted, as he tossed a charred branch at the Shaman's feet. "This is what my body would've looked like had one of your people killed me! Your Queen's decree means nothing!"

Mefakani sat very still, then gave Tani a sideways glance.

"Stalling is what I am counting on now," Temple thought. "And here's the weapon!" Temple was too angry to feel cowardly. He threw a sharp shard of crystal so it stuck in the sand beside Mefakani's feet. The Priest glared back. "How can I prepare myself for your barbaric ritual, when I'm busy dodging these? You deal with these savages first, or I won't go through your bloody Tagheetu ritual!"

Losha's interpretation omitted the slanders, but they all heard the anger in his voice. Temple turned abruptly and walked out of the compound with Losha close on his heels.

Mefakani snapped at his Apprentice. "And where were you?"

"I tried to keep him on the path with me. I suppose we got separated in the fog," the Apprentice explained.

"You suppose?" he growled. "Get out of my sight, you stupid boy!"

Mefakani raised his hand to strike the boy, but Tani rose between them and bowed before the Shaman. "I will see what I can do with Temple Fox."

When Tani had disappeared into the forest, Jabal inched forward with deliberate slowness. "The assassin is dead, my Master. Killed by root snakes, his body taken by the Spirit of the Swamp beneath the mud."

Mefakani turned the spear fragment over and over in his hands, summoning a light trance. "I detect more than just the assassin's hand in this," he warned. "You can bet Sahdon and Cranik are behind this!"

★　★　★　★　★　★

"Are you crazy?" Losha ranted as she tried to keep up with Temple's pace. "You can not talk to a High Priest that way!"

Temple kept walking at a fast clip. "Of course I'm crazy! I'm a god. Remember? Craziness is part of my job description."

Her voice was filled with concern. "You must be careful. The Shaman is a very powerful man."

Temple turned on his heels, the tension of the past few days finally giving way in him. His tone was stabbing. "Look Losha, I don't give a good goddamn what he thinks! Furthermore, I'm not your bloody prophet! All I want is to board a ship, any ship, and get the hell off this lunatic island!" He touched the blisters on his head lightly and winced. "That is, if your people don't kill me first! Or if I survive your witch doctor's barbaric ritual!"

"You are frightened of the Tagheetu ritual?" she finally asked.

She peered into the Stranger's fierce eyes, watching their fire quickly fade until he turned his gaze away in embarrassment. He sat on a rotting log with his blistered head in his hands.

"Would you like me to help you prepare?" she asked.

He eyed her from under his hand. "Not if it means I have to bury myself in the sand and wait for crabs to peck out my eyes." His dark companion blinked in confusion. "That was a joke," he explained dryly. "White men do have a sense of humor, you know. I imagine gods do, too," he added, seeing that he would never be able to persuade her he was otherwise.

"I often wondered," she said and smiled. "Mefakani has such a serious way about him all the time. I sometimes find it..." She struggled for a word.

He raised a singed eyebrow. "Oppressive?"

"A new word for me: O-preezev." She smoothed her skirt and sat down on the log beside him.

Feeling the comfort of her closeness, he asked, "Doesn't he frighten you?"

She tore a piece of fungus off the log and played with it in her fingers. "Sometimes," she answered. "His passion against the Outsiders certainly frightens me. These new weapons he has stolen from the Mountain Spirits, and the old magic he has revived from the ancient traditions, frighten me even more."

"You mean the Tagheetu rite?" he asked.

She nodded. "All the animal spirits used to be honored equally. But ever since Mefakani's Master, Tagon, initiated a resurgence of a fundamentalist theology, everyone has had to undergo the rite with the Crocodile Spirit or risk the charge of blasphemy. I have not gone through this rite myself, of course. Females were excluded from this later on, but Tani says we are better off not having our minds polluted."

"And the spears and shields – you say he stole them from the spirits in the mountain?" His hands were still shaking after experiencing their power first hand.

"He stole their crystals, then made weapons out of them to fight the Outsiders. But it was not until you came that they were used against our own people. It is frightening."

Temple slumped a little deeper in surrender. "You said before you would help me prepare. How?" he asked.

Out of the thicket behind them, a raspy voice called out. "All lies within the divine breath, like the day in the beautiful dawn. It is this you need to learn." Temple lurched to his feet and turned to see the leathery face of the old Healer. She gave a gummy smile and shuffled over to them. "Tai, you do not hear too well. If I were a root snake, I would have made a tasty meal of you by now. Come," she said, "we will go to my hut and I will heal that burn. Then, I will teach you what the gods and I know you already know, but have forgotten."

CHAPTER ELEVEN

Beyond the Swamps

*"I am the Formless One that has become the
many. I am the laughter of children... The wind in
your hair... The scent of jungle blossoms... The
music of the rain and the rain itself... I am
the dance..."*

The Unknown Voice
Makolese Scroll on Magic, Rites and Rituals #102
Makolese Prophecy Scroll #903
The Makolese Scroll on The Education of Temple Fox #11

Armed guards hid in the swamp and encircled the clearing where
Temple sat in meditation. Around the marooned pilot stood the
Interpreter, the Priest and his Apprentice waiting with anticipation.

The Initiate breathed deeply and evenly as Tani had taught him.
Vanished were all his fears and apprehensions. Drawing the Light
inside him with every breath, he pushed it out until an enormous field
of energy built up around him. He felt strong and confident when he,
at last, accepted the second cup of brew from Mefakani's hands.

Temple struggled through the same uncontrollable retching he had
the day before, only this time his mind remained calm and steady.
Holding the giant tooth from the old crocodile close to his aching

body, he took another deep breath then drank the sacred yage. The cool, familiar tingle once again filled his head and he slipped into a trance.

An iridescent cloud of vibrant purple and green obscured Temple's field of vision, until, after several minutes, his head cleared and he could see the steamy swamp again. He looked around him, but Losha, the Shaman and his Apprentice were gone. Mindful of the challenge that lay ahead, the Initiate slid down the slippery banks of the Snake River, without his usual fearful reluctance, and eased himself into the warm brackish waters. He pulled his face down to the level of the water, letting the sun beat down on his head, and waited.

Temple couldn't be certain how much time had passed. Lulled by the warmth of the waters, he closed his eyes for what felt like a mere moment. He heard a strange thrumming in the air. When he opened his eyes again, a huge dragonfly, the size of an eagle, hung in the air before him, its iridescent blue, green and purple wings vibrating rapidly and casting jewel like rainbows in the open air.

"Where'd you come from? You're beautiful!"

The insect hovered for a moment, its bulbous eyes scrutinizing the Initiate. It twisted and turned, moved up and down, and then flew backwards as if to view the pilot from a wider perspective. And then, quite suddenly, it flew directly at Temple, hitting him in the space between his eyes, causing Temple to flinch. It landed on top of his head. The Initiate could feel its sharp spindly legs grip his scalp. Just as suddenly as it appeared, the huge dragonfly shot off down the river and out of view.

"Well, that was interesting. Hope it doesn't have any larger cousins."

After a few anxious moments he noticed what appeared to be a distant bar of black sand gliding forward with barely a ripple. It was Tagheetu. The massive crocodile, whose head alone matched the length of Temple's body, submerged slightly and coasted several yards from the Initiate and no farther, with only its primordial eyes protruding from the surface like two tiny islands. Temple never moved, but waited, the wild beating of his heart causing the water to ripple gently in front of him.

When time had smoothed the surface of the pool, two fleshy eyes and two dreamy reflections stared back, and the creature hung motionless like some dark star in the black night. The giant gazed at the strange man-creature whose thin, pale skin glinted against each eye. Tagheetu slithered closer.

The Initiate raised the giant tooth out in front of him. The reptile stopped abruptly then submerged. Temple did the same.

Beneath the water, Temple's familiar world dissolved. He watched as a well-defined spot of light, illuminating the clouded surface skin of the water above him, formed a column of light that bent slightly in the depths. The shaft of light hit Temple's eye and he drifted in the dream within the dream. And there, in that medium where myths are born, the crocodile swam with swift directness towards its prey. Tagheetu's enormous jaws opened wide, revealing an uneven row of pointed teeth, and issued out a blast of bubbles.

Below the surface of his mind Temple thought he heard a voice that sounded like water. It seemed to say, "Are you not afraid of me, pale creature? Have you not come as other young men... to war with the mighty Spirit of the Swamp?"

Temple remembered what Tani had told him. Nothing could harm him in the vision unless his fear overtook him. He was not afraid, and to prove it he swam closer to the beast and peered through the translucent membrane over its bulging eye. It was there that his eyes held the others. It was there that the dreamer met his primeval self, gazing into forever.

Temple spoke to the Crocodile Spirit in his mind. "I'm here to do battle with the mighty Tagheetu. I'll learn from you. Teach me."

Both surfaced. The crocodile opened its jaw again, crooked teeth dripping with green slime. Temple shut his eyes and stiffened. With one long blast of breath the smell of putrid fish poured forth from the beast's white gullet and the Initiate tensed as he waited for Tagheetu's teeth to clamp down on him. But there were no physical sensations or the sound of crunching bones...only silence.

All at once Temple felt his hair toss gently in a warm, drier breeze. He dared to open his eyes. Before his confused senses were a plain of wavy grasses and a sprinkling of acacia trees. The sky was a rich cerulean blue.

"Temple!" a voice called out in a harsh whisper, "Get down!"

Temple wheeled around to see his father gesturing for him to keep low. He darted behind a nearby bush and gave an instinctive wave back.

"My God! I'm back in Kenya!"

He looked behind him again at the crouched figure of a man wearing khakis and a bush hat. His father nodded his head and tipped up the point of his rifle to signal for his son to advance. Temple looked around him on the parched ground and spied his rifle in the brittle grass.

"No! I can't do this! Not again! Bring me back!" his mind

rebelled.

It was the young Temple's final test of courage, his last chance to prove that all the rumors about him for the past fifteen years had been false. He had waited for this moment because he had been groomed for it. And, for more years than he dared remember, he dreaded it. The nightmares had haunted him for months, as the time grew closer. Now, there was no escape. And, here he was, doing it again. Again!

Fear rose in him like a poison, causing his throat to constrict. He hunkered down lower and clutched his stomach, trying desperately to hold back the panic. His sweaty palm slid across the barrel of the rifle and quivered as he fumbled for a firmer grip.

"Go on!" his father demanded.

The boy's heart nearly burst when he saw the young Maasai guide and old Kikuyu pointing across the plain. Just fifty yards from him crouched a male lion whose face was half buried inside the carcass of a young wildebeest. He watched as the heavy muscled predator pulled his massive head from its prey and licked the blood from his muzzle. Beyond the kill stood a herd of wildebeest, watching the feast from a safe distance, with ears forward and eyes alert.

Temple understood what he was expected to do. He crept forward quietly, reluctantly, knowing he was down wind from the big cat. When he was within shooting range, and was assured the others could cover him, he would taunt the beast until it charged him. Then, and only then, would he kill his first lion!

Temple watched in tense silence as the herd of wildebeest gave out an unexpected bellow, and stampeded, leaving a wall of dust rising from the plains. The lion, curious now, raised his bloodstained head and sniffed the air. He cocked his ears in Temple's direction, but didn't seem bothered and continued to gorge himself.

The boy moved several yards closer and stood up in full view for the beast to see. "Come on, simba. Come on. Let's get it over with," Temple breathed, as he held its massive body unsteadily in his rifle sight.

The lion bared his teeth and growled in annoyance until, seeing that he was being goaded, he rose up at full attention with the back of his mane bristling, his teeth flashing and ready for more than threatening growls. He started to advance, slowly at first, until his pace quickened into a trot.

Temple leaned against the strength of a sudden breeze with his heart pounding out of control. Just as he steadied his aim and slowly tensed the trigger, a heavy curtain of dust swallowed his target. He heard the crack of rifle fire and the gun lurch in his arms just as the gritty cloud descended over him. He blinked back the dust and regained some of his vision, blurred as it was, but the lion loomed larger in his sights.

His heart froze and the lion charged.

Temple fumbled with the bolt, reloaded out of instinct, and aimed. His arm shook uncontrollably. He begged his muscles to squeeze the trigger harder, faster.

Skin and fur rolled over the muscles of the beast in slow motion and the Earth shook.

Temple's head dizzied and his vision fogged.

The lion leapt!

"Now!" He thought. *"Now!"* But his fingers would not obey. Shock waves of sound rippled through his gut and he was knocked to the ground from a massive weight, which crushed his chest, forcing the air out of him in one short blast. He felt the sting of something sharp, something wet and the hot, moist breath of lion. Again and again he heard a deep cracking sound like thunder, overlaid by the sound of ripping fabric. And then, all at once, everything lay still. The only sound was the wind through the grasses and the pounding of feet against the ground.

"Bunya! Bunya, Temple!" he heard the young Maasai guide cry out. But the boy could not utter a sound. He felt the dense weight of the dead lion and its dusty, matted hair against his chest as it was being pulled off of him. He swallowed a mouthful of dusty air, and gasped in fits and starts. A rough hand clasped his arm and dragged him from under the remainder of the lion's heavy frame. He could hear more pounding of feet draw closer and wiped the gritty sweat from his eyes. Conga's weathered, blue-black face loomed over him.

Temple choked on the question. "Did I kill it?"

The old Kikuyu shook his head, scattering the flies from his shiny, sweaty face.

"Where...where is my father?" the boy asked, remorsefully.

The elder guide shook his head again in dismay. "Masta Charles, he head back to camp. Never mind you now 'bout him," he said. Conga motioned for Temple to lie still while he checked his wounds. "Bad cut. Real bad cut. Conga get you to doctari quick!"

The old African sat Temple up until he was able to rip off the rest of Temple's tattered shirt and wrap it tightly around the boy's waist. It was then that Temple got a good look at the lion. There were two shots in its flank and one through its head. It was that shot that finally brought him down. Temple knew none of them were his.

The boy sat beside the dead lion in a sticky pool of blood. "I couldn't kill him." He looked up at Conga startled and confused. "I don't know why. Just couldn't." He was oblivious to the sting of his wounds, but not the large knot that was forming in his throat. He looked about him shaking his head in disbelief, his eyes brimming with unwanted tears. He bit his lip and sucked in his breath. When he could no longer hold his breath, he released a grim sigh until he wept openly, his chest heaving with heavy sobs. "He hates me. Oh god, he hates me."

The younger guide sneered down at Temple, revealing a row of stark white teeth. "For Whites, it is better to be a live coward. For Maasai, it is better to be dead," he sneered with contempt.

Temple watched as the dark, lean figure of the young Maasai walked across the East African plain, becoming smaller and smaller, until in the dry heat of the African day, he quivered out of sight, and once again Temple was brought back, face to face, with the giant crocodile.

"Why? Why did you do this to me?" Temple asked angrily.

"The memories were haunting you in your sleep. They were hunting you down and about to devour you," Lord Tagheetu said. "It was time to look at them again."

"Nothing comes from this, you know. Nothing but humiliation and pain," the Initiate answered back.

"Climb inside my mouth if you dare, pale creature, for there is more to see which might change your mind...."

Temple tucked the giant crocodile tooth in his waistband and, without caring if he lived or died, resigned himself to the fate of his own annihilation. He allowed his body to go limp as the huge reptile gently scooped Temple into its mouth. When Tagheetu's jaws had clamped shut, they sank into the swampy depths together.

Temple descended into a dark, murky abyss, unable to see even his hand in front of him. The only sensation was Tagheetu's smooth, warm, slimy skin against his flesh and the feeling of being in a nowhere place. All at once, Tagheetu's jaws opened and the Initiate slipped out into the darkness onto what Temple could only gather was the grassy bank of the river. At first, he thought his eyes were playing tricks on him. A spark of warm light appeared in the thick blackness and steadily grew in intensity until he could see a distinct orb of orange light approaching. It paused and hovered above the Initiate, then skipped in the humid air, like a stone over water, until it shot up into the sky, leaving an arch of orange light in its wake. Temple followed its path until it disappeared, wondering what it could have been, then turned his attention to the scene appearing before him.

The rich colors of a tropical forest came alive around him. The sound of rustling leaves alerted him and he quickly hid behind a thick bush. From there, he watched a group of people with massive, bony brows, heavy jaws and thick hair covering their naked bodies foraged some berry bushes nearby. Suddenly, all browsing ceased when a pregnant female squatted on the ground and cried out. The small band formed a circle around her and Temple held his breath as he watched the wonderment of birth.

The observer let out a sigh of relief when the ape-like female rested with her newborn suckling at her breast, her fur wet with blood and sweat.

"What am I supposed to see in all of this? Is this the dawn of mankind?" he wondered.

It was when the baby started to cry that Temple noticed something different. The infant had far less body hair than its mother and the heavy brow was absent. He wanted to question Tagheetu, find out where they were and why, when there came a loud explosion. Temple scrambled back to the shoreline and climbed onto Lord Tagheetu's back. Without explanation, his teacher rose in the turbulent air with Temple clinging to him. He secured a firmer grip and the two rose higher. Far below them, they witnessed the gaping throat of a volcano belch dense clouds of smoke high into the sky. There was a shower of spark and, before Temple could blink an eye, the verdant hills below lay smothered in glowing hot magma. The last of the green jungle foliage burst into flame, until it was obscured by smoke and ash.

Temple choked and sputtered, the vision felt so real. While he hung there with his unanswered questions, the land was reduced to a desolate black cinder, in what he could only fathom was collapsed time. Knowing that all he was supposed to do now was observe and listen, he witnessed sprigs of green reappear. In his vision, which caused centuries to speed by in seconds, he watched as the burnt black Earth turned a vibrant green, and the leafy plants and trees rose in groupings here and there, texturing the landscape.

Tagheetu crawled over this new land with the Initiate clinging to his ridged back. They stopped when they came to a wide river and a village crowded with round thatched houses sitting on timber pilings. Tagheetu shook Temple off.

"What're you doing?" Temple asked, pressing the sacred tooth to his breast. He stood on the riverbank dumbfounded, watching his ally slither back into the depths without him. "Don't leave me!" he shouted, his fear real and visceral.

It was then that he noticed a movement behind him. There were people who had gathered on the shores carrying spears and clubs. It was they who had driven his ally back into the swamp. Temple held the tooth out in front of him, towards the people, and shouted for them to stop. But it was too late. The mob let their spears fly. The Initiate dove to the ground, thinking they were aiming at him, and cried aloud when one spear passed through his chest like smoke.

"Bloody hell! I'm invisible!" he cried out. He crawled onto the soggy banks just in time to see Tagheetu submerge and the next vision unfolded before him.

There was a bearded Priest, dressed in animal skins, feathers and ferns. He carried a scroll and a staff made of metal. He set the scroll up onto a podium made of stone and raised his arms high, encouraging the people to chant a prayer with him. When the intoxicating rhythm of the chant reached a heightened pitch, which Temple thought he could no longer endure, the giant crocodile crawled out of the swamp, and the people bowed in reverence.

Without knowing why, Temple felt a sudden sharp aloneness and anger. The Initiate, confused by his own sullenness and despair, moved from the grassy banks, leaving his teacher behind. He walked through the tranquil village, passed round homes made from bamboo and palm leaves. People milled about in fine tunics made from linen and flax, busy with their chores: fishing, tilling, collecting, and storing food, and carving implements made from stone, bamboo and bone. Large stilted granaries dotted the village until the village, itself, grew beyond his vision.

He watched with a quieter, calmer satisfaction as a woman tilled the soil with a hoe made from a sturdy stick and a stone blade. Her two children, a girl and a boy, played by her side. The hazy sunlight rested on her brown shoulders and she prayed to the earth, coaxing it into fertility. Temple felt a stirring, a longing for things hidden and forgotten, and some ancient memory that seemed to flow through his veins and wanted to break like a firestorm in his mind. But the memory only smoldered like an ember.

His attention was called to a long shadow that spilled over the broken soil. He wanted to do something. He tried, but there had been no warning and the cutting blow came too late to move him into action. The woman lay on the ground; blood filling the trenches of earth she had just tilled, her hands caked in moist dirt, drying now. Above her stood the Priest, his sword lowered, looking at the bleeding corpse with a sense of completion, a sense of righteous finality. He handed the sword to the dead woman's son who knelt trembling on the ground. He told the boy what he must do, what was right, what was honorable in the sight of the gods and their Lord Tagheetu. He must do it if he wanted to live. He would be rewarded with the riches and glory of the Heavens. It was his destiny, his right.

The boy took the sword in both his hands and turned to his sister. Tears streaked his dusty face. He bowed to her reverently, but received a reprimand from the Priest. He wanted to do what was right, what would be seen as holy in the eyes of their gods. He ordered his sister to till the soil, do what their mother had done before, only she must plow their mother under the ground. She must cover up the deed so none would know, then continue on with her work. Shivering from fright, the sister obeyed, and, with sad reluctance, buried their mother deep in the earth.

Accelerated time sped forward again and Temple felt helpless and lost, watching the poor child harvest the crops around the patch of ground, which was her mother's unmarked grave. She moved with a methodical slowness over to one of the huge stone granaries, barely able to lift her basket filled with grain. Finally, when she had finished with her load, she sat on the ground exhausted, a thin stilted child with a bloated stomach. Temple backed away when into his vision came what his mind couldn't comprehend. A red haired giant of a man, who was better than fifteen feet high and wore a priestly crocodile skin wrapped around him, approached the pathetic child. She held out her empty hands and pleaded as the giant strolled casually by, oblivious to her torment.

Before Temple could assess the meaning behind the ever-changing vision, he turned to see the village toppled into ruin. The Initiate didn't know what to make of this and the sudden chill that surrounded him. When a tremulous wave rolled beneath his feet, he looked out into the distant landscape. Stark white glaciers rolled over the green mountains and hills, sheering them into a frozen, flat wasteland. Temple saw it all as if each second was a century.

A kind of calm permeated the land when the brutal forces of nature had spent their energies, and time fell in upon itself again, and the ice melted, forming cold, slushy rivers. The seas rose and were dotted with icebergs. As a diffused light pushed its way through layers of cloud cover, the world slowly rejuvenated under its warmth, and again, life flourished.

Temple's eyes grew wide as new villages developed into townships. He witnessed the townships expand rapidly into great shiny cities as far as the eye could see. When he sensed that time had slowed, he climbed a rock promontory overlooking the bright metropolis to gain a better view. Curiosity held his fear at bay when large, round, metallic disks rose from the city spread before him. They flew noiselessly overhead to what he could barely make out to be another gleaming city in the distance that was nestled by the sea. Beams of intense light shot out from underneath the strange airships and great clouds of smoke and debris were thrown into the air. The disks retreated swiftly from their targets and soared back to their home city.

Temple stood on top of the gusty terrace of rock shaking his head in shock and disbelief. He tried to remain detached emotionally as Tani had taught him, but the vision was too powerful. Far in the distance ahead lay an ancient city in ruin; behind him now, the sounds of celebration.

When Temple returned to the victor's city, the streets were full of people dancing and shouting with merriment. Without caring to fight against the tide of people, or the vision itself, he allowed himself to be swept up and herded into a great square building made of polished stone.

In spite of the illusion, out of instinct, he tried to lean out of the way when a parade of servants made their way into the great hall, but their enormous platters, piled high with food, passed through his body as if he were made of vapor. There were people inside clad in fine flowing garb, drinking and falling over themselves and each other. The invisible observer turned to flee and stumbled upon an old man tearing the robes off a woman who had passed out on the floor from too much drink. The old man groped her breasts and mounted her with no heed to onlookers.

Temple moved to the edge of the crowded hall, sweating nervously as he clenched the sacred tooth. Trumpets blared and the sounds of celebration subsided. Servants led a group of slave children into the inner circle and the people gathered around, laughing and clapping loudly. Behind them, muzzled dogs on leashes were brought forth and the people tossed large, gold coins on the tables before one another.

Temple attempted to breathe the way Tani had taught him, struggling to find a detached calm within himself. Try as he might, he could still hear the chinking of gold coins and the incessant cheering. He thrashed blindly over to where he knew there was an exit and opened his eyes when he crossed the threshold. But a patrician woman blocked his way, leaving Temple aghast when she tickled her throat with a feather and vomited on the marble floor beside him.

"Lord Tagheetu! Please release me!" he cried aloud.

Before his inner vision, a large shadow fell over the courtyard of the great hall. Looming above was an enormous dark thunderhead, which covered the entire sky. From it, a silent, silver airship emerged, its size – mammoth, its shape – triangular. The people all looked skyward and cried out.

"Please Tagheetu! No more!" he begged.

He shielded his eyes when beams of piercing light, brighter than the sun, shot out from underneath the silver craft. There was a sound of heat searing through metal and stone. In a flash of collapsed time, nothing remained but melted steel shards in a field of black earth, and the Initiate alone, once again.

He watched in both horror and awe as the airship rose silently away into the heavens, stirring the black dust around his feet. He felt a tight squeezing in his chest and wheezed. He whispered to the tooth praying for the rite to end – pleading for his release.

All at once, a wind blew across the ruins and ruffled Temple's hair with its stiff fingers. The dust and melancholy blew away until both were vanished, and it began to drizzle. Cool, fresh air rushed into Temple's lungs, allowing him to breathe easily again. The voice of thunder spoke and he stood in the rain, allowing the water to wash him clean of the poisonous dust. The thunder intensified, and the ground beneath him grumbled, and he rose into the air with the wet earth below him pressing skyward. Swiftly, his vision was lifted far into the atmosphere, higher than he had ever flown as a pilot, until he realized he was standing on the Moon. From there he watched as the blue ball, known as Earth, shifted and the seas unrolled like a scroll. He witnessed walls of water sweep away the rubble far below, leaving behind vast deposits of mud.

Temple wept when he heard the cries of the dying multitudes far beneath him. Nothing Tani had taught him prepared him for this. The cost to human life had been enormous. He sat on the edge of a crater, unable to comprehend all of the unrestrained destruction he had just witnessed. He wanted nothing more than to sail beyond the stars, but a stirring below caught his eye. Temple spied spinning orbs of glowing light zigzag above the Earth's oceans and the Earth began to dry. The waters drained off mountainsides, which were now appearing above the waves, and were channeled into great rivers. He watched in wonder as a new, harsher sun rose in the eastern sky, casting rainbows over the turbulent seas.

Temple sailed down through the Earth's atmosphere like a comet and cried out in joy when he spied survivors below. Humanity once again flourished, and new species of animal appeared and multiplied, providing milk, wool and meat for the survivors. He saw herds of cattle, sheep and goats with new eyes, and his excitement mounted when he saw vast fields of new grains growing in profusion.

Temple knew instinctively that this was the present era he now inhabited, and yet, beyond the surface of his vision, he also realized that this world would soon perish. Perhaps it was the yage that caused him to know this. Perhaps not. But, before Tagheetu returned to have him climb on top of its back again, Temple witnessed a rapid scene unfold from the rainbow sky, shimmer briefly, then fade away as a quiet breeze dispersed the tiny droplets of rain. He recognized the pattern of events from something that lay deep within him, which had been planted by the Light when he had died. It was some secret knowledge, some forgotten event that, only now, had been unlocked by the magic of Tagheetu. He gripped the tooth tightly and whispered for the Spirit of the Swamps to return.

"I've seen enough," he said aloud, exhausted.

The giant reappeared instantly by his side, basking lazily in the hot sun.

"You have ssseen much for a human," Tagheetu hissed. "And yet, I have only shown you as much as you can handle for now. Soon, you must enter Hollow Mountain – awake."

"Awake?"

"Conscious," Tagheetu explained. "You will experience what many others have experienced...only you will remember some of it. The fear I can stir inside you is no match for the fear the magicians in the mountain can create. Of course, if you so desire, you may stay here to see more in the swamps through me. There is always more to see,"

"No. No more. Much of it has sickened me already."

"That is because you are yet to understand. Do you not know yet who you were and who you are now? And do you not recognize me?" questioned Lord Tagheetu.

"You are the Spirit God of the Swamp and the God of Illusion and Fear. That I know. You are also the Record Keeper of the Past – the Dark Past that is both worldly and personal. Am I right?"

"In part. Go on."

"As for me, they tell me I'm a god, but I don't believe them."

"Ahhh, but if I be a god, why not you? Listen, pale one. You were by my side millennia ago, when the humans came to thoughtlessly slaughter my kind. You fought for an awareness of The One you know as the Light. You fought for my right to be...and my right to die with honor. I have not forgotten your bravery." The mysterious giant crocodile waited for a response.

Temple was stunned. "Then, I'm no coward? And, those people

with the spears were...?"

"They were your sons and daughters, your grandchildren and great grandchildren. You tried to teach them, but it does not matter now. They could not destroy my Spirit. I simply climbed into other skins, many skins in time."

"Are you saying I've lived before? I was..." He paused and gazed into the beast's eyes.

"You were Gadji, my beloved friend, from long ago before your line drove me back into this invisible realm. You have had many incarnations since. You have been the hungry child and the heartless Priest. You powered great ships of destruction and feasted like a famished dog, preying upon human flesh. You are all experience and hold every human emotion within your soul. But it was as the old man, Gadji, that I knew you then. But, old friend, tell no one of what I have just told you about your past incarnations. Only speak of the other visions you have seen."

"I don't understand."

The translucent membrane closed over the crocodile's eyes. Temple gazed beyond the veil, penetrating some secret he didn't quite comprehend. Tagheetu's gaping jaws opened wider until all that Temple could see was the white at the back of his Teacher's throat. The Initiate braced himself, waiting for the beast to blast him again with its hot, stormy breath. Instead, the deep timbre of another voice called out softly. It resonated like a male voice, yet held the gentleness of a female.

"Gadji, do you not recognize me? Have you forgotten me?"

"The Voice!" he called out. "The Unknown Voice! You are the Voice of the Light?"

"Did you not also hear my voice speak to you in the swamp when you were almost pulled under?"

Temple remembered hearing the heartbeat of the Earth and the smacking sound the Earth made when he was sinking helplessly in the mud. "Yes, but..."

"And the sound I made when I was released from the Banyan and changed yet again into smoke, fire and heat? And then I called to you from a bush? Remember?"

Temple gathered his senses, and recalled the popping of the Banyan tree as it burst into flames and the khala bird that fled from a nearby bush.

"I am everywhere, Gadji. I am Everything. I am the Spirit Which Moves in All Things."

"Then...even within Tagheetu, the dark sage, is the Light?"

"I am the Formless One that has become the many. I am the laughter of children... The wind in your hair... The scent of jungle blossoms... The music of the rain and the rain itself... I am the dance... Remember Gadji, I am with you always within many forms. Above all else, remember that what you are looking for is what is looking.

"Go now and tell your Shaman what you have seen. But, for now, speak only of your past lives with the beautiful Swan and wounded Hummingbird, for your Shaman thinks of you as a new god who has no past."

"Swan and...?"

"The beautiful Swan will lead you to the Hummingbird. Trust no others for now. You will understand in time. Temple, I must return you now." Slowly, Temple could feel the voice evaporating once again into the ethers.

The mammoth reptile blinked its eyes dreamily as if waking from a deep slumber then swam up alongside its startled companion, allowing Temple to climb on top its rough hide. The Spirit of Tagheetu drifted back through the dark abyss, crossing a span of immeasurable time and space, until the shore of the Snake River was reached. In a twinkling of an eye, they broke the surface of the water where Temple's physical body sat waiting on the banks.

Temple gasped for air as he broke from his vision.

The Shaman, who was sitting quietly by the fire with his Apprentice and the Interpreter, gathered himself quickly and strode over to Temple. Losha followed. Jabal watched from a distance as his Master removed his own cloak and wrapped it around Temple's quivering shoulders.

"He has broken from his vision," he said to Losha quietly. "Come. He must sit by the fire and warm his limbs."

Temple sat down; his eyes transfixed on only the fire, as Jabal stirred the coals to drive back the chill. Losha handed him a cup of hot tea.

Mefakani leaned forward anxiously. "Tell me, Temple Fox. Tell me what you saw."

Temple's eyes were glazed over and he stared back quite unable to speak of what he saw, unsure if he was still inside the vision or not. He tested the ground with his foot. It felt solid enough, but then so did the vision. It was the eyes of the contemptuous Apprentice that finally brought his mind back into focus. "I saw him," he said dreamily. "I came face to face with the Spirit of the Swamps."

"And did a battle follow?" the Shaman asked through the

Interpreter.

Temple looked into the Priest's eyes. "Not exactly," he answered.

Mefakani rubbed his chin, ignoring the leer of his Apprentice. "He did attack, did he not?"

Losha interpreted quickly. "He does not attack. He forces the Initiate to come face to face with their fear of him…which is the fear within ourselves," she said.

The Shaman grinned and nodded in approval.

Temple spoke to Losha, but kept his eyes on the Shaman. "I wasn't afraid. So, I climbed on Tagheetu's back. I was shown several visions."

Mefakani leaned forward even more, creating an intimate space between himself and the Initiate. "Tell me what you saw, Temple Fox."

"I saw the evolution of humanity, only humanity doesn't seem to progress sequentially," he said. "I saw humanity fall. I was even shown how the world was destroyed."

"How?" the Priest tested. "Tell me how the gods designed this?"

"Volcanoes were opened and the world caught fire. The second time the Earth was destroyed by ice. The last was the Great Flood. Each time was accompanied by the Earth shifting off its axis."

Mefakani smiled knowingly. "What happened right before the Great Flood? Did you see it, boy?"

Temple hugged the cup of hot brew to his breast as if the warmth could vanquish the pain of what he knew, what he had witnessed, even who he might have been then. "Yes. I saw great walled cities with domed buildings. They had flying ships that made war on other cities. Although technically advanced, the people had degenerated back into savages. There was a lot of indiscriminate and brutal sex going on, too." He looked into the fire, then back to the Priest. "Although the cities were destroyed, the Earth wasn't. The gods wouldn't allow that. They promised they wouldn't."

The Shaman gave a painful frown, which opened slowly to a hard smile. "All the men who go through this rite see this," he said, "but it is only the gifted ones, like Jabal and myself, who see it in great detail and with an understanding of what it all means. Only you achieved this the first time you took the yage and not after many years of training. You saw it all, my boy."

Temple remained silent for a moment, recalling Tagheetu's warning about revealing his past lives. A curious tremor ran through his body. He suddenly remembered the vision in the rainbow.

"What were the tablets of stone and the scrolls I saw inside the rainbow?" he finally asked. "I saw it at the very end. If the Spirit of Tagheetu hadn't brought me back, I might have actually been able to read one of them."

"Tablet of stones? Scrolls?" the Shaman asked in a bewildered tone when he heard the interpretation.

"Yes, I saw ancient stone tablets and sacred scrolls being secreted away by the High Priests. The Priests created their own holy texts instead. I saw the people eating these and being sickened by them, but they begged the Priests for more because it was the only thing they knew that could offer any sustenance."

The Shaman shook his head in disbelief. "No one sees beyond the destruction of the ancient cities."

"Yet I saw it just the same," Temple insisted. "Then, I saw them fighting over these texts. The people and the Priests alike forced others to eat them. They even killed each other over whose text of half lies provided the most nourishment, but the people became emaciated all the more.

"Then, I saw one great tablet and one scroll bathed in a beautiful soft light. The first was an ancient tablet. The latter was a scroll representing a holy text written anew, but in the spirit of the ancient tablet. Both will change the world." He blinked his eyes and looked at the silent Priest.

"This, then, is a prophecy?" Losha asked.

"Yes, I think so. The ancient tablet has something to do with the Makolese. It will help the people to reach another level of understanding."

"And the other?" she asked.

"The last scroll is like a road in the forest, a pathway to the Creator, that leads us to the garden we never left. People will understand it on many levels, but it's designed to help the chosen – the volunteers."

The Priest rose to his feet and moved to the other side of the fire, lost in thought. Temple watched him through the dying flames, stilled by the sudden chill. Mefakani paced briefly and returned, holding a serious look on his face.

"Temple, I am the High Priest of an ancient, spiritual people. I have seen many men go through this rite. Yet, none have ever been able to see beyond the destruction of the great cities through our Lord Tagheetu. No man has ever achieved that..." he paused and looked at his Initiate through guarded eyes, "not even myself. I am pleased that your mind is mending and you are remembering some of your magic. You learn at a frightening speed.

"Today you gathered your courage and witnessed the dark past of our world. Tomorrow," he declared, "you will learn discipline. Then, when the moon is void of its course," he paused, "you will go into the depths of the sacred Hollow Mountain for the final test of courage. There, you will find the untold power of the Mountain Spirits, but not without a price, for there are many dangers there. No one but me has ever returned with the powers from the Mountain Spirits. I alone stole some of their secrets. I, alone, faced every danger; and I, alone, returned victorious. And now you," he pointed his crooked staff at Temple, "will go to do the same."

CHAPTER TWELVE

The Power of the Animal

"Every animal has special knowledge and everyone has an animal teacher.... However, you do not need to read this scroll to learn what they teach. Go to the forest, the sea, and the field and see for yourself. Like a river, the animals will talk to you. Go there. They are waiting to teach you."

Losha Ninti
Makolese Scroll on Power Animals #1
The Makolese Scroll on The Education of Temple Fox #12

It was dark and still when a palace guard brought Temple out of his tiny round guest hut to the long portico that ran around the inner courtyard of the Queen's residence. The inner complex was a grand walled village within a larger walled village, each inner and outer ring made of mammoth stones, and each rich with gardens and pathways, springs and a flat level area to accommodate larger crowds. Tall pitched thatched roofs covered broad rectangular pavilions with deep eaves and connected to each other through the network of pebbled pathways. Within the huge inner courtyard grew the royal gardens, lush and fragrant in the balmy, early morning air. Above, a sickle moon cast a thin, eerie light against the backs of the silvered swans that slept in the gardens, their serpentine necks buried deep in their feathers. They stirred uneasily as Temple passed.

The guard led him around the tiled portico to a nearby hut and stood outside as Temple entered.

Inside the hut, Losha arranged baskets of fruit and various ritual objects in front of a small fire. Her hair looked even more disheveled than usual, as if she had just risen from her bed in haste. She never lifted her head when Temple entered.

Temple scratched his forehead where his burn had been healed. "What are you doing here so early in the morning? It's still dark out."

"Come. We have much to go over this morning. And, please, only speak to me in Makolese from now on," Losha said without looking up. "Here. What is this?" she asked in Makolese, pointing to a ritual dagger before he even had a chance to sit down.

He stopped short and smirked. "Well, good morning to you too, teacher," he retorted with sarcasm. "That's a bu-dahl."

"Correct," she said crisply.

"You seem distant this morning."

"And, what is this?" She pointed to a ritual bowl made of tortoise shell.

"That's a channak. Aren't you going to congratulate me for passing my initiation?" he asked in broken Makolese.

"Truly, Temple, I am pleased for you. What is this?" she insisted, handing him a ripe jamalac he couldn't remember ever seeing before.

"You'd never know I was half a god by the way she's acting. She can't even look me in the eye. I passed my initiation, so why is she giving me the cold shoulder?" he thought to himself.

"I don't know," he confessed, and he raised the strange fruit to his mouth to take a bite.

"You may not eat anything this morning," she instructed with the directness of a schoolmistress.

He placed the fruit back into the basket with as much obedience as he could muster without showing his exasperation. "But I haven't eaten in over three days. I'm being starved to death," he complained, then leaned forward trying to catch Losha's eye. "You're people still think I'm the Prophet, don't they?"

"Of course," she affirmed, without raising her head.

"I did do well, didn't I?" he said with a surge of confidence and maybe a little bit of arrogance.

"You went beyond even the Shaman's experience when he was first initiated by Tagon, his Master. You are learning the language quickly, too. Soon the Queen will not need my services anymore."

Temple looked through the mass of hair that shielded her eyes to the heart of her soul. "Would that please you, Losha?"

She looked up. "I am pleased to be of service to you, Temple, but I have personal matters to attend to."

"Your husband?" he reassured, and she nodded. "Will there be a funeral?"

Losha gave him a quizzical look. *"He could not have known, not with all that he had been through in the swamps."*

"I suppose if I did not tell you, you would not know." She let out a grim sigh. "Amron's spirit is surely lost," her voice quivered slightly. "My niece and I have had nightmares. I feel..." she stammered, struggling to control her words, "...I feel he sometimes visits me in the night." She lowered her head, trying to hide her eyes again. "Now it has grown worse. Galana..." When Losha spoke her niece's name, she burst into an uncontrollable torrent of tears.

"Losha," he pleaded softly. "What's happened?"

After a long moment, the young woman wiped her eyes and pushed a thick shock of hair behind her ear, trying desperately to sort herself out. She spoke with deliberate slowness. "My niece has become...possessed by my husband."

"What!?" Temple held a look of horror on his face.

"The Shaman does not know for certain, but he feels Amron does not know he is dead. Or, perhaps Amron escaped from the jaws of Lord Tagheetu like so many others. Somehow he got entangled within the energy of Galana's body." Losha swallowed her words, attempting to fight back a new wave of tears. "She is in great confusion...and here I sit, forced to prepare you for an important meeting with the Queen this week."

"I'm sorry, Losha. I had no idea what's been happening. Tell the Queen I demand she release you from my service immediately."

"The Shaman is speaking with her now," she sniffled. "Jabal has tried to draw the spirit out of Galana, but has failed. The Shaman himself will try tonight. He is preparing you for a purification rite today, but now it seems he will partake in a cleansing as well." Losha bit into her words as her breathing came in shallow gasps. "Tonight...he has arranged for a…a special...exorcism...and wishes for you to watch him. It is to be a...a lesson for you…and...and...."

"Look, Losha. Try to calm yourself. Breathe. Come on, breathe like Tani taught me."

The woman looked at Temple through a veil of tears. Her tongue could not form the words, so she nodded instead and closed her eyes to concentrate. Temple breathed with her to coax her along. She took three deep breaths. A warm tingling feeling coursed up her spine past her heart and throat until it cascaded over top of the crown of her head. It filled her every cell and pushed beyond the limits of her body, spilling into the room. Relaxed now, she sat quietly with her hands folded neatly in her lap. She smiled when she opened her eyes and saw Temple smiling back.

"Thank you, Temple."

"Don't mention it. You would've done the same for me. Now tell me," he said with intentional lightness as he held up the strange fruit. "What exactly is this?"

Losha managed a little giggle and continued with her language lesson. Although somewhat subdued, their moods had brightened. However, it was not to last, for, wedged in the air between them was Losha's anxiety about the coming evening and the day's agenda Temple knew he had to fulfill.

The pilot's mind raced through the blur of his own thoughts. *"I don't know if the Spirit of the Swamps is a thought form or not, but I know for certain that the Voice is real. What about my other visions? And, why, if the other visions are real, is it so important for me to know I lived as Gadji thousands of years ago, other than knowing that I can tap into a tremendous reservoir of courage from my past?*

"Perhaps the Swan will know. So, where is this Swan and how can I speak with it?"

"Can I ask you a few questions?" he asked, interrupting the lesson. He tried to find a way of disguising his inquiries. "Your people often...well...speak to the plants and animals," he finally said.

She confirmed this with a nod.

"Well, when they speak back, can your people understand them?"

"Some do. It is hard to say. It is a most private thing," she said, offering no further explanation.

Temple scratched his scruffy beard. "I know I spoke with the Spirit of the Crocodile, but...what I mean is...do the Makolese converse with other animals like whales, dolphins...and swans, for instance?"

Losha sat staring, wondering at this round of new questions.

"Of course," she conceded. "However, since the Su has been broken, it has become more difficult. Few, if any, have been able to even see Tagheetu. If people do find their animal teacher, they keep the knowledge to themselves and dare not speak of it to one another, unless, of course, there is a reason to share it or it is well known by all. Everyone knows Tani uses the power of the dolphin, for example. But that is because she is a healer."

"Why would anyone want to speak with another animal other than Tagheetu?"

Losha felt grateful for the momentary distraction. "Each animal," she explained, "has special knowledge. You will find the spirit of the whale acts as a record keeper, much like the Lord Crocodile does. The whale holds the history of our ancient past from before we manifested into form, and keeps it in its song. But, unlike the Crocodile, who shows us through our own fear that hunts us down, the Whale Spirit teaches us in a powerful, yet gentle way."

"And the other animals?" he continued to prod.

"The dolphins can teach humans how to hold the Ka within themselves by breathing correctly. They are master healers who are able to enter a dreamtime world, yet they can exist on the same plane of consciousness as we do. That is why Tani could teach you to breathe so well and to hold the light within you.

"The power of the snake can be heavy medicine. Mefakani uses their energy to enter different states of awareness to heal and conjure. When the High Priest, Tagon, noticed Mefakani's great cleverness, intellect, and especially his passion to lead, he referred to him as 'The Snake.' Everyone, particularly Initiates, have an animal teacher, and usually more than one. I suspect your primary animal teacher will come to you soon."

Temple nodded and scratched his eyebrow where his skin was healing. *"What about the Swan? When will she talk about the Swan? Do I dare ask?"*

"How about the swan?" he asked, holding his breath.

Losha's smile radiated warmth that filled the room. Temple was so entranced with her ease and openness that he almost forgot to listen to her answer. "They are a very powerful female energy," she explained. "They teach us to trust and surrender to the rhythm of creation with grace and beauty. If you learn their medicine, you can sometimes see the future. Most of the swans on the island have died off," she added in a troubled tone. "The Councils sees it as a sign that Makol and its people are losing their beauty and the future itself. It is a very grim way to look at things."

"In spite of all that you know, are you more optimistic?"

"Tai," her smile brightened again and the atmosphere in the room seemed to glow. "Some of the swans have moved to the pool beneath the Great Round House. Great Grandfather Okon thinks they are guarding the secrets of the past so the future can still unfold. I know in my heart this is so, for the Snake and the Old Dolphin are optimistic about the power you will gain by undergoing the rite today. The Swan is greatly concerned for your safety, however, for it is a challenging ritual."

"The Swan?" he asked, raising half an eyebrow.

"Yes," she volunteered, without knowing why. "I am the Swan."

"You!?" Temple didn't know whether to laugh out loud or shout. Out of excitement, he reached for Losha's hand then pulled back apprehensively before he had a chance to touch her. Still, he kept his hand close to hers and could feel a distinct spark of some living energy jump from her hand to his. "I should have known all along," he said, allowing only his eyes to smile.

At that moment, a servant entered the room and bowed curtly. Mefakani walked in to find the Interpreter and his pupil sitting close together. He gave Temple a shallow bow and a cautious look.

Temple whispered to Losha. "After the exorcism, we *must* talk."

CHAPTER THIRTEEN

The Renegades

*"They met at night in secret at the Senior Elder's
private lodge. Every one of them I have pulled
from their Mother's wombs. I have bandaged their
wounds, cooled their fevers, and birthed their
children. This I have done for them, their children,
grandchildren and great grandchildren. And, yet,
they plotted against me, the Shaman
and Temple Fox."*

Elder Tani
The Makolese Scroll on The Education of Temple Fox #13

Four Elders sat on mats around a quiet fire and a pot of simmering sha
in the center of Sahdon's lodge. Their Senior Elder paced around them
with a limp. He looked out into the predawn dark for a moment and let
out a troubled sigh. "If only the assassination attempt had not failed.
Now, that white devil has seen Tagheetu and survived unscathed."

Gabu sputtered with a mouthful of sha. "I had not heard. You
mean...?"

Sahdon looked down at Gabu. "He has moved beyond the illusion
and conquered his fears," he said.

Cranik ground his yellowed teeth and spat. "That thickheaded Tani is at fault! She taught him something of her own magic, I am sure of it. And, she taught him too well. Curse her!"

Gabu went rigid. He remembered Tani from forty years before. She was an old woman even back then and he was younger, trimmer, and his hair had not yet thinned. He remembered her clearly as if he had gone back in time. Those small, capable hands had attended to every bruise and sprain on his battered body. He recalled her reassuring smile. He would live, she had told him. He saw those ancient eyes again, etched in tiredness and worry as she healed the wounded, one by one on the blood soaked beach. Tani had been there when he had gotten the news that his wife and children had perished in a fire set by the slavers at the village Common House. She had been his comforter. Gabu remembered, and Gabu would not speak ill of her.

He smothered his feelings in another cup of sha then spoke in a painful whisper. "Please, Cranik. Do not speak ill of Elder Tani. If it were not for her healing powers, many of us would not be alive today." He stole a glance at the melted flesh on Sahdon's leg then looked up into his face. "Is that not so, Senior Elder?"

Cranik snapped. "You stupid fool! She is my enemy as long as the Queen can skewer my head on a spike, like she did to Tekosh and the other rebels!"

Gabu retreated in silence by downing another cup of sha.

Sahdon gave Cranik a look of sullen rebuke, then turned to Gabu. "There is truth in what he says, Elder," he began with skillful calm. "The more Makolese magic Tani and the Priest teach the Wizard, the more power he will gain. It will be harder to kill him the longer we wait. In the meantime, we should do something to keep Tani busy and out of the way."

The others nodded in agreement.

"May I also remind you all," he continued, "that, in spite of our recent setback, much has been accomplished through diplomacy. The Queen has increased her army and has posted more sentries around the island."

Cranik's eyes glared under his bristling brow. "And yet," he interrupted, "some of these sentries have been posted to spy on us. You can not deny that Sahdon."

The statesman leaned heavily on his cane when he lowered himself onto the floor mat, completing the circle of conspirators. "Yes. I know even now they watch us. But truly Cranik, do you not see how useful they are?" He gave Cranik a twisted smile through the cloud of steam that rose from the cauldron of sha.

"What do you mean?"

Sahdon was handed a cup of brew. "How do you suppose I was able to arrange a meeting here this early morning?" He sipped the warm wine, savoring the flavor, then swallowed.

The others looked around at each other and shrugged.

Kulo, who seldom spoke, said, "All I know is I received a short message from a voice outside my window saying there was to be a meeting and it would be safe to attend."

"Same as I," Ikus disclosed, in his gravely voice. Gabu nodded in agreement. "Furthermore, there is something going on at the Shaman's compound tonight – a celebration perhaps. Everyone's attentions are focused on that right now, and not on us," he added in a suspicious tone.

"All true, but there is more," said Sahdon. "I have found, my Elder Brethren, that some of the guards can be reasoned with. Have you looked into their faces lately? What is it that you see? Fear," he asserted. "They are as afraid as you and I of this Stranger who gains so much favor in the court." He ladled out a cup of sha and passed it to Gabu as he spoke.

"I have had some very lengthy conversations with the guard Sumuro ordered to be posted outside my own lodge – very interesting conversations. His name is Ijebu." Sahdon motioned with his head towards the window. "As you saw when you entered, he guards as he is told to, but is well out of earshot." He ladled more sha into his own cup and took a sip.

The wine rolled down Gabu's chin and landed on his fat stomach. "So, you have persuaded him to join us somehow?" he inquired.

"When Ijebu finishes his watch," Sahdon replied, "he will report to Sumuro, as all the guards do. However, what he will report is that I was home all night and all morning – alone."

"What about our guards?" Ikus worried.

"The same," Sahdon responded solidly.

"How do we know they do not conspire with the Queen and act as spies under her orders?" Gabu asked, refilling his third cup.

The Senior Elder raised his cup as if examining the finest brew. "I prize myself as being an excellent judge of character." He took a sip then placed the cup before him. "Ijebu knows who the Believers are among the army and who are not. He arranged for only the Unbelievers to guard our lodges this early morning." Cranik moved his mouth to speak, but Sahdon raised his hand to silence him. "There is more. I have just been told by our informer that Temple is to enter the Hollow Mountain in a month. Mefakani is hoping he will return with perhaps a new weapon or two from the Mountain Spirits. Our High

Shaman, it seems, is blindly optimistic, even though he does not know the true nature of this creature." There were groans from the conspirators, but Sahdon continued unheeded. "Ijebu is going to arrange to have his men guard Temple in the Queen's compound. We will know our enemy better, after the guards learn his weaknesses and such."

"I see a plan in your head," Cranik smirked with approval.

Sahdon matched Cranik's grin. "The Stranger will reside in the comfort and safety inside the Queen's compound for that month, or, so he thinks. And while he is there…" the old man poured some of his wine onto the bed of coals and watched it steam away, "we will smother him."

Cranik smiled. "A good plan. I like it."

Sahdon held his cup up for a toast. "Sumuro will be pleased to have such eager warriors volunteer for such a dreary task." The lip of Gabu and Sahdon's cup met with a dull clunk. "To death!" he declared.

"To death!" they all cried.

CHAPTER FOURTEEN

The Desire

"The key to creation is desire."

Temple Fox
The Makolese Scroll on The Education of Temple Fox #14

Early that same morning Losha led Temple back into the forest. With the amber light of dawn came the first heat of the day, and the jungle steamed and stirred with life.

The occasional twig snapping and leaves rustling alerted Temple to the whereabouts of animals as they played predator and prey with one another in the morning mist. Birds squabbled over their catches and spiders hauled in their morning meals. Somewhere, there were root snakes silently taking on the colors and patterns of their surroundings.

In spite of his desperate need to share his cryptic secret, Temple knew Losha was not ready to take anymore upon herself, not with Galana's problem weighing heavy on her mind. He followed behind quietly as she forked off the trail to the south where a mosaic of reeds and sedge grasses grew. He remained silent, to match her somber mood, until they came to a marsh crowded with orange osier and cattails. Ahead stood a lone cypress surrounded by rows of ornately carved wooden pillars in varying states of decay. Beyond were the mud flats.

The Initiate looked to Losha, knowing the path would lead to the swamps, a place he didn't exactly want to go back to.

She spoke as if she had heard his thoughts. "I have taken the long way, so that I may pay homage to our ancestors. You need not worry about protection, Temple. No one knows we are here, except Tani and the Shaman."

From under her sash she produced a barkcloth bag and sprinkled the pillars with a yellow ash. "People do not live as long as they used to," she said sadly. "We have had twenty deaths on the island just this past week and there are more reports about entire species of plants and animals dying off."

Temple never mentioned her dead husband or the sorrow behind the broken Su. He didn't even question his guide when they left that desolate place and veered off the path again, this time heading west. They coursed their way past ancient pines draped in creeper, then angled off to the north with the sacred mountain to the southeast. When the sun edged over the foothills, slanted beams of golden light filtered through the trees and mottled the forest floor.

The path dwindled to nothing and Losha pushed a curtain of ferns aside, continuing on without explanation, until she stopped abruptly and lifted her head in the air. The sound of water flowing over stones was barely detectable.

Temple's senses became electrified as they wove their way through the forest, the sound of the water growing louder and the strong scent of hibiscus filling the dank air. There was one more wall of ferns, these with leaves as fine as feathers and five times the height of a man. The two pushed past the tall ferns and stood on the edge of a secluded glade bathed in golden light and cloaked in lianas and moss. Giant wild hibiscus and frangipani, the size of elephants' ears, colored the emerald glade in brilliant reds and cast a sweet fragrance through the jungle.

Losha whispered. "Temple, you must enter this glade same as you did the ancient Banyan grove – in silent humility and respect. You must only enter between the two old willows."

Temple stood in silent awe and reverence that he didn't have to fake, for he could feel the strong presence of the lifeforce here. He bowed his head in prayer, feeling small, feeling humble and asked if he could enter the sacred glade. Once he felt he had been granted permission, he strolled around the edge of the pond where the old willows seemed to guard the enclosure, like silent sentries with heads hung down in sleep. He slipped into the warm waters, then splashed his way over to a flat boulder and sat down to rest from the heat.

Losha stepped quietly into the pool with her back to him and let the bubbles tickle her feet. Her eyes lingered on the pebbled shallows and her face changed from worry to an uncertain serenity.

"I used to come here a lot – to be alone." Her voice drifted into a small and distant place.

"Seems like a good place to do that," he said, not knowing what else to say.

She turned slightly, viewing Temple out of the corner of her eye as she wondered, *"How could he understand such things? Divine or not, he was still an Outsider."*

"The Makolese are never completely – alone ," she explained. "That is for healers and priests – not one such as myself."

"Why is that?"

"To want to be alone often is to be considered crazy somehow. Amron thought perhaps I was crazy." She turned her head to gauge a response. "We argued a lot. Although I was in service to the Queen, I chose to live outside her compound – so I could be in the forest. Amron did not like losing the prestige one gets from living within the royal compound. He felt I was spending too much time studying plants and such – and being alone too often."

"That seems kinda unfair. You should do what makes you happy," he said, feeling somewhat uncomfortable with her sudden candor, yet grateful all the same for reasons he couldn't yet identify.

Losha managed a weak smile. "You will make a good god." She looked back into the shallow pool. "Now, I am truly alone," she sighed, as her thoughts drifted back inside her head.

Although the water cooled Temple's feet, the sun beat down on the rest of him. It had been days since he had eaten. He hadn't had anything to drink since the night before and he was bone weary since he arrived. He squinted through the bright sun at Losha and waded over to her. "Your parents. Are they still alive?" he asked cautiously.

"I never knew my father." She looked up at Temple. "He was an Outsider, an Ethiopian."

Temple raised one singed eyebrow. "But you were born after the massacre; after your people no longer made Su with strangers. And they didn't kill him?"

"He sailed ashore alone one evening and was discovered by my mother and no one else. He was a religious man, a Christian. Very mystical, my mother would say. She would often weep when she spoke of him. They spent the night together and then the next day he loaded up with fresh supplies and sailed off. Although my mother had many men after that, she never married."

"That's far to come for a one-night stand," he thought. "I don't suppose your mother is alive?" he asked aloud.

She gave a grim faraway look and shook her bushy head of hair, then looked up into the sun. She spoke with what Temple thought sounded like regret. "I should not delay you any longer. I will give you your instructions now and then leave you, Temple Fox, for this is a man's ritual. Here," she said, and she handed him a small bag made of soft barkcloth. "This is from Tani. She said you are to eat this herb should you fail to be cleansed."

He turned suddenly pale. "What'd you mean? It's not that awful potion again, is it?"

"No," she said reassuringly. She cast her eyes down as if somewhat embarrassed and repeated the Shaman's instructions verbatim. "This is what I have been told to tell you. Listen closely. Shaman Mefakani says you are forbidden to bathe or drink from these waters until you are told to. You must eat nothing, except Tani's herb, should you need it, but even this must be kept hidden from the Shaman's eyes. You must remove your loincloth and stand still on this spot in the center of this shallow pool. He says you are to center yourself and strip yourself of all desires. Do you understand?"

"Well, not exactly."

Losha looked up at him. "You have mastered your fears, Temple. This is a test of endurance so that you may become master over your desires. It is the second stage of your initiation. Only then will you be allowed to enter Hollow Mountain."

"I think I can handle this one," he smiled encouragingly.

"The Priest will not be able to see you again until later. He and his Apprentice are purifying themselves for the exorcism tonight. May the spirits help us all," she whispered then bowed reverently. "Someone will come for you this evening. I take leave of you now." Losha splashed over to the moss covered banks between the two willows.

"I hope all goes well for Galana tonight. I'll see you there," he called out.

Losha turned to face the Stranger a short distance away before drawing the curtain of foliage aside. Her dark mood was intrusive. "Please, Temple. Do not fail," she started. "If you should fail, it would only distract the Shaman from Galana's...."

"I understand. You needn't worry." His tone was intentionally confident.

Losha paused briefly, then nodded and disappeared behind the drapery of jungle.

★　★　★　★　★　★

Temple cast off his wrap and placed it on the moss covered boulder with the cloth satchel of herbs hidden beneath it. He took a full breath and anchored his feet deep in the sand, letting the grains ooze between his toes. And there he stood, naked and ankle deep in the sun dappled pool through the suffocating heat.

He watched insects glide across the surface of the water with their delicate spindly legs. He smelled the scent of wild hibiscus and lifted his arms to catch a rain of red petals as they floated from the heavens to the sparkling pool around him. The gentle breeze from the wings of a white khala grazed him when it swooped gracefully past him, and he laughed out loud as the titwees twittered joyously as they tumbled and darted through the air.

It was in the early afternoon, before the sun had reached its cruelest phase, when Temple's endurance began to falter. There were mosquito bites on top of blisters, blisters on top of bites. His ankles and feet were covered in leeches. To further his misery, his breathing became labored as if he were breathing underwater. With the knowledge that he was barely halfway through the rite, he swayed dizzily through the tropical inertia, swimming in his own sweat with the humidity pressing heavily against his lungs and the emptiness from hunger clawing at his insides. Thinking nothing could relieve him, he scrapped off the leeches and let the liquid heat of the day lull him into distracting daydreams. Although he would lose the thread of his thoughts now and then, and dream of lowering himself to wash the sweat and heat away, he'd let the sweat fall into the folds of his eyes to sting and taunt him.

Lethargy is a slow and creeping thing, however. Once it's gotten its hold on you, it suffocates the life out of time and time moves slowly. Temple was in its stranglehold and all he could fantasize about was drawing one handful of water to his lips. Instead, the willful Initiate purposely licked the salty sweat as a challenge to his thirst and never once lifted a hand to wipe away his tormentor.

Temple Fox knew his only hope was to take a deep power breath, force his attentions elsewhere to strengthen his resistance, and pray for some relief. With his prayer on a thick tongue, and swollen eyes to the mountaintop, he traced the line of weathered rock draped with heavy jungle growth. Looming behind it was a fast moving thunderhead. He focused on the dark cloud until a sudden breeze combed the waters, turning the slick still surface of vibrant green to a rough cobalt blue.

The Initiate sighed with relief when the shadow from the huge cloud mass glided quickly across the glade, shielding him from the boiling sun. A cooler breeze stirred and Temple watched red petals pitch and roll along the surface of the pool like tiny paper boats. Scattered rings of ripples dotted the pond haphazardly until the heavens opened and the landscape blurred. The weary man-god leaned his head back to catch the falling rain and drank from the open sky. Stirring inside him was a feeling of awe for the beauty and the power of the wind, and the rain, and the sky.

As suddenly as the tropical shower began, it blew swiftly to the west leaving the glade saturated in richer hues against a dark blue sky. Temple Fox, rejuvenated now, never moved, but leaned his thoughts towards the music around him, hearing fronds and ferns drip with fresh rain. The moss covered earth crackled as it drew the moisture through its pores. The air, too, was heavily scented with flowers, damp earth, and new rain, and he watched in wonder as a double rainbow arced overhead and disappeared behind the distant mountain.

At first, he was so awed he didn't notice the change. Only, as time moved easily by, he noted that the petals and leaves of all the plants took on a different hue, a soft glow, an undeniable iridescence. There was a distinct hum beneath the silence now, a thrumming in the glory of being alive, and the cells of his body caught the gentle fire; the energy of love, and melded with the energy, becoming one with creation.

Temple whispered a prayer of thanks. "You have done more than relieve my suffering. I thank the Spirit Which Moves In All Things for letting me see you, feel you, taste you."

As if to acknowledge that his prayer had been heard, in front of him, shimmering in a drifting swatch of mist, another rainbow suddenly formed then slowly faded away. Temple smiled with gratitude.

The sun sets early in a glade thickly canopied with trees. When the last light of day had glazed the air in soft pinks, flocks of parrots and parakeets flew screaming to their roosts.

Temple stood without a thought of hunger or thirst, past the time the purple shadows lengthened, and watched the sky turn to Prussian blue and the scant view of the distant hills dim to curved silhouettes. Beneath the deep throaty songs of nearby frogs, and the hum and chirp of insects, he could still detect the powerful, yet subtle, thrum of the lifeforce.

The Initiate had been so filled with the beauty of the emerald glade that, when its colors softly faded, and its varied forms disintegrated in the dark, he was certain he would focus back onto his aching body.

But creation is forever changing and high above him appeared a slice of moon and a sprinkling of hazy white stars. When the starlight grew ever brighter, their smaller companions came out of hiding. Temple found the glade softly illuminated with fireflies that drifted here and there, flashing in imitation of the stars, then disappearing, only to magically reappear in a wholly unexpected place. The Stranger was transfixed as they danced their T'ai chi, gliding through the darkness.

Finally, exhaustion from the constant pressure of the past few days began to find a wedge in Temple's armor. He stretched his arms out in front of him and tensed his painful back muscles. Relief was minimal. The mosquitoes came out in squadrons, taking turns tormenting him again and getting ensnared in the lather of his sweat.

He slapped a cluster of mosquitoes on his scorched neck and cursed. *"Damn bugs! When is someone going to come get me?"* he thought. *"I know the Priest will want to know how I fared before performing the exorcism."* He knew he had passed Mefakani's little test and smiled to himself, thinking how pleased Losha would be.

Perhaps the Stranger's thoughts were overheard, for, shortly after, there was a rustling among the ferns. On the far side of the glade he could barely make out a dark form who stepped into the pool and was slowly drifting over to him.

"Hello," he called out; shattering the quiet of the glade, but the shadow didn't greet him back. He peered again through the screen of darkness, the only light being the moon, the stars and the fireflies. "Hello, I said. Who's there?"

The figure advanced. The voice was a dark whisper. "I have come for you."

"Losha?"

The woman made no sound as she drifted through the shallows. He hardly knew what to do when the young woman came up to him. He covered his nakedness with his hands and squinted down at her. Beneath the veil of night he beheld the soft features of a young woman. Her black eyes were intelligent and serene holding the power of the night. In her long black hair she wore a red orchid. In her hands she carried a small gourd.

A soft whisper fell close to his ear. "You may bathe and drink the waters now." She pulled the stopper from the gourd and the scent of coconut oil wafted in the air between them. "I am here to help cleanse you and guide you back."

"Who are you?" he asked.

"I am known as Wonehcha. Come. I will wash you."

Before he could protest the woman took a handful of warm water and let it cascade down his chest causing his muscles to flinch slightly.

"Please, let me do this myself," he insisted.

Temple knelt down in the water, first to drink, then to bathe. After he splashed the sweat away, he sat in the shallows and let the tiredness soak from his limbs. The dark woman stood close behind him tossing warm water onto his muscled shoulders. When he finally felt himself return to normal, he rose to his feet, accidentally brushing against the woman's breasts. His muscles recoiled and shuddered. He wanted to apologize, but before he could, the woman placed her soft, oiled hands onto his shoulders. The soothing balm soaked into his pores, relieving the burning itch and causing his blisters to instantly heal.

"That's magic," he whispered.

Temple found no resistance from his aching limbs when she pressed firmly into each of his muscles. But his mind scrabbled between total acquiescence to her healing touch and getting about his business. The Shaman would be waiting. He was about to voice his thoughts when the young woman slipped away like a shadow. He turned to find her, but she was gone. Temple remained puzzled when the woman stepped from a deep shadow close by. Her body was bathed in the luminous light of the bright sickle moon, her eyes liquid and dreamy, swimming with fireflies. She ran her fingers down the length of her hair and pulled it off her shoulder, inviting the moonlight to rest there. Then she shifted slightly, her face falling into half shadow. A glint of soft light caught her nipple and she swayed to and fro, allowing it to caress her.

Temple inched closer to the woman, oblivious that he had even moved, drawn like a moth to light.

Wonehcha rolled her hips in a sensual dance and the darkness swirled around her navel.

The curve of her hip rested pleasantly against his eye and his thigh muscles tightened as he drew closer still. He reached out for her. When his shadow enshrouded her, she deflected his grasp and stepped away, grazing his flesh ever so lightly.

Temple's mind danced on the surface of his skin, his senses swirling and blurring all reason. He drifted towards her unrelenting now, caught in her silent spell. Only this time she did not resist, but pushed the fullness of her silken body into his, then pried herself away again teasingly. When he reached out to catch her, she grabbed his hand and placed it gently on her hip. Something outside himself suddenly stirred into his awareness. *"Wait. No!"* his mind protested, but it was too late. His breath came in shallow gasps as his hand answered back with a caress. He drew her closer and buried his face in her hair, drinking in the strange elixir of coconut and musk. He moved his mouth to the base of her neck, gently biting her, tasting her. Then he ran his huge, rough hands down the curve of her back to the base of her spine and round her hips to the jewel of her navel. He loosened her skirt, letting it fall into the shadows, then pulled her rising hips to his. When Temple found his mouth on hers and her breath came too quickly, he knew he had been fooled.

"Blast!" he cried out. "I'm a bloody fool!" He pushed her away and stumbled in the water groping in the dark for his loincloth. "You tricked me!" he panted.

"It is all right," she whispered quietly to calm him. "No one can see. No one will know. Everyone is at the Shaman's compound."

"I will know," he said. "And I know the Shaman will find out. He has his ways. Leave me!" he demanded in a panic.

"Then I will return without you, Temple Fox," she said in a low, cool voice. "And I will tell the Shaman that we made love right here in the water."

"No! Please don't." Temple splashed through the water and found his barkcloth. He wrapped it around his waist, but his penis was hard and the cloth stuck out awkwardly.

"Then you will not make love to me, Temple Fox?" she called out in a sultry whisper.

"No, I will not," he answered defiantly.

"But you still desire me, do you not?"

"Yes. Damn it! And I know that means I've failed the test!"

"Maybe not," she whispered back. "If you can center yourself and can still resist me, you will pass the rite."

"Truly?" he whispered.

"Tai."

"Then I'll try."

Temple ran his hand over the boulder, searching for Tani's magic herb. He tore the bag open and ate the entire contents. When he had swallowed the last of it, he stood back in the waters and struggled to control the wild beating of his heart. He pushed the woman from his mind and cast his gaze on the wisp of moon reflected in the calm black waters, hoping, praying for the bitter herb to work its magic. He took a deep, long breath and closed his eyes, but, when he did, he remembered how the woman's smooth, round hips rose willing to his. He let out a desperate moan. At that instant, he remembered Losha and her pleading voice.

"Poor Galana. I have to fight this temptation! Relax and breathe! Relax!"

Temple refocused on his breathing, but the heat of desire coursed through his veins and the drumming in his breast grew louder. He wanted nothing, especially his failures, to distract the Shaman tonight, and he cried out knowing his weakness had overcome him.

"Someone, please help me!" he pleaded.

Temple didn't want to open his eyes, so distracting was the woman, but he felt a warm breeze graze his face. He opened his eyes enough to catch a glimpse of a bird soaring silently by, its wings awash in moonlight. It landed on a willow branch that overhung the tepid pool.

"Hoohoo, Hoot, Hooo," an owl called out, which so startled Temple he held his breath. "Didn't mean to scare," it said.

"I can understand you!" Temple said.

"And I hear you." The owl blinked down at him with its wide, round eyes. "Called for help?"

"I...I did. I'm trapped in my desires and I must..."

"Been watching and know what you must do. Seen many a man go through this rite. The Spirit of the Owl, Henakaga, can help. I shall relieve you of your burden. Close your eyes," the owl instructed.

Temple closed his eyes and took a deep breath, then exhaled loudly. No sooner did he do this than he heard the beating of wings. Warm gusts of air glanced his body from head to foot and back up his body again, until he felt the familiar tingle fill his head. When he inhaled deeply again, he felt his spirit lift slowly from the top of his head and drift out into the open air. So immediate was the sensation that Temple opened his eyes quickly and looked down, certain he was out of his body and well above the bird perched beneath him now.

He blinked his eyes and blinked again in wonderment at how well he could actually see in the dark. Every pebble, every ripple, each and every tiny leaf, even a lone gnat, came crisply into focus. Never had his vision been so clear! Then he gazed down at himself. Feathers! A warm breeze ruffled his chest feathers and he swayed a bit on the willow branch. When he tensed his feet to balance himself he felt the power of clasping talons.

Temple let out a sharp cry then shrieked again when the foreign sound rose from his gullet.

When the eerie screech had faded, he listened to the night sounds, the scurrying of mice, the breathing of roosting birds, even an insect walking. He cocked his feathery head and gazed into the black pool below, past the reflection of the woman. Beyond her, the stars flashed and wrote their signatures in the pond. Entranced, he watched as the starlight bounced, streaked and rode the crest of tiny ripples like little surfers. All at once, the strange calligraphy became like patterns of beaten silver. Temple deciphered the cryptic language instantly, only to have it safely tucked away in the next moment deep in his subconscious.

The Initiate thanked the Spirit of the Owl silently then stretched out the span of feathers, which once were muscled arms, testing their lightness and their strength. The wind pushed beneath his wings and lifted him high into the air. As if this strange magic was second nature to him, Temple Fox soared effortlessly above the glade with two dark forms, one male and one female, surrounded by fireflies below him.

Temple merged with the river of wind above the treetops and beyond. Soaring to the east, he spied a windy brook that snaked through the forest and flashed like pewter beneath him. He followed the course until he caught a thermal, which rose against the mountainside. This he rode without beating a wing, gliding high above the mountain. Perhaps it was Temple's new vision, perhaps not, but he thought he saw luminous orange balls bounce in the air below him, near the mountain's summit. He suddenly remembered the strange, orange glow in his visions in the swamp and the simian mother and her newborn.

Before Temple could give this anymore thought, he caught a downdraft and sailed towards the island's interior. In the distance, the glimmer of the Shaman's central fire struck his eyes and he flew there on silent wings.

Temple perched in the old cedar overlooking the ritual fire. Tani was there stirring the coals while the Apprentice threw a bundle of herbs onto the fire. Losha, her niece, and the Shaman, however, were nowhere to be seen.

Temple called out, but when he tried to form the words, all that came forth was the strange cry of, "Hoohoo, Hoot, Hooo!"

Tani rearranged a burning ember and squinted up at the bird. "Glad you could come," she cackled, "for tonight there will be a death... a good death."

Temple felt something stir in his gizzard. Thoughts of the exorcism haunted him now and without further delay he flew back to the dark glade using his uncanny sense of hearing and sight.

The Initiate swept past fireflies when he returned with a silent swoop into the glade. He landed on a willow branch and stretched his wings out, tensing them slightly, then folded them neatly by his sides.

When Temple's soul had detached itself from his Brother Owl and had rejoined his physical body, there was something left behind on the surface of his mind. It was something he had never known before, never felt until now. When he traced its perimeters, it held the inexplicable shape of a woman, a silhouette trimmed in the language of the stars. He had remembered it flashing before his owl eyes in the blackness of the pond. Some hidden knowledge lay with the dark seductress, that he was certain of, but there was something more. It wasn't just this one woman. It was all women. It had something to do with the scent of women, the curve of their hips, the curl of their lips, the way they tasted, the way they moved. It was their healing touch, their open heart, the music of their laughter. It was the fire in their eyes and the spirit that stoked that fire. It was the Light! Woman held the Divine in the realm of matter. She was god in form; god disguised in flesh. She was Goddess. She was the ancient Hianna.

If the magnificent Beast of the Swamps could hold the Light; If all the elements: water, wind, earth, fire and the subtle, invisible forces were Divine, then why not Woman? Temple remembered what the old crocodile sage had said: *"'If I be a god, why not you?' And, if not me,"* he reasoned, *"why not Woman?"* Temple held the knowledge to him closely as if guarding a great secret.

"If that's so," he thought, *"then why would I have to deny my desires? It is one thing to be the master of my desires. If I can control them, they will not enslave me. But to deny them altogether like some dried-up celibate priest! It is the Light I desire and the very pulse of life I wish to embrace. Why else would the Spirit Which Moves in All Things have allowed me to feast today on its varied beauty? Which, of course, includes Wonehcha."*

Temple opened his eyes, beholding the figure of the dark woman, who only minutes before held him sway in her spell.

"Temple," she whispered. "I have never known one such as you. I danced before you, sang softly in your ear, even touched you, but you did not respond."

"What a pity," he said. "Honestly, I was unaware of you. I was somewhere else, riding on the wings of an owl," he whispered dreamily. "Should you invite me again into your open arms, at a different time and on a different occasion, I warn you, I might not choose to resist."

"Then it is a matter of choice?" she asked.

"Yes, but only after one has mastered ones' desires." He smiled.

Wonehcha clasped her hands together joyfully and gave a reverent bow. "Come," she said. "I will light your way back to the compound."

The dark figure held her hands out in front of her, placing them apart, one above the other. Then she mumbled a phrase Temple could not discern. Within seconds two fireflies streaked past him and hovered in the center of her palm, flashing their soft phosphorescence rapidly in a steady rhythm. Two more fireflies, then four, danced in the air between her palms, their signal pulsating throughout the glade. Soon, hundreds joined the others until together they all churned into a luminous ball of soft light.

"They will light your way," she said. She looked to the ball of brilliant light and issued a command. When Wonehcha spoke, the ball lifted from her hands. It glided gently over the pond, reflecting in the water with an eerie glow. Temple followed it to the moss covered banks, where the two old willows stood, then stopped to lend a hand to Wonehcha. But when he turned around – she had vanished.

CHAPTER FIFTEEN

The Exorcism

*"During the exorcism, Temple Fox gave a whole
new meaning to the concept of Makolese piercings.
You would have to be Makolese to understand. It is
a Makolese inside joke."*

Jabal, the Shaman's First Apprentice
Makolese Scroll on Magic, Rites and Rituals #103
The Makolese Scroll on The Education of Temple Fox #15

When the echo of drumming drew closer, Temple's tiny companions flew up in a luminous cloud and sailed over the trees tops into the midnight sky. The Initiate raised his head skyward and thanked the Spirit of the Fireflies. Above him, the stars seemed to squint through the humid haze and blink like distant spectators, and the moon sliced a cloud like a scythe. Temple whispered a prayer for Losha's niece and strode towards the Shaman's compound.

★   ★   ★   ★   ★   ★

Mefakani finished painting his face red with an oily finger. "I am pleased, Wonehcha. You have done well." He placed a crown of shiny, black feathers onto his head and tied the chinstrap securely. "Return after the exorcism tonight so I may hear the details of his mastery."

"As you wish," she nodded.

Mefakani adjusted his feathery crown, then grabbed his crooked staff and made his way towards the door. "Afterwards, I want you to administer the same rite to Jabal again, here in my lodge. He has been acting odd lately. Perhaps his purposeful little desires have gotten the best of him."

"But the ritual is only to be done once and has only been performed in the glade so..."

Mefakani pointed his staff at the tiny scar between her breasts. "I order you to, Wonehcha."

"But Master, this is unheard of," she protested.

Mefakani's nostrils flared. "You cannot disobey me! You will be here tonight and dance!"

Wonehcha hid her reluctance behind her heavy lidded eyes. "As you say, Master." She bowed respectfully and then left.

★　　★　　★　　★　　★　　★

A small band of warriors, and a scattering of people, formed an inner ring several yards from the central fire. Temple stood on the outer edge, scanning the crowd for Losha, when, to his surprise, he spied Wonehcha who scurried down the stairs of the Shaman's main lodge and disappeared into the black forest.

The crowd ceased their quiet conversations when Mefakani appeared on the landing of his lodge, a single orchid leaf covering his loins and the crown of black feathers covering his head. In his hand he held the white wing of the khala bird and, in the other, his crooked staff. His bright eyes peered from a greasy, red face and roamed over the gathering until they landed on Temple. The High Priest bowed low with an attitude of both reverent greeting and praise. All turned to see the white Stranger.

Temple responded with a similar bow and the drums beat louder, signaling the beginning of the exorcism.

Temple pulled a man aside. "Do you know where Losha is?" he asked in perfect Makolese. The islander pointed. Sitting on a log far from the central fire was a lone figure draped in blue barkcloth with a hood and veil made of fine black feathers. The figure turned when Temple approached.

He peered through the soft fringe of feathers. "Losha?"

"Please sit," she whispered back. "The Shaman is about to begin."

"I passed the test," he whispered, but she did not respond. "The herbs worked," he confessed, but what he really wanted to say is that he had done it for her.

The black hood nodded, then turned towards the Priest.

Mefakani drew a large circle around the fire with his staff, and then stuck his staff into the ground sharply. He threw more herbs onto the fire and shook the khala wing through the smoke as he began to chant softly. His tawny muscles shone golden against the firelight and rippled with the rhythm of the drum. The light danced against his face, the color of new blood.

Temple drew closer. "Where's Galana?" he asked, quietly.

The hood turned again towards Temple. "They will not let me near her. The Shaman is afraid Amron will leave her body and lodge inside me instead."

Temple shook his head in dismay for the things he had yet to learn and stared in horror as Galana, a slight girl, was carried inside the circle, her hands and feet bound by the strange power of the Apprentice. Her frail body, drained of its vital energy, appeared pallid, and her eyes were wide open with terror. Jabal placed the girl gently onto a bed of ferns by the fire.

The drums beat faster and Mefakani danced around the girl. When his eyes rolled back and he began to jerk spasmodically, Jabal lowered a bolt of barkcloth on the ground, unrolled it and lifted from it a sword, which had a tapered blade and a hilt made of bone. Jabal passed the blade through the smoke to purify it then placed it into the Priest's waiting hand.

With the skill of a swordsman, Mefakani sliced the air above the girl's body, releasing her from the invisible force that bound her then thrust the sword into the ground opposite his staff.

"Come Amron!" the Priest shouted. He leaned over Galana, straddling her feet and fanned the smoking herbs over her body. "Come!" he commanded.

The smoke swirled full circle as he flicked the wing over the girl's body, aiming the smoke near his feet where a nest sat in waiting to receive Amron's spirit. He continued this in a rapid mesmerizing rhythm with his eyelids fluttering wildly and the drums beating faster. His took short steps in place and as the drums beat faster still, he began to undulate his torso like a snake.

"Come!" he called, "RELEASE the child!"

Galana lay wide-eyed and trembling when Jabal picked up a short iron skewer from the barkcloth and waved it through the smoke.

Temple's muscles tensed and he jerked slightly forward, about to bolt from his seat, when Losha's hand held him back.

Jabal let out a sharp cry and pushed the spike through his Master's cheek, but the Priest resumed his dance without showing any pain. The Apprentice took another skewer, purified it through the smoke and thrust it through the fleshy parts of Mefakani's breast.

"Come demon!" the Shaman shouted again. "Come!"

The boy waved yet another iron spike slowly through the smoke. He lifted the loose skin from his Master's shoulder and pierced the skewer through it. Mefakani's eyes flashed liquid white and the skewers moved wildly with the rhythm of his dance. There was a murmur among the crowd, but no one moved, including Galana, who lay there half aware of what was happening to her.

"Stubborn spirit. Why do you not leave this child? You are dead Amron! Dead!" he shouted.

A deep and distant voice issued out of Galana's mouth, causing her aunt to shudder. "I am not dead. I am here! Can you not see me?" a voice bellowed out from the child in smoky tones.

"Leave the girl or you will harm her! Join me and together we will climb back into the jaws of the Lord Tagheetu. I am his High Priest. I will help you."

"No! I cannot go back," the deep voice pleaded back. "If I go, I will die." The girl folded up into herself and closed her eyes. "I am tired," the voice cried out. "So tired…I must sleep…Let me sleep."

"No, demon!" the Priest shouted exasperated. "Leave the girl now!"

There was no answer. Galana's body lay limp and still as if she had drawn her final breath. Mefakani circled the girl for better than two hours, shaking the wing to waken and stir the spirit, but the girl didn't rouse.

Temple listened intently to the rhythm of the drums, the beat thrumming through his body like the beating of distant wings. Nausea overtook him and he began to sway, but caught himself before calling attention to himself.

Mefakani finally slipped to the ground, his chest heaving. Jabal ran over to him before his Master's trance was completely broken and removed each spike carefully, placing them back, with reverence, onto the barkcloth in a neat row.

The Apprentice mopped the sweat from Mefakani's painted brow and handed him a cup of cool water. "I am not defeated yet, Jabal. This stubborn spirit must be slain or he will join with the ranks of the cannibal demons for sure." Jabal nodded in response.

Losha sat rigid with her hands tightly gripped together. "Temple, what will I do? He will become a demon forever and Galana his…."

Losha noticed a heavy, churning energy in the air between her and

Temple. Through her feathered veil, she beheld the Stranger whose body suddenly dropped forward with his head thrown down. She grabbed his hand.

"Temple?"

She heard air rushing deep into his lungs. She held her own breath then screamed.

Temple's hand fell from hers when he rose. He lumbered over to the Shaman's ritual sword and pulled it from the ground, lifting it high in the air with both hands. He swung the blade fiercely and the top of Mefakani's staff splintered and went flying into the crowd. "Who says I am dead?" he shouted.

"Bi Kana!" Mefakani cried, and both he and his Apprentice scurried backwards out of the way of the flying blade. Several warriors bolted to their feet, but their Priest held them back with a simple wave of his hand.

"Who dares to say I am dead!" the voice shouted again. With that, the blade came down slicing the air with a thin whistle.

"I do," Temple spoke in Makolese. Temple's spirit stood by the fire in quiet repose, glowing in a soft blue light.

"Who? Who are you?" Amron asked as he froze inside Temple's body with the sword held motionless in the air.

"My name is Temple. And you are in my body."

"*Your body?* It is my body. And now this is my sword," he argued, waving it defiantly in the air.

Temple spoke with purposeful reassurance. His voice was calm. "Amron. Listen. You died over three weeks ago in an accident. You were on a boat with Noko. You were caught in a squall."

"No. I... I am here. I am alive," he stammered with sudden uncertainty.

"Of course, you're alive. There's no such thing as death. Only, you are now spirit."

"No! This is *my body*," he said angrily.

"Look at the body, Amron."

Amron lowered the sword and looked down at Temple's feet. He raised one of Temple's scraggily eyebrows in surprise. He raised a hand for closer inspection; a hand much larger than his own, and much lighter.

"Are you white, Amron?"

Temple watched as the spirit of Amron animated his face. He looked puzzled.

"Look at your waist. Do you have such a scar?"

Amron eyed the claw marks around Temple's waist. "No," he

answered slowly.

"That's because you're in my body, Amron."

"Well, then I will take it!" Amron swung the sword at Temple's glowing form, but it passed right through him like smoke.

"See, Amron! I am spirit, too, and you can't hurt me. You must leave that body."

"But I will die," he said, with a slight quiver in his voice.

"No, Amron. You must go to the Light. There's a magnificent Light. Look around you. Do you see it?"

Amron looked around him seeing only a shiny tunnel made of swirling nacreous light. It seemed to beckon him.

"You must go through the void to the Light. Others are waiting for you there. Noko is there. If you don't believe me, call him."

Amron peered inside the tunnel hesitantly. He looked back down at himself in Temple's body and eyed the paleness of his flesh. "You are white. This is a trick!"

"Look. You want me to go in first? I've been there already, Amron. It's peaceful. It's safe. There's love there like nothing you've ever experienced before. Go ahead. Call your friend," he insisted.

Amron looked up in bewilderment. "But the whites are our enemy. All Outsiders are."

"Amron," Temple reasoned back, "when you reach this point, there is no race. There's only spirit."

Losha's husband was still uncertain and paced within his stubbornness. "If I go, what will you do?"

"I'll return to my body and live here on your island."

Amron circled the ghostly blue figure and ran his fingers through a beard which was clearly not his own. This added to his confusion. "This is a white man's trick," he muttered, and curled Temple's lip into a contemptuous snarl. He pointed the sword at the shiny blue form. "You are a magician or a demon, are you not? I can see the glow around you." Suddenly, Amron's fear and confusion turned to twisted reasoning. "You trick the Makolese into believing they are dead so you can take our island. You lie!"

"No. Listen."

"Then I will take one white man with me!" Amron threw Temple's body down on his knees in a fury and fell heavily on the sword.

"NOOO!" Temple screamed.

Amron lifted out of the white man's body, leaving the body crumpled like a bundle of old rags. Temple was infuriated. "I needed that body!"

Amron's spirit glowed faintly. "You are still alive – like me!" he gasped with total surprise. He looked past Temple and saw the tunnel beckoning him. He was unsure of what would happen, but he floated closer to the tunnel entrance. "Noko?" he called out. When the stocky figure of a man appeared and shone brightly by the lip of the strange tunnel, Amron jerked back with a start.

"I have been waiting a long time for you, my friend," Noko said softly. "There is nothing for you here anymore. Here," he coaxed, and took hold of Amron's tattooed arm with his broad hand. "I will guide you. Follow me."

Amron's spirit sparkled with a new brightness when he stepped inside the tunnel, and a feeling of peace fell over him. He turned to look at the Stranger. "Are you coming?"

Temple paused and shook his head. "I don't know. Not yet," he whispered. He gazed with longing at the soft, white Light that shone in the distance that permeated the heart of his soul. He remembered what he had lost by leaving the Light. It was everything.

"Here's my chance, at last. I can go home now if I want to, but.." he scanned his surroundings. Galana lay nestled in Losha's arms, the color of health returning to her cheeks. Losha, the beautiful Swan, sat staring in shock and disbelief at the bloodied figure on the ground that lay doubled over the sword. Everyone was still and silent, except the Shaman who stood over the body, his red painted cheeks streaked with sweat. "No! No!" he blustered. "I am ruined! Ruined!"

Temple turned to his ghostly companions. "Go on," he finally said, "Take your chance when you can." In a flippant, lighter tone he added, "Besides, if I go with you, they'll just send me back."

"Farewell, white man." Amron and his companion glided further into the tunnel, and in an instant, vanished into the void.

Temple let out a troubled sigh. Through the force of his will, he pushed the feeling of loss aside and looked only at his present dilemma. He ambled over to his body and walked around it to exam the wound. The sword had been rammed through to its hilt with the blade protruding neatly from his back.

"What'll I do now?" he wondered.

A soft incandescent light flashed before him and coalesced into the form of a man dressed in khakis.

"Dad!"

"Son, don't be frightened," the figure reassured.

"I had no idea you had..." he let his words drop. "Dad, I'm sorry. I've failed you again."

"No, you haven't, son. Listen Temple, it's me who failed you. It's me who needs to apologize. Since I've been here, I've watched you.

I've seen your courage and I've seen your destiny. Please, forgive me."

"But, Dad, look what I've done now," he gestured to the lifeless body that sat slumped over the sword.

"You can't go back to the Light just yet. You must go back to your body, lad."

"I can't," he said defeated.

"Son, you've got to muster all the courage you can now and expect a miracle. We will help you from here."

"How?"

"Just know beyond belief and it will happen. I love you, son."

Temple's spirit filled with overwhelming emotion as he felt his father's energy embrace him lovingly. "I love you, too, Dad." Words were more felt than spoken and Temple smiled at his father.

The old man smiled back and placed his left hand over Temple's head and his right hand over his son's heart. "I've come to tell you, you must return to your body now. Waiting any longer could cause permanent damage. Be brave son. Now go!" The figure vanished and Temple was left with a tingling sensation from where his father's hands had touched him. He looked down at his body again, when a loud screech pierced the air and an owl flew at Temple's head. Forgetting he was spirit, he ducked, and, when he did, his essence tumbled forward into the lifeless body sprawled before him. He returned inside his body with a rushing noise filling his ears.

Temple Fox rose mechanically into a sitting position, like a puppet on a string, and the crowd gasped. With his eyes half-closed in semi-consciousness, he placed his hands up onto the hilt of the sword. In spite of the howling pain, he summoned all his energy, pulled the blade slowly, continuously until the blade was free.

Mefakani froze with his mouth hanging wide open. Temple held the sword out in both hands and offered it to the Shaman, who took it without a word. Notwithstanding, Temple collapsed on the ground.

Shame rose within Jabal when he saw his Master staring blankly into the air, while others swirled past him to attend the Stranger. Tani scuttled over to Temple first and ordered two warriors to carry him into one of the small, round huts. She vanished inside.

Tani quickly bound Temple's wound with fine barkcloth soaked with a medicine that would stop the bleeding. She ever so gently propped his head up and raised a gourd filled with one of her potions to his lips. "I am so proud of the new white Shaman," she grinned. "See, you are remembering your power?" A weak moan escaped Temple's lips and he begged for more of the cool potion. "Powerful, powerful god," she uttered as he drank greedily, sputtered and drank some more. "You slew Amron's spirit."

A trickle of the elixir rolled down his dusty chin and landed on his torso streaked with blood. "Feels more like he slew me!"

"Tai," she laughed, and started to give him a grandmotherly hug, but pulled away so as not to cause him further pain. The old woman leaned backwards and clapped her hands together in delight. "First, you conquer your fears then your desires. Now this! You learn quick, Temple Fox."

"That drug you gave me…was mighty potent," he muttered weakly. "I ate the whole damn bag!" he groaned. "If it wasn't for you, Wonehcha would have...would have..." He tried to pull himself up, but fell back wincing in pain. "For God's sake, Tani, your pujo worked so well I was beginning to think I'd lost my manhood for good!"

Tani sat listening quietly with her lips tightly pulled into a half smile and her eyes brimming with tears.

"You know, Tani, it was easier tackling Amron's spirit than conquering my own desires. But with the kind of help you give, anyone can become a shaman. Anyone can be made to temporarily lose their manly desires if given the right drugs. It only remains to be seen how I was able to become an owl and get back into my own body intact with that sword through me. I had help from those in the spirit world. Who knows ? Maybe your pujo helped me to do that, too. You see, Tani," he concluded, "you made me a god. I'm your creation."

The Healer was silent, her eyes holding back a full smile. "My shaman-god," she cried, shaking her white head of hair. "Tani does not pick man-gods and does not make man-gods. The Divine One chooses man-gods and you accept the offer or not." Then, suddenly, she burst into laughter with new tears streaming down her hollow cheeks. "The only thing that keeps you from being complete is total belief and trust. Master Temple, there were no drugs. No drugs at all." She guffawed again, this time louder.

"What'd you mean, *No drugs*?"

She shook her head and looked fully into Temple's eyes. "Old Tani made a cheat. Tani made a little lie."

Temple tried to sit up again, but eased himself back down from the tedium and raw pain. "What cheat? What lie?" he asked puzzled, as he stared back at the old woman.

"No pujo, for the man with the scar on his forehead who falls out of the sky. No drugs for the future Prophet." Temple was stunned with disbelief. "I only gave a harmless herb that tasted bitter. That is all. That pujo cannot kill pain, make a man leave his body, or make his manhood go limp," she snorted. "You did it," she emphasized with a jab from her bony finger. "You!"

Temple's head spun. "You mean I controlled my...? And an owl really...? And I risked having myself cut in two by...?"

"I only meant to help you conquer your lack of confidence," she cackled. "You left yourself open to possession. But you were completely in belief that you could slay Amron, and you did!"

"I told you, Tani, I didn't slay him. He slew me. All I did was talk to Amron."

Tani leaned forward as Temple explained to her what had happened during the dispossession. He described to her the beauty of the glade, how the blossoms glowed and the lifeforce filled his body, rejuvenating him. He told her what it felt like to be one with creation and how he discovered the divinity in Woman, the divinity in all form. Since it was not to be known that he wasn't a new god, he didn't tell her about the reunion with his father while in spirit, but ended his story by telling her about the Brother Owl in the glade and, again, at the exorcism.

The Elder's eyes sparkled. "The Shaman's only wish was for you to conquer your desires, yet, you have learned all of this. I must get the Shaman so you can tell him all that you have learned."

★　★　★　★　★　★

Mefakani marched slowly over to his array of ritual tools as if sleepwalking. In his arms he cradled the ritual sword. He paused for a moment, trying to recover from his sense of shock. Sticking out of the sand before him was the remains of his staff with the carved head of Tagheetu neatly sheered off. He went rigid.

A crowd of whispering onlookers gathered their things to leave and lit a torch of knotty pine to light their way home.

"Do you still believe this white man has no soul?" someone asked in a cautious whisper. "Does he not sacrifice his own flesh for an ailing child and kill demons?"

The listener let out a disgruntled groan.

"Did you see?" said an old woman in the crowd. "His wounds started healing right before our eyes. He looked no worse for having had a sword run through him."

Another spoke in a hushed whisper filled with awe. "Tai, and he accomplished what our own Shaman could not."

"Tai, tai. I think his magic is greater," whispered the first.

Mefakani overheard this as he wandered through his compound, his face drawn in the inner pain of disillusionment and anger for not having foreseen that Temple's power would exceed his own. He avoided any eye contact with the villagers who remained and, as he drifted in their direction, they scattered when they saw him, finding the trails that would guide them home.

Mefakani pulled his staff out of the ground and stood by himself before the ritual fire, lost in thought, reeling from the dark emotions that pressed down on him. When he fingered the splinters on top of his broken staff, a deeper emotion took root. He spat in the dying fire and watched his spittle sizzle and dissipate, then called for his Apprentice to lock the ritual tools away. "I will go now and speak with Temple," he said.

CHAPTER SIXTEEN

The Rivals

"It was God's gift that I be born a heretic."

Elder Tani
The Makolese Scroll on The Education of Temple Fox #16

Tani plodded slowly across the damp Earth. The sunlight lay in brilliant patches at her feet, causing the ground to steam before her. How many times had she traveled this well-worn path to the Shaman's compound, searching for medicinal plants along the way? Thousands of times? When she reached the summit of a slight incline, she paused to catch her breath and, as the spirits willed it, caught a faint glimmer out of the corner of her eye. Not willing to miss an opportunity, she bent down to talk to the softly glowing plant, noticing her bones creak as she did so. Old age was upon her now and she could feel its slow meanness grate against her. How old was she now? A hundred and ten? A hundred and twenty? With all the many busy years behind her had she finally lost count?

Tani gathered a few leaves and placed them neatly in a bag, being careful not to bruise them. She gave a slice of coconut as an offering of thanks to the plant, then moved on, smiling to herself for the bounty that surrounded her and for the signs of hope that had been given her the day before. Yes, there was much hope brought by the one called

Temple Fox. The old woman's smile broadened when she thought of the strange pale man-god. Yesterday had been quite a triumph for him and she mused at how his learning had been much like an owl snatching its prey, swiftly and in stealth. With that thought renewing her energies she hurried towards the Shaman's private lodge.

★　　★　　★　　★　　★　　★

Tani stood on the landing of Mefakani's lodge squinting in the bright sun. "You sent for me?" she asked as she ambled in.

Mefakani slammed the door behind them, causing the walls to shake. Before the old woman could ease herself to the floor, Mefakani was on her like a snake striking. He jabbed an accusing finger into the air in front of her wrinkled face, tearing into the private space surrounding her.

"Someone has informed me that Temple ate something from a bag he had hidden in the glade yesterday! It was one of your potions, was it not?" His veins popped out on his neck and his jaw tightened. "What was it, old woman?"

Tani stood before the Priest repairing the ripples in her energy field. The stench of stale sha on his breath hung in the air and she forced a sufficient amount of healing air into her lungs. "All I gave him was ground up banalak leaves, nothing more. Temple lacks belief that he has power, so all I did was...."

"Meddle! And conjure! Which is strictly forbidden!"

"Shaman, we work together to bring him to his power," she said with an inner calmness. "This was not conjuring. It was coaxing. No harm was...."

"You never consulted with me on this!" he snapped back. "And worse than your interfering was the fact that Temple did not even kill Amron's spirit." The Shaman shook his fist. "Was that one of your brainless ideas, too, or was he was so full of the false confidence you fed him that he let Amron go into this...this tunnel of Light he speaks of? He has solved nothing! Amron can possess another if he so chooses!"

"That is not what happened," she argued. "Temple says that the Light is where Amron will rest. It is his rightful home after death. Temple says Amron will only return to inhabit a newborn. He can possess no one."

"I am tired of what Temple says," he grunted. "What he should have done is slay the demon through the power of Tagheetu!"

The Healer felt her temperature rise and shook her head in

exasperation. "He never saw a piercing before last night. What does he know of Makolese exorcisms? You young fool. Are you so set in your ways that you cannot learn anything new? Why else would Temple be sent to us, but to do just that?"

Mefakani paced rapidly from wall to wall. "Bi Kana, old woman. He made a good show of it, did he not? He even fooled the people. And you," he stopped and turned to her, "you tried to fool me with your idiotic trickery!"

Tani sidestepped the bite of his anger. "What does it matter as long as he passed the rite and set Amron and Galana free?"

Mefakani leaned into her face. There was sourness on his breath. "It matters to me!" he bellowed. "Amron's spirit never returned to the jaws of the Lord Tagheetu! That is where he would have been purified! Instead, this…this fledgling sends him directly to this Light!"

Tani held her ground and blasted the Shaman's reeky breath from her nostrils, then spit sideways to remove the putrid taste from her tongue. She turned back to look the Shaman in the eye. "If Temple is right, Amron will rest in the Light, think about what he has done in this lifetime, then reincarnate. He will have a chance to conquer his fears then," she said coolly.

Mefakani shook his head and resumed his restless pacing. "Only fools reincarnate. I have spent a whole lifetime purifying people so they do not have to return, or have you forgotten?" he countered, banging his broken staff against the timber floor.

Tani huffed and grimaced at the pacing figure. "You are not listening to me," she barked back. "This is why Temple is here, to teach us new ways."

"Bi Kana, I am here to teach him! There is nothing wrong with the Makolese way. He has yet to come into his power, and I will teach him the right way, and I will teach him alone!" he yelled, until his voice battered the rafters.

"I think you underestimate his present abilities. He conquered his desires on the first try and found his power animal as well."

"Second try!" he corrected with a scowl. "You conjured, old woman, so he would not fail. You interfered!" He tore off a large splinter from the head of his broken staff and threw it into the pot of cold sha, then walked away a few paces to cool his anger, feeling a mite unraveled for having allowed the old woman to rile him so.

"Look how far he advanced through Tagheetu," she chided. "Admit it Mefakani. The old croc' favors him over you." She cackled loud enough to create a power field that would jab him in the ribs.

Burning with jealousy, he shook the remains of his staff at her.

"Old woman, this is the Lord Tagheetu we speak of. How dare you speak of the Lord in common terms? Get down on your knees now," he commanded, "and ask for forgiveness!"

Tani allowed the humiliation to stir the coals of her temper, knowing well what was to come. After all, she was a woman and an old, wise woman at that!

She remained erect. "I honor the old sage," she said softly, defiantly, with her head held high, "but I do not worship him... or his little Priest."

Mefakani froze, his nostrils flaring. "Blasphemy," he finally hissed between clenched teeth. "Your flesh will surely rot in the jaws of the Lord Tagheetu." He raised his staff and pressed its broken tip between her sagging breasts. "I should have known better than to trust a female. I should have taken a piece of your Ka long ago, you stupid old woman," he said with cool anger.

The slits of Tani's eyes widened and fury tumbled from her rankling tongue. "You young dried up, stubborn rump!"

Mefakani's voice was icy. "I will make certain that the Queen knows you are no longer fit to teach Temple."

Tani pushed his staff aside and spit at his feet. "You are hung like a field mouse!"

"Get out!" he snapped.

Tani hurried to the door in a mad shuffle. "Your only lover is your hand, Mefakani! I will see the Queen myself about this!"

"And I will see to it that you are no longer able to conjure, old woman. Now get out!"

★　★　★　★　★　★

Mefakani waited until twilight beneath the hazy stars. It was hot and muggy. He crept sluggishly through the breathless air, stepping mindfully over gnarled roots that had twisted up out of the green swamp muck. He laid the tip of his broken staff vertically against his brow for a moment. The last flicker of the staff's life pulsated gently there, enhancing his vision as he scanned the forest with a mercurial eye. Seeing nothing to attract his purpose, he plodded slowly on beyond the swamps and fertile wetlands,...the only sound, the shrill chorus of katydids.

His senses led him far to the southeast to a copious forest of millipalms, their fine leaves rippling gently in the hot, wet air. He felt a warm, rapid pulse at the center of his brow and slowed his pace. Placing the staff to his forehead again, he turned methodically in a slow circle. A quick, piercing pain lanced his brow when he pivoted to the south. He dropped his staff and grabbed his head from the pain. He sat on the ground for awhile to recover and to scan the area. To the south there was a narrow strip of black sand. When the pain subsided he picked up his broken staff, rose to his feet and strode swiftly in that direction, now that he was certain he would find what he had been looking for.

He passed between colonnades of different palms trees. Some trunks were smooth, some spiny, some armed with nasty spikes till the trees thinned to a small clearing. In the center of a secluded mound of clean, black sand stood the largest acrocomia palm he had ever seen, looking more like a mammoth python with a meal in its belly. Mefakani winced with pain when he touched his staff to his forehead again. The wood grain from his broken staff shimmered, and the trunk of the bulbous palm glowed softly in response, illuminating the space around it.

His breathing became labored from excitement. "Who would have thought?" he uttered with astonishment.

He walked up to the magic tree and placed his hand against its smooth trunk. A subtle vibration moved beneath his palm. Without further delay, he took his short, bone-handled sword, the one he had used in the exorcism, and ripped the belly of the tree wide open. Watery sap came gushing forth, spilling out onto the dark sand. Deep inside, wriggling now that it had been discovered, was the object of Mefakani's quest – a snake, a most magical snake. The Shaman grabbed it swiftly from behind its sticky head, letting it coil around his arm, then stole back into the forest.

CHAPTER SEVENTEEN

A Secret Past

*"People only know how to feed on the energies of
others instead of embracing their own Divinity...
As long as we're in form, we'll always be evolving
splinters of Light, forever seeking the Divine
outside ourselves. When, in fact, as the Voice told
me through Tagheetu, we must remember that
what we are looking for, is what is looking."*

Temple Fox
The Makolese Scroll on the Education of Temple Fox #17

Losha's eyes grew larger. "The reincarnation of Gadji!" she exclaimed.

"That's what The Voice told me. So what does it mean?" Temple asked.

Losha dashed over to the window in the guest hut that faced the Queen's inner courtyard and leaned out. There was no one about, except one guard, a few servants working in the gardens and the herd of royal swans. The opposite window that faced the outer court lent a generous view of soldiers busy drilling new recruits for Palomei's new army. Their marching and their shouting provided a comfortable background noise to obscure any conversation.

She whispered when she returned and put her finger to her lips.

"No one can hear us. Just the same, speak quietly and in English."

He tapped his rib cage absent-mindedly where he felt a slight soreness. "Well?" he asked.

"Temple, if you had told me this before the exorcism I might have told this to the Shaman or the Queen." As her apprehension dangled in the air between them, she started to feel a little guilty. "Well, at least I would have told Tani," she started again. "But since you have released Amron and Galana, I know, without a doubt, that you are the real Teacher."

"You mean you had doubts all along?"

She lowered her head sheepishly. "Please forgive me. I am only human."

"So am I, Losha. I swear it. Believe me; I'm not forgetting the fact that I'm divine as well. Now tell me. Why is it important that I was Gadji?"

Losha took one more nervous peek out the windows and sat down again. "After the world was restored through the magic of Hianna, and people once again populated Makol, the people fell into corruption again. Gadji tried to end the corruption."

Temple felt a need to cough, but with the twinge of soreness in his chest he thought better of it and cleared his throat instead. "What'd you mean – corruption?"

"One Priest taught that the animals were so vastly different from humans that they had no souls. People began to believe the animals were lesser beings than themselves. They were the ones who drove the Spirit of Tagheetu back into the swamps."

"Tell me." he coughed once and winced. "Did Gadji ever restore the spiritual teachings?"

Losha sent out a warm pulse of healing energy towards Temple, who was unconscious of the act. "Our History Scrolls tell us that one High Priest, named Naweze Ka-Seipa, rallied the people against Gadji," she replied. "He finally killed Gadji. They cut him up and fed him to Tagheetu, but not before Gadji vowed he would one day return." Losha's eyes darted back and forth towards the windows. "It has been told that the moment Gadji died, the Earth shook and the Sky blackened. When the Earth mourned his passing, the legends say Naweze was so filled with remorse for what he had done that he used his magic to call Tagheetu back from the swamps. That is why we worship Tagheetu. We do it out of respect for the god Gadji who lies within his belly. To seek Lord Tagheetu in initiation, and in death, is a way of reuniting with the god, Gadji."

Losha secured a strand of hair behind her ear. "We have

ceremonies throughout the year," she explained, "where we sacrifice one of the sacred crocodiles and eat its flesh, hoping a part of Gadji's spirit will join us in body. Much to my people's shame, after several centuries, this ritual became corrupted. Warriors began cannibalizing their foe after they had defeated them in battle. They hoped they would gain their enemies' power, just as Lord Tagheetu had gained power after ingesting the god. However, two thousand seasons ago, Lord Issa came to our people and put an end to that. He taught us to love our neighbors as we would love ourselves."

"Why is it I didn't remember any of this before?" he asked, feeling the pain in his chest dissipate.

"The Gods have their ways of revealing things to us...and in their own time."

He scratched his beard ponderously. "I was truly a god back then?"

"So the History Scrolls say. Every age has their man-gods. I suppose you could have been the reincarnation of Krishram, Boddaloto or the Lord Issa. We all thought you were a new god, only you must be the reincarnation of the great Gadji or the Voice would not have revealed this to you."

Temple leaned his forearms against his thighs with his head held down in thought.

"Temple, can you remember anything else from that vision? You did see Naweze, did you not?"

He climbed back into his vision playing it over and over in his mind. "I saw the Priest, yes... carrying a scroll." He closed his eyes and drifted into a light trance, which made his vision come alive. He watched the Priest set the scroll on the plinth of stone before a crowd of people. Then the Priest taught them a prayer. When the people chanted, the mammoth crocodile climbed out of the water. Temple cocked his head. "The last thing I saw was the people prostrating themselves before their new Crocodile God and Naweze himself."

Losha leaned forward. "Then, Naweze restored the spiritual order?"

Temple pushed the sounds of marching feet out of his mind by forcing the hot, tropical air deep into his lungs. When his trance deepened, he furrowed his brow. "No. No, he didn't. I know this. I can feel it." A dark feeling seemed to cling to him. He opened his eyes and fixed them upon the Swan with the knowing eyes of an Owl. "I'm beginning to remember, Losha. I know what really happened."

"You can see it without the help of yage or the Lord Tagheetu?" she asked perplexed.

"Yes. Don't you see? Gadji never wanted to be worshipped. He...or, rather, *I*, fought against those who taught that the Great Spirit was separate from everyone and everything else. Naweze became frightened when the Spirits of the Earth and Sky rebelled, so he pretended to honor me. What he really did was set both Tagheetu and myself apart from the rest of humanity, as if we were somehow holier than anyone else. Naweze also set himself apart because the people had to go through him in order to reach their new god. Don't you see? He took the spiritual teachings and twisted them.

"He had them written down in that scroll he was holding. Half truths and half lies were tangled together to make his new dogma convincing. As long as people have to go through a Priest to reunite with a long ago god, they'll forever remain splintered from the divinity within themselves and never know the Spirit Which Moves In All Things. Naweze did this all with one simple act. He deified one animal and one man, and raised them above all else. By changing the teachings, he satisfied his own followers and the followers of Gadji alike."

Losha put her hand to her mouth as if to block her words, but they tumbled out in a trembling whisper. "Temple, do you think this is why you have returned? You will destroy the Priest?" She lowered her voice even more. "This is blasphemy and treason...both punishable by death!"

"Mefakani said I was sent to destroy the enemies of the Makolese people. Only, he thinks it is the Outsiders."

"What will you do?"

"I don't know. One thing is certain. I want to stay on his good side. Let him think the only reason I'm here is to win his war. Still, I think there is something else missing from all of this."

"Can you go back into your vision and perhaps see more?" she asked.

He nodded and closed his eyes. When he drew in his breath, the room seemed to tilt slightly as if he were on a slow rocking boat. He let out a moan.

"What is it?"

He grimaced. "My death. But...I don't want to see that."

"Temple, it could be important. If it is one of your fears, you must face it."

A queer feeling overtook him, then panic. "No. I don't want to see it."

"But Temple...."

"No! I said!" He broke into a hot sweat. Unable to control the vision he had set in motion, he clutched a sudden tightness in his chest with his knotted arms and rocked to and fro in anguish. He heard a noise inside his head like the sound of silk ripping, and his mind began to split, darkness spilling into the crevices of his brain. All at once, his memory opened wide.

A tiny spot of blood seeped from the center of his brow and dripped down his forehead. More blood appeared on his arms, then his legs, seemingly out of nowhere, and from no apparent cause. Losha watched in horror as his chest slashed open. She moved quickly and pressed her hands against the wound to control the bleeding. In spite of her swift actions, gaping wounds materialized everywhere on his body.

Temple opened his mouth to scream, but no sound came out.

Losha's intuition told her that she mustn't call for help, so she moved swiftly behind him and cradled him gently in her arms. When she touched him with such compassion, he felt a huge wave of emotion wash over him, at first smothering him, throwing him into uncontrollable convulsions, until his resistance started to drop away. His pain overflowed, like a roiling river of fire. Huge hot tears rolled down his sun burnt cheeks until, at last, the pain eased and his limbs loosened. His head fell back in total trust.

"It is all right," she cooed softly, watching the wounds and blood slowly vanish before her eyes. "It was the past."

New tears; tears of relief and understanding flowed from the corners of his eyes and fell freely down his face onto Losha's arms. "I cursed him, Losha. I cursed the Priest. I hated him," he sobbed. "I was almost a god, a god incarnate – a new god. I saw it. Felt it," he said, feeling cleaner and lighter the more he spoke. "When they pinned me down, he cut me all over, then poured hot poison into my wounds. I couldn't get out of my body fast enough." The memory made him clench his teeth. "And...and the pain," he choked. "I was in so much torment I cursed him! It was my final test and I failed! I fell in unconsciousness because I couldn't understand his ignorance and lust for power. I saw him as separate from myself, separate from the Divine, and I loathed him! That's why I had to return," he cried again. "I'm not here to avenge my death or fight anyone's wars for them. I'm here to gain my godhood. I was sent to that distant time to restore the spiritual order, but I failed myself."

The Swan stroked his hair, failing to hold her own tears back as she listened.

"I was forced to come back, incarnation after incarnation, to experience every human sorrow and every human shame," he said with deep remorse. "I had to learn...experience all. I had to learn so I could understand, without judgment of others, or myself, by *becoming* all others; by living in their skin and feeling what they felt. I killed and was killed. I abused people and they abused me. If I hadn't fallen into hatred that one lifetime, I wouldn't have had to keep coming back…lifetime after bloody lifetime."

"But Temple," she whispered tenderly as she stroked his wet beard. "You know this now and you have understanding. Forgive yourself. In a narrow sense, you have paid your debts. In the eyes of the gods, you have fulfilled their greater plans by experiencing *everything*. Because of this, you can gain your godhood in this lifetime."

Temple wiped his face with the palm of his rough hand and rose up on one elbow. "You think so?" he sniffled.

"Yes." She smiled and wiped her own tears away.

The two sat silently for a long while in the peacefulness that now pervaded the room, watching patches of sun drift lazily across the floor. They laughed as a swan chased a lone lizard through the gardens. Temple held his eye against hers, savoring the warmth of her gaze. He thought of Wonehcha in the glade then looked away guiltily. "I'm sorry I missed Amron's funeral rite."

"You needed to rest," she said quietly, then smiled to reassure him that she wasn't offended. "I needed rest, too. I am glad he is at peace now. I have found peace within myself as well. And all of this I owe to you."

"Please don't thank me again. I'll get a swelled head."

"Swelled head?"

He grinned. "It's a white man's disease."

Losha leaned into the coolness of the shade, her mind filled with new questions that pushed the quiet joy of the moment away. "Temple, why would anyone like Naweze Ka-Seipa want to have so much control over people, do you think?"

He paused as he watched the play of light through the garden ferns. "Losha, it's a desire we're both well beyond. I don't know, maybe you and I have already experienced that in other lifetimes and tired of it. That kind of desire is such a dead end. I do know something though. It was something the Voice spoke of through Tagheetu. I remember seeing it in the waters when I became the Owl, when the stars seemed to speak to me in a language made of light. Everything and everyone holds divinity within them. Everything is made of the same substance of Love. We are all a part of the Oneness. Even Naweze Ka-Seipa. I think it's just ignorance, Losha.

"People only know how to feed on the energies of others instead of embracing their own Divinity. Maybe it's a consequence of being bound in matter. Maybe it's because the soul who wants so much power is a new inexperienced soul. Maybe it's because humanity is only in its adolescence. As long as we're in form, we'll always be evolving splinters of Light, forever seeking the Divine and mostly seeking it outside ourselves. When, in fact, as the Voice told me through Tagheetu, we must remember that what we are looking for, is what is looking."

He got up and looked out the window at the soldiers drawing their swords in practice. "I have this uneasy feeling that after I gain my godhood, there's more, much more to attain at other levels of existence and other levels of awareness."

"You are talking like the strange Unknown Voice that speaks through you, only I know it is you, Temple."

"Beautiful Swan," he said, as he sat down again beside her. "I'm only just beginning to understand. Believe me, I'm far, far from godhood."

Losha smiled. "I have faith in you, Temple."

He looked into her dark liquid eyes. "I failed before," he said then looked away. "Besides, if I'm so damn smart, how come I don't know who the Hummingbird is?"

"The Hummingbird?"

"The Voice that spoke through Tagheetu said I was only to tell this story to the Swan and the wounded Hummingbird and to trust no one else."

"It is unlikely It would omit including Tani as well," Losha said, puzzled. "She is my teacher and friend, and most trusted confidant. Still, I, too, do not have the vaguest idea who the Hummingbird might be."

"Then we must find out."

"How?" she asked.

"Ask the Unknown Voice; the Light," he said. "And, *trust beyond doubt*."

★   ★   ★   ★   ★   ★

Mefakani stood alone by his compound's central fire looking up into the night sky. He shielded his eyes from the glare of the fire and waited for the sliver of moon, known as the crown of Draco, to creep over the horizon. Draco, the Dragon, was Star God to Tagheetu and his ally Zoozaycha, the small dragon or Spirit of Snakes. The sleeping potion he had made had been particularly strong and he was certain his few servants would not waken. He cast a cautious eye over to Jabal's hut and sighed with relief when he heard his Apprentice snoring. This was not a night for witnesses.

Mefakani lit some herbs, and through the smoke he watched the silver crested crown on Draco's sleepy head rise. Deep within his mind he felt the Great Sky Dragon stir. Carefully, he pulled a scroll out of his ritual bag and unrolled the brittle barkcloth to see if he had remembered the archaic script correctly. One word out of place, one action out of sequence, even one second out of focus would shatter the magic and, although Mefakani would not be bodily harmed, he would, without a doubt, lose the greater part of his magic. That, above all, he could ill afford.

The Priest licked his lips nervously and ran the words through his mind again. Then he rolled up the scroll with utmost care. He bowed reverently to Tagon's skull, which sat on a make-shift altar he had just created by the fire. His old Master's eyes stared vacantly back as Mefakani entered into a trance and began his dark magic.

The air above the altar crackled quietly at first. The volume increased, when midway through his invocation, Mefakani took the snake he had found the evening before, now wrapped around his broken staff, and held it up for Draco's blessing. There came a loud static grating in the roiling air and above him a dark cloud formed. The altar fire spit green flames and the moon turned to blood. The dark cloud seemed to suck the life out of the air and Mefakani could feel a heavy weight in his chest as if great, wet slabs of clay had been laid there. He struggled to breath through the incantation, but his focus never faltered and he completed the last verse by tossing the snake and the staff into the fire together.

There was a crack like thunder and giant plumes shot up through the strange vacuous cloud into the night sky. Mefakani was thrown back by the force and hit the ground hard. He lay there, oblivious to the green sparks that covered him and the sickly sweet smell hanging in the air until he shook his head and broke from his trance. He rose swiftly, anxiously, to his feet and rushed over to the fire.

Lying there, hissing in the cold green flames, were the staff and the snake, both writhing together with a brutal kind of beauty. He watched mutely as the force he had conjured swirled around the two until they melded into one. And when the hissing ceased, he thrust his hands, trustingly, into the burning bed of green coals and pulled out the glowing staff, imbued now with more power than before.

CHAPTER EIGHTEEN

Tani

*"The more brutal the man, the more frightened
they are of your power."*

Elder Tani
The Makolese Scroll on the Education of Temple Fox #18

Tani drained the last of the tincture into an obsidian vial and held it up in front of the row of dusty skulls. "Just in case," she breathed in a quiet whisper to the bones of all the Healers who came before her. "This is just in case. May the Spirits grant me courage." The old woman tucked the tiny vial into the folds of her sash and bowed before the altar. Then she held a yellowed scroll before the skulls and whispered, "This prophecy has been fulfilled. May the prophets forgive me." She lit the ancient scroll that she had stolen from the Prophecy Library, and twisted it in the flames to make it burn quickly. Her nerves jumped when she heard the pounding of approaching feet and tossed the rest of the scroll into her fire pit.

Losha was breathless when she closed the door behind her. She bowed to the Elder who squatted in the center of the room stirring a bubbling pot of tea. "I heard you calling me inside my head and came as quickly as I could. I ran the whole way," she panted. "I have heard rumors in the courtyard. The High Shaman had a private audience with the Queen this afternoon."

The old woman stopped her stirring and looked up at the troubled girl. "Yes, we have little time," she said in a low raspy tone. "My only regret is that I did not teach you more."

Losha sat down quickly. "Whatever do you mean?"

Tani spat into the fire. "That stubborn rump, Mefakani, forbids me to teach Temple." She worked up more spittle in her toothless mouth and spat at a nearby mosquito, but missed.

"No! He can not do that."

"Tai, he can. The Queen is sending guards for me at this moment. I can feel it." Tani drew closer and clasped Losha's hand in hers. "There is something I must tell you. Like a small wave that builds into a tidal wave, your learning will grow and cannot be stopped now. It has been prophesied, my child."

"I do not understand."

"Losha, there are many things that the women of old have passed down through hundreds of seasons. Secret things that I have tried to pass on to you. But, I have held one secret too long." She pointed a bony finger at the tiny discoloration between Losha's breasts. "Blessed child, when Mefakani took a piece of Ka from every newborn, and every man and woman on the island, I would not let him take mine, as you know. I was already an old woman and only conjured to heal."

"Yes," the girl nodded anxiously.

"And...he did not take yours either."

Losha's mouth flew open. "What?"

"When I acted as midwife at your birth, I saw something in you, something very special. I know you do not understand what this means, but I knew you would one day become the Swan."

Losha's head reeled from confusion, but in that brief instant there was some clarity. Too long she had held back the knowledge of certain things she often knew intuitively. There was a power in her she never spoke about, tried to hide and forget, fearing she'd be marked as a witch. Too long she was tied to a secret guilt, for she was certain she was a deviant from the true spiritual path set by Mefakani and the Priests before him. Now it seems there was a reason.

"The day you were born, Mefakani came to take a bit of your Ka. I switched yours for another infant's who had just died in childbirth that morning. I reattached your Ka and healed it. That is why you have a scar like all the others." Tani gave a sad, toothless grin. "Losha, no one controls you, not even me." She gazed at the woman who sat in wonder. "My child, do not be afraid of your powers. Do not think this is an evil thing. You are no witch, nor am I."

Losha took the old woman's leathery hands in hers and bowed her head. "You have given me the greatest gift."

"I have allowed you to keep a dangerous gift, which is your birthright."

She squeezed the Healer's hand. "I love you as much as I have loved my own kin."

"I know that, child. I know that." Tani patted Losha's hand tenderly. "Do not be swayed by your emotions. You are on your own now. I bid that you leave me now, quickly, before the guards come."

"No, I will stay with you."

"It is your choice, but I warn you I am marked now as a..." She lifted her head when the voices of men and the clatter of swords shattered the silence of the sacred grove.

Losha turned to her in alarm. "What will they do to you?"

"I have my suspicions. And yet, they might do to me what they did to the Hummingbird."

"Hummingbird! Losha said excitedly.

"Elder Tani!" a voice rang out under the eaves of her hut. "We are entering under the orders of Queen Palomei!"

Losha leaned forward and whispered. "Who? Who is the Hummingbird?"

"Winyon, the Chokahpeiyahpe. The Shaman does not hold her Ka either," she answered back as the door flew open.

Both women raised their heads when Sumuro stepped inside. His imposing figure filled the doorway, casting a shadow over their faces. "I have been given orders to take you to the Queen, under guard."

Losha looked to Tani and back at the Head Guard. "What is she being charged with?" she asked.

"Witchcraft and blasphemy." Sumuro drew his scimitar from his scabbard.

Tani lifted herself off the floor and took hold of Losha's hand. "Force is not necessary, Sumuro. I am but an old woman."

"I hear you can conjure with words alone," Sumuro asserted, holding the sword ready in his hand.

The Elder gave out a hearty laugh. "I have not seen such fear on your face, young man, since I first caught you from your mother's womb. Go ahead. Hold your trembling sword against me if you are so frightened."

Sumuro's eyes narrowed on the frail form and gripped his sword tighter. He glanced behind him and motioned to his men.

Three men entered slowly at first, peering cautiously into the hut, then probed the dark dusty corners to gather Tani's herbs, roots, and jars of potions into wooden boxes. One man paused over the ancestral skulls. "Protect me, Lord Tagheetu," he mumbled under his breath. He reached again for the ancient bones then hesitated. "Perhaps the Shaman should attend to these," he suggested to the Head Guard.

"Very well," Sumuro nodded.

Losha was livid. "You...You have no right...." she started to protest, but Tani held her back.

"Losha Ninti," Sumuro ordered, "you have been commanded to return to your duties."

"What will you do to her?"

"That is none of your affair. The Queen orders you to return to Temple Fox and resume your teaching at once."

One man stopped before the bubbling pot of tea and eyed it suspiciously. "What is this?" he demanded.

Tani grinned from ear to ear. "It will make your penis drop off. Would you like some?"

The guard flushed and kicked the caldron over, causing the coals to sizzle and spit. When they left with the two women in tow, there was not a sound in the empty room except the hissing of steam and the silent keening of ancient healers.

★   ★   ★   ★   ★   ★

Once the private screens were slid into place Owane positioned himself beside his sovereign wife. Queen Palomei sat in her huge rattan chair with her feet propped on the skulls of her old enemies. A bumblebee crawled in and out of the small bouquet of orchids in her hair. She sighed deeply and frowned at the slumped figure on the floor, then nodded to her Head Guard.

Sumuro glanced at his captive uneasily then placed his sword back into its sheath. He bowed obediently and resumed his place against the partition door.

The Queen grabbed her armrest tightly and spoke in a low, troubled tone. "Our High Shaman reports that you committed a blatant act of blasphemy and accuses you of witchcraft...both grave crimes against the Makolese people." Palomei spoke slowly. "Elder Tani, did you or did you not slander the holy name of Lord Tagheetu?"

Tani's disheveled white hair lifted from the floor. "Why bother to ask, Most Respected? My herbs and potions have already been taken. I am deemed guilty before my say."

"You have your say now. Did you or did you not slander the Lord's holy name?"

The old woman looked squarely into Palomei's eyes. "I did not," she proclaimed defiantly.

Palomei leaned forward. "Shaman Mefakani said you refused to kneel before his holy staff. Is that true?"

"It is," she replied with her chin held high, her lips pulled into a chevron.

The Queen shook her head in dismay. "So, you admit to the transgression?"

The Elder lifted her chin higher still. "I do not."

Palomei glanced at her husband, signaling her concern with a flick of her lashes, then looked back down at Tani. "Your future would be better seen if you explained yourself, Elder."

Tani straightened her spine. "I honor Tagheetu as I honor all the animal spirits, Most Respected. However, I do not worship him...or his Priest."

The Matriarch furrowed her brow. "I fail to see the difference between honor and worship, Elder."

"I do not blindly submit to Tagheetu to the point of worship, my Queen. The mighty Tagheetu teaches us and tests us, as all the animal spirits do. He, above all, helps us to face our gravest fears. But to worship him above all others means to give ourselves over to the murky past that binds us, and it is our fears that bind us, Most Respected."

"Surely, by facing our fears we purify ourselves. Is that not what the Priests have taught us?" the Queen responded.

Tani's dark eyes sparkled with an inner fire, but she was careful choosing words Palomei would only half understand or she would get into deeper trouble. "It serves its purpose. Still, My Queen, I ask you, what purpose does it serve to relive an unresolved dark past over and over again at the exclusions of other aspects of the gods we may learn from and even enjoy? It only keeps the men from living in the present," she spoke with audacious candor. "Yes, I honor the Priests of old as I honor Tagheetu. But exclusive worship, Most Respected, is another matter."

The Queen let out a sigh of frustration. "I do not wish to mediate petty bickering between my Spiritual Advisors, or enter into philosophical interpretations of the Makolese spiritual teachings. And yet, the High Shaman seemed to think this was serious enough to exempt you from teaching Temple Fox." She placed her pearly scepter across her knees and stared down at the old woman. "I dare say the charge of blasphemy alone is serious enough to warrant a penalty of death."

Tani placed her head to the floor in supplication again, a silent plea for mercy.

"The Shaman, as you know, is a fair man and a wise man for his season," the Queen stated.

The floor muffled Tani's response. "He is a clever man, My Queen, and most stubborn."

Palomei looked to her husband again and tightened her jaw, then stared back at the small figure on the floor. "The Shaman recognizes the valuable service you have rendered to the people in the past. Your healing has been seen as noble in the eyes of my household. None of us wish to punish you, Elder, and the Shaman pleaded for mercy in your case. The Shaman and I offer you a choice to make amends. In light of the penalties, it is a most generous offer."

Tani lifted her head.

"He insists you make a public offering to Lord Tagheetu."

The old woman squirmed.

"Furthermore, you must consent to having a tiny portion of your Ka taken by the Priest. He fears you might be tempted to conjure again. With a piece of your Ka in his safekeeping you may still perform your healings, but only within the confines of his guidance."

The glint in the Elder's eyes grew dangerously brighter. "If that young rump is so frightened of me, perhaps he should submit to the jaws of Tagheetu again!"

"I do not think slandering our High Priest will sit well with our Lord...or me," the Queen added boldly, and the bee above her head buzzed noisily.

Tani's tone was brash. "I confess, Most Respected, I have no more fears left."

"Very well. Does this mean you chose to make an offering and will submit to purification?"

"No." Tani drew her face into a leathery knot and looked around for somewhere or someone to spit at, but thought better of it. "I refuse to get down on these weary knees to make some grand public huffle just so Mefakani can strut around flaunting his fine feathers like a young pompous cock. I consider it blasphemy!" She reconsidered and spat on the floor.

Palomei stomped her foot and pointed her scepter at Tani. "You are just as the Shaman described you! You have an obstinate streak in you, which is flourishing with age! The Makolese people can ill afford having you interfere in matters of such grave importance! Therefore, you will submit to having part of your Ka removed and kept in the capable hands of Shaman Mefakani. And, you can thank the High

Priest for pleading for your life."

"I have no fear," the Elder said with her head held high. She placed a bony finger between her sagging breasts. "Let him try to take my Ka, but hear me, My Respected Sovereign..." She pointed back at the Queen, aiming her gaze at Palomei's full bosom. "Make certain he does not trick you into giving over anymore of your Ka!"

The Titan glared back at the figure on the floor, then looked to Sumuro. "Take Elder Tani to the Priest...now!" she ordered.

Owane walked briskly over to the Elder and held his arm out to assist her, but Tani turned her head away and lifted herself onto her own feet. Sumuro escorted her as she shuffled out the door in short unsteady steps, her back bent over with age and a sudden fatigue.

When the screen had closed, Palomei turned to her husband. "What a stubborn and ungrateful old woman. I give her mercy and she prattles on senselessly."

"I think it is old age, My Queen."

"What is worse, my husband, is that my Great Grandfather will have to be told of this. Better to hear it from my lips than from some gossiping servant."

"Tai. The news will not settle well with him. He is fond of Elder Tani."

"As I am," she said, gazing into her husband's sympathetic face.

When Tani walked back outside into the garish light, her words caught in her throat and rasped out weakly. "Losha," she murmured. She paused to squint up at Sumuro who towered over her. "Tell Losha to take great care."

"Tell her yourself," he replied. "It is not as if you are being put to death, you know."

Tani's voice rattled inside her throat. "If you only knew," she murmured, as she stumbled slightly and grabbed hold of Sumuro's arm to steady herself.

CHAPTER NINETEEN

The Owl

"Remember the Oneness you experienced before you spiraled into form? It is the space where all that exists is present and yet nothing can be distinguished from anything else. Find that place again. Once there, shift your awareness to the level just below it where identity is first created. That is where you can take on other forms."

Losha Ninti
Makolese Scroll on Magic, Rites and Rituals # 104
The Makolese Scroll on the Education of Temple Fox #19

Palomei's private garden was lush and steamy after a morning rain shower. The rain flowers were open-throated, the purple bells and coral creeper dripping. Queen Palomei sat quietly on a stone slab bench, especially designed for her size, its surface swathed in a thick wadding of wet moss. Seated on a small bench beside her was the lone white man, the True Teacher, though he was still learning as an Initiate. She handed him another jamalac fruit, but he declined politely with a slight bow of his head and a raised hand. The Titan took a huge bite and the juice rolled down the spiraled design on her chin. She tossed the remains to a kaca parrot that sat perched on a gnarled root at her feet. She smacked her lips and smiled, nervously Temple thought, and he watched in polite silence as a bumblebee landed in each of the blossoms tucked into her hair braids.

"You have learned our language quickly," she marveled, licking her huge fingers. "Proof of your genius, no doubt."

"I had a good teacher," he said, returning the smile.

"Ah, Losha. She has been doing well since the exorcism, thanks to you."

He lowered his eyes briefly, humbly.

Palomei's gaze directly engaged him now. "As you might have heard, one of your teachers will no longer be able to instruct you in the disciplines of Makol magic."

"Tani," he added worriedly, straining a little to breathe the hot wet air he was still unaccustomed to. He was anxious to hear news of her, but frightened of what the news might be.

The Queen read the concern on his face. "I have decided executing her would be senseless," she said, and Temple gave out a visible sigh of relief. "Since she is the only Healer on the island, besides our High Shaman, her skills are still needed. The High Shaman and myself have arranged for her to stay in his compound in isolation for thirty days. That will give her time to ponder her crimes and to receive some strict religious instruction."

There was a brief silence and Temple watched as the bumblebee flew off Palomei's blossomed crown and another take its place.

"I will miss her," he said, saddened by the whole messy course of events, especially since he felt partially responsible for them.

The Queen's eyes spoke the same regret.

"It is a hard business being Queen," she confessed, "and deciding people's fate." She looked into the blueness of the white Teacher's piercing eyes and felt the warmth of his understanding pour through them. "Often, there are no winners."

Temple gave a rueful nod.

"'I never knew I would be Queen, you know? Not until I was seven seasons," she smiled again, weakly this time, the burden from years of responsibility showing behind the public grin. "Some feel it is a blessing, a gift from the gods, but it is a curse, Temple Fox."

Temple watched as her countenance changed and the light in the garden seemed to fade. Both the bumblebee and the parrot flew away.

"There is never any time to grieve for the dead," she admitted. Her face was solemn.

"You're speaking of the Great Massacre?" he asked.

"Tai," she replied sadly. "The day after my mother and all her husbands were murdered, they made me Queen. Furthermore, the day after my own daughter was killed I was still busy making war plans. There is little time for anything else these days."

Temple flashed briefly to the lifetime he had led as the orphaned child who had been ordered to plow her mother's body into the ground, only to slave in the fields, as her mother once did, when the deed was done. He wanted to say he understood, but the sound of a distant chime broke the peace in the garden.

Palomei frowned. "Come!" she commanded aloud in her most regal voice. In a moment, her personal servant came around the wall of creeper and whispered in her ear.

"I see...Very well. I will be there," she replied to her servant in a kind, but curt tone, then looked down at Temple with disappointment. "If only my servants would be kidnapped by the Mountain Spirits, they would not bully me so," she complained with a sly sideways glance at her servant, then let out a hardy laugh. "I regret I must leave you now, Temple Fox, but a Queen's duties call from sun to sun." The Matriarch rose from her bench, dwarfing Temple where he sat.

"I look forward to us meeting again," he said as he rose then bowed.

She bowed back. "I am a poor student. I promise the Teacher I will sit and listen next time – without interruption." She smiled again, then left and, despite her height, disappeared behind the shrubbery choked with tropical bittersweet.

★　　★　　★　　★　　★　　★

Temple and Losha sat in his small guesthouse with cups of freshly brewed sha in hand.

"To the Lord, and all his Spirits and our merciful Queen," she declared, as the two clinked their cups together. She sipped her sha then put her cup down before her. "Still," she added, "I worry about Tani being secluded for so long in the Shaman's compound."

"Think of it as a holiday," Temple smiled. "Besides, thirty days is such a small price to pay for the crime of blasphemy, don't you think?" he asked, refilling his cup.

"I still do not think she was ever guilty."

"What about the charge of sorcery?" he asked, with a raised eyebrow that was beginning to grow back now.

"She did give you a potion from the juk blossom. True. The Shaman knows nothing of that, of course. Still, Tani never conjures to harm anyone."

Temple looked over the lip of his cup. "And you? Will you conjure?"

Losha pulled a crop of bushy hair off her face. "Temple, I do not understand what it means to have my entire Ka and to be the Swan. My head is filled with confusion. Tani thinks I am something that I am not."

"Boy, does this sound familiar," he guffawed then downed his second cup of sha.

He gazed back at the dark woman with a warmth that startled him. *"Everything, it seems, has been taken from me,"* he thought. *"My country and its culture have been snatched from me, even though I don't know exactly which country I belong to anymore: England, America or Kenya. My livelihood and, worst of all, my best friend has been stolen from me, too. And what are they replaced with? Strangeness. Adhering to bizarre beliefs are challenges enough, but an Anglo-American having to eat things like raw fish is to declare war on my palate.*

"To add to my discontentment, I am discouraged from speaking my own language and struggle with Makolese, an odd mix of the guttural and sensuous, one minute grating on my throat and insulting my ears, and the next rolling on my tongue like a sweet liqueur. The climate is impossible, too. One day the hot, wet air is sticking to the roof of my mouth, and the next day cold mists are swirling round me forcing me to fantasize about wearing English woolies and wellies again.

"Only the island isn't the worst of it. After meeting the Divine Light, I feel I can't be a comfortable, non-committal atheist anymore. I feel there's nothing I can hold onto; not the strict, religious ways of the Makolese; not even the profound Peace and Love I felt from the Divine, for that, too, had been taken from me when I returned to my body after death.

"So, why am I surprised to feel warmth, or something I suspect is more than warmth, towards this dark woman with the wild hair and dark almond eyes, especially when everything else is awry? Losha seems to know me, understand me, shares my anxieties and doubts. What is left of anything I can feel comfortable with now, but Losha, even though she sits before me now in her own confusion."

Losha interrupted his thoughts. "Truly Temple, I do not know who I am," she professed with bewilderment. "When I was a small child, there were things that used to happen to me. Things I did not understand." She gazed into the boiling pot then poured herself another cup of fermented brew. Temple was still smiling at her warmly. "Once, when I was very young, I found a bird whose wing had been broken. I held it gently in my hand and wished it well. Before I knew it, the bird flew away. I have no idea how I healed it."

"So you've always had these strange powers?" he asked, noticing the loveliness in her eyes.

"As long as I can remember I have tried to stop them. Why, with everyone afraid of sorcery all the time, I felt that I was some sort of witch. I made sure no one saw what I could do."

"You're no criminal," he assured her. "You're as much a part of the Divine Plan as I am."

"Is this the man who speaks? Or the god?" she asked.

He wanted to shake her, hold her. "It's both, damn it! It's time you learn to accept it as I have."

"But I have not been sent as you have." She bowed her head. "I only wish to be a humble servant to you and...."

"Cut it out, Losha. You've got more power and love in you than you realize."

"I beg you to see reason, Temple. I was not sent. You were."

"Without you, I can't come into my full power. You think this is all just a coincidence?" Although he had already had far too much to drink, Temple leaned over and poured himself more brew. "It's easy for you to sit there giving all your power over to me, isn't it? 'Temple, find the Unknown Voice,' you say. 'Temple, please go through the Tagheetu ritual for us.' No one here is taking responsibility for themselves. Including you! When are you going to *Know beyond belief* and *Trust without doubt*? Where's your courage?"

"This is an angry man who speaks," she said, with anger and humiliation churning inside her.

"You're damn right it is. It's an angry man who knows too much!" He put his cup down on the floor with a thud.

"You are very unfair to me. I do not think I have been such a coward. I have lied to protect you and I have watched my family fall apart. And I have, also, watched myself fall apart to the point where I do not even know who I am anymore. Furthermore," she added, "I do not appreciate you raising your voice at me in anger."

Temple stopped and stared. "I'm not yelling at you, Losha. Don't you see?" He leaned forward to see a tear forming at the edge of her eye. He softened his voice. "The god wishes for a goddess. Not a servant."

Losha shook her head in dismay, her mind spinning in a muddle. "I am not ready for this, Temple. For any of this...."

"There's little time to doubt, Losha. It won't be long before I'm sent inside Hollow Mountain. I can't trust the Shaman, and Tani will not be there to help me. There is only you. You have to help me get to the Hummingbird. I've got to speak with her before I do anything else."

Losha pulled her hands through her undisciplined hair as if to rip it from her scalp. "I want to help, Temple, but I cannot think of how to get you to her island without being seen. If you should try and leave, the guards will see you."

"Is there something within your power to render me invisible?"

She shook her wild head of hair. "Temple, you frustrate me so. I have only just learned that I possess all of my Ka and you place this burden on me."

"I'm sorry. You're right. Let's not fight," he said, and sat quite still drowning in his own futile thoughts.

Losha gazed out the window into the imperial gardens and watched a butterfly flit in and out of the creeper vine, weaving its way over to the little tiled pond. A male swan puffed his white chest out and flapped his wings loud enough to hear above the din of marching soldiers.

"Temple?" she asked with a quizzical countenance on her face. "Do you think you could fly there as an owl?"

He scratched his beard and mused over the question. "I could, I suppose, but I know for certain that after my spirit entered the owl that I wouldn't be able to converse as a man."

Losha peered out the window again at the swan. "Powerful shamans can actually become their animal teacher." She looked to Temple for a response.

"I did that," he said.

"No. Your spirit left your body and joined with the great owl, but you still left your physical body behind. What I am speaking of is a total metamorphosis."

"If I did this, you think I could fly there as an owl and then transform back into a man?"

"Yes."

"Have you ever tried it?"

"No, but when I was younger I saw Tani change and swim with her dolphin friends, though she is too old to do that now."

"How's it done?"

"You must compose an invocation yourself, as it must come from the heart of the one who changes. But first, I must teach you the rhythm and how to spin the spell. Tonight we can cast it after all is quiet in the compound."

Temple reached out and caught her hand. "Are you sure you want to do this? I don't want to make you break any of your taboos. You know if we're caught you could end up like Tani, or worse."

"Perhaps too much sha has rattled my brain," she thought. *"Temple is right. I am about to break religious law and, if I am caught, the Queen might not be as merciful. They would mark me as a witch who had corrupted the new god. What would Tani do? Would the old woman risk her very life? Of course she would. In fact, I have been the unknowing accomplice to a conjuring criminal all my life. Although I am frightened, I can only follow my heart."*

"Well?" Temple asked again. "Are you absolutely sure you want to do this?"

Losha took a deep breath. "Tai," she said at last.

★　　★　　★　　★　　★　　★

Losha checked behind the window shade in Temple's guest hut, making sure no one was spying. It was the hundredth time she had done so.

"I'm not sure if I got this right," he complained in exasperation, with his arms falling by his side.

She spoke over her shoulder. "Well, you do remember the words?"

"Yes."

She turned to face him. "And…you remember how to spin?"

"Yes."

"Once you are in flight, can you remember how to get there by the stars?"

"Yes, teacher," he grinned.

"The most important thing to remember is the level you want to reach." she explained. "Remember how you experienced the oneness when you died?" He nodded. "It is the space where all that exists is present and yet nothing can be distinguished from anything else. While you spin you must find it again. Once there, shift your awareness to the level just below it where identity is first created. That is where you will take your owl form. Well then," she gestured to the center of the floor, "begin again, only this time try to say the invocation after you have started the movements."

Temple took a deep breath and positioned himself in the middle of the floor. He began to turn counter-clockwise, slowly at first, with his arms crossed over his chest. He revolved around and around faster and faster with his left foot never leaving the floor.

"Remember to make yourself a center through the middle of your chest," she instructed. "Keep your eyes open."

"God, you're bossy!" he said as he spun faster still.

"Quiet, please. Concentrate and keep your mind balanced between this world and the next." When she saw that he was spinning in perfect balance she whispered, "Now, say the invocation."

Temple refocused his thoughts on the words only and lost his balance till he finally wobbled to the floor.

"When spinning this spell, you must first learn to spin properly," she said, having lost her patience hours ago.

"I think I'd rather drink some of your Makolese poison and puke my guts out, cause if I keep doing this, that's exactly what I'm going to do anyway."

Losha pulled her hair off her face. "Begin again," she sighed wearily.

"I'm too tired," he complained. "This is too much like rubbing your stomach with one hand, patting the top of your head with the other and singing, *God Save the Queen*. Besides, what happens if I fail and I turn into a chicken?"

"Then I will keep you for laying," she said, giddy from fatigue. The two burst into a fit of joyful laughter until they wept.

Temple drew a deep breath to force his laughter to subside. "Oh, my side aches," he chortled. "I need some sha to kill the pain. Here, have a cup." He handed her a cup and she accepted it without any resistance. "Aren't we supposed to be solemn and holier than hell when we do this spell?"

"Please, Temple, do not make me start again," she tittered.

Both slumped on the floor as the sha worked its magic. "I think Tani is right. In order to make things work easily you must first relax. She says if any action requires too much tension, then it is wasted energy. It is so good to make light of things for a change."

"I agree," he said as he lifted himself off the floor. "Well, should we give it one more spin?" He grinned back and helped Losha to her feet.

"One more time," she chuckled. "If it does not work, we can try it again tomorrow night after we have rested."

"I love this *we* business. As I recall, I'm the one doing all the work. All you've done is stand there and boss me around all evening. You're a tyrant!"

Losha was too tipsy to complain. She held her cup up for a toast and smirked. "To my very nasty student."

Temple beamed a warm smile, then placed his left hand on his right shoulder, and his right hand on his left shoulder and began to turn slowly. His spinning became perfectly balanced when his head tilted slightly to the left and back. Round and round he whirled until he stirred up a whirlpool of sound that whooshed past Losha's ear, making the sound of "Huuu" in the air. Faster and faster he turned with his arms slowly pulling away from his body. With his left hand pointing down and his right palm cupped upward, he unfolded like a blossom.

Losha put down her cup of sha and gathered her wits when she sensed an electric pulse in the room. "Now!" she whispered excitedly. "Try the invocation!"

> *Oh, mighty Henakaga;*
>
> *Lord of all the holy Owls;*
>
> *Friend of quick and quiet death,*
>
> *Pray, change me into fowl.*
>
> *Beak that rips,*
>
> *Talons that tear,*
>
> *Wings that lift me high,*
>
> *Eyes that see,*
>
> *Ears that hear,*
>
> *Silently I will fly.*
>
> *Change. Change.*
>
> *So my form may range*
>
> *through the darkest night.*
>
> *Change. Change.*
>
> *So my eyes may take*
>
> *your gift of sacred sight.*

With every phrase Temple quickened the beat and spun even faster. Losha held her breath.

> *Oh, wise and patient predator*
>
> *seeing clearly in the night,*
>
> *Pray, change me with your magic*
>
> *so my wings may lift in flight.*

Beak that rips,

Talons that tear,

Wings that lift me high,

Eyes that see,

Ears that hear,

Silently I will fly.

Change. Change.

So my form may range

through the darkest night.

Change. Change.

So my eyes may take

your gift of sacred sight.

Oh, silent winged warrior,

hear my holy prayer;

Change my swirling, smoky form

from a man to owl with care.

Before her eyes, Temple's form disintegrated into a gray blur within a shower of sparks as the rhythm grew stronger and he twirled ever faster.

Beak that rips,

Talons that tear,

Wings that lift me high,

Eyes that see,

Ears that hear,

Silently I... Hoot Hooo!' he called out, and fluttered his wings until he came to a pivoting halt before his astonished teacher.

"Temple! You did it!" she yelled out with glee.
"Hoo Hoo, Hoot Hooo," he cried and blinked wide-eyed.
Losha held her hand out to stroke the bird, then withdrew it hesitantly. She bolted to the window, pulled the shade up and looked

about the garden. "Temple, you must go! Go, while you still have time." Temple blinked again and cocked his feathery head sideways. "I will make certain the guard and one of the servants sees me leave. I will tell them you have gone to bed."

Temple jumped to the windowsill and turned his head and winked. Off he flew on silent wings and disappeared into the darkness towards the remote island that held the Hummingbird as exile.

CHAPTER TWENTY

The Wounded Hummingbird

"It be the past and yet the past, it rests like a
hungry shark."

Winyon Kneller
The Makolese Scroll on the Education of Temple Fox #20

The tiny atoll was little more than a horseshoe of sandbars with the central part raised into a coral shelf, resting above the high water mark. Temple circled round the lonely isle in an ever tighter descending spiral until he was close to touching down. There he soared inches from the moonlit ground with one talon dragging to draw a circle in the sand. When the circle was complete he screeched loudly, calling for a change, and landed in the middle of it in a flash of bright light. It was only when Temple shook the sand from his feet that he realized he had transformed back into his original form. He flexed his arms to relieve the achiness from the long flight and looked around him.

In the distance deep shadows broke along a bench of coral rock, his eyes penetrating the hidden recess. He could detect no movement.

"Chokahpeiyahpe," he called softly then waited in silence. "Chokahpeiyahpe, please don't be afraid. I come as a friend," he said in English.

Winyon, the Chokahpeiyahpe, woke briefly thinking she was dreaming then rolled over on her sleeping mat.

"Chokahpeiyahpe," he called again, this time a bit louder. *I don't wish to startle her. She's probably asleep. Then again, maybe the old woman died and all I'll find are bones.* " He called one more time and drew closer to the shadows.

Winyon woke fully now and whispered out loud, "Captain?" She rose from her mat and peered from the edge of the cave entrance. In the moonlight stood the lone figure of a man.

Thinking he had heard a response, he called out again.

Winyon leaned against the rough edge of the coral cave and shuddered. She could hardly find her voice. "There be no one I talk to," she replied in pigeon English, then murmured a prayer of protection.

"I'm here to find the Hummingbird," he said, taking two steps closer.

"Who be you?" she called out in the night.

"My name's Temple Fox. I'm an Anglo American. Losha Ninti sent me." He waited a full minute until he spied a movement in the shadows.

"Come," she said, almost anxiously now, "I make you a light."

Temple entered as the dark figure lit an oil jar, which cast an eerie glow against the ragged walls, throwing her features into sharp relief. This was not an old woman as he had expected, but a tall, very lean and beautiful woman slightly past her prime. The Chokahpeiyahpe's gentle oriental eyes creased upward at their edges when she gazed back with a bittersweet smile. She pulled her shawl around her tightly and bowed. Temple thought he saw a tear glistening in the corner of her eye.

"You forgive me," she said in her best English. "Another voice I hear not in over two years. Please, come and sit."

Temple watched the silhouetted figure, with its shadow by its side, slip slowly through the cave, her rough surroundings in contrast to her natural dignity and grace. She gestured with a long fingered hand to the only stool. The hand was callused; the movement polished. Temple sat cross-legged on a mat instead.

The woman nodded, then sat on the stool. She folded her hands in her lap and squinted down at the white man. "Where come you and why?" she asked.

"My story's a strange one and I've little time. I must return to the Queen's compound before the sun rises. I've been stranded on the island for three weeks now. I got lost in a storm like your husband once did."

The Chokahpeiyahpe looked away for a painful moment, pulling a thick mass of her long silver hair through her hands absentmindedly. "Deal you with the Shaman Mefakani?"

"Yes."

"Two years ago my tongue he cursed so no Makolese I speak, and no ears be hearing the truth of him."

"What'd you mean?"

"Mefakani would put to death my husband if not for Palomei's mercy. Sent here he be in exile instead. Wife I be chosen by him, so I go too. Know you what I be? Understand you what be a *Chokahpeiyahpe*?"

"You're, One-who-no-one-wants, or One-who-can-not-bear-children. Yes, I understand. But I also understand your real name is Winyon."

Winyon wept openly when she heard her name spoken.

Temple stuttered. "I'm... I'm sorry. I didn't mean to....'"

"Years be it since last I hear my real name spoken," she apologized.

The marooned pilot looked up at her with sympathetic eyes. "Where I come from, it's not a sin to be childless, and one would marry even if they couldn't have children." He spoke gently. "Besides, most women on the island are barren now."

Winyon nodded at the Stranger with a troubled smile. "To my husband it mattered not. Because I be shunned like he, draw us together close, it did. The Captain was a man very good." Her smile faded. "It be Mefakani who make the trouble for us."

"Mefakani's been acting as my host since I've arrived," he said, his eyes growing more intense.

Winyon's face drew tight. "Sends you not here, does he?"

"No, and that's why I've come at night. Things are happening on the island I don't fully understand. When I went through my initiation, a holy Voice spoke through Tagheetu and told me to only trust the Swan and the wounded Hummingbird."

"The Shaman put through the Tagheetu ritual a white man as you?" she asked in broken English.

"I told you my story was a long one."

Knowing it was to be a long night, Winyon lit another oil jar.

"Please tell me more about the Shaman," he asked.

The woman shook her head. "A shrewd man with great and frightening power he be." Winyon pulled on her length of thick silver hair and looked away into the empty air. "Childhood friends we be,

Mefakani and I. Then Slavers come, and kill his father and steal his mother when only ten seasons we be. Survived the massacre, my parents did."

Temple leaned forward to catch every word and watched the firelight rest softly against the round of Winyon's cheeks.

"Did raise Mefakani as their own, my parents did, and closer he and I grow." She gave the Stranger a long look. "Fall hopelessly in love, we did, and plan to marry." She spoke with a distant sparkle filling her eyes. "Had the gift of healing and sacred sight, he did, even as a boy. Confide to me that the Priesthood be his calling. Longed he that I join him as an Initiate and wife."

Temple squinted harder in the lamplight. "Shaman can marry?" he asked.

"Seasons ago, yes," she replied. "But strict celibate be High Shaman, Tagon, and insist he that students follow his way. Join the Priesthood, Mefakani did, and an Apprentice he be at only thirteen seasons. Of him I be so proud. Made him then a secret vow to me. When High Priest he be in rank, the rules he change, so marry again the Priests could do. Him I love and wait I, patiently. But fueled by hatred of Outsiders he be over many seasons. Desire more power, he did, to destroy them. When High Shaman he be, at last, he ask me to join him as Initiate wife." Her face took on a look of guilt. "So changed he be and no affections did I return. A curse on me he did put, to forever a Chokahpeiyahpe I be unless my mind I change."

Temple looked into the face of loneliness and sorrow, and the face stared back knowing that somehow he understood her pain. "He didn't want anyone else to love you in his absence?"

"Yes." She lowered her head and stared into her empty lap, once again feeling the weight of her despair. "The Captain, somehow, the curse upon me he did break. I still be childless, but no longer I be One-who-no-one-wants, until take away, Mefakani did, the one man who give me understanding and joy." Winyon fidgeted uneasily on her stool and looked away. "It be the past and yet the past, it rests like a hungry shark."

Temple ran a rough hand through his beard. "Then, it was Mefakani who killed your husband?"

Her guilt resurfaced. "Yes, but to blame I be in part. Truth be that the massacre change young Mefakani so. In later seasons, without my affection, an ambitious and bitter man he be. Now he be the High Priest, the position most powerful on all the island."

"But there's the Queen?" he questioned.

"Yes, allies they be for now. But who be saying he not...."

"Take the throne for himself?" he said. It was a frightening thought.

"Secret power has he, that from everyone he hides. Even from the Queen. It be told by the Mountain Spirits to my husband. That be one reason kill my husband, Mefakani did. The Captain knew too much the Shaman fear and he fear that stolen, my husband, the power of the Spirits of Hollow Mountain."

Temple's eyes strained in the firelight. "If Mefakani has this secret weapon, then why does he need my power to win his war against the Outsiders?"

"Power?" Winyon arched an eyebrow.

"The Elder Council and the Queen, and even the Shaman himself, think I'm some sort of new god. I've been learning Makolese magic through his tutelage so that I can finally come into my full power."

Winyon stopped breathing. There was an uncomfortable silence in the cave.

"It appears I've fulfilled some sort of prophecy for your people. They say I bear the sacred mark." He took an oil jar and moved it close to the side of his face. A dark shadow fell into the deep indentation in his forehead. "I've been told by the Holy Spirit to tell the wounded Hummingbird that I'm Gadji returned." He stared up into the woman's startled face.

When Winyon spoke, she spoke slowly, choosing her words carefully. "Told my husband, the Mountain Spirits did, that you be coming. The Teacher you be, who ends the reign of Mefakani. The secret my husband did die holding."

Temple cupped the warm jar, his face suddenly still and grave, feeling the weight of some hidden truth bear down on him.

"Stories we all hear of how magic quartz from the Mountain Spirits the Shaman stole; of weapons from the crystals he did make. Like the Shaman, the Captain seek power too, then plan we to escape this island for good. When back he come from mountain, come he with the weapon greatest of all. Knowledge have he of your timely return."

Temple shook his head in bewilderment. "I'm only just beginning to accept the fact that I may have to end the Shaman's reign. Yet, it's the Shaman who has encouraged my learning his own magic."

"His new magic comes from the Mountain Spirits and most powerful and dangerous they be." She paused and peered deeply at the Stranger. "No understanding have my husband of these things. No words to describe what he see or feel. Only say he that great gods they be and challenge them, no man should or perish."

"If they're so powerful, then why don't they stop the Priest themselves?"

"I know not for certain. The mountain they never leave and must never be seen by mortals."

Temple stroked his short beard in thought. "Maybe Mefakani's fighting on two fronts and needs me to fight either the Outsiders or the Mountain Spirits…or both."

Winyon shrugged her shoulders and pulled her shawl tighter around her in the silence of the lonely cave.

Temple silently thought, *"I wonder if the Spirits inside the mountains are the same as the Voice, which guides me. I always thought the Voice was the same as the Great Light I experienced when I died. Maybe the one who possesses the Unknown Voice is something else; something that lives inside that mountain."* Temple moved uncomfortably on the floor. *"Who exactly are these Spirits and what awesome powers do they possess?"*

Temple looked up at Winyon with curiosity. "You said Mefakani possesses a secret weapon?"

"To my husband the Mountain Spirits tell of more than magical crystals the Shaman steal. Mefakani, they foretold, will uncover the key to one of the secrets he did steal. When he do this, the grand plan the Spirits did plot for untold seasons be greatly altered and thrown in turmoil."

Temple got up and paced, his shadow gliding across the surface of the pitted wall like a dark ghost.

"To my husband you owe your life, Gadji."

Temple stopped pacing and knelt before the woman. Winyon's eyes were sharp, yet kind.

"When return from the mountain, my husband did, Mefakani come and question him. Only after the Shaman did bind and gag me with his magic, and to kill me he did threat, did the Captain be forced to speak. Protect me, my husband did and protect you," she added. "A quick and clever thought he had to save me and upset Mefakani's plans. Of the arrival of a man-god who out of the sky falls, he did tell. Only with the power of this Stranger, all enemies be conquered. Follows our prophecies, this did. But the end of the Shaman's reign be what my husband did not tell." Winyon leaned forward, the tension hardening her face. "Say the Mountain Spirits that the Shaman's rule cannot in violence end. Raise not a violent hand towards him, Gadji, or the cycle of darkness continues, they did warn."

A spark of understanding lit Temple's eyes. "What you say is the confirmation I needed," he said. "It's to do with how my life ended as

Gadji." He gave Winyon a curious glance. "I think the Shaman believes I'm his ally and that all of his enemies can only be conquered with my power."

"Taunt the Shaman, my husband did, as a last defiant act, and to make Mefakani believe as you say." Winyon's face took on a look of profound intensity as if she was reliving that moment again. "Laugh at Mefakani, he did, when he say, 'Furthermore, this man-god is white! You see, you bloody bastard, you need a white god to fight your wars for you!' Mefakani be furious, but I be certain the Captain he did believe."

"Then what happened?"

Winyon twisted her hair thoughtlessly, her voice becoming distant and withdrawn. "Say the Shaman to I, 'I release you, at last, from your wretched burden'...And so," Her tone became almost matter-of-fact. "Cut off his head, the Shaman did. Took he, my husband's head, to be a grisly trophy – a footstool for the Warrior Priest." Her voice grew thinner. "Then whispered he, that he still did love me."

Winyon turned to meet the Stranger's gaze. Her vacant eyes came alive once more, this time with angry fire. "Mad he be! Truly mad!" She trembled slightly, and her face changed again. "I be so frightened, dear Gadji, for the Shaman's boat every new moon sails past this tiny isle. Know I it be him. Feel I his dark presence."

A chill ran up Temple's spine and his flesh turned to goose bumps. He spoke quietly. "Winyon, I'll bring you back to the mainland when I've defeated the Priest. I promise. I owe it to you." He placed a gentle hand on her shoulder. "This life must be a curse for you now."

The woman looked into the Stranger's face. There was a glimmer of joy in her eyes. "Now that you be here, I go in peace when, at last, I sleep eternally."

"When that time arrives, I implore you, good lady, to go directly into the void and there the Light will receive you. Don't linger about on these islands like so many others have."

"I do as you say, Lord Gadji."

"I'm not a god yet and I'm not to be worshipped. I hold divinity as any mortal and yet I'm still only a man, one small man, but a man who can become a god in equal partnership with his Creator. As for you, dear woman, you still have your Ka intact and so have power same as I." Temple remembered his experience as the owl in that star studded glade. "You, Winyon, are divine. You're god clothed in flesh. Do you see that?"

"You be the Teacher who ends the darkness with no hatred and no violence. As for I, know I not what I am. Feel I little power within myself. That be all I know."

Temple reflected, *"I don't know what to say. Who's to say I wouldn't feel the same if I had been through the same circumstances. The only difference between she and I is that I know who I am and she was yet to understand. All the more reason I should gain my full power. Perhaps I'm not some savior after all. Maybe I'm only one who knows myself first, and then teaches the others what I've learned."*

He rose to leave then bowed. "I must leave now before my absence rouses any suspicions." He turned towards the cave entrance, but Winyon caught his arm.

"'There be one thing more my husband did say before Mefakani come for him." She smiled. "Remarkable children you be having."

"Thank you, Winyon." He gave a reverent bow again then vanished back into the moonlit night.

After Temple spun his spell and took on his owl form, he circled where he had left a circular pattern in the sand. He flapped his wings hard against the coral beach and blew away all trace of his visit.

CHAPTER TWENTY-ONE

The Sacrifice

"Let him try to take my Ka!"

Elder Tani
The Makolese Scroll on the Education of Temple Fox #21

Tiv's thin shadow buckled against the rough wall as he moved the apparatus closer to the diminutive figure lying on the table of cold stone. The sound of metal grating against stone echoed throughout the cavern.

Mefakani tightened the straps that bound Tani and smiled inwardly with satisfaction. "For once you are quiet."

Tiv looked down at the tiny withered figure then gazed back at his Master with a troubled intensity.

"It is all right, boy. She has gone into one of her little novice trances."

Tiv shook his head and drew away from the table with a whimper of restrained despair.

"Now, now, boy, I will not hurt her," he said, placing his arms round the boy's shoulders circumspectly. "I will remove all but a tiny bit of her Ka, like I did for you. All right?" the Shaman said in that extra lightness that always disarmed the mute boy's fears.

But Tiv, unappeased by his Master's reassurances, shook his head again and twisted his lips into an exaggerated scowl.

"What is it, Tiv?" he asked now with concern.

His mute assistant pinched his nose and grimaced again.

"A smell?" the Shaman asked, and the boy nodded and pointed to Tani.

Mefakani bent close to Tani's face. A thin black line stained the creases of her lips and a strange smell emanated from her. He moved a swift hand over her Ka above her wrinkled breasts. When he detected no life force, he pulled back sharply. "Bi Kana! No! No! It is too late!" he wailed and beat his fist against the stone slab. He turned to yell at his mute helper as if Tiv had been the perpetrator. "She has ruined it! She is useless to me now!" His veins stood out against his neck and he began to sweat. "That stubborn old woman has killed herself and I know not what the poison is or its antidote!" There was a harnessed tension in his voice as he tried to regain some composure.

He paced around the chamber muttering to himself, tapping his new staff on the floor in nervous thought. "What will I do?" he asked himself out loud. "Everyone will blame me for her death." The Shaman pushed a tall barkcloth curtain aside that divided the stone underground chamber from his private alcove. Deep within the enclosure was a huge chair made of rock, its arms and back a grotesque amalgamation of stalactites and stalagmites. Behind this there was a high wall with thousands of obsidian vials hung from wooden racks, each holding a tiny piece of precious human Ka. "Tiv, put her body in here! Quickly now!" he ordered, as he pointed to a deep stone basin in the darkest corner of the chamber.

There was the clatter of jars as the nervous Priest searched his shelves for just the right concoction, and the sound of stone grinding herbs filled the cavern. Tiv lowered Tani's bony frame inside the basin and waited, immobilized by fear, until the Shaman hurried over with a gourd smelling of bark, root, herb, salt and alcohol. He poured the milky solution over the body haphazardly. "Now, fill this niche with water, boy. And be quick! This will keep her body well preserved and supple until there is time to form another plan." With that he stormed from the cavern yelling for his assistant to lock the door behind him.

★　★　★　★　★　★

Jabal woke with a start when the door to his hut flew open with a bang and the walls shuddered. Standing in the entire frame in black silhouette against the red light of dawn was his Master. He was bristling.

"If that old hag thinks she will stop me, she is wrong! I will continue my work without her!" Mefakani growled with his jaw set firm.

Jabal scrabbled from under his barkcloth coverlet. "What do you mean, my Master? What has happened?"

"I need someone else. Someone who can make it worth my while." He looked down at his Apprentice. "Jabal, tonight go and find me one of the key traitors. Choose an Elder who is easy to capture and bring him here!"

Jabal jumped to his feet, less out of his usual obedience and more out of an impulse to protest. "Does the Queen know that you...?"

"She does not and will not," he answered crisply.

"But...but why?" Jabal complained. "What do you need one of them for?"

Mefakani's eyes narrowed. "It is time we find out what that traitor Sahdon and his faction are up to anyway. That will make it worth my while in case I fail and they should die. I command you to bring one of the conspirators here by midnight. When I am finished with them, you must return them before daybreak."

Jabal shook his head. "I do not understand," he said, chancing a blow from a wave of his Master's hand.

Mefakani's restraint gave way and he snapped at his Apprentice. "You are not supposed to, you stupid boy! I will reveal things to you, if I want to, when I am good and ready. Now go and wake Temple Fox. I have my work set out for us today."

CHAPTER TWENTY-TWO

The Spy

"Even Jesus rested. And when he wasn't resting in the gardens I believe he was with his wife, Mary."

Temple Fox
The Makolese Scroll on the Education of Temple Fox #22

Losha thought she was dreaming when a strong breeze tousled her hair and she heard the beating of wings round her bed mat. She turned her head just in time to see a flash of golden light streak, then fade, leaving her momentarily blinded in the dark.

"Temple," she whispered. She caught his masculine scent first then felt his moist, hot breath cling to the side of her cheek. He had not touched her, but bent down beside her and whispered in her ear.

"I'm back," he said, and in Losha's clearing vision she thought she saw his hand pull away from her face.

Losha lay quite still. Her breathing deepened. She wanted to throw herself into his arms she was so glad he had returned safely. She lingered a moment longer savoring the pulse of his breath against her cheek. "Am I dreaming?" she caught herself saying aloud.

"It's no dream," he answered back, his words forming little tropical storms against her flesh.

"I was so worried," she said dreamily. "I tried to stay awake, but.... Have you seen Winyon?" she asked, more alert now.

"Yes," he whispered, and a puff of warm air teased her cheek again. "It was astonishing, the flight that is. To actually see and hear and fly, even think as an owl. And Winyon, my God, you've no idea what Mefakani has done to her."

Losha listened as Temple explained all that he had learned from the wounded Hummingbird. They talked into the early hours of the morning, until Temple was seized by tiredness and a desperate need to find calm within him.

He paused a moment and leaned back to rest. "I'm glad to be home again...with you."

"And I with you," she whispered back and suddenly found her heart beating faster.

Temple watched a glint of moonlight in Losha's eyes. He could barely make out the line of her lips as her mahogany skin disappeared into the darkness of the night. He leaned closer then drew away hesitantly, reluctantly. Every cell in his skin tingled with her warmth.

"You're a mystery to me," he whispered.

Losha could scarcely control her breath. "What do you mean?"

"You," he said. "The timing of our meeting, and the feeling I've known you before. The Swan," he cooed softly in her ear. "Who is she? Who are you?"

She drew her knees up under her chin, unaware of having covered her breasts. "I do not know who I am."

"Losha." He paused uncertain, his arms wanting to enfold her into himself. But he was mindful of her recent widowhood, and her vulnerability. He was shaken. "I should leave," he said, making a sudden movement to rise.

"Please, no," she begged, and she found herself reaching for him. She caught his hand and he sat back down again.

"I'm scared," he confessed. "Scared of what I've learned about Mefakani." He stopped and searched for Losha's expression in the dark. "I sometimes think I'm scared of you, too."

Losha cupped the back of his hand with her own hand and placed his palm to her cheek. They looked into each other's eyes knowing that, beyond the shadows and the illusion of time, they had always known each other, had always loved each other. Gently, Losha pulled him into her arms and whispered softly in his ear, "The Widow grants permission."

★　　★　　★　　★　　★　　★

It was only two hours or more before the morning light crept inside the hut and nestled beside the dreaming couple. The sunlight inched its way across Temple's muscled shoulders until it caught in the tangle of Losha's hair, like dew drops in a spider's web. Her eyes fluttered when the light pressed against her eyelids and she struggled to wake herself.

Temple could feel her energy shift as she struggled under the weight of his arm. "Are you all right, my love?" he called out, drawing her close to the full length of his body.

Losha's eyes flew open, and she pulled herself awake with a shudder and a moan, trying to regain a sense of normalcy. When she saw Temple gazing at her lovingly, as if he had been doing so for hours, she returned the smile and pushed herself into his embrace, casting off the last of her fears.

"Are you all right?" he repeated.

"Bad dream," she managed to say, and snuggled closer feeling the security of his arms.

"You're safe," he said, as he traced a finger down the curve of her neck. However, the dark thoughts that licked the corner of Losha's brain vied for her attention and she pulled away a little to look Temple in the eye.

"It is Tani," she said. "I dreamt that she was drowning." She gazed back at him with a frown. "I cannot stand the thought of her staying with that murderous Priest."

He put his arm around her in consolation. "I think Tani's capable of taking care of herself, at least for now. Or until I come up with a plan."

She stared back at him. "After all you told me last night, can we be so sure?"

"When I go to the Shaman's today I'll demand to see her."

Losha held a sudden, startled look when she noticed the angle of the light entering the room. "Temple, it is getting late. Go now or the guards will soon find you missing!"

Temple started to rise, then caught himself. "It's too late. I can't afford to let them see me as an owl. In any case," he said, leaning back down again, "I need time to rest and clear my mind before I see Mefakani again. And besides...." He paused, then placed his hand on the small of her back, unwilling to lose the joy he had just found. *"Damn the others for another hour!"* "I don't care who knows about us," he said, defiantly.

"But Temple," she protested.

He rebuked her silently with a kiss and, without any regards for the rest of the world, she allowed the heat of her passion to rise again as it had the night before.

A red spotted gecko, perching unnoticeably on the windowsill, licked his black eyes with his pink tongue. He gave a throaty chuckle then turned for one last look at the couple before disappearing into the forest. There he spied Losha, mouth open, back arched. And Temple, skin glowing like the golden dawn, entwined in the dusk colored limbs of his love, both riding the wave of their passion.

The gecko scurried away into the jungle and scanned the forest floor for enough leaf litter to camouflage his movements. Determined, he raced around, head to tail, whirling among the cold sparks he made, until he transformed back into his man-form. And when he ran off into the forest, the music of the lovers' breathing played heavily in his mind.

CHAPTER TWENTY-THREE

The Sea Bells

*"Coming into your power is like making sha. The
hotter the water, the stronger the sha."*

Old Makolese Saying
The Makolese Scroll on the Education of Temple Fox #23

Jabal wove his way through the labyrinth of tunnels of the cold, dank underground cavern to meet his Master. When he arrived he could see that his Master's mood hadn't changed, for the Shaman paced around his work area wearing an impenetrable scowl.

Mefakani castigated him with a stinging glare. "Why have you taken so long? Where is Temple?" he snapped.

Jabal gave a shallow bow. "Your student is busy," he answered with an impulsive burst of sarcasm, which he immediately regretted.

"What do you mean, 'busy'?"

'The Stranger and the Interpreter are..." Jabal's words broke off and stumbled, "busy...together. What I mean to say is, they spent the night together."

Mefakani's jaw tightened. The heavy circles under his eyes darkened.

"The guards never saw him leave, and both the Head Guard and the Commander are riled. I found him at Losha's." The Apprentice glanced up at his Master's face. "What I witnessed was no language lesson, I assure you, Master."

"Damn females," he said in a tight voice, then fell silent for a moment. "Run back and tell Sumuro and Commander Lobutu that Temple has been found, then go back and bring Temple here, by force if you have to." With that, the Shaman turned on his heels and disappeared behind the tall barkcloth curtain that hid his private alcove.

Mefakani gripped the edges of the cold stone basin. He gazed down through the brine past his own dark reflection to Tani's lifeless face bobbing in her watery coffin. But he was not to witness the expected death mask twisted into a rictus. Instead, he saw the peaceful look of satisfaction on her face, and a cold chill ran up his spine.

★   ★   ★   ★   ★   ★

The sky was a crisp blue and the air was hot. Losha ducked under a heavy cedar branch that was swathed in moss. "Are you certain you do not want to return now?" she whispered behind her, her tone taking on a note of worry. "The Shaman and the Queen will become suspicious with you gone so long." She pushed a thick cluster of ferns aside and motioned for Temple to follow.

"Losha, I need to find a place where I can think in peace." He stepped over a twisted root mindfully. "Everything's changed now. The Shaman possesses powers I know nothing about and here I am struggling to find my own. And there is you." He caught up with Losha and looked into her face. "I need to protect you."

Losha gave him a sad smile. *"This is serious business,"* she thought. *"No time for romance or the pleasures I crave from this curious man, and no time to be a burden to him either."*

Losha guided them through a shortcut of lowland forest until they reached a private lagoon thickly girdled with mangrove. Takamaka trees leaned out at sharp diagonals over the lonely beach and the delicate casuarina pine soughed in the breeze. There was a distinct smell of salt and wet rock.

Losha walked over to an old dugout that was sitting on the beach. "We can use Tani's boat,' she said, and the two climbed inside and pushed off into the clear blue surf. "It is a good day to be out on the sea." She tried to cast off the edge of tension that was mounting inside her and paddled, hoping the gentle breeze that combed the waves would clear her mind.

The boat slowed just one hundred yards from shore, water lapping against its belly. Losha threw over the anchor made of whalebone. "No one will disturb us here," she assured Temple. "The Sea Bells are a very old and sacred place which our people seldom visit anymore." She pointed down into the ocean and shielded her eyes from the glare. "Can you see them?"

Dark disjointed pillars wavered beneath the crystal waters.

"We can swim here if you like, but it is important that you touch nothing. Disturbing this ancient place is taboo." She gave Temple a curious look. "You can swim, can you not?"

'Well of course I can," he answered, feeling too foolish to tell her otherwise. "Look Losha," he spoke this time in a serious tone, knowing that he'd finally found the privacy that he needed. "We need to talk. There are things bothering me...lots of things." He looked up into the cobalt blue sky trying to form his thoughts, his doubts. "Tani's imprisonment, if you want to call it that, is happening because of me." He drew his knees up and pressed his head against them, letting the burden of some long ago commitment bear down on him hard. "Everyone seems to die when I'm around. Winyon's husband died keeping the secret that I would end the Shaman's reign. After that, there was that poor bastard who got eaten by those snakes, some islanders and guards; even that rebel whose head is stuck on a spike in front of the Queen's compound. All of them – dead." He looked into the distant horizon. "I don't blame the man for doing what he did, believing as he did. Maybe that poor sod was right. I'm just a bloody impostor."

He breathed a heavy sigh. "Losha," he appealed to her with a growing ache in his voice, "I'm beginning to think that your husband's death was my fault too." He clenched his jaw and a tear squeezed from the corner of his eye. Then his voice took on a distant tone. "Impostor," he whispered. "I'm just a man, damn it! A pretender. And I haven't the foggiest notion of how to put an end to Mefakani without violence. Right now, all I want to do is rip his bloody balls off!"

Losha moved to comfort him, but her lover did not respond. "Temple, please. Do not question why the gods have designed this so."

Temple made no move to shrug off the tender hand that was placed on his shoulder. He simply withdrew within himself. "You don't need me Losha," he quavered in a pitiful voice. "I'm poison to you. You should never have been dragged into all this." Losha moved her mouth to protest, but Temple cut her short. "I need time alone. And you need time without me. I'm going for a swim," he announced a little too abruptly.

With no time for her to respond, Temple jumped into the emerald waters feet first. The bubbles rose around him, tingling his flesh, and he felt the familiar feeling of being alone like he once did when he had plunged into the sea, when he had died. He felt a melancholy comfort in the sensation, remembering the freedom in drowning, the buoyancy of rebirth. Soon, both the bubbles and his feelings dissipated and the water cleared before him. He noticed that he could see for quite a distance. He floated with his mind suspended between thoughts.

"What have I gotten myself into? And what have I gotten Losha into as well? And what of the Priest? I know my own power is paltry compared to the Priest's, especially now that Mefakani has some sort of secret weapon that no one seems to know about. What power could be used to fight the Priest without violence? And what of Elder Tani? Is she safe while in Mefakani's keeping?" The thoughts just tumbled forth as Temple floated in the crystal clear waters.

The lonely pilot found himself surrounded by vast shoals of colorful reef fish, darting in unison this way and that, matching the patterns of his random thoughts. He swam to the bottom and hovered mindlessly over a razor fish, watching it pluck crustaceans from branches of blue coral till he ran out of air. He surfaced quickly, took a deep breath then submerged again.

He kicked hard, the best he knew how, trying to escape himself – escape his destiny, when the shadowy forms of the Sea Bells came into view. They captured his curiosity as he counted...ten, eleven, twelve rounded columns that looked nothing like any bells he had ever known. Each had varying thicknesses and heights and stood upright in a perfect circle like old sages in the sea. It was then that he noticed that the sea bottom inside the circle of bells was completely bare. *"What power could make a sea bottom so barren that not even a barnacle dare live there? Was it the power of sound? After all, these are "bells"? What secret do the Sea Bells hold? What power?"*

Ignoring Losha's warning, he picked up a good-sized rock and swam through the pillars to where the clean sandy bottom rippled with brilliant sunlight from above. He swam over to one of the columns and ran his hand over its surface. There were no barnacles, no burrs, no weathering or rust. Only the smooth feel of some blackened metal like steel. He was running out of air, but before he surfaced, he took the rock and, without thought of consequence, hit it hard against the column. A single metallic ring pulsated through the crystal waters so strong and pure he thought he was once again hearing the voice of god. The frequency vibrated against the back of his throat which made his brow tingle and his heart ache. He started to surface when, before his amazed eyes, the water around him glowed as if somehow the sound had caused the light to gather.

Pleased at the results of his experiment, he kicked swiftly towards the surface, but not before he was forced into a tumble by a sudden blow to his back, which knocked all of the remaining breath out of him. He groped for a sense of direction, until finally he floated painfully to the surface, only to swallow a mouthful of salty sea before he reached it. He sputtered and gasped as he clawed the air above him, and before he got a second breath he was hit again, this time, in the ribs. Temple detected a shrill shriek beneath the churning waves and felt sleek, smooth flesh brush against him. Suddenly, the light around him grayed, the sea grew rough and he struggled through the obscurity guessing at which way was up. A long, darker shadow passed overhead and a surge of power pushed him down again. Swarms of fins and tails filled the last of his vision.

Losha whistled to the dolphins with a maddening frenzy. Panicked, she tore off her skirt and dove into the ocean.

Temple's spirit offered no resistance, just as it did once before. It simply lifted out his body, this time floating up into the atmosphere into a black thunderhead above. He watched passively as his lover below encircled his body in her arms.

Losha kicked with all her strength until they both broke the surface of the choppy sea. She grabbed hold of the boat with one hand to steady herself and held Temple with the other, but the sea was too violent. She strained to pull herself and her burden into the boat, but she didn't have the leverage and fell back into the rugged sea, losing what progress she had gained. She tried wrestling with the waves again that the sudden wind had churned, causing the boat to pitch precariously, but could find no handhold on the gunwale.

"Spirits of the Wind! Spirits of the Sea! I honor you!" she cried out. Seconds seemed like minutes as she thrashed about, struggling to keep Temple's head above water. She summoned all her power and shouted, "Spirits, please protect us! He meant no harm! We apologize for our transgression!" She clamored for another handhold, but the boat lurched away from her again, leaving them floundering in the storm. Then, all at once, the wind calmed and the sea began to play itself out, allowing her a chance to secure her arm over the hull….and a light burst through the heavy clouds, illuminating the surface of the broken sea. Without a warning, a force pushed beneath Losha and she was lifted into the boat. She whistled back to the dolphin in gratitude and pulled Temple's limp body into the boat.

Losha wasted no time and turned his head to clear his air passages. Temple, who was hovering above in spirit, took the cue and descended swiftly into his body. To Losha's surprise, when she pressed her mouth to his, he responded with a kiss and pulled his lover down on top of him.

"You are alive!" she cried, prying herself from his arms.

"Thanks to you I am," he gasped. "You saved my life –again!"

"Bi Kana! I almost lost you! Another lover drowned, I thought! I would not have been able to face such a thing again!" She hugged him harder and he panted to catch his breath.

Temple raised himself up and sat in the bottom of the boat. "You did it, Losha!"

"Did what?" she asked, offering him the dry bits of her skirt to wipe his hair and beard.

Temple gave a congratulatory grin to his naked companion. "Your powers! You calmed the wind! I watched the whole thing from above!"

Losha sat wide-eyed in astonishment.

"It was a bloody miracle. I'm so proud of you." Temple's patronizing smile gave way to a twisted frown. "It was me who instigated this and for that I apologize," he said with a mixed measure of guilt and self-forgiveness. "You see, my love, I'm very much still just an ignorant white man who's yet to fully understand just how alive all this is." He gestured with an outstretched hand towards the emerald ocean. "To the whites, all of this is dead. Since the war, most of the land, the sea and now even the air is little more then real estate. I'd no idea how disrespectful I've been till now."

"I will not rebuke you, Temple, for you are far too hard on yourself. Still, you must thank the Guardians of the Sea Bells for teaching you. You must also thank the Spirits of the Wind and the Sea as well. I gratefully thank them, too, for I have been the poorest teacher."

"But Losha, don't you see? Without my blunder, you never would've known what power you hold?"

She gave her bearded companion a long look of understanding, then gazed up into the Father Heavens, down at the Mother Sea and at the Guardians of the Sea Bells who were swimming and leaping all around them. She said a silent prayer of deep gratitude. She turned to Temple and smiled knowingly, lovingly. "My old friend," she whispered affectionately. After the two had quieted their rattled nerves with long loving gazes at each other, they lazed together in the sun, side by side, rocking in the calm of the living sea.

CHAPTER TWENTY-FOUR

The Confrontation

"I became the feeling of my desires. I became the outcome. But first I had to learn."

Temple Fox
Makolese Scroll on Magic, Rites & Rituals #104
The Makolese Scroll on the Education of Temple Fox #24

When Mefakani saw Temple ambling through the grounds of his compound, he motioned Jabal away and strode over to the Stranger.

"Where have you been all day?" he asked in a tone indecipherable to Temple's ear.

"I was with the Interpreter. We went for a swim."

"Did you know we were to be meeting together this morning?"

"Play dumb. Act innocent." Temple thought quickly. "No, I'm sorry. I didn't. Your language is still difficult for me. I must have misunderstood." *"Head him off at the pass."* "I apologize for my tardiness. It won't happen again," he acquiesced without blinking an eye.

The Shaman strolled over to the central fire without turning to look at Temple. "You are lying," he said in an easy voice.

"Seeing me with Losha is one thing, but if he knows I've been to see Winyon, I'm cooked. Don't act nervous." "I'm not lying," Temple

said aloud.

"One can lie by omission." The Shaman paused then turned. "Temple, there is a matter I wish to discuss with you."

"He knows. He must. I'm dead! I've got to stop my hands from shaking." The words were screaming inside Temple's head.

"I talk to you as my own Master spoke to me," he offered in a more fatherly tone. "It is about women."

"Bloody hell fire!"

"Women can be contemptible creatures who can charm and conjure with their sex."

"He knows about Losha and I! Oh, shit!"

"It is nothing I would ever want to remove from the female, if I were able to rearrange their Ka so. Even so, it is something that I strongly feel needs to be controlled, you understand, for the good of the people," he maintained.

"Well, that's a contradiction for a start," Temple thought.

"Without their enticements, there would be no Su for our people. Just the same, they can manipulate and destroy a man, particularly when the man is also a god."

"Be forthright. Be calm." "You're speaking of Losha. Am I right?"

"Yes. You have been seen with her."

"But what else has been seen? Has anything been overheard?" Temple balled his fists together to cease their trembling. *"You were Gadji long ago. Show him your stuff. Don't let him push you around."*

Temple looked directly into the Priest's eyes. "I don't care, Mefakani. This is not base lust I feel for her, but a deep love and caring. I don't see anything wrong in what I do, and besides it's really none of your bloody business," he argued, surprised at his cutting tone and his newly found courage, foolish as it may have been.

The tone didn't settle well with Mefakani, however. His patience started to give way to unbridled anger, too long suppressed by his own enforced standards of self-composure. As always, he paused, took a deep breath and reined his temper back. His words came out controlled, rational, disciplined.

"She has corrupted you," he stated curtly. "You know, Temple, you are only still a boy. In a short while, you will understand that the more you waste your precious, vital energies on passion with the female, the more your reasoning powers will diminish! This girl is now your master! And you, a hostage to the powers of her sex." Mefakani started to lose his temper again and shook his staff in the air between them. "Why else do you think I put you through that ritual in the glade? It was so you could learn discipline over your desires. You have lost your mastery over that, and your reasoning has been stolen from you!"

"I can control my desires. I have a choice to act upon them or not. And I have chosen Losha."

The Shaman's tone was chiding. "You do not know what you are talking about. You are still just a fledgling."

"Have I or have I not been asked to teach the people?" Temple pushed ahead. "I can teach by example. And, yes, I've broken the law about shaman taking a vow of celibacy. Furthermore, when I have the power to, I'll change this stupid law." Temple looked into the Priest's eyes to see what response he could draw from them, knowing that the Shaman had, at one time, planned to do the same.

An image of the Hummingbird in her youth formed in Mefakani's mind. His temperature rose. "You think you are so wise and powerful now that you can dictate to me! You may yet remember your full, godly powers, but now you are nothing more than an arrogant child!"

"Love, Mefakani. Love is the power; the greatest force. And, I'm finding my own power through loving a woman. She's not my master, but helps to empower me, for the woman I love is as divine as you, or I, or your Lord Tagheetu. All women are spirit clothed in flesh. Surely you know this?" he said the latter in a taunting tone, as daring as thrusting a pointed finger into the Shaman's face. After all, he was, in a sense, still Gadji.

"Blasphemy! You speak blasphemy, you ignorant...!"

"What? Ignorant god? It's you who says I'm a god. Mefakani, I know who I am and why I'm here. My greatest desire is to help you and your people." Seeing the Priest seethe in anger he softened his voice and searched for compromise. "That's not to say that I don't believe there's some truth in what you've just told me. I know that either sex can enslave the other. With Losha, it's different. I promise you that."

Mefakani scrutinized the Stranger through narrowed eyes, calming his heartbeat with the power of his will. He pointed his new staff at Temple. "You are as belligerent and argumentative as I was when I was Tagon's Apprentice," he declared finally with exasperation.

Temple noticing the new staff for the first time and, feeling an unfamiliar emanation radiating off it, had to muster a bit more of his courage. He got right to the point. "Mefakani there are many things I feel strongly about. Women aren't my enemy. And, Tani's not my enemy either. I'd like to know she's being treated fairly and I'd like to see her," he demanded.

Mefakani was thrown by the question. "She is making amends for her crimes and sees no one."

"What have you done with her?"

The Priest walked into the shadow of the giant cedar so he could see his student better. "Tani has taken a vow of silence and remains in isolation."

"I don't believe you."

Mefakani's hazel eyes shone sharply. "Why this sudden suspicion?"

Temple sat on a log next to the fire. "It's simple, Mefakani. I find that your concern for your own people is...well, how should I put this? Selective." He was seized by a moment of sudden doubt, thinking he had overstepped his boundaries, but the words rolled out anyway. He didn't like the Priest staring down at him, so he rose to his feet and looked the shaman in the eye. "I think you loathe women. Well, I'm here for your people; *all* of your people," he said, renewing his confidence as he spoke.

"He is being noble and proud," Mefakani thought.

"How heroic of you!" The Priest said in a mocking tone. "A child teacher." His voice softened in volume, and timbre. He sat down on a log and pointed his new staff at the fire. Flames shot up another five feet in the air, causing the Initiate to back away. "Temple, you mistake my concern for you, and your lack of good judgment, as being somehow prejudicial against the female."

"That's right," Temple said, somewhat distracted by the show of magic.

"I must stall Temple's efforts."

"I have not imprisoned Elder Tani or harmed her in anyway. In fact, she is free to roam the compound. She chooses, however, to spend most her days in my private garden in quiet meditation. If I allowed you to see her I would have to lengthen her stay as recompense."

Temple stood waiting, not knowing what to say and wondering if he could push the issue any farther.

"Tani is fully aware of her errors. She has made amends by giving several, private offerings to our Lord already. She has made no attempt at anything public, however, for the female, as you will no doubt realize someday, is most stubborn. Who knows, perhaps this quiet time suits her in her old age and she will decide to spend her remaining years here in servitude and quiet contemplation." The idea ignited Mefakani. He raised an eyebrow as if to say, *"In fact, that is exactly what she will decide, and no one need see her again."*

The Shaman rose to his feet again. "Temple," he continued aloud, "respect the female, but never trust her. Break off your relations with the Interpreter now, before your reason flies from you altogether and becomes irretrievable. Your power," he said with a well positioned hand on Temple's shoulder, "Think about your power and the good you can do with it."

A chill ran through Temple's shoulder down into the pit of his stomach, scattering his remaining confidence like dust. He wanted to recoil, but stood steady, knowing he must play the game well or become suspect.

"All right," he gave in, breathing a heavy sigh of defeat. "I'll do as you advise for now."

Mefakani measured his pupil's sincerity with a long probing look. "Good," he said, satisfied at what he sensed in the young man. *The gods have sent a reasonable man.* "Come," he said aloud with a wave of his hand. "I will show you something."

The two walked through the quiet compound, passing the small hut that the Shaman had order to be constructed for the Stranger. It was complete now, but had no occupant, which was something Mefakani still hoped for in time. Jabal stood next to the hut at a campfire, peeling roots and plopping them noisily into a bubbling pot of water. As they passed, the Apprentice shot an icy stare in their direction.

The Priest turned to Temple. "Pay no attention to that sniveling child over there," Mefakani said loudly so Jabal could hear him. "You see the energy field around him? It is green with jealousy." Mefakani let out a short, cruel laugh.

Temple saw a strong glow around Jabal, but could detect no color.

"It is a good test for him," the Shaman said in a muffled aside. "My present duties force too much responsibility on him lately and he longs for my attention. Although the magic I have taught him has been growing stronger within him, I have given him menial tasks this week. Hopefully, his temperament will match his powers someday. Still," he said, trying to rouse a response from his new Initiate, "he is a good deal more advanced than you."

Temple didn't rise to the bait. He was too occupied on focusing his unfocused eyes on Jabal, until he was able to see the murky, green glow around him.

"Come," called the Priest. He led the way behind his own lodge and gestured towards the entrance to a cave situated inside a tiny hillside made of black rock.

Temple ducked his head and found himself in a cramped shelter with two dark passages leading off to either side.

"Tiv!" the Priest called out and his voice echoed.

The boy with the deep scar on top of his shaven head appeared from around one of the dark tunnels. He handed Temple a stick of knotty pine so his Master could light it with the power from his new staff. Once lit, the three coursed their way through a cool underground passageway, until they dead-ended into a pitted wall of black volcanic rock. The Shaman placed his hand on the edge of a fault in the stone and pushed. A large crevice appeared and a monolithic stone pivoted noiselessly on its hidden axis. The torch flickered and dimmed when a chilly breeze escaped from the enclosure.

"My important work is done here," the Priest explained, and he motioned for his pupil to enter first.

Temple remained guarded. *"I hope this isn't a trap, or some test."*

He squeezed through the narrow doorway into the dark, dank chill. The cavern was barely visible, yet he could detect a subtle, natural light coming from above, from what appeared to be an air vent.

Tiv lit some oil pots and slowly the deep cavern came alive with the grotesque shapes of onyx stalactites and stalagmites, taking on a glow of their own. In the half light, Temple made out a stone slab, waist high, used as a table, he imagined, and next to it, a primitive still sitting on another bench of stone, and a kind of wine rack where scrolls were stored. He took careful note that several power shields were stacked in the corner in various stages of assembly or disassembly.

Within a deep shadow, in another chamber to the far side, Temple spied a large glistening block of lumpy rock that took on the shape of a high backed chair of some kind, formed, no doubt, from centuries of the dripping and evaporation of water and minerals. Behind this, he could barely make out a deep, horizontal niche carved from an outcrop of rock. A thin stream of water coursing through a narrow gulch in the stone had been diverted and flowed into the stone basin. The earthy smell of herbs and roots, salt and alcohol filled his nostrils. As the light grew brighter, Temple detected hints of torchlight glimmered off row upon row of vials made from onyx and obsidian on sturdy wooden shelves. He looked to Tiv for an explanation of what he was seeing and the boy pointed to the tiny scar on his own chest.

"The Ka, of course," Temple thought. *"That's where the Shaman stores them."*

Mefakani saw Temple eye the enclosure and barked at his servant. Quickly, the boy pulled a curtain across the dark alcove.

"Careless boy!" the Priest grumbled, and he raised a hand to strike the boy, but the boy cowered and distanced himself from his Master. He lowered his hand and sighed. *"I must show restraint. Besides, Temple saw nothing."*

The Priest strode into the lamplight and picked up one of the wheel-like power shields, then called his servant over. He handed the shield to Tiv. "Temple. Come, I will show you how this works."

Tiv positioned himself behind the metal frame and winced.

"Watch." Mefakani picked up a pebble and lobbed it at his assistant. Tiv's face creased with painful concentration, but the pebble fell through the shield frame and hit the boy on the thigh.

"Now watch again." The Priest positioned himself behind the shield and motioned for Tiv to throw a heavy rock at him. This time the rock magically bounced off the air in front of the shield.

"It is the crystal sphere from the Spirits of the Mountain that amplifies the will of anyone who uses one of these shields," the Shaman explained. "I ask you, Temple Fox, what is the power source for these?"

The Initiate scratched his beard in thought. *"He wants me to say it's the crystal ball."*

"Well, the mind; the will is, I suppose," Temple answered.

"No," the Shaman countered. "It is *emotions*. Emotions fuel the imagination of our thoughts. The mind or thought merely directs the energy. Merged together they can create intense, focused feelings, which set the outcome."

"I don't understand. Aren't emotions and feelings one in the same?" Temple asked.

"No," the Shaman said. "In this case, raw fear, which is the desire to protect oneself, becomes the force that drives our imagination to the outcome, the outcome being protection."

"But…." the Initiate began then fell into an uneasy silence.

"Whoever tries to protect his life with raw fear, will lose it," Temple wanted to say. *"With so much negative attention placed on protecting one's life, wouldn't one be creating circumstances that would, in fact, put one's life in jeopardy? And wasn't that the reason why so many of the more ruthless Outsiders had been attracted to the shores of Makol? The people were sabotaging themselves."*

"Are you listening?" the Shaman asked annoyed. The Initiate nodded his head and the Priest walked over to another shield and held it up in front of him. He motioned for Tiv to stand behind him.

"Behind you," the Shaman said to Temple, "is a device retrieved from the Portuguese barbarians. Get it!"

Resting against the wall was a rifle.

Temple drew back with hesitation. *"Now is my chance to blow the Priest to Kingdom come, if I want to. Unless this is a test – a trick? Maybe the Priest wants to see if I'm an impostor."*

"Take the fire stick," he ordered. "Aim it at me, and press that curved mechanism."

Temple picked up the rifle and ran his hand along the cold, smooth barrel. He raised it to his eye slowly, reluctantly. His heart started to pound and his arms began to tremble. In his mind, he saw the lion all over again, bounding over the dusty, African plain.

"Do it!" A voice shouted inside his head. *"Trust!"*

"Do it!" the Priest commanded, echoing the voice inside Temple's head.

"But...." *"There's to be no violence!"*

"Do it! Now!" the voices demanded.

Temple shut his eyes, trusting the two voices, but not knowing why, and squeezed the trigger. There was an explosion of sound, which thundered throughout the cavern. Overlaid in this was a whizzing sound as the bullet bounced off the force in front of the shield and ricocheted off a stalagmite, until it impaled itself inside the wall of soft rock opposite the Priest.

Temple unfolded from a crouch on the floor. "You could've killed me!"

"And you could have killed me," the Shaman replied coolly, "if my feelings and my will had not been strong enough. But my feelings and will are strong, you see; so strong that I do not even need such a shield. I have invented these, however, for those who do not have my power."

"Well, you should have, at least, warned me!"

"Do you not trust me?" he snorted. "All warriors, Temple, are not only taught to protect themselves, but to angle their shields so the pellets from the fire sticks ricochet off and strike their enemy. They do this by imagining or feeling they have already struck their enemy. They do this even before the pellet has been deflected. You see, Temple, the best warriors do what I have just demonstrated as their final test of courage. Only, they do it in a great ceremony with seasoned warriors volleying the ricochet back and forth, aiming it at the new warrior, who is continually fired upon. Now you know why our elite army has been so small." Mefakani offered the shield to Temple. "Would you care to try a round?"

"No, thanks. I don't think I'm ready for that yet."

"Ahh, so the young god does admit there are things yet to learn?"

Temple couldn't argue. He had been shown up.

"From now on, I want you to practice with a power shield with the new recruits at the Queen's compound. It will strengthen your body and mind. You will learn to focus until you, unlike my warriors, will be able to volley a pellet with a mere flick of a hand. Believe me, Temple, after I teach you, and you come into your power, we will be able to defeat the Outsiders. It is written in the prophecies."

CHAPTER TWENTY-FIVE

The Player and the Played

*"I was a patriot with a just and moral cause. I saw
the larger picture, and saw myself through the eyes
of history. I would be a hero. There would be
songs sung about me, a festival in my honor and
my name written in the History Scrolls.
I was eighteen."*

Jabal, the High Shaman Mefakani's First Apprentice
The Makolese Scroll on the Education of Temple Fox #25

Sahdon sat bent over a low table in the middle of his lodge, his withered leg twisted awkwardly and painfully beneath him, the dying fire from an oil jar crackled by his side. He was so absorbed in studying a copy of the Queen's latest laws that he never noticed the rhythmic scratching sound behind him. It wasn't until the hairs bristled on the back of his neck that the startled statesman lifted his head. A tiny circular blur on the floor grew higher into a swirling plume of red smoke. Out of the funnel of obscurity and sparks, a dark form stepped up behind him from the shadows.

The Elder spun his head around and clutched his chest. "Bi Kana, you gave me a start!" He gave a little nod and one of his political smiles. "Greetings to you, Jabal."

"And to you, Senior Elder," Jabal bowed low.

Sahdon peered out the window mindfully, but the eyes of his guard were cast only on the reflection of the moon in the quiet bay. "Since all of your visits always bear such valuable information, tell me what important news you have for me this evening?"

"Bad news, I am afraid," the Informer confessed.

"Oh?" Sahdon gestured for the boy to sit away from prying eyes in the darkest corner of the room.

"I do not understand what is going on," Jabal began. "Without Queen Palomei's consent, the Shaman has bid me to kidnap one of the key Unbelievers and bring him to his underground cavern tonight."

"For what purpose?"

"I do not know, Elder."

Sahdon frowned disapprovingly. "You must tell me boy. Our plans for killing the Stranger may be at stake."

"My Master denies me access to his private cavern. He only allows the mute, Tiv, to assist him. I think he is using magic he stole from the Mountain Spirits. It is only a guess."

"No hostages will sway us from our purpose. Surely he knows that. And to question one of us without the Queen's knowledge, perhaps even killing one of us, would be foolish for him. It would only instigate more violence among the Unbelievers in the villages."

"I do not think that is his plan. I heard him say that whoever I brought him would be returned before dawn." Jabal tensed as he leaned forward and touched the tiny scar in the middle of his chest. "It was a command. I can not return to the Shaman's compound tonight without bringing back one of our lead conspirators."

Sahdon's eyes narrowed on the boy. "And this will be done in one of his secret chambers, you say?" The boy nodded. Sahdon got up painfully and paced the floor with a heavy limp, his one hand held behind him and the other bearing his weight on his cane. He ran his hand through his wavy, gray hair, thoughtfully, then bent as far as his pain would allow, pouring himself a cup of hot sha from the simmering pot in the center of the room. He breathed in the steam and, after a measured moment, he took a sip, then turned to face the Informer. "Does the secret weapon he has been developing, the air boat, as you call it, have anything to do with this, you think?"

"The air boat is almost complete now," Jabal said, "but I do not know if it is related to what he is doing now. All I know is that he plans to send the Stranger inside the mountain to steal more crystals so we can build a fleet."

Sahdon rubbed his brow as if he suddenly had a headache. "Have you been able to exercise any influence over your Master yet, Jabal?"

"He burdens me with women's work so that I hardly ever see him, but I have tried," he stated. "I am not altogether sure he remains steadfast in his false beliefs any longer. After the exorcism, I sensed doubt about him. Still, in the end he blamed Tani for corrupting his pupil."

"Yes, I have heard the charges brought against her and it has fit well into our plans. Without her influence over Temple's education, there is a chance our Shaman will learn it is the Stranger himself who is corrupt and bends the natural laws. If that is true, then Temple Fox and Mefakani will come to blows soon enough."

"Respected Elder, I must inform you that just today we had a breeze of good hope blow our way, which might rekindle the doubt within my Master. I spied on the Wizard this morning. He has broken the sacred vow of celibacy with the Interpreter. I told the Shaman, and heard him quarrel with Temple, and yet..." he hesitated, "I fear he creates too many excuses for the Impostor. He might only blame the woman for Temple's weakness. I do not know what it will take to make him see the truth."

"You have done well, Jabal. I will count on you to drive a deeper wedge between Mefakani and the Stranger. Still..." he paced again unsteadily, "we have little time to wait for our High Shaman to see the light of truth. I had hoped, with perhaps an unreasonable measure of optimism, that this would have already occurred, and that both you and the Shaman would have joined forces by now." He paused, the full weight of his gaze bearing down on the young Apprentice. "Now, there is only you."

The boy stared back wide-eyed and listened obediently.

The Elder lowered his voice in confessional affectation. "I am worried, Jabal. The assassination attempts have failed, and the Stranger gains powers we are uncertain how to handle. I am afraid this business about teaching the Wizard has gotten out of hand. It seems no one remembers that the prophecy states that even the elite can be fooled by false prophets. The Stranger should have been killed long ago. Our High Shaman should have been preparing the army, going inside the mountain himself to steal the crystals, not this..." He gestured with his arms outstretched then let them fall with the silence. "It is blasphemy!" he whispered.

In the moment after the tense silence, the Elder did something uncharacteristic of himself. He eased himself down on his good knee onto the mat in front of the boy, a most humbling, yet calculated gesture. He clasped his hands on the head of his cane for balance and spoke softly, directly. "I realize it hurts you, Jabal, to know that your Master; our own respected Priest, can not see the truth in this matter. He is a most courageous and powerful man, but…" he peered into the boy's eyes with contrived candor, "he has failed us."

The Apprentice moved uncomfortably on the mat and lowered his eyes.

"You and I know, deep inside our hearts, that your Master lacks the wisdom and insight one would expect from a High Shaman." Sahdon forced Jabal's eyes to lift and to look squarely into his own. "You, Jabal possess the kind of intelligence that carries wisdom and insight, and you, Jabal, will someday be the next High Shaman. It is you we turn to for help now."

The Apprentice stared back, feeling a mixture of grief and a surge of righteous anger building within him. *"It was true,"* Jabal thought. *"I have waited too long for my Master's muddled thinking to clear. Shaman Mefakani has sold himself to The Beast in man-form, and coddles The Beast like a child. I do not know how to kill the Impostor…not yet, but I know it is time my Master was stopped before the white Wizard gains more power."*

Jabal inflated with righteous anger. *"It is time to claim my place as High Shaman!"* He shouted within himself. *"With the Lord's divine help, I will set the task of destroying the Wizard myself, before it is too late!"*

Sahdon sensed his words were working on the boy. "All of us are helpless, Jabal, for none of us can conjure. Your Master does not yet know about your ability to spin, and does not know how powerful your own magic has become. I pray that you will help us. Is it possible for you to learn what it is your Master will be doing in this hidden cavern you speak of?"

The boy was far ahead of Sahdon's plan. "I can change myself into a chameleon and hide within the chamber tonight," he avowed with sound confidence.

"Then see to it that Gabu is taken."

"Gabu?"

"Yes, he will be the easiest to capture. When last I saw him an hour ago, his belly was full of sha and he was stumbling on the beach heading towards his lodge on Snapper Creek. Jabal… observe what your Master does with him. Learn all you can of your Master's secrets and I will deal with Gabu myself when you return him. I will find out if he has made any deals with the Shaman or has been enticed to spy on us."

"I will not let you or the people down, My Respected Elder."

The Informer stood up and gave a sharp bow, then took a step from the dark corner. There he sang his invocation and spun, filling the air with a crackling static.

When Sahdon's eyes readjusted to the darkness of the room, he spied a red spotted gecko scurrying out the window. He lifted himself off the mat and took a sip from his cup of warm wine. With a smile of satisfaction, he held his cup up to toast the new alliance he had just forged with Makol's future Shaman.

CHAPTER TWENTY-SIX

Smoke and Blood

*"Details of this controversial scroll have been
purposely eliminated so those who are attracted to
the Dark will not be tempted into cruelty, and so
that those who have a leaning toward the Dark will
not accrue any Karmic debts, which may lead them
into a life where they, too, are victimized and
enslaved, be it in their present incarnation
or the next."*

Losha Ninti
Makolese Scroll on Magic, Rites and Rituals #105
The Makolese Scroll on the education of Temple Fox #26

Temple ached to steal himself away from the Queen's compound so he could tell Losha all that he had learned, especially his plans to sneak inside the underground chamber that night to find Mefakani's hidden weapon. Until he could fly to his lover's arms again he chose to use his time wisely and exercise the strictest discipline with the power shields.

When the precocious pilot repelled his first rock he heard a joyous shout in the distance. Palomei's giant form stepped from the shadows of the inner courtyard gate. She bowed to the Stranger.

"Beginners luck!" he yelled to the Queen, then returned the bow.

He trotted over to her and, after exchanging a few pleasantries, strode off to the guest hut alone, knowing that the renewed confidence he was feeling from this latest victory mustn't lull him into a false sense of security. Mefakani was a murderer, a corrupter of the true spiritual laws. All he could think about was how he was going to stop him. And yet, in spite of all his worries, the marooned pilot sat down to a meal of raw sea urchin, pretending with all his heart that it was a hot buttered scone shared with Losha by his side.

★　　★　　★　　★　　★　　★

The heavy scent of burning herbs found its way up through the air vent of the underground chamber nearly choking the Owl-man. Temple shook right down to his hollow bone, thinking all that he had just witnessed below him in the smoky chamber had affected his nervous system. The nerve in his eye twitched again until he realized that he was catching a jerky movement out of the corner of his eye. With talons clasping the rough rock, he poked his head down through the hole and twisted his feathery head around just in time to spy a tiny chameleon scurrying through the smoke to a shallow ledge on the cavern wall. The creature camouflaged its skin and blended into its rock surroundings. Temple's gizzard growled annoyingly, but the thought of food only made him feel sicker after what he had just witnessed.

Elder Gabu was still strapped to the tablet of stone with the dark Priest and the young mute bent over him.

"Listen, boy. If this last experiment works, then all of the suffering I put you through would have been for the greater good."

Tiv touched the scar in the center of his chest and blinked back innocently.

"Watch his pulse," he said, blotting the bit of blood that stained his lips. He leaned closer to his captive. "Can you hear me, Gabu?"

The Elder rolled his head to and fro, but was unable to reckon where he was.

Mefakani stepped back for a thoughtful moment. "Ahhh, I feel it working." He walked over to the hidden alcove and threw back the curtain. He settled back in the throne-like chair made from dripstone. After several minutes a sour smirk spread across his face. "Despicable creature. Jabal should have been more selective. Brings me a drunk. Meat-faced glutton." He patted himself on the stomach. "Absorbing all his foul desires makes me thirsty. Tiv, make me some hot sha," he ordered.

Tiv lit a small fire on the floor below the air vent where Temple was hidden. He pulled out a large gourd of wine from a dusty corner and quickly warmed it on the cauldron over the fire.

Mefakani downed his first cup of sha in one gulp and held his hand out for a refill.

"Bi Kana, it is working! I possess Gabu's every thought and emotion, boy. I can feel it through my veins. Now I own his power, what little there is of it, poor slug." He drew the cup to his lips then paused puzzled. "But what is this I see in his memory? Secret meetings with Sahdon and other Unbelievers. The fools. Did they think I would not find out?" He leaned back examining the pictures that ran through his head, then swilled his sha and licked his lips. "Another cup, boy!"

Tiv rushed over with more brew and cast a worried look towards his Master.

The Priest closed his eyes as if listening to a distant conversation. "They speak of an informer who spies from within," he grunted. "A male. But Gabu, poor worm, did not know who he was." His face tightened in concentration when all of a sudden he let out a long groan. "Bi Kana! Another plot to kill Temple Fox...and with some of our own soldiers as traitors!"

Both Jabal and Temple stifled their choked cries as they clutched onto their ledges of cold stone.

The dark Priest leaned back and snorted, then downed his cup of brew. "I will weed these warriors out soon enough and add them to my new army." He laughed, then belched and called for more sha. Tiv hurried to his side.

Mefakani took another swallow and the wine dribbled down his chin. "I see Sahdon and his rabble discovered not even swords can wound this young man-god. Damn fools! You cannot kill a god! Only I possess the power to deal with Temple. Me!" he shouted, spilling a little of his drink. "When I finish with him he will be like a plump shiny plum. And then...when he is just ripe... just ripe, I will take his Ka, and his power, for my own!"

Temple's claws froze on his rock perch, his wide eyes transfixed.

"Then I will send this shell of a god to those godless creatures in the mountain! You hear me, boy?" he slobbered then tottered from his dripstone throne. "With all that power and no one to stand in my way I will sssoon..." he slurred, "turn my people into elite assassins for our blessed Lord."   Mefakani staggered. "They will only obey one force...and that is the mighty Lord's God-Priest – God of Law & Order! And then, Tiv," he bent to dip his cup into the wine cauldron,

"I will take the Chosen People beyond the Barik Limits to cleanssse the outside world!"

The lizard lost his camouflage and turned a brilliant yellow as he shuddered on his stony ledge. Temple, still hidden, held his breath.

Mefakani's head reeled and he swaggered over to the stone basin where Tani's body lay. He draped his drunken body over it and spat. "Ta damn with you, old woman!" he said with a string a drool clinging to his lip. "Curse yer kind! You'll never boss me 'gen. Never!" His head dropped. "No Hummingbird," he whimpered and swooned. "Tender arms, cold heart. Soulless females! Thieves!" he shouted. "Ne-ver!"

Temple watched the little ripples subside inside the basin. With his uncanny vision, he was struck dumb when he suddenly spotted his old friend bobbing lifeless below.

"Foul," the Priest whispered when his vision blurred and his stomach turned over. He wobbled over to Gabu and leaned into his face. "Are you shtill alive? You will not remember any of this." Mefakani swayed back a step and dropped his cup. "Should put you out of your misery, you ssspineless...." But before he could finish, Tiv grabbed hold of his Master's shoulder and led him back into his chair.

Mefakani sat groaning for over an hour, trying to stop the chamber from spinning through his head. "I do not wish to hold your power any longer, Gabu, for it putrefies me, and yet now it is mine forever." The dark Priest held his aching head and peered from under his hand. "Tiv, unbind our guest. It is time I finished and sealed him." The Priest rose unsteadily from his chair as Tiv unlocked Gabu's arms and legs from their metal bindings.

"Do you know your name?" he asked as he made his way over to the Elder.

"Gabu. I am Gabu Kestrel from Snapper Creek," the captive answered in a hollow tone. The Elder's mind was dulled and unable to make out the shapes in the room or where the voice was coming from. He pulled his hands free from his restraints and felt the hard, stone table beneath his numb hands, trying to feel something cold, something real.

"Good. Now listen, Gabu." He leaned closer into the old man's face, his voice smooth and monotone. "You will remember none of this. You understand? You will forget you were ever brought here. You will, however, remember everything that Sahdon and any Unbelievers say. You will report back to me when I call you. Do you understand?" Gabu nodded. "Good. We have an understanding, you and I. My bewildered Elder," he said with a gallows' smile, "do not worry, for I have left you enough of your Ka so that you may live out your life in blissful unawareness. You see, it is a great gift I give you. The mind will sleep and you will no longer have to grapple with the more difficult decisions in life. Those you leave to me, your Master. Are you feeling any pain?"

The Elder didn't answer. He wasn't sure if he could feel anything.

"I will heal this incision for you, but if anyone should ask what it is, you tell them you had too much to drink, and stumbled and cut yourself. Understood?"

Gabu nodded slowly in what felt like syrupy time.

"Now, there is one more thing I must do to complete you." His tone became accusing. "You have been disobedient. You, and Cranik, and Sahdon and the rest. You must learn respect for our Lord. He loves you. He knows what is best, Gabu. You must give yourself wholly to Him. Since He and I are one in Spirit, I am your Master now. Surrender your fears to me and join me in the old Mal-Sudaik rite." Mefakani forced the Elder to drink a dark, sticky, sweet liquid from a nearby bowl.

"It is a sacred trust we establish here between us. I have your thoughts already, Elder. Now I must bind you to me forever. Roll over, Elder. I will seal you now."

When Gabu rolled over on his fat belly without protest, Tiv darted into the nearest corner to hide. The Priest lit another bowl of herbs and put on his heavy, crocodile skin to invoke the powers of Lord Tagheetu.

"You will be like an innocent babe again, Gabu. And, I will be your father, your Master," said the Crocodile Priest. "I will love you as my Master loved me, as the Lord loves you now; and once sealed, you will love me as your protector, your shield." Mefakani reached out and slipped Gabu's loincloth down around his knees. "I will anoint you now," he said in a gray tone. The dark Priest pulled the stopper out of an oil jar and spilt a little of its contents into his thirsty palms, then ordered Gabu to spread his legs. The drugged Elder responded with a whimper as Mefakani gently massaged the oil into the pucker of his anus.

The Priest's voice rose above the smoke, his trance deepening. "Sweet child, I do this for you, for the Lord loves you. Your father loves you." His well-greased palm slid up under his own barkcloth, under his Priestly garb, and gently stroked his own penis until it was slippery and hard. He spoke his invocation with a smoky voice. "Anointed, we are, with the semen of our Lord Tagheetu. Blessed, we are, by His sacred seed. Untainted, we are, by the female, for we are the Race of Men. Pure, we are, in His sacred sight. And obedient, we are, so we may serve Him." The Crocodile Priest climbed on top of the cold, stone slab and crouched on all fours over the Elder, allowing his power to rise into his loins. Then he committed the unspeakable act that caused Temple to lose his dinner on the chamber floor below him.

Still panting, Mefakani released his clutch on the Elder and his mind slipped out of a deeper darkness, back to the surface of the world. The old man lay splayed helplessly with his Master's semen glistening on his thighs.

"The Covenant is sealed," he declared. "You belong to the Lord now." He noticed the Elder was silent and motionless. "Gabu," he called out, but the Elder didn't answer. "Boy!" he called to the corner. "He has passed out. Rouse him and clean him up, then go and fetch Jabal. I will have him take Gabu back, but not before he gets a harsh reprimand."

★　★　★　★　★　★

Jabal, having escaped when Tiv swiveled the rock chamber door open, retreated into one of the distant tunnels. He made a quick transformation and stood in stunned silence, the damp, rough stone pressed against his bare backbone. It was then that he started to shake uncontrollably and a wave of nausea overtook him.

"My Lord! The Shaman is mad! He possesses a power more dangerous than any power Temple Fox could ever have! By the Lord Tagheetu and his Legion of Spirits, what am I to do? If he steals the entire Ka of the white Wizard, his power will multiply!" The thoughts were screaming inside of Jabal's head. *"But Bi Kana! My Master is already corrupted by his own power now! Look what he has done to the Elder and poor Tiv! Experimented on them like caged rats! If my Master finds out I am the informer he will surely do the same to me! My Holy Lord Tagheetu, what will become of me? What will become of any of us? In his hands he holds the power to enslave us all!"*

Jabal heard the echoes of shuffling footsteps and pulled his shoulders straight. Tiv came sliding around the corner. He gestured for the Apprentice to follow, but Jabal, still shaking, grabbed his arm. Tiv pulled away and held his arm up in defense.

"I am not going to hit you," Jabal whispered, and the slow thinking boy stood there half guarded. *"It could have been me,"* Jabal thought. "I am sorry," he cried, "so, so sorry."

Tiv stared back. Although the light of understanding was absent from his eyes, Tiv saw the torment in the Apprentice's eyes and gently patted Jabal on the shoulders in sympathy.

Jabal stood quite still – equally as silent as the mute, stunned by the compassionate gesture. A deep shame suddenly darkened his soul for how he had treated the Shaman's former Apprentice. He let out a deep sigh to release the pain, but his whole being was still laced with grief. He placed his hand on Tiv's shoulder like Tiv had done to him. He stared at the former Apprentice with what felt like an eternity. Finally, he drew back his tears and wiped his eyes, knowing he had to face the inevitable task ahead. "Come on. I will take Gabu back now."

CHAPTER TWENTY-SEVEN

The Little Brother

"The Elders say, 'to know the forest you must get lost in it many times.' Were it not for my new friends, I would still be roaming the forest of my life."

Jabal, the Shaman's First Apprentice
The Makolese Scroll on the Education of Temple Fox #27

Jabal waited just out of sight of Sahdon's lodge with the drugged Elder by his side. He hid his face beneath his barkcloth cloak when he saw a dark shrouded figure approach him.

"I will take him from here," a voice insisted. "Elder Sahdon is waiting for you inside." The Apprentice watched the figure grab hold of Gabu's elbow and lead him into the dark of the forest until they disappeared.

Jabal stood anchored to the ground. The images of what he had just witnessed seared into his memory – the smoke, the blood, the perverse ritual.

"Poor Gabu. Poor Tiv," he thought. Nausea over took him and he began to sweat and shake again. *"What can I say to Elder Sahdon? That our High Shaman is a madman worse than the Wizard? That I have no power to deal with my Master, let alone Temple Fox? That I*

do not want to be a Shaman? That I am scared?"

Jabal stepped back into the cover of jungle and sat on a damp log, feeling sick, alone and more confused than ever. *"The past few weeks my Master has talked as though Temple were the real Teacher, even in spite of the latest argument between those two, even tonight with too much sha loosening all his inhibitions. Could I have been wrong all this time? If Temple were the real Teacher, might he have come like the prophecy said, to destroy the enemies of the people, meaning the Priest was the enemy? Bi Kana, perhaps Temple is no impostor after all!*

"By the Lord Tagheetu, I am in trouble deeper than I ever imagined!" In total despair, he dropped his head into his hands and began to weep.

In the distance, Jabal heard the door to Sahdon's lodge open and the murmur of voices. His fellow conspirators would be waiting for him. Jabal wiped his eyes with a dirty hand and stared into the darkness.

"How can I be certain that this Temple is not an impostor? Where has all my insight gone? And where is my magic now? Vanished into the night?" Sensing his distress, a tiny skink leapt from a nearby tree on top of the boy's shoulder, giving Jabal a short start. The tiny creature nuzzled his cheek and Jabal pulled it off and cupped it carefully in his hands. "I feel as small as you, little brother. What power do we have now, eh?"

The lizard slid its head out from between Jabal's thumb and forefinger, and forced its way out of his grip. It jumped down and slithered onto the moonlit path. The skink performed a series of little push-ups then turned to look up at Jabal. The Apprentice stooped to pick the lizard up, but it scurried off a few paces, and then stopped, waiting for the boy to catch up.

"You want me to follow?" he asked puzzled.

The lizard moved in a jerky kind of circle then hurried down the brightened path. Jabal followed blindly for about two hundred yards down to a shoulder of beach. He stood at the water's edge and listened to the sea breathe, the air ripening with expectation. A silver light stirred in the waters as something surged below the surf. Jabal waited breathlessly as several dark forms cut the moonlight and fins broke the surface. In the bay, a school of dolphins whistled their welcome.

Jabal threw off his cloak and walked into the shallows, the warm surf pulling at his ankles. He whistled back and walked further into the water. The school surrounded him and in the darkness he could feel their warm skin glide gently under his outstretched hand. He stroked them with awe, unaware that his problems had momentarily melted away. Deeper and deeper, they coaxed the boy into the surf, until one of the largest Guardians swam under him, catching him off balance. Jabal grabbed hold of the dolphin's fin and, under the moonlit and starry sky, the school escorted the boy to the far off island exile.

CHAPTER TWENTY-EIGHT

The Snake

*"Had I the power, I would have killed the
Priest myself!"*

Losha Ninti
The Makolese Scroll on the Education of Temple Fox #28

On the main island of Makol, thunderheads hugged the sacred
mountain, smothering the predawn light. And, in the eerie stillness of a
remote ravine, where Snapper Creek ran through only an hour before,
the dry, polished, creek stone thirsted for the sound of water; and the
land beneath the dry bed shifted slightly. On the parched banks the
stilted roots of the screw pines ceased their fruitless search for water,
loosened their hold on the Earth, and fell from their crumbling ledges.
And, the mournful cry of a kestrel pierced the air.

★　　★　　★　　★　　★　　★

A heavy breeze, foretelling of an approaching storm, cooled the beads
of sweat on Mefakani's brow as he raced to the Queen's compound.
Although he rushed to warn Temple about the assassins, his step was
confident. Soon he'd learn who the rebels were, and when he did, he
planned to take their Ka's, too, and add them to his new army.
    The Warrior-Priest pushed past the guard at Temple's guesthouse

and stepped inside. Temple's bed matt was empty!

Mefakani gave the guard an interrogating stare. "Where is he?"

The guard looked puzzled and looked inside the guesthouse himself. "He never left. I swear it!"

Mefakani ran out into the courtyard and pulled a servant aside who had overheard the conversation. "Get me Lobutu! Now!" he snapped, with the last of his hangover pounding his brain. The servant ran at top speed.

Commander Lobutu came around the long, tiled portico, his ponytail bouncing in his stride and his feathered headdress ruffling in the stronger breeze that blew now. He greeted the Shaman with a shallow bow. "I was just told Temple is missing."

"I should have your head!' the Priest threatened in a low voice, out of earshot of the guard. "There is a conspiracy brewing within the army. There are Unbelievers among you who have arranged to guard Temple so they may learn his weaknesses. This rebel faction has also volunteered to guard Sahdon and his gang so they can plot in private. They have been scheming to assassinate Temple!"

Doubtful that such a scheme could have escaped his notice, Lobutu lifted his Roman nose in the air and eyed the Priest on the slant. "How did our High Shaman come about this information?" he asked.

"Ask the soldier called, Ijebu. He is the one who heads this little band of renegades. He takes his instructions from Sahdon. Bring him to me, Lobutu, and I will find out who the rest of the traitors are. In the meantime, only use your most trusted men, for besides these soldiers there is one other among us who acts the spy for Sahdon."

"Any idea who?"

"Probably someone here within the Queen's Council, someone who knows too much. As for Temple, leave him to me for now." The Shaman rubbed his sore head in thought. "I have one more place to look for him. If he is not there, then we will send some men to search for him." The dark Priest turned on his heels abruptly and took off out the gate in full stride.

Lobutu grumbled beneath his breath, angered and humiliated at the thought of traitors among his own men. He turned to draw his sword against the soldier who had guarded Temple, but the guard had vanished.

A short distance from Losha's stilted hut, Mefakani spied a dark object sail through her window, then the figure of the Interpreter pull down a bamboo shade. The Shaman crept stealthily across the sand up to the window and watched in horror as an owl spiraled into a tight blur, electrifying the air. Out of a luminous puff of smoke emerged the white Stranger.

"Bi Kana! He spins!"

Temple grabbed Losha by her upper arms. There was terror in his eyes. "Losha, he's crazy! Bloody crazy! Mefakani's found a way to steal almost all of a person's Ka! Their primary life force! He somehow removes it and does something to their brain! It's like surgery! It's sorcery! It's, it's..."

"Slowdown," she said. 'And keep your voice low."

Temple took a deep breath and whispered what he knew.

Unable to hear them any longer, Mefakani murmured his spinning spell underneath the little house, and turned and turned, creating a circular pattern in the sand beneath him. In the half light, Mefakani's reptilian form slithered across the sand to one of the timber pillars.

Temple flashed a concerned eye towards the window. "What was that?"

Mefakani froze against the piling, taking on the color and texture of the wood.

Losha moved to the window and pulled the blind aside, then did the same to all the other windows. She watched for a movement in the twilight of the forest.

"I see nothing," she said. "Perhaps a bird."

"Something's wrong." He stood quite still, listening to the silence.

"The land is out of balance. I sense it, too," she said.

"The birds are not singing, and they always sing..."

"...at dawn, especially when it is going to rain." The two exchanged glances. "It is unnatural," she said.

He whispered back. "It's Mefakani's new power that...." His sentence broke off and dangled between them like a hangman's noose. "It's the Shaman who keeps the Su broken and the island..."

"Dies."

The Shaman wound himself around the pillar and twisted up the side of the hut.

Temple spoke in a quiet tone, but he was clearly still panicked. "Mefakani can steal another's entire will power, and yet keep the victim alive and functioning!"

"What do you mean?"

"He can make them do anything he wants! He plans on creating a whole new army of warrior-slaves! I heard him and I saw him do this to an Elder, one of the Elders who is aligned to Sahdon! The fat one!"

"Gabu?"

"Yes. He's done it to the mute boy, too, only he didn't have the power perfected then! That is what really happened to Tiv! He was experimented on like a frog!" Temple was breathless. "And, oh god, he…he rapes them! It's part of some dark ritual."

Losha fell silent, immobilized by fear for what she knew she was about to hear next.

Mefakani crawled inside the window cautiously and ever so slowly adjusted the pattern of his skin to mimic the bamboo slats.

"By stealing Gabu's thoughts, he uncovered a plot by Sahdon's gang to kill me. But Mefakani wants me alive so he can take my power. After he takes my entire Ka he wants me to do his dirty work for him and go inside the mountain to steal more crystals. It's his way of fulfilling the prophecy. And Tani…" He stopped.

"What about her?" she asked, horrified.

His voice softened. "Losha…she's dead. I saw her. He keeps her pickled in a vat. I think he must have…"

Losha clutched the windowsill opposite from where the snake was hiding. "He…" she stopped and choked on the unspoken word. It was unthinkable, so unthinkable that Tani would befall such a fate that Losha's mind fogged over from the shock.

Temple moved behind Losha and held her shoulders. "I'm sorry," he said, "so sorry. I think he took her power to add it to his own."

Losha dropped to her knees and placed her head to the floor. She allowed enough of the fog to lift from her brain to feel the pain. "My Lord, My Lord," she sobbed, holding herself and rocking.

Temple paced the floor. "That's why he's been teaching me all along. The more powerful I became, the more powerful he'd be in the end. But he's already got ultimate power. Christ! What more does he want?'

Mefakani coursed his way up the wall of pressed palm leaves, slowly masking himself as he went.

"On top of that, he plans to use this army of mindless slaves to take on the outside world."

Losha raised her head. She was speechless.

"Yes, Losha. I heard him say it to Tiv. It's exactly as Winyon told me. He's totally gone round the bend!"

When Mefakani heard Winyon's name, he stopped cold and his twitching tongue went suddenly dry.

Temple was frantic. "What am I going to do? What power could I possibly have to deal with this?"

"You must stop him without violence," she warned.

"No, Losha. He must be killed!" He grabbed her arms again. "Losha, it's the only way. Even if it means I lose my chance for godhood! Even if it means I have to reincarnate a thousand more times!"

"Temple, you must find the Voice within you and ask It for guidance," she argued.

"You think I haven't tried? Before I flew here I sat up in a tree and pleaded for the Voice to speak to me."

"And?"

"Nothing. I sensed nothing. I've been abandoned!"

"Then what will you do?"

"I don't have the power to do this alone. I must go to the Mountain Spirits, and ask for their help, or steal their power if I have to."

"But Temple. They are dangerous, more dangerous than the Shaman.'

"No, listen! It was their crystals and now this dark power he's stolen from them in the first place."

"Curse you!" The Shaman thought. *"They make no deals, you stupid boy! You cannot escape your destiny! I will take your power now!"*

Mefakani inched his way along a roof beam to position himself within striking distance.

"I do not know," Losha said. "You are much too uncentered and full of fear. We both are. I do not think you will find your power inside the mountain. Everything you have learned says your power lies within. I feel you must ask the Light within you for help," she said with calmer reasoning. "Ask first, align yourself and allow the answer to come."

Temple lost it! "If you're so bloody right all the time, so spiritually correct," he snapped back, "then you go and stop the Priest yourself!"

The snake crawled to a spot above Temple's head.

Losha remained composed. "I will help you, Temple, but I must insist we calm and center ourselves before we act."

Temple stared into her languid eyes for a brief moment. "I don't want you involved in this. I want you to find a safe place to hide until I come back."

"I will go to Tani's hut," she said. "Maybe I can brew a tonic or a sleeping potion of some kind, and somehow get the Priest to drink it. Something to give us time to think clearer."

He nodded his head reluctantly; sorry for the danger he was putting her in. He kissed her tenderly. "I've got to go," he said.

Temple placed his hands on each of his shoulders and began to spin.

Mefakani's scales loosened their grip on the rafter and he lunged with his jaw open, fangs glistening with just enough venom to paralyze his prey. But the power field whipping around Temple in a whirlwind was so strong it stopped the snake mid-air, forcing Mefakani back up against the rafters with a hard thud. And with one beat from Temple's powerful wings he lifted swiftly into the air and soared out the window.

The Shaman dropped to the floor. Losha drew back in horror as the root snake coiled into itself, becoming a blur of rattling scales. And out of a burst of cold light the Shaman stood before her bristling with anger.

"Damn you and your lover!" he cursed, wiping the river of blood from his forehead.

"You murderous parasite! You killed Tani! You killed her!" she shouted back and picked up a bone knife and threw it at him with pinpoint precision.

The Shaman held up his hand and the knife bounced off the force field in front of him. "Call me whatever you wish," he dared, binding and gagging her with his magic. "We will see what happens when your lover finds I have you."

PART – III
THE ASPIRING MASTER

CHAPTER TWENTY-NINE

The Swift, the Bat and the Owl

*"I bore 'The Mark' all right, but it was beginning
to look more like a bull's eye."*

Temple Fox
The Makolese Scroll on the Education of Temple Fox #29

A diffused sheen lit the drizzly dawn. Fog banks pulled aside like great curtains of shredded silk, allowing the Priest and his hostage to pass through the Queen's palace gates. The Thunder announced their arrival by pounding the Heavens and the Earth.

Losha could hear the reedy babble of swans beneath the din of rain as she was led past the imperial gardens to the sheltered portico. Her heart jumped when she heard the scimitars of Commander Lobutu and his next in command, Bundugen, rattling by their sides as they ran to meet the Shaman. She fumbled furiously, but unsuccessfully with her invisible bindings.

The two bowed quickly to the Warrior-Priest. The Commander spoke. "My men are not back yet from arresting Sahdon," he said. "We have arrested Ijebu though, but he is not talking."

"Take your most trusted men and go to the entrance of Hollow Mountain at once!" the Priest ordered. "I have found Temple and have told him to proceed with his mountain quest since his life is in danger here. Block the entrance with nets so no one else enters. And hold Temple under protective guard when he returns. I want you to capture all owls in the net as well, whether they are inside or outside the mountain. Understood? Now, I will take this Ijebu for questioning."

Lobutu gave a sharp bow then stood quite still, narrowing one eye on the bloody cloth wrapped around the Priest's head. He looked askance at the Interpreter without knowing she had been bound and gagged by Mefakani's magic.

The Shaman pulled the Commander aside, away from Lobutu's first in command. "Temple will be most vulnerable when he returns. Remember, I want only your finest men to guard him," he said in a conspiratorial whisper.

Lobutu caught the Priest flick an eye of concern towards his First Man. "Bundugen," the Commander said with indignity, "is my most trusted officer...and a close friend," he added.

The dark Priest acquiesced with a nod, then turned to leave, but the Commander, noticing now that Losha had been bound and gagged by magic, stood waiting for more information. "I will have to report this to the Queen. What of the girl?" he asked.

"She is part of the conspiracy to assassinate the Teacher," Mefakani lied. He gestured to the blood smeared cloth around his head. "As you can see, she is vicious."

"This, then, is the Informer you spoke about?" Lobutu asked with a puzzled frown.

Mefakani had not anticipated the question. "No," he replied quickly. "There is still another. This place festers from the inside out. I will take Ijebu and the girl now." When the Priest turned abruptly to leave without a bow and without further explanation, the swans grunted loudly from the sedge brakes.

★　★　★　★　★　★

Flying allowed the panic in Temple to subside. He sailed on the day's immeasurable dome far above the caldron of the storm. Below him, branches of lightning illuminated canyons of dark clouds. A deep roll of thunder shook the air beneath his wings and he soared higher still – above him, the sun, calm and inviting. He squinted at the fiery sphere, letting the fingers of warmth find their way beneath his feathers. He pretended for a moment that the sun was the Divine Light and he was heading home. With the feeling of Divine Peace still lingering in his soul, and the heat of the day lulling him, he let his mind drift.

"Oh, what I would do to go home to the Light again. Or sail above

the madness and keep going till I reached the Seychelles or Mombasa. Buy another plane and start where I left off doing supply runs again – and tell no one, no one, of what I've seen. No more swamps and spinning spells, no more yage, no more smoke and blood and dark rites, no more..." An image of Losha suddenly filled his mind, the warmth of her embrace and her dark, intelligent eyes. *"Losha is the one who's saved my life, has urged me on and has helped to bring me to my present power. Is she safe? Has she hidden in Tani's sacred grove of Mother banyans?"*

A branch of lightning flashed below him and the memory of Mefakani's jagged tattoos usurped his thoughts. *"What of the Priest and his new, unholy powers? He has taken the very heart of his people – a fragment of their essence, and has shattered the Su so completely that now he is even killing the land."*

What frightened Temple more than anything was that the clever Priest had chipped away at the people's sovereignty with their own consent, under the auspices of his religious fundamentalism, and the law and order it was supposed to provide. Now the wizard priest was planning to sacrifice his own people, his Chosen People, in his zealous mission of madness so he could crown himself as the ruler of the world. Temple shivered at the thought of a plan, so righteous and Utopian in the Priest's eyes, that it spelled genocide for the rest of the world.

"And what about me? The Shaman is going to use me, too – use the rightful Teacher to fulfill his own twisted version of one ancient prophecy in order to fire his crusade into action." Temple's thoughts drifted as he flew. *"I bear The Mark all right, but now it's beginning to look more like a bull's eye!"*

If it weren't for the sudden force of thunder, the chatter inside Temple's head would have overtaken him. He jolted back into his daytime senses and eyed the mountaintop, rising from the sea of clouds below him. He knew what he had to do and set his course.

Temple glided inside the mountain cave with wet spray against his back. He perched on a rocky ledge and shook off the rain from his feathers. A flock of Swifts, agitated by the sight of him, screamed their warning call and fled into the tiny holes scattered around the cave walls. The Owl-man swooped through the heavy air in a graceful arc and skimmed through the roiling swarm. He snatched up a Swift with his talons then landed back on his perch, one leg pressed lightly over his squirming prey.

"Please do not eat me, Owl!" cried the Swift.

"Tell me how to get to the Mountain Spirits and I'll let you go."

The bird looked up with frightened eyes, its heart about to burst. "What kind of owl are you? Owls eat their prey! They do not make deals with them!"

Temple felt the bird tremble and loosened his grip altogether. The Swift stretched a wing, testing it to feel if there was any damage. "I'm an Owl-man," he said. "The Spirit of the great and wise Henakaga grants me this form from time to time."

"A Shaman!" The bird let out a sharp chirp. "Well, why did you not say so before? Why does the Owl Shaman seek the magicians in the mountain?"

"If you must know, the Snake Shaman, known as Mefakani, has broken the Su. His strange power is robbing the life out of the people and poisoning the land. I need to find the Spirits who dwell inside the mountain to ask for their help."

The Swift blinked both beady eyes and shivered a bit. "But I cannot help you! I do not know the way to where they hide! I will tell you this though. When Initiates come here, they first choose one of seven passageways to begin their journey. Some never return. It is a dangerous quest."

Temple eyed the seven tunnels. *"How do I choose?"* he shuttered. "Which one do you feel will lead me to these Spirits?"

'Perhaps the Bats will know. Ask them. They come and go out of the third and fourth tunnels."

"Well, that narrows it down to two for a start," Temple thought.

The third tunnel was wide and lit by a diffused light that reflected off the cavern walls. Its walls were hacked rough. The forth shaft was the darkest and Temple's owl vision could scarcely penetrate beyond a few yards. The entrance was narrow and partially blocked by broken stone. Its walls and floor were worn smooth and even. Temple remembered the slick tunnel of darkness he had passed through when he made his transition into the Light. From this he made a quick decision. "Thank you, Swift."

"It is I who am in your debt, Owl-man. I will warn the others of what you have spoken," it said then flew away.

Temple prayed to the Spirit of the Wind for its divine assistance. "Trust!" he hooted. And with that solely in his mind, he flew at the wall of stone that separated the two tunnels. The Owl heard a frightened cry from the Swift, but he soared on, forcing his muscles to slacken over his frame of hollow bone, the stone wall looming closer in his sight. Within three yards of the wall, the wind shifted sharply and Temple's body tilted to his right, his wing tip catching on a jagged edge of rock. He slipped down the dark passageway, listening to the

Spirit of Thunder, the Spirit of the Wind, and, with quiet satisfaction, to the noisy chatter of cave Swifts whose voices echoed off the nearby walls.

He soared the length of the narrowing passageway with the ease of a glider until he came to a split in the tunnel. Again, Temple felt a wave of calm flow through his body and let the wind choose his course. His left wing angled towards a ragged ceiling so he could veer to the right again. He rode on a musty breeze a short distance until he came to a staircase cut from rough stone. He landed, and then paused at the top of the stairs to ease the pain from his damaged wing. Temple rearranged a few broken feathers with his beak until a sound stirred him to attention. Behind him, in the distant corridor he had just traversed, he caught the whistling sound of air pushed hard through narrow rock. The Owl-man, not wanting to miss an opportunity, climbed onto the back of the Wind and coasted down the spiral stairway without mishap.

Despite the sharp pain in his left wing, he flapped his wings furiously the last hundred feet or so, then landed, his feet cold against the hard flat bottom. Spread before him was an enormous dripstone cavern. Here, time and space meant little. Deep within the bowels of the Earth there were great fluted columns and canopies glinting in shades of rose pink and amber. Stalagmitic masses of dripstone hung like blankets with white, cream and rust-colored bands and delicate lacework, some taking on the appearance of an ancient waterfall frozen in time. Wavy shawls of stone shone in translucent white and the floor and ceiling glistened with drusy quartz.

Temple paused to capture the beauty, the sense of timelessness. It was another world. Alone, with no one but himself and perhaps some frightened Bat hidden somewhere, Temple still had a sense of being watched by some other invisible eyes. It was as if he could feel all who had ventured here before him, as if he could hear them breathing, hear the history of their footsteps. But he also sensed he needed to move on. He could feel the air press down with the musty smell of damp rock and mold. A trickling sound pricked his ears and he hopped in fits and starts over to its source. A tiny waterfall played its delicate music in a shallow basin made of limestone-crystal. Temple paused to slake his thirst there, then raised his head and eyed the spiked ceiling, searching along the edges of his senses for a Bat or two. After a patient moment, he detected an ultrasonic tweak and the flitting of leathery wings. Temple sent out a cry to locate his target, then, with one stroke of his wings, darted after his prey. But the Bat, using its evasive sonar, zigzagged an impossible path around the stalactites and disappeared into a secret crevice somewhere.

Temple's great talons rested on an arm of wet stone and there he sat for a fitful moment, waiting for a movement, a sound.

The Bat peered from behind a tusk of limestone and sent out a purposeful cry. When he heard one beat from Temple's wings, he took off through a hole high in the wall behind a massive stalactite, and disappeared into the darkness beyond with the Initiate in pursuit.

The Owl folded his wings and glided through the short tunnel that led to the hidden cave, this one hollowed smooth and round. With pupils and talons both open and sharp, he tensed, clutching at the acrobat, but missed. The Bat flitted upward and slithered into a fissure in the rock.

"I won't hurt you," Temple called out loud. He thought he heard a shrill chuckle beneath the echoes of his own cry. "Rat faced Bat!" he cursed beneath his breath, but his voice rattled off the walls all the same.

"Who dares to call me 'rat faced'?" This was said in a squeak, which seemed to come from all directions.

The name of Gadji bounced off a nearby wall and rolled around the cavern, causing the Bat to shiver, regretting he had spoken in haste.

"Spare me!" said a thin voice, its words returning again and again to mock him.

"I'll eat your liver if you don't tell me where the Spirits of the Mountain live!"

The Bat wedged himself deeper into the shelter of rock. "I've 'eard of 'em. But don't know where they live. I swear!"

"Listen, Bat. The island's Snake Shaman has gone mad. If I don't get to the Mountain Spirits your life will be in danger – everyone's life will."

A deep shadow in the cleft shifted slightly. A tiny head popped out and flicked a pointed ear. "You'll spare me if I tell?" asked a tiny voice.

"If you don't I'll..." the Owl-man champed on his beak.

"Told ya, don't know any of these spirits, but I do know this. 'Eard this wall 'ere move before."

Temple traced his eye along the lifeline of the cave above him. It dead-ended into a wall. Knowing what he must do, he let out a screech and dove high into the air. He circled around in an ever-tightening spiral, until he managed a bruised wing tip to the soft bat guano on the ground to draw his magic circle. When the Owl-man cried for a change, the cave filled with light, and spark and a churning cloud of guano.

Temple stepped out of the swirling debris in his man-form and sank up to his calves in bat shit. "God! What's that awful smell!" He raised one foot up caked with muck. He cupped his hand over his face and stumbled over to the wall. Blind and unsure of himself, he ran his huge palms across the coarse stone haphazardly, searching for the secret door, until he fell into a coughing spasm.

It took nearly an hour to wait for the dung to settle so he could take a deep, stifling breath to calm him. When he felt calm enough, he ran deft fingers over the stone to search for a fissure in the rock. It took a layer of flesh off his fingertips before he found the crack, discovering it ran the height of the wall from ground to ceiling at sharp angles, forming a perfect square. Quickly, he scraped the fissure clean with a fingernail then formed a buttress with his shoulder. He gave a good heave.

Nothing!

Obviously, there was more to opening this secret door than brute force.

He paused to think amid the putrid air and caught the light of an idea. He didn't know if he could do it. There was no one or thing to assist him now. Tani and her magic juk blossoms were a thing of the past, and Losha, his precious friend, was nowhere to lend her sage advice. So alone and doubtful as he was, he lowered himself painfully to the ground and folded his legs beneath him. He groaned. The pores of his flesh crawled in rebellion against the touch of guano.

Summoning all of his energy and centering it, he pushed the distractions of the cold, damp ground and the stench of excrement from his senses, and shut down all his nerve endings. Then he whispered a quiet prayer and drew the Divine Light down through the crown of his head. The light spiraled down his spinal column, activating every cell, until the energy vortexes within him spun and unfolded, causing a deeper calm to flow through him. When he, at last, had pushed the light beyond the perimeters of his hands and feet, past the limits of his skin, he drew his attention to the other side of the secret door and slowly, ever so slowly, lifted out of his body.

CHAPTER THIRTY

The Captive

*"There were miners and sheiks, Eskimo
dogsledders and one poor woman who looked like
she had spent her life in the sewers
beneath Paris."*

Temple Fox
The Makolese Scroll on the Education of Temple Fox #30

The dark Priest signed his name with a flourishing brush stroke then allowed the ink to dry. "Tiv, go and fetch Jabal. Be quick!" he ordered.

The mute unbolted the door made of monolithic rock and pushed on it, allowing a small enough opening for him to squeeze through. The Shaman bolted the chamber door behind him.

A sinister smile spread across Mefakani's face when he eased himself back into his stone throne. He peered into a mirror made of polished obsidian, past his own image to the renegade soldier behind him. Ijebu was sitting quietly on the ritual table of stone, recuperating from a dark rite he no memory of. "You have restored my energies, Ijebu," Mefakani called out. "With a few more like you, I will have all the vigor's of youth. I am pleased...but not as much as I am delighted by this." The Shaman looked in the mirror at himself and rubbed a finger against the wound on his forehead. He laughed. "Who knew that there would be two that would fulfill the ancient prophecy. The ancient prophets were geniuses! Brilliant poets! And I, their metaphor." He refocused his gaze onto the distant figure in the mirror. "After I have taken the Teacher's power, I will take a little ride in my new air boat. Sound prophetic, Ijebu?"

"Yes, Master," Ijebu said in an empty tone.

The Priest lowered the mirror and swung around, holding his full attention on the renegade soldier. "Are you feeling well enough now?"

The answer was dull and hollow. "Yes, Master."

"Good. I will need you to help me round up your rebel friends; seeing you should make them more compliant." The Shaman hid his wound beneath a swath of cloth tied around his head when a signal rap echoed through the door.

"Ijebu, let them in."

Ijebu walked unsteadily to the door and unbolted it. The mute stumbled in alone, wincing with apology.

"You can not find him?" the Shaman grumbled. The boy shook his head. "He has been missing ever since I had him take Gabu back to...." A sudden suspicion came over him like an axe blow. He leapt out of his chair and paced the chamber floor.

"Not once has Jabal openly approved of Temple, but I have dismissed the boy's attitude as mere jealousy. Is my own Apprentice an Unbeliever? Is he the Informer?" Mefakani tapped his staff against the floor in thought. *"Jabal is a boy of stubborn dedication, so stubborn that if he did not see things my way he just might betray me and wish to take my place as High Shaman."*

"It would be just like that old shark, Sahdon, to set Jabal against me," he thought out loud. "Perhaps the boy thinks he can replace his Master. Most Apprentices try...at least once," he said, casting a mean eye towards Tiv.

He eyed the bark paper scroll before him and tapped a light finger against his scarred forehead in thought. Without further hesitation, he added Jabal's name to the list of conspirators, then rolled up the paper.

"This is too important a task for you, boy." The Priest threw on his cloak and hid the scroll inside it. "I must go myself. But first," he stopped and stared at the renegade, seeing that his height and build was much like that of Tiv, "we must disguise Ijebu or his appearance will confuse the others."

★　★　★　★　★　★

Tiv and the masked renegade trailed behind their Master in the dank musty corridors, until the dark Priest stopped. He growled a complaint as he paused by a heavy wooden door, bolted from the outside with a block of timber.

"I will deal with her later." He turned to the mute. "Tiv, I command you to disassemble the air boat and reassemble it in my private garden as I have taught you. Lock the garden gate behind you. Then I want you to come back here, right here, in front of this door." He handed the boy his dagger. "I order you to kill anyone who tries to open this door – even if it is Jabal. Understand?"

The boy gave a reluctant nod and recoiled when the dagger was placed into his hand.

"Do it, Tiv! It is a commandment!" he bellowed, seeing the boy's hesitation. "Come Ijebu!" The Priest motioned behind him without looking.

Ijebu, disguised in a cowl made of soft barkcloth, hurried after his Master back through the cool, twisted corridors to the surface of the world.

★　★　★　★　★　★

The subtle particles of Temple's spirit body passed through the dense molecular structure of rock as if he were sugar melting in warm water. He drifted into an empty corridor, which had a slick glazed finish to its well-defined walls, ceiling and floor. It was as if the rock had once been molten, pushed into smooth clean angles and then allowed to cool and solidify. It was man-height, curving gently to the left and was dimly lit by a source he couldn't detect.

He paused, delighted with the sensation of new freedom. He flapped his invisible arms like a bird, realizing in an embarrassing second that he couldn't control his movements. But when he willed himself to rise, he rose. When he willed himself to the left, his spirit obeyed without the need of acrobatics. Flying was easy. Temple willed himself still for a moment. Before he scouted for the Mountain Spirits, or a weapon he could find, he reminded himself of how cramped his physical body would feel after sitting so long in the foul excrement behind the wall. With the promise of returning to his physical body soon, he slipped down the empty corridor, lighter and freer now than when he had been in his owl state; independent of any friction or force; flowing like a streak of light against polished silver, beyond the curve where his vision had earlier been impeded.

It didn't take long before he came upon several rough stone archways that honeycombed the main corridor. He stopped in mid-air and pondered on which way to go. His curiosity pulled him to the left and he floated through the archway into the tunnel. He had only traveled a few yards when the tunnel narrowed to a dead-end. He started to will himself backwards when a sudden thought came to him. *"Why am I going through these tunnels? If I **am** without a body, why not just go through the walls like before?"*

His ethereal body paused for a moment, turned toward the rock wall and he willed himself through it till he felt he was inside another enclosure, this one cramped with needle-like dripstone. *"I'll get lost if I keep doing this,"* he thought. *"I should go back, and yet...why travel at all? Why not simply think of the place I want to be? I desire to be where the Spirits of the Mountain dwell. No,"* he thought, correcting himself. *"I **am** where the Spirits of the Mountain dwell."*

No sooner had Temple thought and felt this and he suddenly found himself hovering below a high arched ceiling in a vast open chamber. It was dark, except for hints of light glistening on something that looked like glass. Temple swept over the enclosure past orderly rows of rectangular glass boxes, highlighted by islands of bright light from an undetectable source. He eased himself down by one of the cases and peered inside. A sudden, nervous paralysis overtook him when his gaze met the immobile stare of a Makolese warrior with a war club held high by a brawny tattooed arm. He drew backwards to escape the blow, not realizing that his spirit had penetrated the glass case behind him. When he turned to flee, he was jolted by the rigid stare of a Maasai warrior, eyes wide, mouth parted set to shout. But the shout never came.

Temple drifted back again, slowly this time, for a closer examination. The Maasai's head was framed in a lion's mane. His left hand was about to throw a spear. His right hand held up a cowhide shield brightly painted with diagonally crossing bands. His feet wore sandals and were set slightly apart, one foot forward and one back for balance.

Temple gave a quick and panicked glance all around him. Suddenly, he realized, *"I'm surrounded by bodies! But are they dead bodies? Or are they replicas like at the wax museum I once visited in London as a child?"*

His spirit inched closer to inspect an old Buddhist monk robed in yellow silk. The monk's one hand gripped his prayer beads; in the other – a silent prayer wheel. Temple was greeted with a stony stare. The lines etched in the old man's face were authentic enough. The texture was of human flesh.

The scene seemed so strange Temple felt his physical body

tugging at him to return, but he sped through the rest of the chamber past a Kikuyu woman poised with a grain pounder in her hands, a Turkish merchant selling tea; hundreds of people, each frozen into predetermined poses encased in glass boxes.

Temple Fox circled around the body of an Egyptian wearing a fez when, without the slightest sensation of having traversed through space, he slammed back into his body. His head filled with a static screech, as if his astral body had come to a skidding halt and the sound was still echoing in his ears. There had been no passage of time. One moment he was there examining the bodies and the next he was back in his own.

But now he felt a new sensation. Tiny hands, lots of tiny hands, warm, yet cool, fleshy and somewhat clammy, blind folded him. They grabbed his wrists, forearms, ankles and thighs, even his hair and dragged him across the threshold of stone. He could hear the sound his flesh made when pulled across soft excrement and gritty earth onto the polished corridor floor. His heart was in his throat and he couldn't find his voice, his primal voice, so he forced the muscles in his throat to swallow dry. He moved his mouth to scream, but only animal sounds came out.

CHAPTER THIRTY-ONE

The Paper Coup

"Limbs!" he began to cry. "Limbs! Heads!"

Bundugen, First Man to Commander Lobutu
The Makolese Scroll on the Education of Temple Fox #31

Sheets of rain poured from the eaves and spattered noisily against the mosaic tiles of Palomei's inner portico. Lobutu ran through the downpour to intercept Mefakani just as the Warrior-Priest stepped under the deep eaves. The Commander shook the rain from his feathered headdress and straightened his golden sash around his chest. He cast a dispassionate eye at the masked and hooded stranger, who stood at full attention out in the obscurity of the rain, then gave a stiff and shallow bow to the High Priest. The droning rain muffled his voice. "The Queen wants to see you right away," he announced in a formal tone.

The Shaman peered from beneath his rain hood. "I will deal with the Queen later, but first..." He produced the scroll from inside his cloak and handed it to the Commander. "Here is the list of conspirators. I want them all captured, bound and brought to my compound for questioning immediately."

Lobutu's jaw tightened. "The Queen says I am to take their heads and bring the heads to her."

The Priest touched the point of his staff against Lobutu's golden sash. "I am ordering you to bring the rebels to my compound – unharmed."

Lobutu raised one defiant eyebrow. "I only take my orders from the Queen."

"Inner bickering! Bureaucratic squabbles! Too many leaders and not enough followers!" The Priest shouted inside his head. *"Curse you all for wasting my time!"*

The Priest raised his staff as if he was going to strike Lobutu just when a conch sounded, blasting his angry thoughts away and turning both men on their heels. A swarm of guards ran out the inner gate, and the Commander, with hand clasped firmly on the hilt of his sword, trotted out into the rain.

In the outer courtyard three blurred figures came into view – two soldiers carrying a third. "Bundugen is wounded!" someone shouted. A crowd gathered around the soldiers.

They carried Lobutu's First Man under the closest eave and gently lowered him to the wet tiles. Bundugen's wounds came alive in brilliant scarlet with the rain no longer washing the blood away.

One of the soldiers spoke. "He refused to speak to anyone, but you, Commander."

The Commander knelt beside his unrecognizable friend. "Bundugen," he gasped, but his voice lost its power in the downpour. Lobutu touched the mangled hand of his first officer, a knot constricting his own throat.

"Ambush," Bundugen whispered hoarsely, his swollen face twisted in pain. "Mumbula,...and, and others..." The officer's throat struggled against a wave of rising blood, his rasping voice turning to liquid. "Surrounded us." The First Man gurgled and winced in torment.

Lobutu leaned further, his feathered crown plastered to his soaked hair. "And the troop? Our men?"

"Limbs!" Bundugen began to cry. "Limbs! Heads!" he sobbed.

Lobutu motioned to his men with a flick of his head and they carried Bundugen away. He yelled out orders and heard the conches blow. The sound of feet pounding wet sand against the gray noise of rain was suddenly cut by a cold voice behind him.

"He will not live. Spirit of the Wind must have been to his back for him to have made it this far," the Shaman said in an unattached tone. "I suppose if Sahdon and his little army want a fight, we will give it to them."

Lobutu wheeled around sharply and aimed a stabbing eye at

Mefakani. "And does our High Priest still want these murderers captured and bound?"

Mefakani stared back with a quiet intensity. "I promise you, it will not be necessary."

Lobutu's tone was searing. "Then I will make it necessary," he said. He turned to the nearest officer and ordered them to inform the Queen about what had happened. When the Commander turned back towards the Priest, the cloaked figure was slipping away behind a sheet of rain. "Where are you going?" he called out.

"I will bless the troops when I return." The din of rain swallowed the Shaman's voice and he and his cloaked companion disappeared.

★　★　★　★　★　★

Mefakani laid his brush down on the inkblot and rose from the writing table. He looked through Ijebu's slotted mask into his lifeless eyes. "Do you understand what I am ordering you to do?" The figure nodded. "Speak to no one, but myself. Tiv is mute. They will think you are him." He made certain the ink was dry, then rolled the bark paper and fixed a beeswax seal on it. "I will call a courier. Come."

The dark Priest handed the scroll to a servant just outside the Queen's library. "Be certain the Queen knows it came directly from me." The courier bowed steeply and the Shaman watched as the man edged his way around the courtyard and disappeared behind a wall of shrubbery.

★　★　★　★　★　★

The Commander and the Crocodile Priest stood side by side before their rain soaked troops. Mefakani raised his staff and the warriors fell to their knees with their heads touching the wet sand in submission. "The Lord Tagheetu grants you courage and strength," he began, and while he continued with a prayer of protection, Palomei's guards gathered around Lobutu.

One guardsman spoke. His tone was clipped. "Queen Palomei wants to see you immediately, Commander, and orders you to bring the list of conspirators."

Mefakani gave the Commander a little nod of pardon and continued with his speech about how the men would be pitted against their own friends – each equally skilled in the art of war as they were. And when Lobutu was well out of earshot, he told his troops what they must do – protect the Teacher at all cost, be merciful and capture their treasonous brothers.

★ ★ ★ ★ ★ ★

The Commander marched back through the Queen's innermost complex, his walk punctuated by an audacious gruffness, an impatience to return to his troops. The guards ushered him into the Grand Lodge, beyond the private screens, past a row of Palomei's elite guardsmen. The Head Guard, Sumuro, stood in front of the sovereign, facing the Commander.

The Matriarch sat on her throne with her first husband standing tense and alert by her side. Lobutu glanced up at her; a shrewd, judicial pucker on her lips; brows knit above a crisp eye and white knuckled hand grasped firmly on her scepter. He delivered a hurried bow. When he rose, the chamber filled with the clamor of swords forced from their scabbards. Sumuro stepped forward and towered over the Commander, his massive, tattooed jaw set firm, his eyes narrow and hard. He held the two points from the tip of his sword blade inches from Lobutu's troubled eyes and motioned for one of the other Guardsmen to take the Commander's sword. "The list of conspirators," Sumuro demanded, with his large hand held out in waiting.

Lobutu pulled out the scroll from his cloak and handed it to him. Sumuro, in turn, passed it on to the Queen who unrolled it and read quietly. The only sound was the mad buzzing of bees from Palomei's crown of blossoms and the incessant rain outside, until a sudden wind pushed past them all and rattled the private screens, making Lobutu start for the briefest moment.

From her side the Queen produced another scroll and compared the two in silence. Then, without a word, she nodded to Sumuro. A keen slash whistled through the air and Lobutu's golden sash fluttered to the floor. Another whistle cut the air and Lobutu's head fell.

★ ★ ★ ★ ★ ★

The rain had played itself out and all that remained was drizzle and patches of drifting fog. Mefakani waved his staff with ceremonial flourish. He bowed to Boran, the new Commander he had chosen, and then to Sumuro, the Commander's new First Man, who the Queen had appointed.

"In spite of the delay due to the change in command," he stated, "I desire a private meeting with you, Boran. I will expect you at my compound shortly." Mefakani started out the gate with the masked stranger trailing behind him.

Boran, a popular hero known for his skill in battle, stepped forward. He fingered the golden sash he wore across his tawny chest when he spoke. "But High Priest – why not meet here at the Queen's compound?"

Mefakani turned sideways without looking at the new Commander. "Questions. Always questions, when one has so little time. Why can no one simply do what I command without questions? I said 'a private meeting,' did I not? The traitors still have sympathizers in this complex. Make haste!" he said, and headed for his own compound.

CHAPTER THIRTY-TWO

The Con

*"Am I not the Priest of Tagheetu – Breaker of
Men's Bones?"*

Mefakani, High Priest and Shaman
The Makolese Scroll on the Education of Temple Fox #32

Mefakani's army stopped at the base of the mountain on a gently sloping bench of earth, the wet ground littered with sharp rock. Above them in the mists rose the tall cliff, which hid the traitors. Rain cascaded down the cliff face, leaving a beaded curtain. The runoff turned ravines into rivers, bare earth into mud, and tried, out of instinct, to purify the land again. But the blood of war was unrelenting and soaked into the earth like a fast moving poison; and so the energy signature of war still clung to the hills. It hid in the stones and rode on the mists like lost men, dead men, ghosts – the dross of battle.

Sumuro, the new First Man, crouched down behind one of the many outcroppings of green, wet rock. He stopped to listen. The silence was as thick as the fog, except for the steady drip of rain. In the shadowless light, stones took on the shape of the crouching enemy; a stand of trees became the band of renegades. He loosened his buskin from the mud, making a loud squelching sound, then stopped short and listened in tense silence. His muscled shoulders shivered slightly under his sodden cloak, but he dared not move. He waited until he gained a brief glimpse between the sheets of moving mists. No enemy about. He whistled like a tit-wee bird as a signal for the Priest and the new Commander to move to the next cover of boulders.

With his Master by his side, Boran, the new Commander, moved stealthily through the fog to the shelter of boulders where Sumuro awaited them. Although Boran hadn't been the highest ranking warrior, before his sudden and unexpected promotion, he was the best of soldiers, a clever man whose skills in the art of war had been doted on by the Queen herself. He was fearless without being careless or impatient, exhibiting the extraordinary ability of sensing where the enemy was and dealing with them before they struck. Boran understood he had been chosen because he was highly respected by all ranks and yet, when the new Commander had his private meeting with the Priest, the seasoned warrior had been told that there was another reason why he'd been appointed. Although the Commander's memory was foggy now, he remembered the Priest had told him that the Lord himself had chosen him to lead the troops, and that he was to follow the Warrior-Priest's every command – without question.

Boran lifted his golden sash off the tender wound in his chest, and fingered it absent-mindedly. "I have sent scouts out, but I doubt the traitors had any time to make traps for us," he whispered to his Master.

The three watched as scouts bent low searching for footprints in the mud, a misplaced rock, anything to tell them where traps might be hidden.

"They probably have little in the way of supplies too," Boran whispered.

"So why not wait them out?" Sumuro asked.

"No," the Shaman replied without further explanation. *"We have lost twenty good soldiers already,"* he thought, *"and dare not lose another if we intend to slay the impending Arab armada and the Outsiders later on. Too many funerals to perform. Too little time. And then there is the question of Temple's return."*

"They may not have food, but they have the shields," Boran pointed out. "They have stolen several of them along with many power spears. I think they will make the first move."

"I agree," the Shaman said. "Still, there may be one way to avoid bloodshed. Their leader is a statesman who has no head for war. Through him we could negotiate."

One of the scouts whistled a signal call to his superiors. The three hunched down low with their bodyguards ahead and to their flanks. Together they climbed the muddy slope to a well beaten trail marked by puddles of blood and a thick cluster of flies. Set squarely in the path was a living tree that had recently been hacked into a stake. Impaled upon it was a head, a rictus twisted on its rheumy, tattooed face.

"There are several more like these," the scout whispered with contempt.

Sumuro turned around and eyed the Shaman coldly. "Negotiate?"

"Your trust in our Lord wavers, Sumuro. We will not lose another man, I promise you." Mefakani loosened his belt and handed his sword to Boran. "It is time I paid a little visit to the other side."

The First Man raised an eyebrow in alarm. "But they will kill you!"

"Am I not the Priest of Tagheetu – Breaker of Men's Bones?"

"Tai, but...."

"Faith!" he breathed between his teeth as if issuing an order, then moved off the trail beneath a rocky ledge.

A damp breeze caught between two boulders with a deep-throated groan and the air became electrified with an icy light. The new Commander and his new First Man shielded their eyes and stepped back against the barrow of rock, witnessing their Priest's flesh transform into a blur of scales.

Mefakani uncoiled himself and took on the color of the ground as he wound his way past the shelter of rock into enemy terrain. He slithered past tufts of spiny undergrowth, hiding as he went, using instinct and the fog as cover, until he felt rockier ground beneath his underbelly. When he reached the base of the vertical impasse, he searched for a wide crack, a ledge, anything he could hold onto. His muscles hugged the slick wet surface and he coursed his way up.

It was only after he seized the lip of the clifftop that he was able to move to level land. He lifted his scaly head and examined his surroundings. He sniffed the air for human scent with his flickering tongue and tested the ground for vibration. There was nothing; and far below in the distance? The serpent's beady eyes detected no movements in the fog and no sound from his well-hidden army.

He darted into a cluster of dianella, and his skin took on the pattern of the small blue flowers. It was faint at first, but he felt a tremor in the ground and caught the scent of men. He watched between two leaves as a pair of feet went plodding by. When the vibrations had all but faded, he zigzagged his way over the muddy terrain with lightning speed then stopped to sense the air and ground again. To his left and right grew thick patches of stinkweed; before him a screw pine. He made his choice and spiraled up the screw pine for a better vantage point. Far ahead sat a small group of villagers mending the net that would snare the boy-god, and beyond them, at the wide mouth of the cave, a rebel soldier conversed in hushed tones with Elders Sahdon and Cranik.

The serpent climbed higher to increase his vantage point, until the thin bough beneath him began to bow. The traitor's encampment was made up of an alarming number of villagers, perhaps one hundred in all. Both men and woman stood behind boulders and makeshift walls of rock, guarding all paths that led from the hill far below to their clifftop fortress. They were armed with only fishing gaffs and simple clubs, but Mefakani could sense the determination in their spirits. *"Hold off the ignorant Believers and kill the Wizard when he returns"* was written in the signature of their group energy.

Mefakani strained his tiny eyes to see as far as his snake eyes would allow, trying to take into account the twenty renegade warriors he had learned about from stealing Ijebu's memory. A third were perched on ledges above the cave entrance; perfect locations for scouting out the Believer's army below, despite the fog, but also strategic posts to launch an ambush against Temple should he escape from the mountain. *"And the remaining warriors, could they be inside?"* he wondered. Mefakani could only guess that those most skilled in their profession congregated inside the cave at each entrance to the seven tunnels.

As a last act to gather as much information as he could, the Snake Shaman flicked his tongue in a coded rhythm only he and the Spirit of the Snakes understood. Jabal's energy was distinctive and the dark Priest tested the ethers for his Apprentice's whereabouts. Surprised that the possible informant was nowhere to be felt, he spiraled down the screw pine, planning his strange and dangerous strategy as he went. *"My only real gamble is if Sahdon and his rabble somehow figured out what I had done with Gabu in my underground chamber."* But Mefakani was a man who took risks and he was betting that the Lord, who bestowed the sacred mark upon his brow, would guide and protect him.

The Snake Shaman burrowed beneath some leaf mold and slithered in a wide arc towards the gaping mouth of the cave. When he reached it, he eased himself around its edges by disguising himself as leafy creeper, until he was well behind Sahdon, Cranik and the rebel soldier, and deep within the twilight of the enclosure. The rebel warriors were to his back. He raised his head to check the small holes in the walls around him, marking exits for a quick escape, should he need it. The right moment arrived and he coiled into himself, casting sparks into the air like ice crystals aflame. The rebels turned aghast when Mefakani rose out of a swirling column of blue smoke before their eyes.

"Sorry to interrupt your meeting." Mefakani gave a twisted smile, but kept his eyes unfocused to keep his attention in all directions, especially behind him where he was most vulnerable.

One of the renegade soldiers, a tall, wooly-headed man, called out. A dozen warriors came running, spears held horizontal like spokes in a wheel with the Priest as the hub.

Mefakani didn't flinch and continued in a smooth voice. "Foolish, this business of civil war. Reckless!"

"You would do better performing funerals, Priest!" Cranik snapped acidly, and the other Elder conspirators came out of hiding from the dark recesses of the huge cave.

Mefakani spoke boldly. "I am here to negotiate a truce."

"A truce?" Sahdon staggered forward. His hair was disheveled, and his eyes were jaundiced and bloodshot.

Mefakani spoke only to Sahdon. "And an alliance."

Cranik spoke scornfully. "You must be mad, Mefakani! We are here to end your stupidity once and for all, even if it means we die in the process."

"That can be easily arranged, Cranik, since we have three times as many men as you do."

"Your army and the Wizard are all sitting targets."

"I do not think you will hold to such an irrational mind-set when you hear what I have to say," Mefakani said.

"There will be no negotiations here," Sahdon retorted. "You and the Wizard are finished!"

"Really? And, have you planned exactly how you are going to kill the Stranger?"

Sahdon, Cranik and the wooly headed soldier, Mumbula, looked to one another. "Well, we can certainly do away with you, traitor, and put your head on a spike!" Mumbula shouted back.

"Can you? Funny that I should be standing here well behind enemy lines and be conversing with you now. Eh?"

Mumbula blustered and Cranik shouted. "Take him!" he ordered.

The warriors lunged forward with their lightning spears, but the Priest was well into a spin, his blurred form discharging a shock of tiny stars in all directions. The men pressed forward against the force field, but it was the unlucky man on the extreme left who ventured too close. An electrical arc struck the tip of his spearhead and shot its way through the shaft. The man was thrown back in the air eight feet and fell to the floor convulsing uncontrollably, his hands and legs burnt raw where the current had entered and exited. The nauseating smell of burnt flesh permeated the air.

The warriors backed away and Mefakani twirled slowly to a halt. "Is this what you want, Sahdon? Death and more death?" He pointed to the helpless man jerking spasmodically on the ground. "If I can do this, what do you think Temple can do? Only I know how to kill him."

"You!" Cranik started, "Kill him?"

Mefakani made eye contact with only Sahdon. "Are you ready to listen now?"

"What are you talking about?" Sahdon asked, limping a step forward.

"False as it may be, an admission of guilt is what they need now," Mefakani reasoned with himself.

"It is true, I had made a terrible error," he confessed. "If the Queen knew of this she would have tried to take my head. If she knew of my error I would have been fighting the entire army instead of correcting my error in judgment. Go ahead, Sahdon, call all your men and kill me if you dare try, but with me dies the secret of how to kill the Wizard."

"This is total nonsense," Cranik complained. "He is lying!"

"Listen Sahdon, I want no bloodshed among our own people. I have come up with a plan to kill the Beast." The Shaman continued with seeming sincerity.

Sahdon pointed his cane accusingly at the Priest. "You sent him into the mountain to retrieve power from the Mountain Spirits."

"That is what I told Lobutu to prevent bloodshed between us. I sent his best troop here to trap Temple myself, but your men killed them all! Do you not see that the Wizard came here on his own accord? He hopes to ripen into his power so when he returns he can kill all Unbelievers and take the throne. It is true," he added convincingly.

Cranik's eyebrows twitched nervously. "You are playing games, Mefakani. We have a reliable source who has told us you coddle the creature."

Mefakani ignored Cranik and coaxed Sahdon back into the conversation with his eyes. "Do you not see how I was forced to? I have acted as his advocate to learn the secrets of his invincibility. Truly Sahdon, we must act in haste or our entire culture will be at stake." He beat his staff against the ground. "We are wasting time! We must gather our forces to capture Temple now!"

"Capture!" Sahdon turned to Cranik and Mumbula, and the other two Elders who had gathered during the commotion. He turned back to the Priest. "You are lying! We must *kill* the Wizard!"

"Do you really think you can kill this creature with only swords and spears?" the Priest argued. "Only the Priest of Tagheetu can kill him. All I am telling you to do is capture him first, then bring him to my underground chamber." He balled his fist. "That is where I will kill him myself."

Sahdon kept his eyes on the Priest, the creases in his weary face deepening. "There is something wrong in all of this," he whispered to Cranik.

Mefakani called out again. "If you do not believe me, then you must speak with Ijebu, before your myopic vision kills us all."

"Ijebu?"

"He is waiting below disguised as my servant boy. Blow two blasts on a conch and he will come."

"This is some sort of trick!" Cranik shouted back.

Mefakani opened his arms wide in a gesture of surrender. "You have me as your hostage."

Mumbula and the other Elders gathered around the Senior Elder. Sahdon looked to Mumbula. "The Priest is not invincible. We would lose quite a few men, but we could take him, could we not?"

"Tai," Mumbula nodded in agreement.

"Then, tell the people to hold their arms," Sahdon said.

A conch wailed twice, echoing deep within the cave and over the misty chasm below.

Boran's army stood in bewilderment as the stranger with the cowl and rain hood stepped from behind a cover of boulders. The Commander held up his hand to keep the call for silence as Ijebu walked boldly up the craggy slope. Ijebu plodded without shirking, with no fear of retribution, his only thought to serve his Master.

When the masked figure made it to the top, he ambled across the clifftop past stinkweed and screw pine with his old treasonous friends gathering around him with spears. They escorted him into the twilight of the cave. He bowed to Mefakani first, then Sahdon and the others, and unmasked himself.

"What happened to you?" Sahdon asked, hobbling towards Ijebu. "We assumed you were dead."

Ijebu methodically explained all that the Shaman had drilled him to say. He told about the details of his imprisonment; how he had been tortured by Lobutu, but never divulged any information about the renegade band. Ijebu spoke in gratitude about how the Priest came and saved his life; how the Priest plotted to capture the Wizard with the help of both armies aligned together. He told the Unbelievers how the Priest played the Queen against Lobutu by sending the Queen a message accusing Lobutu of treason so Mefakani could gain better control of the army.

"I am alive to tell this story," he said, with finality.

Cranik was not cajoled and spoke bitterly. "Whatever the Priest tried on you, he also tried on Gabu. Gabu conspired with the Priest as well. When he refused to talk to us, we killed him. You understand Ijebu? We killed one of our own. So tell me, what has the Shaman offered you, Ijebu, to carry out this con?"

Ijebu answered plainly. "I am offered the assurance that the impostor will be destroyed. I know so because I know who my Master is now." He paused and pointed to the dark Priest. "It is Mefakani. He was the True Teacher all along."

"What!" they all cried in total disbelief.

The Shaman took a bold step forward into the light and unwrapped the cloth from around his head. "I have just received the sacred mark," he said calmly, and Ijebu lowered himself to the ground in supplication. Mumbula and the Elders stood quite still, but the warriors lowered their spears and assembled among themselves, mumbling to one another in confusion.

"It was a miracle that this should happen in time to rid our people of the impostor," Mefakani said assuredly.

Cranik whispered to the others. "This is a hoax! He made the mark himself!"

"You see, good men, I must kill the Beast first, before I present myself to the people, for if they know who I am now, there will only be more chaos and more bloodshed. If the armies can align we can prevent that. We must stay united, for after the False Prophet falls we will still have the Outsiders to deal with. Or have you forgotten?" The Unbelievers all looked to one another in a tense silence. "But first I will demonstrate my powers to you, and by doing so fulfill the prophecies. I need only to return to my compound. I promise my prompt return with the means to coax Temple out. And I will return with the signs that will prove that I am the True Teacher." He looked into Sahdon's troubled face. "Do we have a truce?"

Cranik whispered in Sahdon's ear in a strangled aside. "I do not trust him."

"He has gone to great risks so none will be harmed. He is being fair-minded," Sahdon whispered back then looked to the Shaman again. "Do your troops know," he paused, pointing at Mefakani's scar, "that you think you are the True Teacher?"

It was a timely question. "Only Boran knows. Boran is my new Commander."

There was a rise of excited chatter among the warriors that echoed off the cave's walls. Boran's promotions had continually been denied by Lobutu. The former Commander had once explained that Boran was too valuable as a lower ranking soldier to be granted anything higher. Now it seemed under Mefakani's wise leadership that even a lowly soldier could have a chance to lead. "Boran, an Unbeliever and a Commander!" they whispered among themselves with smiles, forgetting they were traitors.

Mefakani saw his plan working. "I want you and your bands to know about me before my troops are shown a demonstration of my powers. I do so because I need your support first. I cannot trust my own troops at the present. They do not know Temple is the impostor and know nothing about the divine destiny that our Lord has bestowed upon me. I have ordered them to kill no one. They are here thinking they will capture your small band and escort Temple back to my compound when he returns. I have told them we must prevent civil war. Still," he frowned, "there is much animosity over the slaughter that just occurred. They have no idea how insightful you all have been. Naturally, I recommend a truce until I return."

"He is mad!" Cranik whispered. "Our army will not be satisfied until their men ride their funeral boats."

"I am a god!" Mefakani's voice ricocheted off the rock walls. "I bear The Sacred Mark. But still, I am half human. I am not invincible. But neither is the Beast. Only with my power can he be slain. But we all must act together. He is clever and must be caught unawares."

Sahdon spoke to Cranik. "If he truly has this remarkable power, he would have used it on us by now. Instead, he risks his life to negotiate. Do you not see?"

After a short meeting among the Elders, Sahdon moved forward addressing the crowd.

"Let him go," Sahdon said to the others as he limped over to the Priest. "We have a truce for now. Mumbula and Ijebu will escort you back. Return to your compound and we will wait to see this demonstration of power."

"Power indeed," the Shaman smiled to himself. *"When I return, you will fall to your knees. And, if you do not...I will take your heads! But only as the very, very last resort."*

CHAPTER THIRTY-THREE

The Little Blue Man

*"When you awaken you will remember only bits
and pieces of a shattered dream, and, of course,
the details of the ritual dance we will teach you –
so you may mend the Su after you succeed in
stopping the Priest. Since he has stolen our
secrets... our people have found few good
specimens for our work."*

Shu, the little blue man
The Makolese Scroll on the Education of Temple Fox #33

He was dropped on the hard, smooth floor. The patter of feet faded into the distance. When Temple came to his senses he eased a sore arm up to his face. He pulled the blindfold off and with it came tiny balls of excrement that clung to his hair. He laid back for a moment trying to figure out where he was. Above him stretched a high ceiling which seemed familiar. His shoulder ached and he rolled to one side, hesitantly, only to be shocked by the sight of a pair of brown brogues and legs dressed in knee length stockings standing before him. Bewildered, he drew himself up with his good arm and looked up. In front of him, behind a sheet of glass, stood a middle-aged man, obviously a Brit, with bowler permanently tipped in greeting. The man wore a tweed suit, and a tattersall check waistcoat with the chain from his watch looped from pocket to pocket. In his other hand he held a walking stick, its handle handsomely carved into the head of a fox.

Temple stared in confusion and pulled himself to his feet.

"Do you find this educational?" a voice sounded behind him with a high-pitched resonance. The words were in English, but the voice was not human.

Temple swung around seeing nothing, until he lowered his sights. Before him was a tiny hooded figure wrapped in a fine blue robe. Temple stumbled backwards with a start.

The child-sized figure asked again. "Our museum – do you find it educational?" Temple froze with his mouth open and his heart racing. "I am Shu," the voice said, from deep within the hood.

He gathered enough saliva in his dry mouth to swallow. "I... I'm Temple Fox."

"I am designed to interact with Surface People," said the reedy voice.

"Designed?"

"Yes. Engineered. You are a Caucasian container: half American, half English, somewhat like this container here." He pointed to the figure behind the glass. "A handshake is customary," he declared in a mechanical kind of tone, and thrust out his tiny hand offering it to the Stranger.

Temple drew away from the three-fingered hand. "Why...you're blue!" He clasped the creature's hand reluctantly. It was warm.

"Our skin coloring is consistent with our sun."

"Your sun? You mean? Then you...you're not from here? You're..."

"That is correct." The creature's voice was even, unemotional. "We are from a planet far beyond your Milky Way."

"Holy Christ! This isn't real!" Temple shouted in his head.

"I did not mean to startle you. We intend no harm."

Temple struggled to maintain composure as his legs began to wobble.

"So you have come to steal some of our devices."

"Certainly not," he lied. Temple mustered all his courage and lowered himself a bit to steal a peek at the face hiding deep within the hood, but the hood tipped lower in response to Temple's movements.

"That is why they all come. I can read your thoughts."

"Oh terrific! A midget mind reader from another planet. Who's ever going to believe this?"

"No one will, I am certain. You will not be allowed to take

anything and will remember only what we want you to."

Temple tried to close his mind down.

"There are things I am permitted to show you, however. Come."

He followed behind the tiny figure down a narrow, curved corridor made of glazed stone. Temple was chilled to the bone with fear. "Your friends nearly killed me back there."

The blue hood tilted up slightly. "We mean no harm," said the squeaky voice. Shu stepped aside when the corridor dead-ended, waiting for his apprehensive guest to catch up. Without any indication that it might be anything other than a wall, the wall in front of them began to soften like chewing gum and dissolved into a fine mist, leaving a wide berth for Temple to pass through.

Temple, overwhelmed by the strangeness of the experience, took a hesitant step inside and found himself in a vast, cavernous chamber, larger than any he'd ever seen. Within it, floating before him in all its splendor, was an oval-shaped airship. The pilot's eyes gleamed with amazement and he inched closer for a better view. The hull was divided by a horizontal seam, its sheen, metallic. A susurrous sound filled his ears and he sensed something whirling inside. There were rectangular portals, several in fact, and underneath – the familiar crystal spheres pulsated with an orange glow. Temple caught his breath when the ship's color changed into a scintillating array of hues, ending with a radiant corona of blue-white light.

"It's beautiful!" is all he could say through the shock.

"Beau-ti-ful? We do not know, *beautiful*," Shu disclosed with a mixture of innocence and curiosity.

"How does it work?"

"It is based on the natural laws of harmonics." The creature raised its arm and the air quivered and swirled in front of them. A vertical screen of light formed before their eyes.

Shu explained the basic principles in meticulous detail on the holographic screen suspended in midair, complete with mathematical equations and diagrams in three dimensions. When Shu was finished he waved his blue hand and the screen vanished in wisps of chalky light.

Temple shook his head in frustration. "Create a vacuum at zero degrees using magnets? Free electrons? Look, Shu, I'm an airplane pilot and I don't understand any of this."

The little blue creature raised his hand and, like before, light gathered out of thin air. The light appeared to solidify into a transparent sphere inside the creature's hand. Shu opened his hand and two steel balls winked up at them.

"If my explanation was unclear to you, Temple Fox, please observe." Shu threw both balls high in the air together at a precise forty-five degree angle. "One spins at four hundred and fifty revolutions per second. The other is static. Quickly now, will they rise and fall simultaneously at the same rate of speed?"

"Why, yes. It's Newton's Law of Gravity."

"Incorrect. Observe." The spinning ball rose faster, went farther and fell quicker than the ball that was not spinning.

Temple was awed. "Why are you showing me all of this?"

"When the time is right the Chosen will lead your people to create wonders before the world. Devices that can be created from this knowledge will not only act as power sources, but heal and clean your atmosphere with no strain on your economies."

"I must be dreaming," Temple thought. *"None of this is real."*

"Temple Fox, we will not make it easy for you to dismiss our existence. Others who have not undergone the trial by fire, that you are about to go through, will say we do not exist. But you will know because you will have suffered and survived the burning."

A wave of goose bumps ran over Temple's flesh. *"What burning? What does he mean by suffering?"*

There was a silent pause as if Shu had heard the question inside Temple's head, but there was no answer. He led the Stranger back through the slick corridors where the thrum of machinery grew louder. When they came to the first set of doorways the creature pointed to his left. "This is our nursery, which has been empty since the Su has been broken." He pointed to his right. "Over here is our main laboratory for brahmatic experiments."

Temple brushed a clot of excrement from his beard. "What kind of experiments?"

"Brah-ma-tics," Shu pronounced slowly, "involves the study of life. For homo sapiens, acids and subtle forces act as carriers of brahmatic information by directing the synthesis of proteins and energies. Brahms have purposely been designed to be a fragile substance, which is a common component in all life on Earth and in many life forms beyond your world." Shu never took a breath, if, indeed, he was even capable of breathing.

"Each brahm holds a light code to the life force, which can determine a multitude of characteristics. One single brahm can hold the secret to the biological components, which determine a predisposition to a particular emotion or disease. Or one single brahm could hold a code to a specific characteristic which might protect the biological container from their environment, or the development of consciousness," he continued mechanically.

An eerie feeling crept over Temple. "So what's this have to do with me?"

"All of the Makolese are by far the most biologically diverse. They hold all the secret codes from human and Other World races, both multi-dimensional and interstellar. However, few Makolese are biologically complete, especially since the Su has been broken."

"Huh?"

"In your ancient past brahmatic diversity was intentionally designed for humankind. If one race succumbed to a deadly disease, for instance, humanity would still survive through another race." Shu paused waiting for his captive's mind to catch up.

"Each race and racial subgroup have successfully flourished in isolation. In order to continue the brahmatic flow, races have been brought into contact with each other, but have often clashed. At this period in your history this clashing will grow in intensity. Although we desire the intermingling of races, it will reach a critical point. This is especially true since your recent world war, which will be the first of three such wars."

The Stranger scratched his head and remembered the prophecy the Voice had given of the second Great War. "Three world wars?" he asked.

Shu droned in a robotic monotone. "The last will be different than the first two. It will be worldwide war on revered and respected life itself." Shu checked a device and continued where he had left off. "There are presently no *pure* races. There has never been such a thing. Even so, certain racial groups, who think they are *pure*, are seeking the savage annihilation of one another. Your people call it *natural selection* and *survival of the fittest*. If we allowed this to go unchecked only the barbarians would survive and would rule your world. The consciousness of humanity would then collapse and years of our work would be ruined."

Temple moved his mouth to speak, but Shu answered his question before he had a chance to ask it.

"To prevent the death of your species, we have conducted an experiment that continually and deliberately modifies the organic composition of the Makolese containers. Our goal is to combine the strongest brahmatic components into one race, which comes, in fact, from all your races. They and their progeny will be the Teachers, the Chosen People. They are already scattered around your world, many of them having been taken as slaves by barbarians."

Temple thought the experiment was purest in itself, until he remembered the vision of the ape-like woman in the primeval forest who had just given birth to an infant looking more human than her.

The blue hood nodded in agreement to Temple's thoughts and said, "We cannot emphasize this enough. The Chosen of the Makolese, meaning those who have been tried by the fires of life, must develop the higher emotions such as love and compassion. Once developed, this resonance will become imprinted biologically."

The captive listened hard to what the little blue man said next. "Those who have not been able to adjust to the finer emotions; who have been pulled down in a quagmire of coarser human emotions, such as envy, greed, shame, guilt, fear and hatred, have degenerated to such a degree that they have stagnated the growth of those who otherwise would have adapted. Your people are learning the hard way and must master their fears, metamorphosing them into the finer emotions. When they succeed, this knowledge will be incorporated into the cellular memory of the body and will then be replicated. Do you understand?"

Temple scratched his dirty beard in thought. "I think I understand a little more about why I'm supposed to end the Shaman's reign – without using his own violent methods. It's because my knowledge and my emotional state become embodied in my cells. Is that what you mean?"

The hood bobbed up and down in agreement.

"That's why I've come – to ask for your help in ending the Shaman's reign of terror."

"We can not assist you," Shu stated matter-of-factly.

Temple panicked. "But I can't do it unless you give me something to match his power!"

"Have no fear. The forces who oppose you have recently broken into factions and have been fighting among themselves. Now you must follow me. We need you for some laboratory work."

"Laboratory work?"

"The brahmatics I spoke of. We need a sampling of your codes to strengthen our brahmatic storage bank. Please follow."

Temple followed not knowing what to think or what to expect. He was numbed by what he had seen already. He turned a sharp corner and stepped into a long, sterile looking room. The two walked past panels of strange machinery that was like nothing Temple had ever seen before. There were lights flashing and electrical waves passing through the air and then vanishing. Shu brought him over to where a young Makolese man was strapped to a chair with his chin and his head gripped in a tight metal brace. The young man's swollen eyelids were pulled open with claw-like wires, and a small hooded lamp shone an intense blue light in his eyes. The man's teeth were clenched in anguish.

Temple was beside himself. "What've you done to him!"

"This one has been selected for his physical endurance, a most desired characteristic we wish to preserve. He is a man we found outside the entrance today. It is a foggy day – a good day for collecting specimens."

Temple's jaw tensed and the veins in his head beat wildly. *"This is not the place where the Unknown Voice dwells! Losha warned me! How stupid can I be!"* he thought.

He wanted to flee, but he knew the creature would be reading his mind, even now. He made an effort to relax his muscles and forced life renewing air into his solar plexus, but his calm couldn't be sustained for Shu led him over to another of their cruel experiments.

A male figure floated lifelessly in some kind of gray liquid inside a vertical, glass aquarium, his body entangled in tubes that ran from all of his orifices to a black box in the floor. It was the main hose, however, that made Temple wince with both sympathy and revulsion. A hose attached to the man's genitals was hooked to a throbbing pump that drummed out a mad rhythm.

The blood from Temple's face drained and his head began to spin.

"Even though the soul from this container has been disengaged we can still activate the hypothalamus to maintain voluntary functions such as breathing and eliminating," Shu explained with cold objectivity.

Temple squinted through the thick liquid. An unusual pattern of tattoos ran from the man's cheek down to his arm. A realization clicked inside his brain. It was Amron!

Instant adrenaline balled his fist. "Why you bastard!" He swung, but the creature, having caught Temple's thoughts, jumped out of the way in a split second motion, even before the captive had completed his swing. Before Temple could throw another punch he felt hands, tiny hands, numerous hands, clutching, clawing, pulling him down. His face was squashed against the hard, cold floor and the shuffle of tiny boots grated against his ear.

"We're not your goddamn guinea pigs!" he screamed.

Shu spoke calmly without emotion. "Although you have the capacity to know all, we realize you are not complete yet in consciously understanding the full meaning of what we do. In time, we are certain you will understand the full measure of love and trust, and living as an Awakened One. We aspire to the same." The blue figure droned on without pause. "It is your capacity for understanding which seeds our hopes now, for we are not able to contain the knowledge that you carry. If you behave without violence, we will release you now. Remove your loincloth."

"Like hell I will! Do you know who I am, or who I was? I was Gadji! You understand? Gadji!" he yelled.

"We will not harm you. Take off your loincloth," Shu said to the figure still lying on the floor.

"Go to hell!" the captive screamed back.

In a blur of blue, several of the robed figures forced the Stranger to his feet. They surrounded him in a huddle. Shu ripped off his loincloth.

"What're you doing!" The Stranger stood naked with his grimy hands cupped around his genitals.

"We have prepared a bath for you. Come."

Temple shivered from the damp cold and the fear growing inside him when the beings pushed him out into the corridor. He was a caged rat now, like Elder Gabu had been, and as helpless. Escape was futile, so the captive didn't struggle as he was led down a wide sloping corridor with the band of blue hoods bobbing alongside of him. They rounded a curved corner and led him into a large, round room lined with numerous metal tables and three giant vats made of what looked like stainless steel. There was a smell of disinfectant.

Shu spoke behind his captive in an empty tone. "Do not resist. It will only waste time."

Without touching him, they lifted Temple into the air by some invisible force and swung him high above one of the steel containers. "Wait, no!" he protested, kicking his legs helplessly in the air.

He was dropped, perhaps a bit too quickly, into a vat of thick, pink-gray liquid. He struggled to keep himself from going under, but when he tried to clutch the sides, he found they were slippery smooth and he slid down beneath the ooze. After a few panicked minutes, he was levitated out of the vat and lowered gently to the floor, feet first, his skin taking on a kind of oily sheen, although he didn't feel oily.

"You son-of-a-bitch! I almost drowned!"

"We will not harm you. Come – over here," Shu gestured with one hand. "Lie down," he said in a smooth, but commanding voice.

"Fat chance!"

The white man screamed when the creatures converged on him in unison again, blue hands and claws stretching from their sleeves. But he never felt a scratch, for they simply levitated him again and lowered him down on a cold metal table that sat low to the floor.

Temple tried to rise, but found himself pinned to the table by an invisible force. "What're you going to do to me?"

"We are going to measure you for light."

One of the beings held up a device for Temple's scrutiny. It was wedge-shaped, like an oriental fan, and edged on two sides with rods pulsating with a rose-pink light. He cringed, expecting pain, but felt only a pleasant tingle undulate through his body.

Shu's voice spoke from under the deep hood. "You are a very interesting container. Your pineal and pituitary glands are open already, but are not operating at optimum levels. We will need to go inside to make adjustments."

"What! You mean go inside my brain?" He tried to rise from the table, but the force held him down.

He keened when the beings bound his head tightly in a cold metal brace, further immobilizing his movements. His eyes flickered wildly from side to side as he watched the blue robes roll a strange machine behind him. A huge overhead lamp was brought down close to his face, its intensity blinding him. He saw only red through his thin eyelids and he screamed a quick prayer inside his head, pleading for the Divine Light to rescue him.

Temple felt no pain when the little blue surgeons made a neat incision around the perimeter of his skull with a laser light cutting tool. The top of his head lifted off with a liquid, squelchy sound.

He was filled with indignation. "You can't do this to me! You've no right!"

"We do have the right," Shu said.

"You're not allowed to interfere! It's not permitted!" Temple hollered. *"The Voice said so! I remember! They're breaking the Law of Non-Interference! I need to calm myself, find my center, and access the Voice! I must speak to the Voice!"*

"Voice? What voice do you speak of?" Shu asked.

"It's God, you bloody arsehole! The Light! The Love! Where the hell have you been?"

"We know your God. It is the same as The One," explained the blue hood in a smooth, dispassionate tone. "The One is all energy. Energy is information. That is what we seek. That is what we eat. Knowledge is nourishment. However, Love, as you know and experience it, is another matter."

"I don't understand. All of this…this power you have and you don't know anything about Love? What're you, an idiot?"

The squeaky voice was emotionless. "I assure you Temple Fox; we are an ancient race, very advanced in our learning. We love you, but we express it differently. It is true we know nothing about emotions, however. We have not the capacity. We have bred it out of our people in the pursuit of pure intellect."

As his skull was reattached with the same laser tool, and his incision healed, Temple felt a warm current flow through his brain. The overhead light was dimmed.

His eyes flew open. "You're monsters!"

One of the hooded beings, a taller one, came close to him and looked directly into his eyes. Temple snatched his breath. The eyes beneath the hood were enormous, almost bug-like, and were so penetrating and black, they held no light. The creature backed away and was handed a surgical tool by another smaller being in a blue robe.

Temple felt the chill of fear race through his skin. "What're you doing now?"

"Your flesh is needed for a biopsy," Shu answered without feeling.

Before Temple could protest, a clawed hand took a sharp instrument and gouged a hole, a half-inch deep, in his left calf. He clenched his teeth to bear the pain. "Please, no more!" he groaned.

"These procedures are necessary. We care about you."

"You liar! You're hurting me! Why?" he cried. "Why?"

Shu clasped Temple's hand. "To make you remember. You are a physical being. You retain your memory through physical sensation. Your body remembers."

The creatures pushed Temple's knees up, spread his legs apart and, with no hesitation, inserted a long, flexible wire up inside his rectum.

A wave of humiliation overtook Temple and he screamed uncontrollably. "Stop it! You can't do this to me! You can't!"

Shu bent down, leaning close enough into the captive's face to reveal the same, strange, black eyes. "We can and we must. We are placing a device inside you that will allow us to track you wherever you are."

"No!" he protested. "I won't let you! You can't!"

The huge eyes were cold, unexcitable. "Yes, Temple, we can," the eyes said. "We can shift the Earth off its axis with a single blast from one of our ships. We can create a nova. We can alter the physical structure of man. We can form matter and..."

Temple broke out in a cold sweat. "You're godless things! You're the Beast!"

"Beast?" asked the eyes. "Unlike homo sapiens, we respect all life. We do not kill or maim out of pleasure or greed or thoughtlessness. We do not lose our minds in fits of passion, or erupt into violent anger. We do not possess the capacity to be perverse like your species. We are not corrupted by the emotions, and could never conceive of destroying a planet, which the barbarians of your species will attempt to do by the beginning of your next century. Although we cannot reproduce by natural means, we do not squelch or squander our precious seeds like humans do. We share them. It is the life force. We have come light years, risking our lives, to take the seed from your containers to engender our own with this – emotion – this Love as you know it."

The captive looked into the eyes beyond the coldness they reflected, to the inner being. There was no warmth in them, which he understood as love. What he felt was a thought, and it was caring, though detached, and yet it was still love. "You mean...?"

"That is why we are here – to take your brahmatic template of light to entrain our own; to seed the heavens, and upgrade your species in the process. Emotional love is something we knew long ago, but lost along our evolutionary journey. So you see, what we do is allowed. It is our right. It is our way of paying a debt, for we destroyed our own world eons ago. It is possible that this will happen to your world, too. If this occurs, all the universe will fall into disharmony."

"I don't understand."

Shu looked away for a moment and consulted the taller being. The being nodded, then withdrew the wire that had been pushed far up inside Temple's intestines. Shu turned back around and leaned down near Temple's face, the creature's huge eyes filling all of the captive's vision.

Out of the corner of his eye, Temple saw one of the beings move behind him and felt a sudden, sharp pain behind his ear. In an instant, before his eyes a vision of the Earth appeared from far beyond the Moon. He watched in horror as the seas turned red and the atmosphere above the Earth caught fire. Beyond the flames he could see coastlines altered in the Western Hemisphere. Most of Florida was missing and parts of the states along the Gulf of Mexico were gone. The Mississippi River was vastly wider and split North America in two. He could barely see the west coast because of the cloud cover, but it appeared as though California was greatly reduced in size and was further north than he remembered it on maps. Arizona looked as if it was the new, west coast. And Britain? Temple could see nothing, but an expanse of water where the Isle had been.

Then there was an explosion of such magnitude that it shook the very foundations of the Earth, shifting the planet off its axis. Mountains collapsed, oceans were displaced and a dark ominous cloud filled the atmosphere, obliterating all light. A feeling of doom and inevitability fell over Temple like an oppressive weight on his chest. In his vision, a chunk of the Moon shattered, flying off into the black sky, sending the Moon tottering off its axis. And a wave of some dark forbidding force pushed past him, heading for the other planets in the solar system. When his vision cleared, he looked up into the creature's face. Although it was hard to read what was behind the emotionless gaze, Temple sensed a profound sadness, like his own.

"We can not allow this to happen," Shu said.

Temple was overwhelmed by what he had seen. "Then fix it! Save us!" he pleaded. "You have the power!"

"While our species works in concert with other Outer World species, we do not have the power to change an event of such magnitude, for a portion of the event is of a grand natural cycle. We are also not allowed to save your planet from a dilemma which your people drew to yourselves, much like the Makolese have drawn the slave ships to their shores. We must work within the confines of Divine Law. If humankind grows in consciousness, much of this can be prevented, Temple Fox. If your ignorant species succeeds in enfolding its consciousness upon itself, however, it will kill all life on your planet. That is why we have taken the seeds – the life force – the germ plasma from both our species and have altered them to create a new race elsewhere. Although the seeds have been altered, this was designed to ensure the continuation of your species. By doing so, we upgrade both our species."

Temple closed his eyes and saw the battered Earth in his mind again. He watched as the seas receded and brown patches of the new coastlines, that had been rolled flat, slowly turned green with new vegetation.

"What are you doing?" Shu asked.

Temple watched in silence as a new light appeared within the solar system, a light brighter than any planet, yet far smaller than the sun. It was a dazzling bluish-white light and exquisitely beautiful – like a star. A profound peace fell over Temple and a feeling of magnificent, all pervading Christ Love permeated the entire new Earth. The captive let out a deep sigh.

"What have you done?" the creature asked.

Temple opened one eye. "I am seeing beyond what you only wanted me to see," he replied. "You're the one who adjusted my pineal and pituitary gland to maximum."

Several more creatures entered the room and there was silent mind chatter between them. Another machine was rolled across the floor and placed by Temple's legs. "We have agreed to give The Chosen, the

Makolese, the ability to learn what we know," Shu announced, as if nothing out of the ordinary had just happened. "We are hopeful that they will teach the world about the Oneness, about Spirit, to put an end to this mindless destruction. You call the Oneness: Love, Light, God."

Temple caught the sight of a being just a second before it pushed a long needle into his scrotum. His back arched in agony. "The pain! *Please!*"

Shu waved his hand over the captive's forehead, making the pain disappear instantaneously. Temple's muscles relaxed and his body fell slack against the table. He opened his eyes again and watched the black eyes stare down at him, closer.

"Your fear creates an interference pattern, which causes the pain. Do you understand?"

"Yes," he whispered. "I understand."

Temple groaned as probing hands cut shocks of his hair from his head and his beard. They poked him with another needle and drew a vial of blood. Tiny three fingered hands pressed hard against his lower abdomen.

"Losha warned me about the dangers here, but she said nothing of what you just told me."

"Lo-Sha," Shu pronounced slowly. "The container you speak of has a great capacity for love and the more sympathetic emotions. We bring her here often to teach her, for she has been our finest specimen thus far, with the exception of her parents and the two old ones, Tani and Okon, but there are others."

Temple couldn't believe what he had just heard. "Her parents? Even her father?" he questioned with new doubt. "But her father was only here one day! And besides, the Shaman said only Initiates, only males, come here. They come as a test of courage and to steal your power."

"Your Shaman has been purposely misled. All have been here, Makolese and foreigners alike. That is how we take your seeds. We take the women when they come to the mouth of the mountain, bearing offerings to insure fertility. The men we steal away during their initiation. Others we take in the fog we create. But, you see, we have the ability to make people forget."

"Will I remember?"

"You will remember very little."

"Then why are you telling me at all?"

"We want you to remember certain things at appointed times. We only allow you to remember what you can handle without losing the balanced mind."

"When then? When will I be able to understand and consciously remember all of this?"

"We cannot calculate in your fractured time measurements. We are not of a focused time. To us time is a singularity."

"I don't understand." He felt a tiny prick on his left arm.

"Now you must go into a kind of sleep. When you awaken, you will remember only bits and pieces of a shattered dream, and, of course, the details of the ritual dance we will teach you – so you may mend the Su after you succeed in stopping the Priest. Since he has stolen our secrets, and this fine love vibration has been suppressed, our people have found few good specimens for our work."

"Your work," Temple's voice blurred, "it's important...so big. But how can I trust you? Maybe you're here to take us over."

"If we wanted to take you over, we would not have gone to such lengths to do it this way."

Temple felt tiny hands all over him and the room shift out of focus. "But how can I stop the Priest?"

"The Makolese have an old saying, 'To help the chrysalis tear its binding, is to kill a wingless butterfly.'"

The beings made some adjustments on the device by Temple's legs and nodded to Shu.

"Will you assist us?" Shu asked.

"What choice do I have?" he asked back, his voice fading.

"You chose to assist us before you manifested into form," Shu said. "You volunteered to have your freewill taken should you not comply willingly with us now. Still, it would be easier if you agreed to help us." Shu leaned nearer, his eyes looming larger. "Do you remember now?"

Temple peered into Shu's strange bulbous eyes. In them was a sense of familiarity and the look of a love starved child.

"I know you," he whispered, "don't I?"

Shu nodded and gazed back into Temple's sharp blue eyes, drawing him deeper into his own. "Yes," he said.

"I love you," Temple said, dreamily.

Two beings attached a hose to Temple's penis and, when he fell unconscious, they milked him of his seed.

CHAPTER THIRTY-FOUR

The Swan

Tani held a yellowed scroll before the skulls and whispered, "This prophecy has been fulfilled. May the prophets forgive me." She lit the ancient scroll that she had stolen from the Prophecy Library, and twisted it in the flames to make it burn quickly.

Reference to the Makolese Prophecy Scroll #18
The Makolese Scroll on the Education of Temple Fox #34

A feeling of wild ecstasy gripped Mefakani as he stepped inside his private garden and locked the iron gate behind him. He scanned the walled enclosure. Canna lily and payanke edged the crooked path that led to clusters of medicinal plants. Nigella, koket and periwinkle grew in abundance in well-tended beds with sprays of coral creeper surrounding them. He quickened his step around a sharp curve in the path where orchids perched in niches of a thorn apple and vied for the sun under a mantle of ipomoea. In the far corner of the garden, a bwa tangin tree suffocated under massive curtains of Makolese vine. Beneath this he caught the gleam of metal. He smiled to himself. Tiv had hidden the airboat, fully assembled, under a cover of leaves.

He ran his hand over the smooth burished side of the wrecked airboat he had salvaged over twenty years before. Half of the top had been ripped off clean, but the main mechanism was still intact, even though it took Mefakani twenty years to glean its secrets. He inspected each crystal sphere with nervous alacrity, making sure none of the orbs had been chipped in transport. When he was satisfied, he secured each back into their brackets with fastidious care.

"Who would have guessed all this could happen? Two who bear the sacred mark."

He stilled himself for a moment and lightly touched the scar on his brow. He drew in a deep breath, a sigh almost, filling his nostrils with the heavy scent of jungle blossoms.

"This is supposed to be the happiest day of my life. Supposed to be. I bear the sacred mark, which has sealed my fate, confirmed my destiny. I conned the opposition and have powers beyond anyone's wildest dreams. Or do I?"

The thought of Temple inside the mountain gnawed away at him.

"The Mountain Spirits would never form an alliance with a human. I know that, but Temple does not. But what if the boy does succeed in stealing their power? Impossible as it seems, Temple will be a threat to me then."

Mefakani envisioned the Initiate stumbling blindly in the dark and was paradoxically both delighted and frightened. Delighted because the Priest, having missed an opportunity to take the boy's unripened power, wouldn't have to worry about Temple returning with power to destroy him. Mefakani's fears, however, were another matter. *"The boy-god had been so unprepared, so undisciplined, so...cowardly at times. Will the boy even survive the creatures below the mountain?"* he pondered. A wave of worry fell over the Priest. *"If the boy survives and returns with new powers, will I be strong enough to steal his Ka and take this power? Will the old prophecy ever be fulfilled?*

"It will happen soon, so soon I feel my head beginning to spin. I feel like shouting to the world, embracing it. And yet I feel so remote, so alone, so marked for greater things."

The mixture of anxious desire and his darkest fear gripped hold of his heart and plucked his jangled nerves. It was like a poison, a potion of love, an exhilaration that one only gets when one dances on the knife-edge of death…and life.

Mefakani took a deep breath again to center himself. Satisfied that all was in order, he left his private garden and locked the gate behind him, then hurried back to where Mumbula and Ijebu stood by the central fire.

He shook off the worry that threatened his focus. "We must go now. Mumbula," he said, without looking directly at him, "I want you to see something in my underground chamber first. I want you to see how I will kill the impostor so you can report to Sahdon all you have witnessed. When we are finished there, we will go and get the bait that will draw Temple out. You can be sure he will come out willingly when he smells his female."

Unaware of the horror that awaited him, Mumbula followed behind Ijebu and the Priest through the dark underground tunnels.

★   ★   ★   ★   ★   ★

"You have had enough rest." The Shaman rallied Mumbula, leaning down into the rebel's flushed face.

Unsure of where the voice had come from, the soldier opened his eyes and let out a little groan. His rectum ached and his head was still spinning, but he couldn't remember why.

"We will go and fetch the girl now. By the time we return to the mountain, the potion I gave you will have worn off. You understand? Get up!" Mefakani wrapped Mumbula in a cloak and led his two converts out into the maze of corridors.

Tiv was slumped on the cold ground in front of the bolted door that held Losha captive, waiting just as he had been ordered to. When the Shaman rounded the corner, the boy jumped nervously and hurried to attention.

"You have been a good boy, Tiv. Now move," he said, shoving Tiv aside.

The mute gave an awkward bow and shuffled sluggishly out of the way. His Master unbolted the door. The Shaman's heart pounded with renewed confidence as he stepped inside, but...the cell was empty!

The force of Mefakani's anger ricocheted off the cavern walls. "Tiv! Was Jabal here?"

Tiv's head tossed from side to side frantically.

With both hands, the Priest grabbed the boy by the arms and shook him hard. "Did someone else take the girl? Tell me!"

Out of Tiv's mouth came a silent cry, his moist eyes answering, "No!"

"Then how did she escape! How!" He threw the boy to the ground and cast a keen eye to the cavern walls. High above him was a single air vent, too high for anyone to escape from.

Tiv wiped his wet face with a gritty hand and motioned to his Master.

"What is it?" he grunted sharply.

Tiv pointed.

A circular pattern had been swirled onto the dirt floor and was stained with drops of blood. In the center of this circle lay a lone white feather.

CHAPTER THIRTY-FIVE

Widow's Wisdom

*"It is time to remind you of what you already
know, but have forgotten."*

The Voice
The Makolese Scroll on the Education of Temple Fox #35

Mefakani's library of prophecy scrolls seemed to tower over him now. He scanned the shelves recklessly. "I know this," he kept repeating with the swan feather crushed in his hand. "This sign, I know I have seen it before!" He hurried back and forth the length of the shelves like a caged animal, searching for the right prophet who would stir his memory, explain the meaning behind the intense vibration he felt in the empty cell. "Adiwan A'geed...Likeze...Wambli Galeshka..." He murmured the names as his fingers ran across the shelves. "It must be someone obscure; one of those self-proclaimed, female prophets, no doubt!"

He raced to the darkest, dustiest corner and ripped the shelves apart. "Beata...Cabiria...Dakini... That is it! The obscure prophetess Dakini knew!" Mefakani pulled the stone casket off the shelf and flung the lid open.

Empty!

He dashed the casket to the floor and pulled out others, tossing their lids open and tearing off their shark skin casings. He unraveled them quickly and read.

"No! No! No! It is not here!" He paced the floor, cold sweat trickling into his eyes. "Why is this happening *now*?" He clenched his fists in frustration. *"But think. Calm yourself. Center yourself."*

"But there is no time!" he cried out loud. "Nine hundred scrolls!"

Mefakani forced himself to sit on his library floor and lit a bowl of herbs beside him. By using the energies of Mumbula that he had just claimed as his own, he quelled the new fear that mounted in him long enough to center his own energies. He gently rested his staff against his brow and invoked the Lord Tagheetu, asking that his doubts and fears be taken from him. As he sat in silence, he thought about the one scroll – the missing scroll that attracted his attention.

After several minutes of quiet prayer, Mefakani felt the room pulsate with new energies. His eyes flew open. He yelled for Ijebu and Mumbula and instructed them in the new plan he had just devised.

★　　★　　★　　★　　★　　★

The night was clear and the stars drew close. Mefakani, strapped in his airboat, waited patiently behind a dark cloud, watching Mumbula's signal fire at the mouth of the mountain cave. No one had seen him circumvent the island, so slowly had he hovered over the black forest tops, skirting behind low flying clouds when he could. But now was different. He wanted to be seen. He drifted with the cloud, waiting to position himself and his airboat alone with the full moon at his back.

When the last cloud slipped away, and he perceived the moment was just right, he broke through its wispy tail, framed in all his glory in the silver light of the moon. He aimed the airboat above Mumbula's fire.

Soldiers, Elders and villagers – all the renegades, tilted their heads towards the heavens to witness what they thought was an odd looking cloud looming larger in their vision. Several of the rebel warriors raised their weapons, but Mumbula ordered them to put down their arms.

The Priest hovered above the cliff and locked his steering pole in place to hold the airboat steady and to free his hands. He mumbled an incantation and touched a lightning spear to his magic staff. Flames leapt into the air, illuminating him to the crowds below. From his podium in the sky, he shouted to Sahdon and his faction on the clifftop.

"I am Mefakani, Lord Tagheetu's Highest Priest, Snake Shaman,

Healer and now, by the Divine Will of the gods, I am god in flesh!"

There was a rising murmur of excited voices from the clifftop as the rebels left their posts and people pushed against one another for a better view.

Mefakani held the torch close to his face and shouted, "I have been touched by Lord Tagheetu and the gods, and have received their sacred mark upon my brow. With this sign comes holy wisdom and vision." No sooner had he said those words than the ground began to moan and quiver, setting off a series of screams throughout the encampment. He touched the spear tip to his blazing staff again, making sparks fly out in all directions like shooting stars.

The masses below him gasped in wonder at the figure floating ablaze in the night sky and hushed one another so they could hear.

The Priest waited for the excited chatter to ebb before he spoke again. "I have brought you magic before as your High Priest; weapons superior to any on this Earth. Now, I will bring you a legion of airships and, together with my blessings, we will fight the Outsiders...and we will win!"

The people shouted and cheered. Sahdon and all the Elders' eyes held a hint of silver light. Out of the corner of their liquid eyes they watched as villager after villager, and soldier after soldier, dropped to their knees.

"I am your Lord and Prophet. Praise my name and be blessed for all eternity. See my works through new eyes, for my works are great magic. Join my army and become 'The Chosen' who will heal the world...and hear this prophecy." His outstretched arms caught the fiery light. "Together we will capture the Wizard, and then..." he paused, waiting for the noise from the flood of devotion to subside so he could drive his words into their savage brains, "I will kill him!"

Without noticing he had done so, Sahdon fell to his knees, tears streaming down his weary face, his sobs drowned by the rebels' chanting, "Praise God! Praise Mefakani!"

A loud storm of exaltation dove off the cliff and rolled down the hillside, reaching the ears of Commander Boran and his troops.

"What is happening up there?" Sumuro asked his Commander.

"It is the Master Teacher," replied Boran, confident that the Priest's plan had been executed. "I have seen his power firsthand. I know."

Sumuro's eyes blazed in shock. "You mean Temple Fox has returned? And the traitors praise him!"

"No, Sumuro. It is our High Shaman, Mefakani. He has received the sacred mark. He and Temple Fox will teach and rule together like twin stars in the heavens, but it is to be our secret for now. At this very moment he is winning the traitor's hearts with mere words." Sumuro was struck dumb. "You see, he was right," Boran stated flatly. "He has calmed the rebels and won them over without losing another man. He has done exactly as he promised he would."

★   ★   ★   ★   ★   ★

Temple woke up lying in a pile of guano with his head pounding and his penis aching. It was dark. Completely dark. His mind was sluggish and his movements unsteady when he tried to sit up. He knew where he was by the stench, but wondered how he had gotten there. He had been with the Spirits of the Mountain, that was certain, but hadn't remembered returning to this awful place.

"Have I brought back any power to defeat the Priest?"

For a moment he forgot himself and searched the filth around him. There were no weapons, no devices lying beside him. Then he remembered what the beings wanted him to remember – the dance. They had taught him the ritual dance that would mend the Su. Temple took a fistful of excrement and flung it into the air in anger. Feeling defeated, he positioned his weary arms across his chest and sang his song of changing, his voice rebounding off the walls in a melancholy chorus.

The silence was total when the walls mimicked the last of his song then faded, and his bird-form spun to a halt in a whirlwind of guano. With his owl vision returned, he flew through the narrow tunnel the Bat had originally led him through, only to find he had exchanged one stone prison for another.

Temple perched on top of a stalagmite, a dull, cold fear slowly filling his chest, when he realized he had no plan to deal with the Priest. He cursed the Mountain Spirits whose power to manipulate seemed empty to him now.

The Owl-man ignored the flutter of featherless wings when they came dancing by. The fearless Bat attached itself upside down onto the nearest stalactite to Temple's right.

"The rebels 'ave blocked all the exit tunnels, Owl-man."

Temple's head pivoted around. He cast a crisp and dispassionate eye towards the voice.

"They've cast nets out for ya, too," the Bat warned. "And your Swift friends 'ave been beatin' themselves against them for five days now. Without success," he added with a piercing shriek.

"Five days! I've been in there with those creatures for five days?"

"'Fraid so," the Bat replied as he flared his nostrils and sniffed the air, recognizing the smell of fear, which, in his experience with Initiates, usually meant the fear of death. "It is but a small death for the greater learning," he said, offering a little of his Bat wisdom.

The Owl-man turned away, settling deeper into his self-created miasma. "I've died already…and more than once."

"Then yer unafraid of death?"

Temple gave an Owl sigh. "Death doesn't frighten me. I'd happily die if I knew it would help, but I'd hate to abandon Losha. She'd be twice widowed in a sense." He turned a vexing eye towards the Bat. "It's ending the Shaman's rule which worries me now. The Spirits of the Mountain gave me power to mend the Su, you see, but nothing to stop the Priest. I've no power against his," he lamented with a pessimistic groan.

Temple thought he heard a voice. The voice was not so much heard as felt. Like a delicate tendril of thin light aimed straight inside his brain, the unheard voice seemed to penetrate his mind and then unfold itself like the branching root of some flower, weaving neurological pathways never formed before. Temple didn't dare move, mindful he'd break so fragile a connection. At the edge of his vision he saw a ghost of a movement by the side of his head. Hanging from a gossamer thread was a spider. Temple took a deep breath. He did not want to be distracted. But the more he focused on the spider, the stronger the communication became. It was as if the detractor was saying, "It's me!"

Temple turned his head to fully face the Spider, his Owl eyes wide open in the obscurity of the quarter light.

"Well, what *do* you have then?" The voice seemed to say.

"Huh?" Temple looked around him, seeing no one else but the Bat.

The Black Widow Spider lowered herself on her silvery thread to the level of his eyes. "Well?" she asked again.

The ground trembled slightly and Temple blinked both round eyes at the Spider as her dragline vibrated above her. "You know the island's dying? Makol's Priest is having a power feast?" he said to the tiny intruder.

"My threads are made of mercury," she answered.

The Owl stretched out his bruised wing, tensed it then folded it under him. He remained deep in thought. "What do you mean, 'What do I have'?" he asked. "I have, or at least had, Losha," he said, the thought of possibly losing her causing his heart to sink deeper.

"Yes, go on," the Spider spoke encouragingly.

"Which means...I have love," he added. "Losha's love."

"And what else?" she asked, coaxing him along.

"Well, I suppose I might still have love from the Great Spirit," he added, doubtful now and a little annoyed at the question.

"And?" she pushed.

"And...I don't know. What's the point?" he asked irritated.

"And courage?" she asked. "Do you have that?"

He let out a tetchy hoot. "I've drowned, been nearly burnt and buried alive, stoned, poisoned, run through with a sword, and as of late, poked, prodded and almost pickled! Need you ask!"

"My 'e's touchy," said the Bat, slipping his tongue into one nostril.

"And what else do you have, Owl-boy?" the Spider prodded further.

Temple was exasperated. "You're so damn smart. What else is there?"

She lowered herself another inch. "Trust, birdbrain! Trust in the greater power! Trust in the Source! Have you lost that?"

He hesitated. "Well,...almost," he whispered back.

"Almost trusting is like being a virgin now and then," she said, lowering herself onto a pulpit of flat limestone. "Think the gods brought you here to listen to you whine and pout?"

The Owl glared back with smoldering anger. "That's all I need right now – more pressure. Thank you *very much*."

"The Spirit Which Moves in All Things hasn't abandoned you," she said more sympathetically.

"But I don't know what to do!"

"Relax," she said, dreamily.

"Relax, nothing! I have to bloody well find out what to *do*!" Temple was almost screeching now in panic.

"Do! Do! You don't have to *do* anything, boy, just *be*."

The newly formed tendrils of thought connected with something inside his head and the realization hit Temple's brain like a bullet of light. The feeling of some hidden truth instantly prickled his flesh. *The moments I have **been**, as the Spider might have put it, were the happiest moments in my life, especially when I died. I didn't have to do anything then, just exist in the **Now**. In the Light there were no expectations, only joy, total acceptance.*

"But since then I have felt little or no joy, except when I breathed as Tani had taught me. Or in those rare, easy moments with Losha when the two of us were silent in each other's company; when I could just be and was not judged or prodded to perform by her, or especially myself; when I held no preconceived images I needed to live up to,

especially the image of 'savior' which I have a total disdain for. But were there any other moments?" He paused to think. *"There was the time I drew out of myself while my body floundered in the sea, and I watched Losha and the little tossing boat in detached silence. What drew me back then? Was it Losha? Was it an obligation to finish what I agreed to come back to do in this lifetime, even if it meant fulfilling other's expectations of me?"*

Forgetting his companions, Temple closed his large round eyes, remembering the mystical experience he had had in the glade. There he had found perfect joy and the mystery of self through the brilliance of the sun as it danced on the waters *(when it wasn't blistering him)* and the thrumming of insects *(when they weren't biting him)*. There was the scent of jungle blossoms, the touch of a woman, and the songs of the birds. He felt and knew the stars in the heavens, the fireflies, and the breath of the wind itself when he rode on its back as the Owl for the first time.

Temple opened one eye briefly then slipped back into his bliss. He remembered how he had soared above the storm in his Owl-form just five days before, when he had lingered above the mountain before he had entered it. It was another brief, but jewel-like moment of *being*; of being disengaged from the drama, that artful theater that had unfolded below him; that illusion that he most surely created for himself for perhaps some deeper need he had to experience all life.

*"So do I know **being**? Yes. But only as a respite of sorts, so I can briefly touch the original reality again, the primal reality, before it had become sullied by my own limited thinking. And why have I experienced **being**? So I could remember it, savor it, and to gain a loftier perspective before finishing the role in a part I somehow agreed to play in this murky world of illusion."*

No sooner had this realization played in his mind when Temple opened his Owl eyes. Suddenly, the new light in them grew dim again.

"I find *being* to be a fleeting experience," he finally said. "And I don't see what it has to do with defeating the Priest, anyway."

The Bat gave out a tacit squeak. "This is what we all get for our efforts! After all, they sent us a mere boy – a novice!" he complained.

There was a deep rumble and the sound of pebbles shattering on the stone floor. The Black Widow swayed back and forth on her dragline. "The Snake Shaman is causing havoc on the island. It's time," the Spider announced calmly to the Bat.

"Yer right, it is time," the Bat agreed, looking at a trail of grit that trickled from a fissure in the rock above him. "If there's still time," he added worriedly.

"Time for what?" Temple asked, puzzled.

"The Spider Spirit, Wakazoontei, sends Her blessings…and Her wisdom." The Black Widow bent four of her eight legs to give a little bow a she spoke.

"Are you leaving me?" Temple asked, his anxiety smothering what little light was left in his eyes.

"In a manner of speaking. But I'll return before long…in a manner of speaking," she said cryptically.

The Bat shook off the powdered stone that had landed on his stomach. "She's a weaver," he explained, "talks in riddles sometimes."

Feeling abandoned, Temple hugged his dark mood closer until the Widow spoke in another voice, a voice he knew well and couldn't dismiss as his imagination. The Voice seemed to smile and say, *It is time to remind you of what you already know, but have forgotten."*

Before the Owl-man could respond, his teacher climbed back onto her silvery dragline. She swung like a trapeze artist, over to a stalagmite made of onyx, leaving a streak of rainbow light trailing behind her. When she produced one viscous droplet of liquid silk to secure a line there, the stone glowed with translucence.

Temple stretched his neck to the limit, anxious to see her spider magic.

The weaver pulled a gossamer thread from her abdomen and swung from her dragline over to another stalagmite, leaving a wave of silver light in her wake. Again she attached a slender strand of light and again the onyx glowed. This she did from stone to stone in a circle, casting a ghost of light behind her. Then she worked her nimble spinnerets and spun a web, not an ordinary web, but a tightly woven web made of a soft silvery light; the color of ice on a full moonlit night. It illuminated the small space around her.

The pupils of Temple's eyes contracted.

Just when she had finished, a male Spider, much smaller than she, appeared on top of the web. Temple sensed there was an exchange of vibrations, a patterned ritual of sorts, as the male and the female tugged and tapped their legs against the webbing. He couldn't guess when, but there must have been an exact moment when the male received the signal of consent and approached. Only then, with the female's permission, he bound her with her own silver filaments and immobilized her.

The Bat and the Owl scarcely breathed for fear of creating the slightest eddy that might tear the fragile web. They watched in tense silence while the male clasped hold of the female's tight fitted waist with his spindly legs – then mated.

When the male had finished and inched away, and everyone was breathing again, without the slightest warning, the dark mistress broke her bonds and snatched her black companion in a death hold, keeping him struggling between her deadly pincers until she had pumped her venom gland to satisfaction. And then, without apology – she devoured him!

"Ruins yer appetite, don't it?" said the Bat.

Temple's gizzard groaned in protest.

However, the magic was not to end there. The Widow snapped off several of the silken strands, which she had attached so expertly to the circle of stones. With agile legs she grabbed hold of their ends and drew them together, making the web curve curiously. She pulled another thread of light from her abdomen and bound the loose ends to the plinth of stone, creating a bubble of light around her. A curious, soft glow pulsated from the gossamer dome.

The down on Temple's brow ruffled from goose bumps and he felt a slight change in the air. It was a subtle feeling; a sense that time was altered, somehow condensed. His keen eyes penetrated the translucent dome again and watched the shadow of the Widow inside spin once more.

"What're those?" he asked.

"Hush!" said the Bat. "She's makin' her egg sacs."

With light and time bent by her warping magic, Temple watched through the gauzy haze as the scene played out in collapsed time…and a hundred Spiderlings tore open their silk casing and spilt out onto the web with their mother following behind them. They flexed their fragile legs and scrambled over to their mother. The Widow immediately rolled over, revealing a red hourglass marking on her shiny black abdomen. And, without the slightest sense of horror or regret, she allowed her babies to nourish themselves on her flesh.

It was as if lighting hit Temple's brain. The luster of life returned to his eyes and he gave out a cry of understanding. With reverence for the Widow and her magical teaching, he sang out a prayer of thanks to The Spirit Which Moves in All Things.

CHAPTER THIRTY-SIX

The Challenge

"There is no one here but you."

Temple Fox
The Makolese Scroll on the Education of Temple Fox #36

Temple heard the sound of sandal against stone and the echo of men's voices in the distance. He waited as calmly as new wisdom would allow, bracing himself for the inevitable.

When Mefakani reached the bottom of the stairs with the huge cavern spread before him, he scrutinized the deeper shadows with his sixth sense. There was a presence, an unmistakable presence hiding – somewhere. He called out, issuing his challenge, his voice ricocheting off the cavern walls.

"Temple, I know you can hear me." He allowed his voice to echo and fade. He spoke slowly. "Ever hear the old Makolese saying about the death of a loved one? 'Grief locks its jaws around the blue song of a dying swan.'"

The Owl-man, who was hidden behind a pillar of stone, became suddenly more alert.

Mefakani signaled for Mumbula to put down the crate he was carrying. "I have a swan here with me now, Temple Fox." The dark Priest stuck his staff inside the cage and jabbed the bird until its cries vibrated every stone. "I have thirty-four cages of swans, Temple. Do you know what that means?"

Temple stopped to think. *"Losha once told me there were only thirty three swans on the entire island. She had told me that she was the Swan. Had she transformed herself into one? Had the Priest captured her?"* Temple maneuvered like a war pilot, dodging the stone teeth in the upper jaw of the cavern, and flew in an ever-tightening spiral until his wing tip drew a magic circle in the dust. When he touched down, he cried out for a change.

Mefakani heard the echoed cry and spied a flash of light in the distance. He held his staff up for a quick defense and called out. "Did you know that we have kept detailed reports on the population of every species on this island since the Su was broken?"

When Temple spoke, it was as a man. "No thanks to you, Mefakani! You're the one who's smashed the Su to hell!"

"Our records show we have thirty-three surviving swans. Thirty-three," he repeated. "And yet right now I hold thirty-four swans. Do you understand?"

"I hear you," Temple replied.

"Then you will also hear this." Mefakani waved his magic staff in a tight circle, causing the air around him to ripple. The carved wooden snake that was wrapped round his staff lifted its head, its beady eyes catching a hint of torchlight. It slowly spiraled down the staff and slithered across the floor towards the caged bird.

Temple waited, his ears filled with the sound of his own heartbeat, giving an even greater edge to the unnatural silence.

Mefakani pointed his staff and the obedient serpent crawled inside to where the cramped bird beat its wings against the cage. The swan struggled to strike the invader, but the slates of the crate proved too tight against its neck, thwarting its defense. The snake struck swiftly, until the bird's last haunting cry echoed throughout the cavern.

Mefakani made sure his voice was loud. "Bring me another cage!" he commanded.

"Don't do it!" Temple shouted. "Can't you see, your Priest is mad? He's been deceiving you from the start!"

Mefakani shouted back at his adversary. "You are wasting your energy, Temple Fox. If you do not give up without a struggle, I will kill each and every swan!"

The heat of Temple's anger pumped through his veins and he recognized the destructiveness of the emotion from a lifetime long, long ago. *"This isn't what I want,"* he cried. *"Not again!"*

He thought of Losha being tortured and felt his anger form into a hot iron fist. He straightened his shoulders and took a long deep breath. *"Mefakani will take my power first before he kills the last swan. So there's still a chance. Still, if I do battle with the Priest, I'll have already lost, simply because I've engaged him."*

Temple drew in another power breath, trying desperately to find his center, his balance, a semblance of peace. For a few moments he flashed onto the massacre that had distorted the Priest's mind when Mefakani was but a small boy. There were reasons for madness it seemed; reasons – not excuses.

Temple inhaled again, taking in more of the lifeforce. *"No matter what he does to me, I'll not stoop to his beastly level. It's what he's counting on. Well, I won't hate this lost soul. The creatures in the mountain taught me that. If I can love them, I can handle one little priest. We're all one and we're all souls of the Divine Light,"* he reasoned. *"We are ultimately the same spirit, the same mind of God. I must trust and do as the Widow, both Widows, have taught me and remember what the Voice had said, 'Above all else – Forgive and Love.' But forgive and love a fractured soul who is about to murder my lover?"*

Temple heard the echoed cries of yet another dying swan, and forced his eyes to close and jaw to slacken. He remembered who he was and repeated in his mind. *"I am not my body. Please God help me."*

With his feet firmly planted on the stone slab of Mother Earth, he breathed deeply, evenly, focusing his mind on the center of the Earth. When he allowed the slow beat of Her heart to creep up his legs to the base of his spine, a pleasant tingle filled his body. From there the golden rhythm spiraled up his spine and gathered at the base of his brain, grounding him like a lightning rod. He extended his love, feeble as it was at first, into the vast universe. It was a love for all beings no matter what they looked like, how they expressed themselves, no matter what their motivation. It was love without judgment.

The deeper his trance the higher his spirit rose, past the vast cavern, and the encampment around the mountain entrance, to above the green island. His consciousness stretched higher, far above the Indian Ocean, beyond the ball of blue Earth, rising past the scarred Moon to the outer limits of the solar system. Pluto and Neptune blurred past his sacred vision and his mind grazed the stars. Stars flashed past him like bullets of molten silver; suns unheard of and yet secretly known to him, until he could no longer feel the edges of himself. All sense of defined borders blurred together. All sense of time and space vanished. His body slowly broke apart into miniscule particles of light and scattered until he could no longer distinguish himself from anything else. It was then that he melded with the stars and became one with them. And as he danced in the heavens, the planets whirled around him like dervishes, spinning joyously, harmonizing, and singing tunes so piercingly pure one would have thought angels were playing on crystal harps.

"You are wasting time, Temple Fox," the Priest shouted, and there was a clamor of wings and painful cries shaking the stifling air.

When Temple suddenly shifted his focus onto the Priest once more, he found the limits of his love, a sick pain growing in his heart. The sensation of wholeness vanished.

"Is there nothing to be done?"

He stopped amid the stars and took another power breath. He had to return to the place of forgiveness and love within him, a place of wholeness. With divine intent in mind, he visualized Losha's face out among the stars and the energy of love was set in motion again. He allowed the powerful feeling to wash over him until his heart was full.

Even though his heart easily ripened with the fullness of love once more, he purposely allowed the vision of Losha's face to dissolve before him and another face take its place. He deliberately chose a stranger's face, someone on the island who was merely an acquaintance. The feeling of love already coursing through his heart stabilized into a beam of bright light and he allowed the love for the stranger to overflow within him. The feeling of love seemed to magnify.

"Bring me another cage!" the Priest ordered, taunting Temple.

An inner peace suffused the space around Temple when he let the vision of the stranger's face dissipate and replaced it with the image of Mefakani's face. The strength of divine love that flowed through him held firm and bright inside his heart.

"He is me," he whispered to himself. *"He's an aspect of me. I feel that. I know that now."* Tears formed in Temple's eyes at the power of the realization. He let out a deep sigh and spoke softly for no other ear but his own and that of the Holy Spirit. "Dear God, ...I forgive him. And I forgive myself for this broken fragment of myself I've created." With that declaration, a deeper peace enfolded him like the wings of an angel; like the profound peace he had found in the Light after death, and he became that peace.

When Temple's compassion stretched until he felt an even greater fullness, he stopped, sensing both his own expansiveness and limitation. But when he stopped – the world didn't. There was a sudden gathering of light that poured inside his stilled brain. Or was it the other way around? His mind seemed to split open, spilling and unfolding like a blossom bursting forth into resplendent light. It was then that Temple knew he had entered his true self by stepping over the threshold of heaven's gate, the doorway to his shining soul, becoming the Divine Love – the Voice, now fully known. And this God of his Living Being strengthened him and gave him refuge. Although It had been there all along, the soft flame of Christ within him merged into an awakened consciousness, and there it formed a fortress, sealed in faith, trust, truth and divine compassion. Temple's beauty radiated throughout the heavens.

Focused elsewhere, but still able to move his physical body, Temple walked out into the opening, slowly, cautiously, keeping the sacred light centered within him. As he walked closer towards the tiny glow from the Priest's torchlight, Temple, once a cowardly boy, now a god realized in man-form, faced his personal lion head-on with only a single weapon. He held the secret of the Widow's wisdom, the knowledge he had always known, close, ever so close to his expanding heart.

He took a confident step forward and looked into the Priest's worried face. *"Mefakani and I are the same being. We are one. There is no one here but me,"* he thought. Temple recognized a raw kind of beauty there and embraced it with his heart, openly, fully. He paused to feel the truth more fully, without shame or guilt, seeing his other splintered self as Christ would – in love and total acceptance. Then Temple smiled and raised his arms in surrender.

A dangerous smile spread across Mefakani's face. "Temple is mine!" he murmured.

Within the darkness of the cavern an iridescence swirled around the Stranger's body and the dark Priest drew back.

"That light around you, what is it?" the Priest asked, pointing his staff at him.

Temple's spirit, that had left his body just a few short minutes before, moved his lips to speak, his voice taking on a somewhat sardonic note. "A mirror," he answered.

"It is your power! Then you *did* come back with something!" Mefakani was ecstatic and frightened all at once. "Well, I will take it!" he hissed.

Beneath the Priest's sibilant voice the Earth spoke in a strange, low frequency, and Temple listened. There was a distant rumble and the feeling of something racing towards them like a speeding train. Understanding what was to occur, Temple swiftly strengthened the golden light that ran through his spine, anchoring himself to the Earth.

His spirit watched from a place outside his body as the Earth shook the Shaman and his warrior-slave off Her back and off their feet. Temple remained erect, having levitated a few inches off the ground seconds before, but the Priest and his slave were thrown to the stone floor. The cavern groaned all around them and the three were showered with grit from white limestone above.

Temple's body, now covered in white chalky powder, hovered there like a ghost, waiting for the last of the tremor to play itself out. He looked down calmly as the bewildered Priest rocked helplessly on the ground. Beneath the cacophonous rumble, Temple detected a stony, cracking sound. His eyes darted upwards to a sharp stalactite as it came hurtling down towards the unsuspecting Priest. Without hesitation, he did what he knew he had to do. His spirit animated his muscles and he thrust his arm out, exerting a force through the ethers that was aimed at the falling stone…and the stone was held in mid-air above the Priest.

Mefakani was paralytic when he saw what Temple had done. He slid from under the threatening stone, then pushed his will out through his staff, allowing the sword of stone to complete its fall and shatter on the hard floor beside him. Mefakani, paled now by more than white powdered stone, lay there wondering at what manner of god he was facing.

EPILOGUE

CHAPTER THIRTY-SEVEN

The Awakening

"Show me what you have made of your life."

The Divine Light
The Makolese Scroll on the Education of Temple Fox #37

The meek and silent Temple Fox lay splayed on the Shaman's ritual table, looking less a victim and more like a corpse about to have an autopsy. There was no readable expression on his chalky face when the bands were locked around his ankles with a short metallic click.

The crowd shuffled against one another as they squeezed through the chamber's stone door, struggling to catch their last look at the white Wizard. Ijebu and Mumbula pressed their shields against the mob and drove them back into the corridors; but Sahdon, who was unnoticed in the commotion, slipped past the two warriors. He limped to the darkest corner of the chamber and hide behind a pillar of rock.

"God or no god," Sahdon thought, *"I will watch Mefakani kill the Wizard with my own eyes, to make certain the deed is done."*

Mefakani drew the last strap across the Stranger's forehead with trembling fingers. *"Temple could have let that stone fall and be done with me,"* he thought.

He secured the strap tightly, then drew back for a moment and gazed in awe at the complaisant god. *"He knows,"* the Priest thought. *"He knows he has to fulfill the prophecy; give me his power; combine our powers so I can cleanse the world. It is by the will of our Lord and the gods that I have been rightly chosen."*

He filled a bowl with a dark, sticky, sweet liquid and forced Temple to drink. "Ijebu and Mumbula!" he called out. The two turned their heads towards their Master. "You both stand guard outside. Tiv will stay inside to assist me." The two nodded and pushed the last of the mob through the doorway. "Tiv," he ordered in the same rigid tone. "Bolt the door!"

Mefakani looked down at his captive with a half smile. "You belong to me now, Temple Fox.'" But Temple's astral spirit was somewhere far off in the invisible realms, barely aware of his physical body.

The Priest invoked the Spirit of the Lord Tagheetu in a low discordant song and beat a black, bird wing against a bowl of smoking herbs. As he droned on, the Elder watched dizzily from behind the pillar of stone with his nostrils burning from the acrid smell.

The Shaman positioned himself behind Temple's head. He held one of the magic quartz spheres in his left hand, beside the left side of his captive's head, and closed his eyes to summon his power through his song. The sphere slowly lifted from his hand and hung in the air. Mefakani did the same with the second sphere, this time to Temple's right side. Again the second crystal rose a few inches from his palm. When both seemed stable and evenly spaced from Temple's head, he gave them both a little twist and set them spinning in the opposite direction from each other and contrary to the natural flow of Temple's brain waves. Then the singing Shaman shut his eyes and called forth his powers with his wand by placing it between the two revolving spheres and aiming it at the center of Temple's head.

A galvanic shock leapt through the space between the crystals and entered Temple's skull then collided at the base of his reptilian brain. Temple's body jerked on the table, but the greater part of the captive's essence felt nothing.

The Priest changed the rhythm of his song to match Temple's altered brain waves and, while still in trance, stepped dreamily over to the captive's side. He took his magic staff and made a tight counter-clockwise motion through the smoke. A low hum filled the chamber and the wooden carving that was spiraled round the top of his staff came alive. It lifted its head up and flicked its tongue. The dark Priest offered his forearm as a perch, and the serpent undulated slowly off the wand until it wrapped itself snuggly around its Master's arm. The Priest let out a primal cry and threw his staff high into the air, twisting his wrist as he released it. And there the staff hung horizontally over Temple's body, twirling slowly. The Priest waved two outstretched fingers at it and the staff began to spin faster.

Sahdon's light mahogany colored skin paled to the hue of well-oiled pine when the wave of strange energy rippled through the chamber. His head suddenly began to throb and the smoke stung his eyes. When he blinked back the tears, and could focus his eyes again, Mefakani's staff was whirling madly in a glowing red blur. A more rapid pulse of energy pervaded the room and Sahdon felt a force push him against the wall.

Mefakani uncoiled the serpent from his arm mindfully and held it upside down under the whirlpool of energy. Over and over again he stroked it from tail to head until the snake's undulating body went slack and dangled straight in front of him. And, when the energies ripened, he let go of it and the snake hovered in the thick air.

Sahdon was still pressed against the cavern wall, his eyes fixed on the snake in spite of the intensity of the building energies and the burning in his eyes. Between the moist and heavy smoke, and the fine electromagnetic current, came a colliding of electrons, a friction, and a release of energy before his eyes. The snake quivered for a moment and Sahdon thought he caught the glint of muted light against metal. The smoke cleared away and a dagger of peculiar design appeared, cast in the cold cauldron of magic, hanging motionless in the red smoke like a specter. Its blade was tapered thin and sharp, and when the Shaman cried out, it plunged into Temple's chest, making the chamber reverberate with the sound of metal against bone. Sahdon clutched his own breast and gave out a muffled cry of triumph.

The Priest waved a deft hand over the knife and it rose out of Temple's chest, leaving only a tiny wound. When it hung back in the air, its point glistened with a speck of crimson flesh. Mefakani caught the knife and fingered the hilt between his fingers. With his eyes rolled back inside his head, he tilted his head back and opened his mouth just in time to catch a drop of warm blood. Remaining deep in trance, the Shaman invoked his dangerous magic.

Temple, hovering somewhere between the invisible planes, knew all that was happening. He followed suit and prayed.

Mefakani spoke. "Our Lord Tagheetu; Dark Spirit of the Swamps..."

"Our Mother - Father God who is in Heaven..." Temple recited

within his mind.

"Eater of Fears; Breaker of Bones," the Shaman prayed aloud.

"sacred is thy name."

"May I restore your Righteous Order..."

"Your Kingdom has come. Thy will is done..."

"and your Holy Law..."

"on Mother Earth as it is in Father Heaven."

"Worldwide..."

"You provide us, Lord, our daily sustenance..."

"as I become entrusted with all Sacred Powers..."

"and forgive us all our offenses..."

"and become the Molder of Mankind..."

"even as we forgive our offenders."

"and Lord of the World."

"Let us not enter into temptation..."

"As I hold all hidden knowledge..."

"but separate us from error."

"for mine is the Kingdom..."

"For yours is the Kingdom..."

"over all Life..."

"the Power..."

"The Lord..."

"and the Glory..."

"And I..."

"forever and ever."

"are now One."

"Amen."

Mefakani pried the piece of flesh off the blade with his teeth and ate greedily. But when he swallowed, all of Temple's knowledge and experiences, all the emotions of the past, every sorrow, guilt, humiliation and joy slipped down his gullet. Temple's essence pumped through the arteries of the Priest's heart and moved like hot daggers of white lightning, darting here and there, tumbling against his jangled nerves, piercing his body and electrifying the neuro-circuitry of his brain.

Mefakani fell to the floor with his fist pushed against his stomach. Although he fought against it, there was a sense of collapsed time for what he was experiencing now. Embarrassment overtook him and he found himself running from his tormenting friends. His heart lodged in his throat when Temple's old, childhood fear leapt on the hot, dusty African plain. He struggled to breathe on the sticky ground under the weight of a dead lion. Unable to control the depth of what he was experiencing, he fought to retain his own feelings. But humiliation stung his eyes just the same as he watched Temple's father, now his own, walk coldly away.

The Priest's mind twisted into confusion when years blurred past him in seconds. A force of air dried his tears and the de Havilland Moth lifted off the dirt path into the blue heavens. Joy stretched his mouth and soothed his uncertain heart. But, all too soon, the fears returned, registered in gripped teeth when the Priest relived the moment Temple jumped from the Moth into the unknown.

Sahdon watched dumbfounded as the Shaman thrashed on the floor. It wasn't until Temple, and now Mefakani, plunged into the growling sea that stirred Sahdon into a slow panic. Mefakani flayed his arms madly, drowning in the smoky air, and slowly – ever so slowly – let go of life. His arms fell silent by his side, his mouth open, eyes wide and vacant.

"Is he breathing?" Sahdon worried, panicked.

The Elder stroked his gray head of hair nervously, waiting for the Priest to show any signs of life, a flutter of an eyelid, a twitch of a hand. There was nothing. He hobbled over to him then stepped back in horror when he spotted the Priest's toes turn dark and a blackness creep up Mefakani's legs.

"Mefakani?" he breathed, then looked from the Shaman to Temple's still body. "You poisoned him!" he shouted.

Sahdon's world was revolving in such sudden madness that the white blur above his head went unnoticed. He threw his cane aside, picked up the magic dagger from Mefakani's lifeless hand and stormed across the chamber towards Temple. He raised the knife to deal the deathblow, but a weight fell hard against his shoulder and there was a flurry of white feathers. The Elder lost his balance and fell to his knees, and the knife went spinning into a corner. He scrambled towards it, but when his fingers found it, the assailant returned, this time delivering a thunderous blow to his back. The knife, its magic having been broken, jolted in his hand and its metallic finish transmuted furiously into reptilian scales. It pressed into Sahdon's clutches just as the Elder regained his composure and calculated how quickly he could move before the next blow. In spite of his struggle, when he rose on unsteady legs, the dagger swelled beneath his white knuckled grip and willed itself free with a sharp bite. Its fangs dug deep and, when Sahdon could take no more of its poison, he collapsed dead on the floor.

The Swan circled round the chamber once, the beat of her powerful wings offsetting the magic staff that spun above Temple's body. The staff came crashing to the floor, splintering into hundreds of thorny fragments. The spinning crystal spheres slowed their revolutions, until, having lost their momentum, dropped to the table, rolled off and shattered on the stone floor in an explosion of crystalline light.

Losha landed quickly, her deep-throated song calling out for a change. Another burst of soft, white light suffused the chamber, and when her transformation was complete, she rushed over to her lover's side.

Having been shaken off the Swan's back in the commotion, Jabal stepped out of a plume of green smoke in a dark corner of the chamber and shook the dizziness from his head. He called out when the room stopped spinning, "Is he alive?"

"Yes," she answered. Losha took a blood soaked cloth that was wrapped around her head and wasted no time. She pried Temple's teeth apart and twisted the bloody rag until seven red droplets stained her lover's tongue. Tenderly placing one hand over his heart, the other over his head, Losha called forth her powers of healing.

Something rose to the surface of Temple's mind, pushing him to semi-consciousness. He opened a weak eyelid and the bushy-headed figure looming above him blurred in and out of focus.

"Losha," he whispered feebly.

"Hush," she said. "Lie still."

Temple strained to open his other eye and set his gaze upon the deep gash across Losha's brow. "The Mark. You bear the sacred mark!"

She reclaimed the rag and wrapped it around her head to staunch her weeping wound. She smiled back. "I had, what you would call, a prophetic accident while learning to fly."

His eyes widened as he struggled to sit up. "It was *you* all along? You're the true Teacher?"

"Tai," she said and gently lowered him back down on the stone slab. "And you as well – both of us. Remember, 'Two multiplies the power ten fold'," she smiled, reciting a fragment of the old prophecy. "I do not see why both of us cannot fulfill the prophecy."

"Really?" he whispered, half dazed.

"Truly. No one person can do it alone."

"Do it?" he asked dreamily, drifting through the twilight world between dimensions.

"Change the world," she answered. "Only we needed each other as triggers to remember who we were. Without each other, neither of us would have come this far. Tani knew before any of us did," she said, while working to bring her lover back to ordinary consciousness. "She always knew. But I had to find it out for myself."

Temple looked up at her with both relief and awe, the color returning to his cheeks. "And to think I was worried about your safety."

"Tai, I was too at first." Losha glowed, knowing her healing powers were working. "Fortunately, I had help from the Swans. They told me to fly to Winyon's where I would gain more of my power. At last, I too can spin," she grinned. "I found Jabal at Winyon's teaching her how to do the same. By the time I had gotten there, he had broken the curse on her. She insisted on coming with us to help you, Temple."

"And the Priest?" he asked, more conscious now.

"I do not know. I feel we should let him be." She looked down at Temple lovingly. "You need to rest," she said in a smooth commanding voice.

★　　★　　★　　★　　★　　★

Mefakani floated down a tunnel of nacreous swirling light. At the other end – the Divine Light. But when he encountered the Light, the experience was no longer a shared experience. What the Priest felt was a Light so clean, so pure, that he could hardly stand the sight of It. He tried to squeeze his eyes shut, but there was no escape, for inside his mind, his eyes were still open and he heard a voice call out to him.

"Show me what you have made of your life," said the Light.

The Priest clutched his breast, twisting in his spirit body spasmodically, trying to escape the torment of truth. All the same, the pain bored through him, for he relived the massacre, the murder of his father and abduction of his mother all over again. He saw the face of every Apprentice he had conjured against as he vied for greater power. He witnessed himself taking tiny portions of everyone's Ka, robbing them of the essential component that kept them young and vital. He saw all the lives he had ended too soon as a consequence; opportunities he had stolen from them; the grief he had caused their families; the chaos. In flashes of red and green, he relived the time when, in a moment of jealous rage, he had taken the head of Captain Kneller....And then there was Winyon, his beloved Hummingbird, the one he thought he loved; her life ruined by the never-ending bitterness and sorrow he had created. For the first time he felt her pain and the sting of her hatred upon him, and his heart felt it would burst.

He turned to escape from the visions, but when he did the Nature Spirits converged on him and showed him the island in its death throes. *"Have I done that too?"*

The Spirits of the Earth, Wind, Rain and Rivers, the Spirits of the Bald Egret, Snake Kite and Swan, the Spirits of the Snake and Acrocomia Palm all swirled round his spirit crying out to him. Then he saw Gabu standing next to Tani who glowed with a brilliant luminescence. She spoke to them briefly. His guilt and shame deepened and his soul struggled as he pulled at his chest, as if he could rip out the anguish. His life had been so destructive, so utterly wasted!

He looked before him into the Light, instinctively knowing what lay before him, but the dark Priest was not to escape yet. The rest of his life flashed before his eyes and he watched himself as he tricked his former Apprentice, Tiv, into drinking a cup of his dangerous brew. The lethargic boy was bound and soon there were flashes of light bouncing in all directions. There were miscalculations and an experiment gone wrong, and the stench and taste of burnt flesh and warm blood returned to Mefakani's senses.

Without being able to turn from the horror, he watched himself don the heavy garb of the Crocodile Priest and push the boy down on the ritual table. He witnessed the violation over again, until his own face turned into the face of his Master, Tagon, and the boy beneath him became himself.

Mefakani screamed in anguish until his spirit gathered itself together. "Was there nothing of worth I have done?" he cried.

There was an immediate flash of blue white light and before him stood the young Mefakani. The Priest eyed the boy, hardly recognizing this stranger from the past. The boy's hazel eyes were keen, his limbs supple and quick. There was an innocence about him and a brilliance in his countenance. Quick scenes flickered before the Priest as he observed the boy in his daily life. He watched the young Mefakani talk to the birds and the snakes, and sit by his Master's feet asking never-ending questions. He observed the boy's selfless devotion, witnessed him foretell the future; heal the sick, no matter how busy he was or how small other's problems seemed.

As he grew older he saw himself as a genius among the people, excelling in math and science, astronomy and astrology, physics, the healing arts and as a ceremonialist. He was Master Tagon's ambitious protégée and unrivaled First Apprentice, who moved through each sacred rite of passage to become a High Shaman faster than any had done before him. He was brilliant and clever with intelligence as sharp as the spine of a puffer fish and just as deadly.

The scene faded rapidly and Mefakani was left with only his feelings. Most of the good he could feel about himself, he realized, was before the massacre; before his thirst for knowledge had turned to myopic ambition, before his love and devotion had turned to obsession; before his trust was betrayed during the bizarre initiation forced upon him by his Master. Regrettably, it was before he had witnessed the power of the little Gods in the mountain, who he had secretly worshipped – until now.

"God, forgive me," he whispered.

When the pure, clean Light of Divine Love gathered force, swirling round the deepest chambers of Mefakani's heart, there it made a home. It licked his wounds, accepting him for who he was, as he was, without judgment, without punishment or blame.

"Let me go. Let me go," he whimpered. "Please. I am not worthy," he cried. But the Light held him all the tighter in Its embrace.

The Light spoke. *"Mefakani, before you incarnated into form, you volunteered to help Temple Fox and Losha Ninti come into their power. You are a part of who they are, just as they are a part of you. And you are all a part of the greater heart of God. You have never been judged by me. You have judged yourself. Know that there is nothing you could do that would make me stop loving you?"*

"Let me go!" he begged. "I am nothing!"

The Voice rang out again. *"I will teach you what it means to have a great soul; a soul with a tremendous capacity to love, and to live in the moment in simple joy. For you are my son and possess the same spirit as I. You are worthy of my love, Mefakani. I have always been and will always be inside you forever."*

Mefakani felt the darkness inside him drop away and he collapsed into the Light. And for the first time he allowed himself the one thing he had always, unknowingly, fought against. He allowed himself to be fully and divinely loved.

When the Creator was satisfied that the Warrior-Priest had completely surrendered, he spoke again. *"Now you must return. Go and complete yourself."*

"No!" he panicked when he saw the Light withdraw. "No! Let me stay. Do not send me back!"

Without a way to act against it, Mefakani felt himself suddenly cartwheel helplessly through the void and then squeeze into something dense as if he were putting on an old wet cloak that had grown heavy with mildew. When he came to, he was slumped on the floor, weeping.

Tiv appeared from the sanctuary of a distant corner. He sat quietly by his Master's side and placed a hand on his shoulder to console him.

Mefakani sobbed with his head held down, feeling the shame for what he had done to the boy. "You have more love in you now than I have held my entire life," he wept.

Unaware that he was the focus of his Master's anguish, the boy pointed in the air to call his Master's attention to the curious thrumming around their heads. Mefakani lifted his head to catch a quick flash of iridescent feathers and a swirl of colors. A thin column of rainbow light rose in the center of the floor and his glassy eyes met those of the wounded Hummingbird.

"I have known her bitter pain. I have experienced her sorrow as my own. What can I say to her now?" "Winyon, I have seen It. I have seen the Light," he managed to say.

Winyon stared back dumbfounded.

"I have not taken your Ka, but I have crushed your spirit all the same. Please," he cried out. "Please kill me, Winyon. It is your right. Return me to the Light."

Winyon eyed Mefakani with both loathing and pity. *"I have dreamed of this chance. Hundreds of times I have plotted his death. But before me now is no monster, but a broken shadow of a man."* She shook her head.

"Kill me, please!" he pleaded. "Let me go home!"

Winyon looked down at the crumpled figure on the floor. "Better to let you live," she said, acidly. "Better to let you suffer as my husband did – as I did."

"Please forgive me, Winyon," he begged.

Seeing what had transpired, Temple nodded to Losha and she helped him to his feet. He walked slowly over to the Priest, his energies rejuvenating with each step. He bent down before his adversary.

"Now you know beyond belief," he said softly. "And, now you'll have to build on a whole new foundation just like I had to."

The Priest hung his head in shame, nodding, unable to control his tears. He whispered weakly. "I have much to learn...so much."

Losha and Temple knelt on the sweat streaked floor beside the fragile Priest. In spite of her abhorrence to him, and despite his own protests, the Swan placed her hands on the crown of Mefakani's head.

A pronounced tingle entered his skull and poured through his brain like warm oil.

Temple didn't speak until he felt a shift of energy in the room and Mefakani's sobbing subsided. "There is much healing to be done," he said, "healing for you and many others."

The Priest nodded his head, but kept it low. "He betrayed me," he whispered. His breath came in hoarse, shallow gasps. "Made me think...it was right."

"You are talking about your Master?" Temple asked.

"Yes," Mefakani said. "The ritual…It was wrong. *I* was wrong."

"You are not to blame," Temple said. "You were young. He drugged you."

Mefakani looked into Temple's eyes. "I thought he knew everything. He was like a father to me. I wanted to be like him – all powerful."

Temple smiled down at the Priest. "We all have strange notions when we're young. You know, before I had my experience with the creatures in the mountain, I had thought those crystals, and your power, were the greatest powers."

Tears came back to the Priest's eyes. "Please, Temple Fox, I have felt the love of the Divine One. That is the greatest power. Those crystals are only a fragmented reflection of the Divine, as are the spirits in the mountain." Temple nodded back. "And to think I secretly worshipped them and tried to steal their power," he whispered in confession.

"But how?" Temple asked, curious now as to how the Shaman had succeeded in stealing what he couldn't.

Mefakani wiped an eye. "One of their airships had crashed on the other side of the mountain. I…I had constructed weapons from what I could salvage,…applying what I had learned from my spying on the creatures while out of my body."

"You *are* a clever sod, you know," Temple said with honesty, "even though you were…."

"Foolish, dangerously ignorant, self-focused, delusional. I know that now," the Priest admitted, critically, candidly. "The creatures are an empty race and yet I know they are from the same source, equal in the eyes of the Divine One. Their power is paltry compared to…to Divine Love." He almost burst into tears again, but held them back against a trembling chin. "You should have let me go, let me die."

Temple winked at Losha and smiled at the Priest. "Now we couldn't do that. Could we, mate? That would have been too easy for you. It's harder to live, you know? Besides, now you know there's more than a part of the Divine Love inside you. The Divine Love *is* you. It has always been that way. And there's a part of my love inside you, too."

"But I am unworthy," Mefakani argued.

"You're god, too, Mefakani. You're our brother," Temple assured.

Mefakani spoke with his head held down in supplication. "I will be your servant, your slave. Please let me serve you. Please."

"I want no one to worship me. It's not *the Way*."

He looked up at Temple with swollen eyes. "Then what should I do?"

"You must be true to your Divine Self...and serve the Earth and all Her kingdoms. You must give back all the tiny portions of Kas you have taken."

The Priest wiped his rheumy face with the back of his hand and nodded in agreement. "I will do it, but Ijebu, Mumbula, Boran and..." Mefakani's face suddenly fell in pain. "...and the boy, I can not. It is not possible. I will try to heal them all, but...but I have damaged Tiv's brain permanently."

"That is not so," Losha said. "If we combine our healing powers, I am certain we can restore Tiv back to normal."

"If that is true, then I will try," he answered back. "Still, there are those I cannot help. Gabu is dead," he said calmly now. "I saw him in the Light, but I did not kill him. I swear. Yet, I am responsible for his torment and death." A deep groan came from the depths of his soul when he remembered what he had done to the Elder. "Oh, I want to die. Please!"

"Sorry, Mefakani. We still need you to help us mend the Su," Temple said.

"But how?"

Temple took hold of Losha's hand. "Do as I've asked, then leave the rest to us."

Jabal moved forward cautiously now and prostrated himself on the floor before Temple and Losha.

Temple sighed. "Get off the floor, Jabal, and please don't ever bow to me again. I know the difference between honor and worship."

"Then I will bow to you in humble respect and beg you for forgiveness."

"It's you that must forgive yourself, not I," he advised, and Jabal nodded with understanding.

"May I ask what it is I can do for the great Teachers? Ask anything of me."

"Prepare funerals for Elders Sahdon, and Gabu and all your fallen brothers."

"And Tani?" Jabal asked. "Should we arrange a High Shaman's funeral for her?"

"We'll see to Tani ourselves," Temple replied. He cast a sympathetic eye over at Losha as she got up and walked over to the stone coffin that held Tani's body. He came up behind her and wrapped his arms around her, but she remained sullen and silent.

"There's something I need to tell you," he started.

Losha spoke with a quiet, but sharp resignation in her voice. "You will say her death was by the god's designs – like Amron's. Am I right? But still...." She stopped, tears forming in the corners of her eyes.

He gently turned Losha around to face him. "That's not what I was going to say." He gave the Priest a brief glance over his shoulder. "Isn't that right, Mefakani?"

Mefakani got to his knees, then rose to a wobbly stance. He walked over to the basin where Losha stood brooding.

"Tai, Master Temple," he said. "Please do not grieve Great Lady, for I have seen Tani in the Light and have spoken to her."

Losha raised her head to meet the Shaman's eyes. The malice his eyes once held was replaced by a glint of warmth, edged, she noticed, by the dark painful look of guilt.

His voice was laced with both sorrow and hope. "She told me to mix a potion using one grain of anakealo and a handful of bruised prubal leaves, so we can bring her back."

Losha pulled herself from Temple's arms and raced past the Priest over to his shelves of herbs and potions.

"To the right," Mefakani pointed excitedly, as he rushed to join her. "It is an antidote for a concoction she took to give her the appearance of death."

Losha looked over her shoulder at the Priest. "Then you did not...?"

"I did not kill her, no! And I did not take her Ka. It was her ability to breath like a dolphin that kept her alive. Still, she was in this vat too long and drowned only recently."

Losha and the Shaman found the right herbs and crushed them with his mortar and pestle. Then they mixed them with some coconut oil into an obsidian vial, holding the concoction over an open flame to fuse the ingredients. Losha diluted the potion and shook it vigorously. With the vial in hand, she hurried over to Tani's body.

"You must place it under her tongue," he insisted, "and pray! We all must pray hard!"

Losha did as she was instructed with Temple and the Shaman by her side. They were joined by Winyon and Jabal. Tiv, too, felt the excitement and the positive, loving wave of energy that filled the chamber. He squeezed in around the others, emulating them with closed eyes and hands held out over Tani's body.

The brine Tani floated in vibrated rapidly and the basin filled with a soft pink glow. The old woman sputtered and spit then sucked in a deep noisy breath. The water splashed over the basin when she shook her head as if casting off a deep sleep. "What are you trying to do, burn my tongue off!" she complained. She rubbed the gunk from one eye and spit out a mouthful of salty water then looked up at the Shaman. "You fool! You nearly drowned me!" Then she noticed Losha, and Temple and the others all gathered above her. "Well, do not stand there! Get me out of this soggy pit before I mold!"

Temple and Losha lifted the old woman out of the salty stew and sat her on the edge of the basin, dripping. Tani wiped the gunk from her other eye and blinked up at Losha for a long, silent moment. She raised a feeble hand up to the bloody cloth around Losha's head, but was too weak to complete the gesture.

Losha came to her rescue. "Yes," she whispered. "I have The Mark."

Tani let out a deep sigh and grinned from ear to droopy ear, knowing her life's mission had been successful. "At last," she said merrily. "At last!" She clasped Losha's hand, then Temple's, and pulled herself to her feet. She grumbled when her barkcloth skirt, which had since turned into goo, slowly slid off her in great slimy patches. "Bi Kana! I am naked in a room full of eyes! Get me a wrap! Quick!" she shrieked.

Temple couldn't contain himself and started laughing, which sent Losha tittering. Yes, even old Tani, healer and holder of many secrets, was back from the dead!

★   ★   ★   ★   ★   ★

The morning light streamed through the window like a welcomed friend. Mason, the Scribe, laid his ink brush down on his writing table. He read the last passage of what he had just written and let out a deep sigh of satisfaction. He stretched his aching legs out from where he sat then laid down on his bed mat for a short rest while the ink dried. Images raced through his head of the dripstone chamber filled with smoke, of Swans and Lizards, Hummingbirds and Snakes. He didn't notice he had fallen sleep.

Temple, the old centurion, crept quietly into the hut. He saw the scroll and picked it up. He read the last passage, where the Scribe decided to end his story, and rolled up the barkcloth scroll and placed it in a shark's skin casing for safekeeping. Temple gazed down at Mason as he slept and smiled. He leaned down and gently covered his friend with a blanket and left the hut to enjoy the new morning air.

★ ★ ★ **End of Book I** ★ ★ ★

AUTHOR'S NOTE
Or What Might Happen When You've Been Poisoned and Your Brain Has Been Deprived of Oxygen

There are always stories within stories, especially about the making of a story. *The Education of Temple Fox* didn't start as a book. It all started when my former husband and I left our home in Santa Fe, New Mexico for a two-week "working vacation" in El Rito, NM, home to the Hispanic "low riders" in the early '80s. Our dear friend, Donna Lucker, gave us access to her adobe getaway in a town where the locals still hung cattle in their trees for butchering. The tiny boomerang shaped adobe was made of thick timbers and was half buried in the ground. It was a one bedroom, one shower, but no bathroom arrangement with an outhouse down a path in the wood. The outhouse had no door, but featured an ornately arched entrance that looked like a confessional. It was in this setting that I started the book.

My husband, Phil, was rewriting a book at the time. Since this was a "working vacation" I brought watercolors and a box of sculptor's Victorian wax, along with the tinfoil to melt it in so I could work on a portrait bust of Phil. It was November and it was already cold in the mountains. Our cozy adobe was heated with a wood stove, which also functioned as our cooking stove and a place to melt my wax.

One day I was so absorbed in painting, and Phil with writing, that neither of us noticed that we were working in a thick cloud of smoke. I brought this to my husband's attention. He's not a fix-it kind of fellow, but after he climbed up on the roof he discovered the pipe was blocking the flow somehow and needed a section replaced. So, off he went to the general store in town, which sold food, car parts, clothing, candy, sodas, cigarettes, boots, kerosene, gas, hardware and stove pipes! It was *the* only store in El Rito in 1984.

I had no idea I had been poisoned, not until early the next morning when I woke with uncontrollable dry heaves. The oxygen had drained from my brain and I was as white as a sheet of paper. The carbon monoxide poisoning had left me helpless on the floor and with a headache that rivaled Marie Antoinette's. In spite of the snow falling outside, Phil opened all the windows and piled blankets over me so I wouldn't freeze. And there I lay for two days, gasping for fresh air and relief from the excruciating pain.

While I lay in bed I had remembered something I once did when I was a kid and had the flu. While vomiting in the bathroom sink I decided I could detach from the illness by thinking of something else. I was in college at the time and had just read a book on Einstein. So I thought about the theory of relativity while puking up my breakfast. It seemed to work pretty well, so I tried this when I was in El Rito laying in bed incapacitated and in anguish.

That is how the book was born. First it started as a thought of where I'd rather be at that moment. I saw myself on a sunny island with indigenous people who hadn't encountered Whites before. I scribbled down these random thoughts and the thoughts grew into a short story. I took it home with me and worked on it more. And, then,…well,….it just grew. Five years later I had my first novel.

Ya just never know what you'll do when your brain is deprived of oxygen.

It's been sixteen years since I resurrected this book. And yet, *The Education of Temple Fox,* Book One of the series, *The Last Scroll,* feels as fresh to me as it did sixteen years ago. This spiritual fantasy adventure reflects my deepest thoughts and the fantasy world I inhabit in my imagination.

Pat Christy
Dec. 28th 2011

PATRICIA S. CHRISTY was born with a silver spoon in her mouth, which tarnished beyond recognition by age 6 and was hocked for rent by age 21. At age 15 she began to *wake up*. It was from that point on that she knowingly interacted with those in the invisible realms. It would be accurate to say that she is a resident on this Earthly plane, but also resides in other places beyond fractured, focused Time. Call her a traveler, but one whose passport has been temporarily confiscated.

CHRISTY holds a BFA, cum laude, from the Maryland Institute, College of Art and is versed in some of the Healing Arts. She presently works as a Spiritual Counselor. In addition to being a writer, she also plays the roles of sculptor and poet. CHRISTY lives with her partner, two dogs and a cat in Black Mountain, North Carolina.